Praise for *Mother's Day*

'*Mother's Day* is terrific. So dark, so twisted and one of the most batsh*t crazy characters you'll ever meet in Marlene.'
Harriet Tyce

'Superbly written and darkly funny, *Mother's Day* is an epic psychological thriller that revels in the visceral horror of family relationships. So brilliantly and horrifyingly executed I simply couldn't look away. Abigail Burdess is a refreshing and original writer – don't take your eyes off her.'
Janice Hallett

'*Mother's Day* is so dark and so shockingly, fabulously funny. I absolutely adored it.'
Daisy Buchanan

'Dark, funny'
***Guardian* Books of the Month**

'This dark, crazy thriller is one hell of a ride!'
The Sun

'Dark, brilliant, and completely and utterly compelling.'
Jenny Colgan

'Fast and funny, dark and beautiful – I loved every page.'
Robert Webb

'A startlingly original, pitch dark page-turner'
Claire McGowan

'Deliciously dark, dripping in malice and drenched with razor sharp wit. Burdess is a writer to be watched – and feared.'
John Marrs

'A twisted, gruesome and diabolically funny exploration of motherhood that I lapped up like a feral cat. Dark, weird and brilliant, *Mother's Day* will haunt you – particularly Marlene, a jaw-dropping creation, the mother of malign mothers.'
Beth Morrey

'A brilliant debut with all the twists and turns of Du Maurier and a stunning ending that leaves you breathless. Astonishingly good.'
Robert Thorogood

'Messed up motherhood at its darkly funny and twisty best – what a debut thriller.'
Cesca Major

'A fresh and complex story about the many layers of motherhood that twists and turns until you really can't imagine what might happen next. Startling and instantly intriguing.'
Katy Brand

'*Mother's Day* is completely gripping and quite terrifying, an addictive story about motherhood and madness. I was utterly blindsided by its twists and turns.'
Lucy Porter

'Fantastic: so funny, so human – you won't be able to put it down.'
Isy Suttie

'Read this book only if you can drop everything else in your life until you've finished it.'
Marianne Levy

'Wickedly dark and devilishly funny, I loved this original take on the "mother daughter" relationship. A must read for 2023!'
Sophie Flynn

'Had me absolutely gripped from the beginning. A dark and claustrophobic tale.'
Ingrid Oliver

'Wickedly dark'
Crime Monthly

'An absolute corker. Twists and turns abound in this sharp psychological thriller that will make you sweat.'
Glamour

'Dark and delicious'
Magic Radio Book Club

'A sharply written, darkly funny, twisted page-turner about motherhood and madness.'
Platinum

'A striking look at motherhood and mental distress. Just when you think things can't get any more shocking, they do.'
Socialist Worker

Abigail Burdess has written for and acted in various comedy shows for the television, radio and stage. She also sometimes writes TV for kids, as well as plays and musicals. She lives in London with her husband, Robert Webb, and their two children. *Mother's Day* is her first novel.

MOTHER'S DAY

Abigail Burdess

First published in 2023 by
WILDFIRE
an imprint of HEADLINE PUBLISHING GROUP

First published in paperback in 2024 by
WILDFIRE
an imprint of HEADLINE PUBLISHING GROUP

1

Cataloguing in Publication Data is available from the British Library

ISBN 978 1 4722 9555 2

Designed and typeset by EM&EN
Printed and bound in Great Britain by Clays Ltd, Elcograf S.p.A.

Headline's policy is to use papers that are natural, renewable and recyclable products and made from wood grown in well-managed forests and other controlled sources. The logging and manufacturing processes are expected to conform to the environmental regulations of the country of origin.

HEADLINE PUBLISHING GROUP
An Hachette UK Company
Carmelite House
50 Victoria Embankment
London EC4Y 0DZ

www.headline.co.uk
www.hachette.co.uk

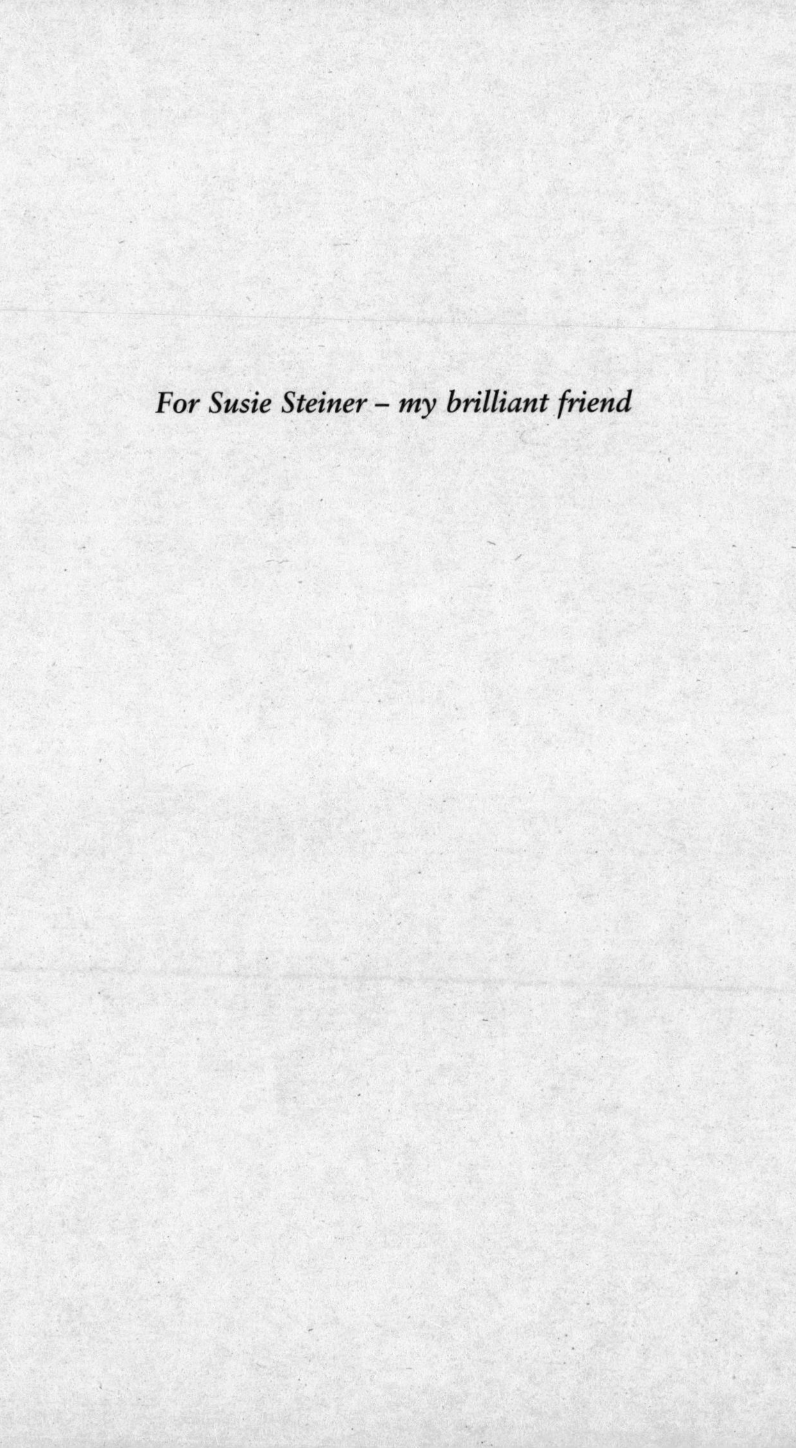

For Susie Steiner – my brilliant friend

‘The wild beasts of the desert shall also meet the wild beasts of the island, and the satyr shall cry to his fellow; the screech owl also shall rest there and find for herself a place of rest. There shall the great owl make her nest, and lay, and hatch, and gather under her shadow: there shall the vultures also be gathered, every one with her mate.’

Isaiah 34.14–15

‘How dare you climb over into my garden like a thief and steal my rampion!’

Rapunzel, The Brothers Grimm

AFTER BIRTH

'Skin to skin contact really helps with bonding. Once the cord is clamped, you can continue to cuddle your baby.'

She tasted iron as she pushed the baby into the void. She felt something float free inside her cheek and probed it with her tongue. Was that part of her, or did it belong to the baby? On to the slab she spat a piece of knotted, bloody flesh.

There was blood too, on the baby's tiny body. Blood was crusted across the head. Blood had dried on the fingers. Blood bubbled black from the cord. The first light of dawn shone through the tiny ears. Some waxy stuff made the baby's skin a mottled grey. She pulled the towel over the body in a hopeless attempt to keep it warm.

She thrust the basket forward once more into the stony coffin. A freezing draught came from above and, as she looked directly into the blackness, something scuttled over the baby's legs, something with claws. 'Push,' she thought, 'push.'

Stone scraped on stone. As the bundle disappeared into the shadows, the baby jerked, as if falling, and she strained every sinew to shove the slab across, burying the baby alive.

'Please,' she prayed with her whole being. 'Please be quiet. Please don't make a sound.' For a moment, all she could hear was her own ragged breath. But then, from inside the tomb, came a reedy mewling cry.

FIRST TRIMESTER

1

CONCEPTION

'Pregnancy happens when sperm enters a vagina, travels through the cervix and womb to the fallopian tube and fertilises an egg. Conception occurs up to five days after having sex. Your weeks of pregnancy are dated from the first day of your last period.'

Anna was in the dark. 'Dermot?' His shoulder was in her mouth. 'Dermot!' Anna jiggled her shoulder a bit. He was a dead weight on top of her. Dermot let out what was, unmistakably, a long snore. Anna shouted, 'DERMOT!' But it was no good.

Anna fumbled to get her phone from the pocket of the jeans she'd dropped by the side of the bed. She just about reached them. The smashed screen lit up the tiny bedroom. She scrolled down her friends' 'Happy Birthday' messages, while eighteen stone of Dermot pressed on her bladder. Anna counted. Sometime after ninety-one Dermot woke with a snort, muttered something incomprehensible, like 'Noughts!' and rolled off her. As he unpeeled, Anna's freed right hand shot down to keep the condom attached to him, rather than her. That was a first. He'd fallen asleep while she was in the bathroom, or getting water, or going between the sofa and the bed, but never actually during sex itself. Had he even finished? Anna suspected that he faked it quite regularly. Ever since they'd had a fantastic Saturday afternoon demonstrating their come-faces to each other, Anna had been unable to shake the suspicion, at the crucial moment, that Dermot was doing the face on purpose.

'It's all right,' Dermot had woken up enough to know there was some incomplete task, though not necessarily enough to grasp it was to tie a knot in a condom. 'I'm doing it, I'm doing it!'

Anna rolled out of bed, grabbing Dermot's huge towelling dressing gown from the hook on the back of the bedroom door. It was one of those hooks without screws or any other fixings, so they can be moved from flat to flat. Anna had bought it three flats ago – two of those had been with Dermot. Once upright, she noticed she couldn't get the floor to stay still. She headed straight for the toilet. Four minutes of throwing up red wine later, she managed to get into the shower.

The water pooled around her feet. The plug was blocked again, a consequence of being in what her boyfriend described as 'A Wookie Union' – Dermot's chestnut shoulder-length hair and beard, and her Disney Princess plait. It took her ten minutes to twist the barbecue skewer down the drain and get it working. The shower was an impregnable expanse of beige tiles. Why was every rental bathroom designed to be hosed down after a murder?

When she came out of the shower to dress in the tracksuit bottoms and hoodie which were her usual pyjamas, Dermot was still dead to the world. He was flat out on top of the duvet, naked, his conker-bright curls merging with his dappled beard, and his long, knotted left arm flung across the bed in an expansive gesture: a beached Viking. In the neon light from the window the pale down on his skin traced his outline, making him almost luminesce. Anna briefly considered trying to cover him up but knew from bitter experience she couldn't lift him: he was over a foot taller than her and twice as broad across. They made a classic double act: Laurel and Lardy, Dermot said. Sometimes strangers would start laughing just at the sight of them together. She took the phone out on to the balcony to check her email. It was an iPhone so old they had a running joke that no mugger would want it. There were three emails from a job recruitment site called Charity Career she'd signed up to ages ago just in case. Maternity cover for a fundraising job in a refugee organisation in Glasgow (five years' experience required). That looked interesting. That was far enough away, but not insane. She was finishing her cigarette when . . .

'Aha! Caught ya!'

Anna yelped and dropped her phone, adding to the network of cracks across the screen.

'I thought you'd given up,' Dermot said.

Dermot, all six foot five of him and both his chins, was ducking under the balcony door.

'You know you won't be allowed to smoke when we're married. I shall forbid it!' Dermot made a small cross with his two forefingers, sliding his voice from his natural deep Sligo to that of a high-pitched, censorious English bishop.

'When we're married?' Anna wondered if the red wine was going to come up again. She fought to keep the blind panic out of her voice. 'Are we getting married then?'

'Well, if you're asking. Are you asking?' Dermot perched on the table, which looked way too small to support him: a giant on a toadstool. ''Cause I feel like you should at least get down on one knee, or both. Both knees is fine, too. No?' He raised his eyebrows suggestively. 'All right then! Give me a minute to think about it, OK?' Dermot swept his hair off his shoulders. 'I just can't be rushed!'

The phone was hot in Anna's hand: a tiny glowing doorway to somewhere else. Could she say she had five years' experience? If you added it all up, sure.

'Look,' Dermot was still doing his shtick, 'stop *pressuring* me, OK? I will marry you when I'm good and ready, and not before! Got it?'

'You're right,' Anna deflected. 'I wouldn't expect you to say yes. I'd think less of you if you did. It's not like I've made any sort of effort. I should go down on one knee! I should get a ring! I should maybe wait an hour after we've had crappy sex!'

'It wasn't that bad.' Dermot looked sheepish.

'You fell asleep.'

Dermot caved instantly. 'OK, it was crappy. So, what you're saying is . . . it's not the perfect time, ask again, right?' He grinned at her. On Dermot's front tooth was a star-shaped patch of lighter white, like he was a cartoon, constantly twinkling. 'I mean, you're going to ask me again?'

A baby screamed, as if burned, from the darkness, and Anna started.

'Jesus!' said Dermot, putting his hand on her back. 'It's just an owl! What's got into you?'

Anna perched on the wall on the edge of the balding lawn, balancing her paper plate, piled high with stuffed vine leaves and pistachio pastries. Cherries from the tree overhead spattered the brick. She'd tried to find somewhere out of the path of the children, who were bombing around the tiny back garden. Layla sat next to her, dressed in a white shirt, as she was every workday, although her usual NHS jacket was balled up beside her in concession to the baking sun. It was a black jacket, standard issue of some spun plastic, the kind of fabric that turns meadows into dust bowls, easily wiped, with a little name badge which read, 'Dr Layla Pasdar'.

'There are so many of them!' Anna said, gesturing to the skinny kids who were whipping each other with wet towels.

'There are three.' Layla raised her voice to her nephews, 'Hey! Twats! Knock it off!' She turned back to Anna. 'What's the big favour?'

'Would it be OK if I put you down as a reference?' Anna asked.

Layla's face congealed, 'No!'

'What?' Anna maintained total innocence.

'Don't tell me you're doing this,' said Layla.

'Doing what? I'm just applying for a job.' Anna glanced around the garden.

'Where? Where are you applying for a job?' Layla interrogated her.

'Glasgow.'

'Great! I thought you'd finished with all this.'

'All what?'

'Have you even told him you're moving to Glasgow?' Layla threw down the question like a gauntlet.

'Who?' Anna asked.

'Don't be a dick.'

Anna blinked. Layla was a Londoner but could swear for Scotland: the worse the word the better she liked it; hanging around with her was just swimming in a stream of shits and fucks. Anna assumed it was a hangover from teenage rebellion.

Layla's father was an Iranian shopkeeper, and her mother was a beautician, probably the most beautiful and, crucially, ladylike woman Anna had ever met. She was currently illuminating the buffet in Layla's back room. Her nails were a burnished gold, shaped to a point, her black hair was always highlighted and low-lighted various shades of caramel, her eyebrows threaded into two perfect commas, quotation marks around the eternal worried question mark between her eyebrows, etched in her skin despite the Botox. 'What's gone wrong now?' her face seemed to say. 'Whatever it is, I'm prepared to face it waxed.' Layla had conformed in many ways, becoming a clinical psychologist: '*Almost* a doctor!' as her mother would say. 'I *am* a bloody doctor,' Layla would mutter murderously. 'Look at my fucking jacket!'

Every time Layla cursed like a trucker with Tourette's, Anna thought of the phrase 'You kiss your mother with that mouth?' and pictured Layla's mother's endlessly worried face offering her perfect cheek to be kissed. Layla was not groomed, nor was she risk-averse. She climbed rock walls and jumped out of planes. On Saturdays, she punched strangers in some modern sort of martial art with a fancy Japanese name for beating the crap out of people. It was as if she was trying to fulfil her mother's conviction that something terrible would happen to her the moment she was out of her sight. Layla also had sex with good-looking and much younger men, who presumably she swore at like she swore at Anna, but calling Anna a dick was fairly direct, even for her.

'No, I haven't told Dermot. I'm not going to get the job. What's the point in worrying him?' Anna said.

'Bullshit. You're going to leave him! I bet the poor bastard doesn't have the faintest clue you're fucking off!'

Anna lowered her voice, 'I'm not anything off. I probably won't even get it.'

'What about me?' Layla was indignant. 'What am I supposed to do with you in Glasgow?'

'I'll be back in six months! It's maternity cover!'

'Oh! So, you're getting the job now?'

Anna was bewildered. 'I mean, not if you won't give me a reference. I honestly don't understand why we're fighting. Dermot's not going to be upset if I get a job . . .'

'Fuck! You're so fucking infuriating.' Layla's paper plate upended, tipping kofta on the cracked earth. She stood up. Then sat down again.

'Did something happen?'

'Like what?'

Layla narrowed her eyes at Anna. Anna tried hard to keep her face open. But then looked at the grass.

'He proposed, didn't he? Fuck a woodchuck chuck! He fucking proposed!' Layla crowed.

'No! Yes, but as a joke. It wasn't real!' Anna protested.

'So it was an unreal proposal,' said Layla.

'No . . . yes . . . it was . . . don't make a thing of this!' Anna said.

'Did he or did he not ask you to marry him and have his little babies?'

'Yes!' said Anna. 'But I can't, can I?'

'You aren't seriously saying that to me, are you?' Layla was in her fourth round of IVF. 'Why can't you? 'Cause he's not Jewish?'

Anna almost did a double take. Where did that come from?

'No, I don't even know if I'm Jewish! That's the whole . . .' Anna struggled to articulate what she had never said aloud to herself and fell back on practicalities. 'I'm a temp. Dermot doesn't have a real job.'

Layla snorted, 'That's not a real reason.'

'Okay, what if I have some . . . genetic disorder? Some family history of something awful?' Anna asked.

'What if you do? Why does that matter?' Layla countered. Anna looked at the fold-out table, where Layla's loving mother was doling out home-made pudding in the sunshine. Layla did not have the first clue what she meant.

'Why don't you adopt, then?' Anna said, surprising herself with the aggression in her voice.

'What?'

'If it makes no difference whether your family is biological, why don't you adopt a baby instead of putting yourself through hell to have one?'

Layla's response was silence.

'Exactly! It matters. I don't know if I'm a . . . I don't know anything . . . I don't even know my name!' Anna said.

'Yes, you do!' Layla exploded. 'It's Anna. You're allowed

to be happy. You're allowed to get married. You're allowed to have kids. Even if your mum can't be there when you do.'

'Oh my God, Layla!' Anna replied. 'I just came for a reference. If I wanted the full psychoanalysis I'd have, you know, paid your insane fees!'

'What have you done that's so bad? Why are you punishing yourself? Why can't you marry him?'

'I think there's a fairly good argument that if I actually wanted to punish myself, I *would* marry him.' There was a wail from the back room. Anna and Layla looked across the scrubby London grass to see Dermot comforting one of Layla's nephews, who he had clearly just whacked in the head with a can of Stella. Dermot saw them both looking at him and did an elaborate apologetic shrug.

'You see? I can't marry him,' said Anna decisively. 'I'd kill him.'

'Look on the bright side,' said Layla. 'He might kill you.' And she leaned back, knocking her jacket off the wall. As the bundle fell, Anna saw in it the shape of a baby, and a tiny skull, cracking against brick. She started forward to catch it, then shook her head like a dog trying to get water out of her ears.

Layla put her head on one side. 'Are you OK?'

'Yes!' said Anna. 'Are you going to give me a reference?'

'I don't know,' Layla jutted her chin out. 'Are you going to tell Dermot you're leaving him?'

'I'm not leaving him!' Anna almost yelled. Then added, 'I don't think.'

The only other person who could give her a reference was her line manager Yanni, but it didn't go well from the moment she asked for a quiet word. Yanni closed the door silently and put his head on one side.

'How are you doing? Mental-health wise?' Anna knew with a steely certainty that if she showed a moment's weakness Yanni would use it to cut her hours. Anna was currently temping, having moved from job share to short-term contract at the same organisation, and she had ended up, after eight years and four or five 'specialities', being paid almost the same as she had at the start.

'There's no shame, you know, in having mental health,' Yanni said.

'I have mental health,' said Anna.

'You have mental health?' Yanni got out his special ballpoint.

'Yes,' she said. Yanni looked pleased. He clicked out the nib. Anna clarified, 'I mean, I don't have mental illness.' Yanni looked blank. Anna spelled it out, 'I'm doing OK!'

'Oh,' Yanni deflated a little. 'I'm going to sign you up for four support sessions anyway.'

'Please don't do that.'

'The nature of the work can be very challenging. We have a duty of care to all our staff, even temps.'

Great, now she would have to talk to one of the psychiatrists who littered the place. At various points, it had been Anna's job to interview them, and they were bastards to a man, including the women. They treated Anna like a schoolgirl. She was pretty sure a couple of them had thought she was on work experience. Last year she'd spoken to one of them and he'd gone straight to Layla, who was managing her at the time. 'There's some girl saying she needs to interview me?'

'Fuck that dick!' Layla had said. 'Hasn't he heard of "I Am A Man"? He can't treat you like a child. Sexist shit-sack!'

'Yeah,' said Anna, making a mental note to google 'I Am A Man' as soon as she was alone. Layla had 'drawn senior management's attention' to this alleged slur and now Anna found it even harder to schedule meetings with the psychiatry team. She couldn't imagine telling her darkest secrets to any one of them.

'Thank you so much for the offer but . . .' she began.

'You're very lucky to have this level of input from such highly qualified doctors,' Yanni told her.

The 'support' scheme was a new and informal attempt to address the fact that people were constantly going off sick with mental breakdowns. Anna didn't know if the job did it to them or if the place itself was a psycho-magnet. Yanni loved the scheme because the psychiatrists had to do it for free.

'I don't need any support,' said Anna, 'there's nothing wrong with me! Everything's fine! Everything's perfect!'

But he signed her up anyway, making her late leaving work.

Anna hurried along the Finchley Road, checking the time on her phone. A text appeared from the Moon app: 'You are in your fertile window!' and Anna said, 'I know!' out loud to her phone. She needed to get the morning after pill before six. Something about the pill's ticking clock always made her faintly hysterical. Seventy-two hours! Seventy-two hours to make it to Boots! It was a bit like being in the TV series *24*, but three times as long and fighting blastocysts instead of terrorists. Though in a way an embryo was a tiny terrorist, hijacking your womb and driving you headlong into a mountain. Her 'birthday' celebrations had been Friday night. Now it was Monday. It hadn't been her actual birthday, but she had no idea when her real birthday was. Her parents had nominated the twelfth of July. Dermot always took the piss because it was the day of the Orange march.

'All across Northern Ireland,' he'd say, 'they celebrate your birth by beating up Catholics!' When she was in her twenties, earnest young men with unkempt hair would ask her, 'What's your star sign?' and Anna couldn't say, 'I don't know,' so she said, 'Cancer! Means I'm a sceptic, apparently.' They never laughed. It was five to six when she got there. 'Have you taken the morning after pill before?' the chemist said. Anna nodded.

It was all right, she reasoned to herself, as she let herself into their seventh-storey flat, she was taking the pill, there was no cause to panic. Dermot had probably forgotten about the whole proposal thing, and if he hadn't, she could laugh the whole thing off. But when she went into the front room Dermot was dead.

He was white as milk and lying on the kitchen floor, where it met with the living room, his mouth gaping and drool pooling on the lino. Anna dropped her shopping bag and an inarticulate bark came out of her. She rushed to him, and as she got closer she could see there was something white falling out of his mouth. Should she try to breathe for him? Her stomach turned over as she looked at the pale stuff on his chin. She paused over his breathless body, willing herself to put her lips on his spittle-flecked beard. That was what you were supposed to do, wasn't it? The lights in the kitchen were throbbing, she could hear the transformers buzzing in the ceiling like deranged wasps. Anna swung her leg across Dermot's body to straddle him and put both her hands together to place all her weight on his heart, like she'd seen people do in the movies. Where was his heart? Somewhere in the region of his pocket, she guessed, and she crossed her hands over it, then transferred all her weight into his middle, pushing hard on his third button down.

'Jesus!' said Dermot, suddenly shoving her full in the chest.

Anna flew backwards off Dermot's erstwhile corpse and banged her head against their Klippan IKEA sofa.

'What the fuck are you doing?' Dermot yelled, wiping the drool on his face with his lumberjack sleeve.

'I'm sorry!' said Anna. 'I'm so sorry!' and she rubbed the back of her head.

'I'm sleeping here!' Dermot was groggy and slurring. He must have passed out.

'I thought you were dead!' Anna protested.

Dermot was now sitting up, orientating himself by groping the fridge like some blind plaid yeti.

'Why in God's name would you think that?' he said.

All Anna knew was that her adoptive parents had got her when she was a few weeks old. She'd been left on a traffic island in an orange handbag.

Anna's mum, her adoptive mum, had been a lovely woman. Fat. Fat was always the first thing Anna remembered about her – lovely fat arms holding her, the rolls of her lovely belly, which Anna used to bury her little hands between, while her mum told her off. 'Get off! Get your hands out of there, that's not for you!' she'd yell jokingly. Even today Anna couldn't help associating fat with kindness, even when Dermot would say, 'Arseholes can be fat too, you know!' And name all the nasty people in the world who were fat: Kim Jong-un, Eamonn Holmes (while he patted his own round belly). The association of fat with love was early and unbreakable: her lovely, kind, sweet-smelling, fat mum. They had a special way of curling up, Anna draped across her mum's fatness on the sofa, like an ill-fitting belt. She used to hold her hand in a special way too, sort of hooked around her baby finger. It was a silent communication that said: you are mine. She held her hand that way when she walked her to the local school, where she was a teacher.

Anna's mum didn't want her in her class – she was scared she'd be too strict with her – so Anna went in the other class, run by the lady who also taught RE. She was a weird, nervous person who made jokes only she got and then laughed at them too long. In this class Anna was sat on the 'Robin' table. Another Robin asked her, 'Do you speak Jewish?' and Anna was about to explain it wasn't a language it was a religion when the teacher interrupted and started laughing too much again. 'What a question!' she said. Anna saw her mum at lunchtimes when she'd sneak her a cuddle. When Anna told her mum about the RE teacher her mum was cross.

Anna's mum had a temper. Sometimes she got really angry with Anna about little things and Anna would be sad, but then she'd say sorry and do a routine acting enraged about everything. 'Stupid fridge!' she'd yell. 'Stupid stapler! Stupid coffee table!' and she'd pretend to beat stuff up, like she was a wrestler, and Anna would laugh, and everything would be better. And Anna would sneak her little fist in between the layers of Mum's lovely flesh under her armpit and she'd feel safe.

But she had died, Anna's mum, when Anna was in the last year of infants, the classroom at the far end of the school, next to the field. A lorry hit her. She was pulling Anna home on a sledge. The bastard psychiatrists would draw looping arrows on their A4 pads as if one thing led to another: pearls on a string. After school Anna would go into her mum's classroom and read a book or play with Lego until her mum was ready to go. In the winter they tried to get home before dark. That day, Anna had been sent to see the head. There were two tiny grassy swells in the playground, which the kids used to call 'the humps'. To seven-year-olds, they seemed like hills. It was behind the cover of these mountains that Kevin, a kid whose claim to fame was that he wore adult size five shoes, had asked Anna if she was a boy or a girl. 'A gel,' Anna had replied: under the little boy's threat her Peckham accent had intensified.

'I don't think so,' Kevin had said, 'you've got short hair.' Kevin checked with his two sidekicks, Big Matthew and Little Matthew, that they'd caught this brilliant piece of observational stand-up comedy.

'I am!' she declared. 'I am a gel!'

'Pull down her pants!' yelled Kevin. 'Check!'

Big Matthew hung back: he clearly didn't want to. Anna used the pause to say, 'I'll smash you!'

'Girls don't fight!' declared Kevin. Anna thumped Kevin in the face. Kevin Size-Fives touched his bleeding nose. 'Cor!' he said. 'You're strong for a girl.' Anna had been, as her mother put it, 'cock-of-the-hoop'.

The head had given Anna lines; she'd had to fill two sides of A4 with the sentence 'I will not brawl with my little classmates' until her hand was cramping, and her cockiness was somewhat dented. But her mum had said she had to finish the lines before they went home. 'I expect you're proud of yourself, are you?' her mum had said. 'I expect you think you're clever?' Anna had a dim sense that if she could just tell her mum why she had punched Kevin in the nose, her anger might have abated quicker. Her mum often became enraged, and then ten minutes later she was all hot chocolate and puns.

'I wasn't fighting, really!' Anna lied.

'Are you going to fight me now, Anna?'

Anna's face felt hot. Sweat made her school shirt stick to her.

'No.'

'No,' said her mum, 'you will learn, as you get older, that fighting will only heap more trouble on your back.'

'What about the Warsaw Ghetto Uprising?' asked little Anna (her mum usually liked it when she brought up the Warsaw Ghetto Uprising).

'Don't you Warsaw Ghetto me!' said her mum. 'There'll be trouble enough in your life without seeking it out. I have never been ashamed of you,' she said, 'but I am today.'

By the time they had gone home in the snow it was getting dark. Her mum had hooked a rope to a green plastic sledge like a tea-tray and was pulling Anna home. Anna could still just see her mum's glorious auburn ringlets glint six feet in front of her. She hoped her mum had forgiven her and a lorry skidded off the road in front of Anna and smashed into the side of her mum and her mum's head rebounded against the side of the lorry as if it were going to fly off. It stayed connected to her neck, but it hung down all wrong. Anna got knocked too – she never knew what by – but she skidded across the ice into some brambles at the side of the road and she'd sat there in the cold looking at the broken pieces of her mum and the snow on the branches until the paramedic spotted her and took her into the ambulance to treat her for the cold which had got inside her. She'd picked up the plastic tray she had been sitting on and walked along the rope, along the line of the rope that had led to her mum, but it had just stopped. There was the end of the rope in the bloody snow. Her eyes had been drawn to her mum, lying lifeless in the headlights. Anna hadn't wanted to leave her there. She'd wanted to go and hold her mum's hand in the special way they had, and bury the other hand in her fat, but the paramedic said Anna had to go to hospital. 'She'll be so cold,' thought Anna, as the doors closed.

Anna's much older father forgot to book her a haircut. Anna's hair began to grow, and Anna decided not to bring it up. So what if her hair grew? At least nobody would pull her pants down. And she wouldn't be tempted to smash anyone in the nose. Nor did he arrange dentist visits or trips to buy clothes or even, in any recognisable way, an evening meal. He began to eat boiled eggs and soldiers and liver every night of the week, making Anna a little matching tray, and before her eighth birthday he told her she would go to boarding school, first just during the week, and then, when she proved to be 'academic', on a scholarship, to a massive public school. Once at public school, it took her about six weeks to erase her Peckham accent completely.

'And we'd never have known,' said her father, 'how academic you are. If what happened to your mum hadn't happened, you would just have carried on going to the village school so, in a way, it's all turned out for the best.'

Anna didn't agree that the discovery of her 'academic' potential was worth the pieces of her mum lying in the snow, but she nodded and smiled because she didn't want her father to be unhappy. Neither did he. He didn't want to be unhappy so much that he decided not to feel anything at all. Sometimes he would pat her awkwardly on the shoulder, especially if she got some recognition – the Science Prize. 'Not bad,' he'd say, 'for a kid with PTSD!' That was what the health visitor had said, after the rope in the snow, that she might have 'PTSD', and her father had laughed at the idea and assured them that technically a child couldn't suffer from anything of the sort, since children were pre-social. Mental illnesses were for grown-ups, whose personalities were already formed, not for children, whose experiences simply became the foundation of the construction of their self. Anna wouldn't *have* PTSD, she'd *be* PTSD, as it were. That would just be Anna.

So it was only two years later, when Anna was trying to get to sleep in the public school, lying in a dormitory of twenty-four girls, with plyboard 'walls' between the beds, listening with the weariness of an old salt, dry-eyed, as the new eight-year-olds cried for home, that she began to think about her other mother, the one who had left her on a traffic island as a nine-week-old baby, and wonder where that mother was, and if she was growing into the sort of little girl that that mother would be proud of, and if that mother was alive, and if she was fat.

Anna was going to beat the final boss. She'd done four Divine Beasts and climbed laboriously to the top of Hyrule Tower. Dermot lay asleep in the bedroom, and her bag lay where she had abandoned it. She glanced at the cracked screen of her phone as it notified her of a new email, subject line: *Your Fucking Reference.*

> *To Whom It May Concern: My name is Dr Layla Pasdar. I line-managed Anna Rampion for six months while she completed a project charting the efficacy of CBT in survivors of torture and organised violence. She is highly intelligent and articulate. Her written work is of the highest standard. She is punctual and extremely hard-working. She's also a fucking arsehole. She runs away from any relationship and leaves every job. She's completely fucked up about being adopted. In my professional opinion she got survivor's guilt from losing her mother and that's why she wants to work with survivors, and also why she almost certainly shouldn't. If you give her a job, she will just leave it. Anyway, Good Luck!*

It took her a moment to grasp that Layla seemed to think she was not inherently a bad person. In Layla's mind, there was nothing essentially rotten at Anna's core. It was certainly a theory. Anna replied immediately, *Got Your Fucking Reference!*

And Layla came back with, *The phrase you're looking for is thank you!*

By the time Anna looked back at the screen, she'd fallen from the top of the tower into a pit containing a ten-thousand-year-old evil and died. Anna reloaded the game at the last save. She couldn't go forward and she couldn't turn back. She could always stay where she was. She felt a sharp pain in her stomach, like a mosquito had bitten her from the inside.

2

FIVE WEEKS GONE

'Changes to your sense of smell are a side effect of oestrogen. If you feel like every little fragrance around you has been magnified, this could be an early sign that your body is getting ready for a baby.'

Anna sniffed at her wine. Something smelt weird about it. Was this what people meant when they said wine was 'corked'? Dermot always said corked was just a word posh people had to make working-class people feel small. What was the smell? It didn't smell appetising. But she'd spent her last five pounds sixty on it. She'd never noticed that the pub itself smelt cacophonous – moulded upholstery, vinegar and, from somewhere close by, oestrogen and blood. Three folkie women with purple highlights were clustered six feet from her and Anna realised that at least one of them, probably all three, had their period. Christ! Could other people smell when she was bleeding? She was two days late. She wouldn't be. She never was, but she should buy another test, just to be sure. Maybe she could still use the one sitting in her bag. Her nose wrinkled at the thought. One of the women gave her a chin-jerk in greeting. Try as Anna might to dress like these women, in leggings and high-tops, they always had her pegged as an outsider. Although she'd seen the leader before, it was likely she knew she was Dermot's girlfriend. As if in confirmation, the woman leaned into her two friends and whispered something, and all three glanced at Anna and raised their Strongbows in her direction. Anna tried to nod back, but felt her skin flame up. She checked her face in her phone camera. Despite the tree of cracks across the screen and the concealer, a horrific bruise on her right eye was already clearly visible. She swallowed a mouthful of wine and identified its bouquet: dental anaesthetic. Five pounds sixty.

Dermot (fiddle, Hardanger fiddle, vocals, guitar) was half of a folk duo – confusingly named The Byrnes Trio. Technically they had been a trio when Brede (vocals, guitar, whistle) had been with them, but she'd had a massive folk hit with an American band and was touring in the States. She still occasionally dropped in to play and the other fifty-one weeks a year it was just Dermot and Neil (vocals, guitar). The duo/trio had some actual, hard-core fans – the kind who made it their life's work to go to every gig and to buy anything the band were selling – just not very many of them. In fact, Dermot and Neil seemed to know most of the fans by name. Anna respected the fans' dedication; their willingness to choose something and define themselves by liking it. She had never been able to do it. Anna had never put up a poster, never bought someone's merchandise. She downloaded the odd song on to her ancient phone but it seemed to Anna an act of supreme confidence to declare oneself a fan, unilaterally subscribing to a group that may not want you back. Dermot's thirty-something followers called themselves, with some ironic detachment, Byrne-outs.

Dermot's bandmate Neil brought the drinks over post-gig. It was a regular monthly thing, and some of the payment was in beer. The oestrogen was suddenly and decisively replaced by the smell of fresh sweat. Folk music is hard work, not, as Dermot said, compared to mining tin but to, say, Anna's job. Neil's T-shirt, which read 'Folkies Fuck Better' was soaked. Neil got involved in a lot of accidents. He referred to himself as 'part-machine'. His jaw had been smashed up in a cycling accident and sometimes he'd scare kids by pulling aside his lips to reveal some metal infrastructure. But, despite the Bond villain jaw, or maybe because of it, Anna had always suspected he did, in fact, fuck better. Better than most people, anyway. Then, three weeks ago, Neil had looked at Anna.

They were outside, trying to keep an eye on Dermot in case he bothered the wrong guy for a cigarette. Neil and Anna stood either side of the double doors, at least one metre twenty centimetres apart by her reckoning. Anna had loosened the plait she always wore her hair in, to let the air in at the back of her neck. She had done it unconsciously, but, looking back, it was an intimate gesture, too intimate a gesture to perform in front of someone you'd never had sex with, and Neil had levelled his green eyes at her, silently, and Anna felt a desert wind blow her skirt off. She'd instantly broken eye contact and gone inside the pub, but she knew that Neil knew that something had happened. For the last eighteen months Neil had openly flirted with Anna. 'Christ, you're gorgeous!' he'd say in his undiminished Dublin accent. 'When are you going to leave this arsehole and let me have a crack at you?' And it had felt safe, cosy even. Dermot never seemed to care because it was so blatant, or maybe he just didn't notice. But three weeks ago, on her birthday, the look that Neil had given her hadn't been safe. And nor had what had happened afterwards, in the tiny windowless room that held the coats. Anna was almost sure it had been a very unsafe sixteen seconds. And here he was, elbowing in a tray full of pints, setting the purple-haired women fluttering like pigeons. Neil immediately clocked her cheek.

'What the hell happened to you?' Anna put her hand up to cover it.

'It's nothing.'

'It's not nothing!' Neil put his long fingers round Anna's wrist and tugged her hand away from her face. 'Did someone hit you?'

'What's all this?' Dermot saw Neil's hand around his girlfriend's wrist and didn't blink.

'Someone's hit Anna!' Neil's voice rose.

'No, they haven't!' Dermot dismissed this nonsense with a wave of his huge hand.

'It wasn't hard,' Anna protested. 'I'm fine!'

Dermot looked bewildered at this news. 'Who hit you?'

She'd bought a pregnancy test during lunch hour and taken the bus back. On the seat in front of her a woman was talking loudly to a friend to her left, and as Anna was about to get off the bus she noticed, jammed between the two seats and sticking out at a weird angle, a doll's arm. Anna leaned forward to look at it and as she did, the tiny fingers convulsed.

Anna stood up and tapped the woman on the shoulder. 'Excuse me!' she said, and the woman whipped round, irritated. 'I think your baby's stuck.'

The woman shouted at her about minding her own effing business until Anna had gone way past her stop. It would have been quicker not to have taken the bus at all and just walked back to work directly. So, she was in a hurry, not really concentrating, when the teenager asked for directions to the tube. It was quarter past one in the afternoon.

'You go down the end of this street and take a . . .'

'Where's your phone?'

'Sorry?' said Anna. The girl had a thick accent, but Anna couldn't identify it. She was about five foot one, a little shorter than Anna.

She spoke slowly like Anna was a stupid child. 'Your phone! Where's your phone?'

Why was she asking that? 'I don't know. It's here somewhere . . .' Anna began to feel her back jean pockets for her phone.

'Give your handbag.'

What? None of this made sense. 'I don't have a handbag!'

Rage flashed across the young girl's face. 'What's that then?'

'A shopping bag?' Anna said.

'Looks like a handbag,' said the girl.

Anna's eyes fell on the girl's right hand. She was holding a wrench.

'Oh,' Anna's thoughts were running slow. 'She's mugging me. Shit, I wish I had my phone to give her.' Anna began to search even more feverishly, patting all the pockets of her jacket. The girl looked too young to be a mugger. She couldn't be older than twenty.

'It's just got shopping in it,' said Anna, shaking the bag at her. The teenager reached out to the bag, but it was across Anna's body, diagonally, and the girl's tiny fist with its perfectly painted nails made contact with Anna's belly. Anna felt an electric shock and her right hand automatically shot out, as if a circuit had been completed, and punched the girl in the mouth.

The girl blinked, and her front teeth were bright orange. She lifted up her hand to her bleeding mouth.

'Sorry!' Anna said immediately. 'I'm so sorry! Oh my God! I've hurt you! Are you OK?' Anna raised her left hand towards the girl's face, but she batted it away in a powerful parry.

'You hit me?' Her arms were stringy but strong, covered with raised keloid scars, the flesh spat out again by her own body.

'I didn't mean to!' Anna said. Anna looked at the bloody heel of her hand, where the imprint of the girl's teeth was clearly visible. The tiny mugger looked at it too and punched Anna, very very hard, in her right breast. Anna was knocked down, on to the side of the road, as she thought, 'I deserve that.' Anna kept watching the wrench in the kid's hanging right hand, which hadn't moved. She must be left-handed. Thank God. At least she hadn't hit her with the wrench. At least she wasn't using the weapon.

'You want to fight me?'

'No!' Anna cowered, covering her head with her arms. As she squatted, the phone fell out of her pocket. 'My phone! I've found my phone!'

'Give it to me!' the girl demanded.

Anna picked up her phone and handed it to the robber. She looked at it for less than a second. 'I don't want this.' She threw the phone back on the ground, where the screen crunched into even more pieces. 'Bag!' she said.

Anna pulled her canvas bag over her head and handed it to the mugger who casually looked inside it. 'Where's your wallet then?' she asked.

'In my pocket,' Anna said.

'Give it!'

Anna reached into her back pocket with her right arm and the girl used her left hand and smacked Anna across her now unprotected head. Anna toppled sideways and felt the stones of the pavement scrape her left cheek.

'Please don't hit me! Don't hit me! I didn't mean to hurt you!' Anna found herself pleading.

The kid smacked her again, round the side of the head, big brother like. 'You thought that hurt? Look! I'm hitting you! I'm hitting you! What you going to do about it?'

Anna silently offered up her empty wallet to the tiny mugger, stretching out her arms and ducking her head, a Wise Man to the baby Jesus.

'Pathetic.' The girl put down the wrench to look inside Anna's wallet. She kept a toe on it, as if Anna might pick it up and attack her with it. She had perfect make-up: her cheekbones and the bridge of her nose highlighted like she was in a forties movie, constantly followed by a spotlight in her daily life. Anna couldn't tell if her lips were swollen from the punch, or always looked bee-stung. 'How weird,' she thought, 'that the feminine ideal is to look like you've been smacked in the mouth.'

'There's no cards, nothing!' the girl complained.

'I'm sorry!' Anna could hear herself almost whimpering, 'I don't have any money.'

'Fuck!' The girl made as if to punch Anna again but instead threw the wallet back to her. 'I'm taking this!' she said, waving Anna's canvas bag at her. Anna felt a pang. Dermot had given her something in it, some perfume she'd hated, and she'd added long straps and sewn over the original branding.

'Take it!' Anna gestured wildly, like this tiny, perfectly turned-out mugger didn't understand, like she needed her permission. The girl picked up the wrench and she was gone.

Anna touched her face. It was grazed, and she was pretty sure bits of gravel were now embedded in her cheek. As she drew her hand away, she saw blood on her fingers.

'Oh crap!' she thought, as the pavement tilted towards her.

Anna was woken by an older woman.

'Are you all right?' she was asking.

'Yes,' said Anna, 'I just . . . I haven't had lunch.' This was true. She hadn't had lunch. She should eat lunch. Wait! The little fucker had taken her sandwich. This small loss affected Anna as the rest of the experience had not. She'd taken her sandwich! And she didn't have enough money to buy another. She stood up, trembling slightly, and headed back to the office.

By the time Anna reached the front door a few minutes later her breathing was even and her head was killing her, where a small egg had swollen under the hair. The important thing was not to touch it. If she didn't see the blood she'd stay upright. She stopped by the rubbish bins and her eyes fell on a canvas bag, her canvas bag; the bag which she had just been mugged for, sitting in the bin. She leaned forward and picked it out. She could just put it through the wash. Next to it was the pregnancy test Anna had bought only twenty minutes before. Was it OK to use it? The cardboard was relatively undamaged. She didn't have another eight pounds ninety-nine. She was only going to piss on it anyway. Anna picked it up too.

Dazed, Anna walked into reception, where clients of the charity she worked for waited for appointments with the doctors and lawyers in the offices upstairs. The building was ancient and ugly, entirely unsuited for its current purpose, and the clients were packed downstairs on top of each other in the makeshift waiting room. Directly opposite her, as she came in the door, was her tiny assailant. She had her feet up on the municipal rectangular chairs, and in her hand was Anna's Boots sandwich, half-eaten.

Her eyes met Anna's. She recognised her immediately, and, with no sense of urgency, as if quite sure Anna would do nothing to denounce her, pulled her feet down from the chairs, stood up and crossed the couple of metres which separated them. In that time it struck Anna that the girl was, in all likelihood, a former camp follower, a child kidnapped by the military and held against her will, her accent, the scars along the inside of her arms – whipmarks – all pointed that way. She was just a kid.

The receptionist, Prudence, clocked Anna's grazed cheek.

'Anna! Are you OK?'

'I'm fine,' Anna said, keeping her eyes on the mugger – the girl, Anna corrected herself. Inside the office, she looked much younger. Her make-up seemed like the make-up of an eight-year-old, playing with face-paint. She must be older than eight. How old was she? Twelve? Thirteen? Anna couldn't catch a breath. Shit. Shit shit shit. Anna had hit her first, hadn't she? From the girl's point of view, she had been defending herself from Anna. Anna had smashed a child in the teeth. A child who'd more than likely been tortured. She could go to prison for that, couldn't she? She'd certainly lose her job. What was the girl doing? She was raising her left hand. 'Oh God,' Anna thought, 'she's going to tell everyone. She's going to tell everyone what I am.'

'It was . . .' Anna told Neil, 'just some kid.'

'What did he look like?' Neil demanded.

'He . . . I didn't really get a good look.'

'I'll kill him! I'll fucking kill him!' Neil was next to her. He smelt like coal tar anti-dandruff shampoo, and it was helping. Neil's mouth was a square of rage. This was savage enough to draw Dermot's attention.

'All right!' Dermot shrugged. 'No need to go nuts!' He rolled his eyes at Anna.

'It's really fine!' Anna tried to smooth over Neil. 'Didn't have anything worth stealing.'

Dermot was giving her an impish look.

'No,' she said to the unasked question, 'they didn't take my phone.'

'Course he fucking didn't!' Dermot couldn't stop himself laughing. 'Sorry! Sorry! It must have been scary.'

'Have you gone to the police?' Neil demanded, all jaw.

'Ah, come on,' Dermot batted away the possibility, 'the police aren't going to do anything, are they?'

'You have to report it! The guy might be dangerous!' Neil thumped the table, making the tray of drinks shiver and clink.

Part of Anna, a part she was ashamed of, wished Dermot would punch Neil in the face. She wished Dermot would stand up, sweep the glasses off the varnished wood, say, 'For fuck's sake, Neil! She's my fucking girlfriend! And I'll defend her!' and kiss her hard while her jeans soaked up the Doom Bar. Anna imagined Dermot punching Neil, just leaning across the table and swinging those big arms of his, smashing into Neil's head.

'Do you want to report it, Anna?' Dermot asked.

'Not really,' she said.

'There! So can we all just calm down! Drink? Drink?' Dermot had stood up and was pointing at everyone down the table. 'Oh God,' Anna thought, Dermot was about to spend their rent. Dermot caught the look on Anna's face.

'We get two each free!'

'I'm fine,' said Anna, 'but can you get me some pickles?'

Dermot bowed elaborately. 'Your every wish,' he said, 'is my command!'

Neil leaned forward, his ridiculous chestnut leather bracelets almost exactly the same colour as his skin. Neil's olive eyes were resting on the little dip at her clavicle.

'Where's your flower?' he asked.

'What?'

Anna wore a tiny silver necklace in the shape of a bell-flower, with a pearl embedded in it. It was a Rampion: her surname. It had been given to her by her mum when she was four years old and she never, never took it off.

'Your flower necklace? Where is it?'

Anna's hand came up to her neck. Neil was right. Her neck was bare. She must have lost it in the mugging. Immediately her other hand came up to cover her reaction.

'I left it off today.'

Anna was profoundly grateful that, despite Neil's proximity, she hadn't wanted him physically. Anna paid close attention to the minor details of her physicality; whether she was sweating, or had a pain in her temple, or an ache in her back. She wasn't very good at that thing that other people, especially other women, seemed to do so easily, saying, 'I'm sad' or 'I'm angry.' She'd had, she was aware, the very best education in the world, in suppressing her feelings until she was no longer able to recognise what her feelings were. Boarding school, they said, built character. 'It does build character,' Anna thought, 'it's just the character Kathy Bates plays in *Misery*.' So she scanned her body for clues to her mental state. She was not reacting to Neil's too-close body. She observed Neil's forearm, just inches away from her own; although the hairs on his arm were alive, hers were lying flat. Neil was covered with goosebumps. And she was unaffected. Then he lifted his hand, his index finger hovered over the spot where her flower should be, and came up to her face, landing on her jaw like a butterfly, tilting her face into the light, and she felt herself go over a humpback bridge. Her womb thudded up, her pulse was in her groin and she was wet.

'It looks really bad,' he said.

It did look bad. Was anybody else seeing this? This was

out of order, wasn't it? Where was Dermot? Outside, smoking, she guessed. Maybe she wanted to hit Neil. Maybe she didn't want Dermot to. Maybe she wanted to thump Neil over and over again, her fist smashing into his beautiful lips, making them swell.

'Thanks very much!' Anna said lightly. 'I'm combining a bashed-in eye with a nude lip.'

'I'm sorry,' Neil said.

What did that mean? He was sorry he'd looked at her in the doorway? He was sorry whatever had happened, happened. Maybe he didn't mean anything. He did this stuff all the time. Maybe she wasn't wet. Maybe it was just blood she could feel. She should check but right now she didn't trust her legs.

Anna put the orange handbag on the table in front of her. She didn't know why she'd brought it. What if it got lost? Her canvas bag was still hanging on the radiator drying. Dermot had suggested she take this one as she was trying to fit a bag's worth of stuff into her pockets – 'Why don't you take *the* bag?' – and for some reason it seemed like a perfectly reasonable idea. But now she was scared of someone spilling beer over it. She clutched it to her under the table.

'New bag?' Neil asked, nodding at the leather. 'Aren't you veggie?'

Anna shrugged. 'The other one got a bit fucked up.'

Dermot appeared with more drinks.

'That bag, right . . . wait for it . . . Was the bag she was left in when she was a baby!' Dermot was triumphant. 'Oh shit!' he said, as he saw Anna's face. 'Was that a secret?'

'Not any more!'

Dermot smacked his forehead. 'You know I can't keep anything quiet! It's why I'd make the world's greatest husband. You can be sure I'd never cheat. Because I can't lie, baby!'

'Husband?' Neil raised his eyebrows. 'Are you going to make an honest man of him?'

Anna held up her hands, palms out. 'Move along, lads! Nothing to see here!'

'She's going to put a ring on it. She just doesn't know it yet.' Dermot leaned across the pair of them. 'Anyway, that's the bag!'

'What are you talking about?' Neil was having trouble following Dermot's slightly slurred speech.

'You know, when she was, not abandoned, but . . .'

'I think abandoned is fine.' Anna stared into her wine.

'OK! Abandoned. It was like, "A Haaaaaandbaaag?"' Dermot did a startlingly good upper-class English accent. 'That's it! That's the fucking handbag!'

'Really? You were left in this? Jesus, you must have been tiny,' said Neil.

'About nine weeks old,' Anna said.

'Have you ever tried to find them?'

'Who?'

'Your birth . . . your biological . . .' Neil floundered.

'You mean her real mam?' Dermot interjected.

'I think the standard phrase is birth mother. Or first mother,' Anna suggested.

'You can join DNA sites now,' Neil volunteered.

'Can you really?' Anna said. 'I had no idea!'

Dermot narrowed his eyes. 'Ah right!' he said, like he was a brilliant detective cracking a case. 'Sarcasm!'

'Did it all years ago,' said Anna.

'Did you?' said Dermot. 'Why didn't you tell me that?'

''Cause nothing came of it,' Anna replied lightly.

'Can't you just do it on Facebook?' Dermot was over-excited. 'People put up signs like a Bob Dylan video and their families turn up, out of the blue.'

'A Bob Dylan video,' said Anna, 'is that your most up-to-date reference?'

'Dylan never gets old!' Dermot was indignant. 'Dylan's immortal! Dylan's a god!'

'What about *Love Actually*? That's at least in the last twenty years. Doesn't the guy stalk his best mate's wife with some cue cards in that? It's a meme!' Anna raised her drink carefully over the leather.

'He's not stalking her, is he?' Neil observed carelessly. 'He's just letting her know how he feels, without hope or agenda.'

'Oh my God!' Dermot cracked up. 'He knows it off by heart!'

'Damn right!' Neil thumped the table. 'Best Christmas film ever! Plus, she fucking kisses him, so it's not stalking!'

'The guy's an arsehole,' said Dermot, 'and the woman's a right slag.'

Anna tried to steer the conversation away from the sexual ethics of women who kiss their partner's best friend. 'I'm not looking for my family. I mean, what would I say? I don't even know my mum's name. "You didn't want me thirty-five years ago. Do you want me now?"'

'She's not going to just fall in your lap, you know,' Dermot told her.

'You can't not try just because you're scared of being rejected,' Neil said. 'I mean, what's the worst thing that could happen?'

Anna saw Neil's glass topple off the table and smash, and the broken splinters cutting tiny feet.

'Guys,' said Anna, 'I would like nothing more than to find my mother, but if it hasn't happened by now, it's never going to happen. Did you get the pickles?'

'Ah shit!' said Dermot, and he went haring off to the bar again.

Anna looked at herself in the pub toilet mirror. Her reflection looked the same as always. Like herself, not like she was pregnant.

But she hadn't looked pregnant last time. Anna remembered the waiting room. There'd been a young girl sitting there with her boyfriend. Anna had been alone. She'd ended up chatting to the girl about football – she was wearing an Arsenal T-shirt – while they waited. The boyfriend had been totally silent. She remembered thinking, 'This abortion clinic is the only place two women could have a conversation about football without a man offering his opinion.' Afterward, when she'd been bleeding, she'd bought an Arsenal T-shirt herself and worn it while she watched *Obvious Child* to cheer herself up.

She didn't want to repeat the experience. But she wasn't a mum. She wasn't a beautiful, big-hearted woman with auburn ringlets and a great big voice. She was small and dark and she liked quiet. Thirty-five years old but from a distance easily mistaken for a twelve-year-old boy, except for the hair. The hair was 'long enough to sit on'. That's the phrase that was used. Anna hated it. It made her think of pubes.

Her breasts ached inside the sports bra she always wore. Aching breasts was a sign of pregnancy, wasn't it? Or a sign of a sports bra? She obviously couldn't have a baby. What did babies even eat? She fished inside the bag for her phone and googled it. Milk! Of course! They drink breast-milk! How much? How much do they do that? 'Babies can suckle for between ten minutes and an hour.' An hour? An hour a day? It's got to be more than that. On TV they always said, 'He's ready for a feed.' A feed: like vampires. 'Babies can feed for up to ten times a day.' An hour? Ten times a day? Is this a joke? Ten hours a day just feeding a baby? For a moment, clear as day, Anna saw a baby drowning in the Butler sink. She couldn't have a baby.

Anna washed her hands again. The mugger had not denounced her. She had dropped Anna's half-eaten sandwich into Anna's palm.

'It's disgusting,' the girl told her. Dumbly, Anna had taken the sandwich. She'd turned and climbed up the narrow stairs to her floor. It was only when she got there that she noticed the sandwich was squashed into her palm, the fingers clawed around it, stuck shut. She'd had to unfurl the fingers of her right hand with her left, to drop the sandwich in the bin.

The test was poking out the top of the bag. It hadn't been earlier, had it? The cardboard packet was damaged by its adventures with the mugger. She was struck by the stupidity of doing it here, when they were both twenty feet away. It wouldn't be positive. But if it were, would Dermot be able to tell? Would Neil? But as Anna let herself into the cubicle, hanging her bag carefully on the back-of-door hook, and sat down to pee on the stick, she saw blood in her underpants. As always, she looked up rapidly and took a few breaths. Sometimes even the sight of her own period could make her pass out. Well, that was over. At least she could throw away this disgusting pregnancy test.

Anna checked her body for symptoms of emotion. There was no egg in her chest to indicate sadness. So she was relieved. She must be relieved.

By the time she got back Neil had brought her pickled onions. There couldn't be a surer sign, could there, that she was not about to follow him out into the street and kiss him on the mouth.

'What about the bag? Weren't there any clues in it?'

'Clues? You mean, like, a scarlet pimpernel and a poem?' said Anna.

'No, I just meant,' Neil shrugged, 'I don't know what I mean. That'd be cool, though, wouldn't it?' He tried to meet her eye and Anna resolutely avoided it.

Dermot loomed in, balancing beer. 'She might be a gajillionaire! Maybe she'll give us a yacht. And a castle. And a billion quid! Who knows?'

'I mean, I don't actually want a billion quid,' Anna said.

'I bet you could find her. I mean, with the internet and everything,' Neil said.

'The internet isn't a magic mirror, you know.' Anna noticed she was snappier than usual.

Dermot butted in, 'Ah now, I would argue with that. That's exactly what it is! A magic mirror that shows you what you want to see . . . like in that show with the hats.'

Neil and Anna took a second to process this. Anna got there first.

'Harry Potter?'

'That! Harry Potter! Who's for another?' Dermot tapped his glass on the table.

'I think if we're forgetting the name of Harry Potter it might be best to sit this one out,' Neil suggested.

'I don't want to!' Dermot gestured wildly. 'Are you accusing me of drunk?'

Dermot's beer arced across the table. Anna snatched the bag up out of its trajectory and Neil was half up in his seat as the droplets caught his T-shirt. For a second Anna's eyes were level with Neil's belt and she glimpsed the hard muscle ridge that led down. Neil's scent rolled towards Anna like a tidal wave, ready to drown her. Anna kept the bag up to her face to defend herself from it.

'I mean . . . well, I am drunk! Free beer!' Dermot shrugged. 'I'm arse-holed. Do you think I should sit this one out, Anna? Anna?'

Anna was sitting completely still with her face in the bag. It had her bag smell: make-up and mints, and the smell of the old leather itself. She was profoundly familiar with both these smells. She had held the bag many times before, rubbing the leather against her top lip, skin to skin. But now, defending against Neil's powerful pheromones, she smelt something else – something different. It was a bad smell, a rotten smell. How could she have missed it? Had Neil slipped something into the bag? Was this a trick? What was that smell? Had Dermot's beer caught it? She inhaled deeply and ran her hands across the sides and down to the base, but the bag was dry. And then she knew what it was. It was unmistakable. The fusty smell of paper that was once wet. Her hands were guided to the metal ridge which protected the bag's base. Fluidly, and as if it had done so every single time she'd touched it, the metal support divided into two, to reveal a hitherto unseen pocket in the bottom of the bag. Anna exhaled slowly. She slid her fingers into the fold, and immediately felt the skin on the tip of her index finger spring apart. As she sucked the cut, with her other hand she pulled out what was inside – a small booklet.

It was a school report card. The paper undulated where it had recovered from some long-ago storm. A darker line separated the handwritten report from the pupil's identifying details. Across the top it said first the name, and then the subject, then the grade.

Marlene . . . spelt like Dietrich, L and the surname was illegible. Waters? Mather? Walter? English, A. Anna held it up.

'This was in the bottom.' Her face was pale enough to get both their attention.

'Jesus!' said Neil.

Anna began to flip the pages. In subject after subject on the handwritten report, the student was described as Marlene L W, or maybe, Marlene L M, but her surname didn't appear again.

'Marlene was well prepared for her A-level and I expect her to have done well. She might have done better had she not, unfortunately, missed so much school with her ailments this year.'

'Marlene, alas, has missed more of the lessons than any of us would have liked this year, but despite this, I expect her to achieve a high grade.'

'Marlene seems to have a good grasp of her religious studies, despite her unseemly brawling with her classmates.'

It must be her mother. Her mother was called Marlene. Marlene L Walters? She'd been 'brawling with her classmates'. And she'd been missing school. Why? Because she was pregnant, of course. She was pregnant with Anna. Anna found herself staring at the little bowl of pickled onions in front of her, like eyeballs, wet eyeballs, and she lifted her hand to her face to find water was running freely down her own cheeks. She must be crying.

3

SIX WEEKS GONE

'Changes in your libido are common in the first few weeks of pregnancy. You may experience an upturn in your sex drive. This is due to your hormone levels fluctuating and is completely normal. If, instead, you want to have sex less than usual, this is nothing to worry about.'

'Doing a little genealogy project, are you?' Nicholas asked. 'Why would that bother me?'

'No reason, I just thought you might want to know that I'm looking for her. It doesn't mean anything. I mean . . . I don't want you to think it's because . . . of anything.'

Anna was propped in Nicholas's kitchen, though at first glance it might have been taken for an over-full garage or, possibly, a recycling centre. Only the tap rising from the sea of objects on the worktop marked it out for food preparation. Anna's adoptive father, who she called Nick, saved everything.

He blew on his cup of tea at the same time as Anna blew on hers.

'What's prompted this?' he asked.

'Nothing really,' Anna said.

'I quite understand you digging up your roots, as it were,

though I have to say, you probably won't have much luck; there wasn't anything left with you, you know, so there weren't any leads. I've learnt a bit about this recently as I've been doing the same thing myself.'

'I'm sorry?'

'I've been looking for my biological parent also, coincidentally,' Nicholas added.

'Oh!' Anna was dumbfounded.

As far as Anna knew, Nick had never met his own dad. His mother had left him at a home for waifs and strays. The story was that his father was a pilot killed in the war, but the payment due to RAF kids – there was some sort of official stipend – never turned up. The Barnardo's staff therefore assumed Nicholas was illegitimate. 'A bastard,' her father said, raising his eyebrows. It was the only time he swore. Nicholas liked saying 'bastard'. He even let Anna say it, so long as she was using the word correctly. She wasn't allowed to say, 'Lucky bastard!' or 'Stupid bastard!' but 'bastard' was just fine. Nicholas spent his childhood moving from foster home to foster home.

Magically, one of the homes stuck. But then there was some sort of argument with his biological mother. She'd turned up to take him for a weekend out when he was six, just a weekend out from the home he'd known for all his conscious life: the home he thought was his and the people he knew as Auntie Sal and Uncle Eric, but who had changed his nappy and fed him and hugged him when he fell off a wall – the people who were, to any sane eye, his mother and father. His birth mother was called Baby, of all things: a family nickname that had stuck. Baby had turned up against the foster-parents' wishes. Nicholas had later been told it was because 'Baby' didn't want him attaching too strongly. Apparently, his foster-parents had said, 'If you take him out, don't bother bringing him back.' Baby took him out and the foster-parents, true to their promise, sent him back to the children's 'home': poor little bastard, poor, poor little bastard.

Then he bounced around in care, until Baby took him in at eleven. By that time, she'd had a couple more kids, and was working as a midwife. He was given the choice: a scholarship to the Choir School or live with his mother. He'd chosen his mother. It hadn't worked out. His much younger half-brothers fought constantly, and Baby treated him as if he was the same age as them, sending him to bed at half past seven while he tried to study for his 'O' levels. She was irritable with him. Everything her dark, handsome son said annoyed Baby. Anna knew how handsome her father was because people constantly commented on it – even the nervous RE teacher had asked what it was like having such a 'matinee idol' for a father, although he was twenty or thirty years older than all the other dads. Good looks don't sit right on some people. There is a disconnect between the way they look and who they are. Anna knew her father had never grasped how good-looking he was, and how it changed the way people treated him. He didn't understand why women were always so stupid: giggling, blushing. 'You're the only sensible woman, Anna,' he would say. And those good looks, presumably like the biological father who'd knocked up 'Baby' at eighteen, made his mother cruel and negligent. It took Anna a long time to understand that his time at 'home' was why, when he sent her away, after her mum died, her father regarded it as some special privilege he was bestowing, rather than a punishment. She was living his dream, away at school, on a scholarship, far from family, with their complicated, difficult feelings, in a world of pure reason. But here he was 'doing a genealogy project': looking for his father.

'I can lend you a book if you want.' Her father fetched a white bound book with a silver title, *So You Want to Find Your Family?* The cover's saccharine style was entirely incongruous in his hand. 'It warns you about the possible pitfalls.'

'Any luck?'

'Yes, I found him,' Nick nodded. Anna coughed on a biscuit.

'You found him?'

'But, dead of course,' Nick added cheerily, 'hanged in a US military court in the fifties. Murderer! Terribly dramatic!'

'Oh my God!' said Anna. 'How . . . does that . . .'

Nicholas batted away Anna's implied question. 'Oh, none of that! Criminality isn't genetic, though traits like aggression can be. I think if I was going to turn out to be a cold-hearted killer it would've happened by now, don't you?' He waggled his eyebrows.

'Still . . . You must have hoped to meet . . .'

'I hadn't hoped anything. Always best not to hope for anything, then you can never be disappointed.' Nick clasped his arms behind his back and wheezed, 'Much the most sensible course of action.' Anna became dimly aware that he was trying, in his own distant way, to protect her. She attempted a strained hug. It was, perhaps, the fourth or fifth time she had hugged him in her life. 'Goodness! What have

I done to deserve this?' he said, patting her ineffectually and turning away to put the kettle on again.

Anna took a deep breath. 'Actually, I think I found a name. It was on a report card in the bag I was left in. I think she's called Marlene.'

Nick was now completely motionless.

'My goodness!'

'You aren't upset, are you?' Anna asked.

'No, no!' He remained with his back to her.

She had upset him. 'You don't want me to find her. You think I'm letting Mum down.'

Anna knew without seeing his face that Nicholas was wearing the glazed look he got when he was trying to process emotion. Conflicting feelings often shut him down for a few minutes, like an old desktop. Anna could almost see the spinning, coloured wheel. She took over making the tea while Nicholas sorted through the tangled connections in his brainstem, perching slowly on the countertop amongst a collection of old spoons.

After what seemed like minutes, Nicholas was ready to speak.

'A name might well be enough, these days . . . the wonders of modern technology! But I'm reminded of the old adage: just because we *can* use a technology doesn't mean we *should*. Some people aren't cut out to be parents, Anna.' He shook his head ruefully.

What did this mean? Was he apologising for his own distant parenting? Was he more hurt by the idea of her mum being replaced than he could admit? Or was he disturbed by the discovery of his own family history, despite his levity?

Anna opened the book. In the first pages was a 'Fill in Your Own Family' chart, with empty rectangles branching off from each other. In the 'Father' box, Nick had pencilled in a name in his unreadable scientist writing. He had also turned the little box into a 'Hangman'. He saw her looking at it.

'You can always rub that out.' Nicholas leaned forward and gripped Anna's hand. 'Promise me you won't do anything without telling me? About your mother,' Nicholas said. 'Promise me?'

Anna's right hand was wet. She didn't look at the mugger lying on the floor because her head was caved in, but she did look at her right hand, soaked, as she knew it would be, in blood. The blood ran off automatically as if rinsed by tap water to reveal her own lily-white skin. She was clutching a sandwich. Her eyes drifted to the corpse, shrinking rapidly now, until all that was left was the body of a baby.

Anna woke up, sweating. Her right hand was between her legs. Dermot slept beside her. He was making the strange staccato suckling noise he sometimes made when he'd drunk too much. She'd have to be up for work in an hour and a half anyway. She threw back the duvet and went into the bathroom. The light above the mirror made her black eye bloom. It was just as well she had promised her father. No mother, surely, would want to see this creature crawling out of the woodwork?

God, she could murder a pickle! In the 'kitchen' – a recess carved out of the front room – she was confronted by rows of ancient cans: some previous attempt of hers at organisation had left them in a strict system which now made absolutely no sense to her. She started to unpack them all, maybe there was a jar of pickles in here somewhere. She was now making a hell of a racket, but nothing could wake Dermot once he was down: nothing. Salt! At least there was salt. She poured salt into the palm of her hand and started lapping at it like a cat.

Rooting around down between the sofa cushions for the remote control, Anna found her vibrator, abandoned for some months. It wasn't branded as a vibrator on the box, but as a massager for sports injuries. Anna made the same joke every time they used it: it *was* for sports injuries, if the sport was wanking. It was velvety black, like a hole in the fabric of space time. She thought it might take the pressure off Dermot. The last time she'd tried to make it a part of sex, he had pretended it was a Dalek prison ship, releasing the Daleks every time she tried to switch it on. They'd both been on the floor laughing but it had killed the mood, which she assumed was what he wanted.

Maybe she just needed to come. She generally operated on a need-to-come basis, only bothering with masturbation in extremis. She'd never seen the point of the old suds and candles routine. Why would you bother running a bath for yourself or taking yourself out to dinner? You knew what you were after. You weren't going to turn yourself down. She could use the vibrator. She was going to come but she was going to do the right thing and come to a nice wholesome Dermot fantasy. She tried the concealed button. It was out of juice – of course it was. Dermot didn't want to have sex with her, even by proxy.

She found the charger in Dermot's desk drawer, in his box of cables-which-have-no-known-use. Was that safe, to use it plugged in? Well, she'd find out. There was still salt on her palm. She lay on the sofa and pictured Dermot, lovely Dermot, funny Dermot – but the second the machine touched her, Dermot's face turned into Neil's and Neil was all she could see: Neil Byrne on top of her, pushing into her, his bare brown shoulders against her cheek, his long fingers stuffing something round into her mouth, something round and veined. Neil Byrne, part-machine, was fucking her and . . . filling her mouth with pickles? The vibrator stopped suddenly. The TV was black, not a light in the flat. The electricity key must have run out. Anna screamed silently into the sofa cushion. What was the point in having the bloody thing if she didn't have the power to use it?

Seething with frustration, Anna stumbled blindly into the kitchen. As she counted her in-breath, she remembered the tin she'd hidden under the sink – the last place Dermot would look. In it were two folded twenties, smelling of Brasso.

Anna came back half an hour later. She pushed the electricity key into the slot. As the overhead flickered into life, Anna stood stock still. She knew what she had to do. It was very, very wrong. But she was going to do it anyway.

The mugger girl had been in the waiting room at two on a Thursday, when it was full. Anna surmised she must have been waiting for a group. She dropped by reception and asked which groups were running on Thursday afternoon – she wanted to book a large room. Anna noticed that as she lied through her teeth, she sounded completely normal. Prudence, the grandmotherly receptionist, handed over the timetable, pointed at Anna's eye and said, in her deep Zimbabwean accent, 'You should have seen the other guy!'

'Right,' said Anna, forcing a smile. There were two groups – Art Therapy and Mothers and Babies (for the mothers of children born of rape). Short of stealing an infant, Anna didn't see how she could investigate the Baby Group, but it was easy to sneak into the Art Therapy room. On one of the Formica tables were piles of paintings signed by the clients. One pile was of self-portraits in charcoal. Most of them were entirely abstract or completely unrecognisable but two-thirds down the pile was a strikingly good likeness of the girl who had punched Anna in the tit. The Art Therapist had helpfully added little white labels with people's first names on. It said, 'Samyra'.

The database was a mess but a search by first name and likely country of origin revealed only two Samyras. One was eleven years old. Could the girl have been that young? The other Samyra had no recorded age, but was under the Child and Adolescent team. Sweating, Anna let herself into the stuffy file room, which was a regular haunt, clutching a piece of paper with the file number on it. Technically she wasn't allowed in here, as a temp. But since she'd been 'temping' for eight years, the data manager, a Persian God named Darius, whose perfect skin peeped out in tiny brown petals between each button of his tight white shirt, knew her and nodded her in.

Anna found the no-age-recorded hard copy first. It was the mugger. Her age was scrawled in Sharpie on the top right-hand corner – twenty-one. Before she could change her mind, Anna took out her phone and photographed the cover page with the mugger's address. Then she saw a question mark next to the age. Often the age of kids who'd arrived alone was disputed. Anna started to read the file from dirty foolscap cover to dirty foolscap cover, sitting on the floor amongst the shelves of files. She had the sense, as she often did reading the cases, that she was standing at the doorway to hell. She was on earth but looking through to the underworld. The girl's story, framed in the fiery doorway, shared characteristics with hundreds she had read: all of them escapees from Hades, crawling out from a pit of bodies and running, running for the border. The girl had lost her family. She'd watched as her mother was murdered, and then had been separated from her twin brother and two younger sisters. She had been the wife/slave of a captain in the militia which ran the north of her country. She'd been impregnated at fourteen, tied to a tree while pregnant, and the baby had been taken, where she didn't know. There were photographs of her scars, great keloid scars branching across her back. But of all the things that woke her at night, it was the loss of her twin brother which haunted her most. She knew he was dead, and he visited her in her dreams, calling for her, begging her to save him.

This girl's childhood was long over. She went to put the file back and had to take out several others hanging in the same divider. She checked the three files to make sure the names were alphabetised: an error in storing them could jeopardise the survivors' legal progress. They were a mess. As Anna sorted the files, she noticed that the file fourth or fifth down had a similar family name. A passport photo was clipped to the front of a kid who looked a lot like the mugger – no, exactly like her. Picking up the file, she realised he had the same birthday. Not just the same birthday, the same year of birth.

Anna opened the boy's file: the murdered mother – a missing father – two younger sisters. The boy had been recruited as a child soldier. He was – he had to be – her twin. Anna noticed her hands were shaking violently as she flipped to the back of the files where their key-worker contact details were held to take a photo. The boy had a shrink – Dr Alec Higham. The girl had a lawyer. It's possible the shrink and the lawyer had barely met, never mind discussed their cases. He lived here, two miles from his sister. She was the only one who knew. Well, she had wanted to know who had hurt her. What was she going to do?

Anna made her way to the locked door of the file room, where a small glass window criss-crossed with wires provided a view through to Darius's antechamber. He was bent over his computer, his sleeves pushed up to reveal veined arms. He got up and shimmied round the desk like a ballroom dancer to let her through.

'Hey Anna!' he called through the door, as the lock clicked open. 'What are you signing out?'

Anna slipped her phone into her back pocket.

'Nothing,' she said.

Three days later, Anna found a painting on her desk. There was also an envelope. The letter she found inside was written on the back of lined A4 paper. 'To the person who found my brother. I just want to say: thank you from the bottom of my heart. I don't have anything to give you, but I painted this picture of how I feel and I thought you might like it.'

The twins had reunited in front of everybody. The plan was that they should meet in the scrubby bit of garden the charity had at the back, for privacy, and to protect those who weren't about to be reunited with their long-lost family from pain. But both twins went to reception at the same time, so anyone who was there witnessed their reunion. Anna was not there, but Layla was, and she told Anna about it, how they had pulled together as if magnetised, how they had held each other, shouting for joy, how they had fallen, as one, to their knees, still holding each other, for minutes, long minutes, how all the unthinkable losses these children had suffered, of their mother and father and homeland, of their little sisters, of their innocence, had for a moment evaporated in this unexpected return. How the rest of the refugees waiting had turned to each other and embraced, their many differences for a moment erased, and their own losses for a moment put aside. What was lost had been found. Restitution is possible. Blood will out.

The painting was in acrylics. It was a vivid yellow and white earth and a massive black and grey root system which reached deep into it. The root system had produced what looked like a red flower, a mass of red dots. Behind the stem was a band of blue sky, and the blossom was framed against clouds in green and gold. It was a fantastic painting, an incredible painting, a painting which said, from deep roots grow beautiful blooms, and it had been given to her.

Layla said, 'If this is not a message from God that you should find your birth mother – I don't know what is.'

Anna saw a baby, naked and crying, on the cracked earth.

'Are you kidding?' Anna replied. 'You don't believe in God! And you just gave me a massive lecture about how biology isn't destiny!'

'Still,' said Layla, 'look at it.'

It was Mather: Marlene Mather. Marlene Mather was Anna's mother. It took her about half an hour. The name kept coming up in the Facebook posts of a woman called Hebe Williamson.

Hebe was twenty-eight and looked very similar to Anna. She looked, in fact, just exactly like her, only prettier. She looked like Anna if Anna were sold as a doll on Etsy. She had a fashion bob with a short fringe that was halfway between model and village idiot, and Anna's brown eyes. She wore unflattering jeans and bulky sweaters and flat shoes – the kind of clothes that twenty-somethings wore as a sort of challenge, a fight between the ugliness of the clothes and the youth and beauty of the wearer. At the moment Hebe's loveliness was winning.

Anna, on her desktop, scrolled through Hebe's photos expecting a thousand beautiful artsy friends in dungarees with blue highlights and mocktails, but there wasn't much, just a few selfies taken on a home computer and an endless stream of half-focus shots of London: men combing their hair outside Polish supermarkets at night, an old woman in a tea-cosy hat walking alone down the middle of the road, a single owl on an iron railing – images of loneliness. She was faintly relieved to see that Hebe wasn't a Facebook moaner: no oblique references to people who'd hurt her, 'You know who you are,' or boaster: no cutesy trailers for an unspecified 'announcement' she was about to make, 'Really exciting news! Can't say much more now but watch this space,' and none of those narcissistic 'experiments', 'Only my real friends will read to the end of this post.'

Anna reflected briefly on Dermot's description of Facebook as the Mirror of Desire. Was she just seeing what she wanted to see? This was her sister, surely, and she didn't want her sister to be a wanker. But there were no red flags, just re-posts of funny videos, links to the odd left-leaning article about libraries or mental health and the endless photography. But then, sandwiched between a close-up of a Marlboro packet in a torrential gutter and a picture of a rat on the tube, there she was. They were proper photographs, the kind you had to develop in a chemist and then scan into the computer, of, it had to be, her mother: her mother, posing in a hat, her mother, lying on a bench in the sun, her mother, in a sheer shirt, the shadow of her nipples clearly visible. And Hebe had captioned it 'Ladies and Gentlemen, the one and only . . . Marlene Mather.'

Her mother was not fat. She was muscular and startlingly symmetrical. The photographs spanned decades, probably the decades of Anna's life. In each one her mother was completely different. She appeared to view clothes as costumes, almost personalities, to be put on and taken off at will. In one her hair was red and short and she was dressed in a ballgown. In another she wore a large perm and white leather boots, in another a pixie cut and a riding outfit. The last photo was a posed close-up of her arresting face, clearly taken by a professional photographer. Her eyes looked up through long straight lashes – brown eyes with a yellow starburst around the pupil – directly at the camera, as if she were finding whatever the photographer had just said to her both outrageous and appealing. Her chin had a very slight cleft in it, reminding Anna powerfully of somebody. Who was it? Anna realised with a jolt it was herself.

Anna hovered over Hebe's page. The silver title peeped out from under Dermot's lyrics next to the keyboard, *So You Want to Find Your Family?* Could she send Hebe a blank message? Was that too weird? Did she have to friend her first? But if Hebe received a friend request from a stranger who looked like her, what would she do? Turn it down, probably. Anna didn't accept anyone she didn't actually know. Anna looked at a photo of a suited type, clearly drunk, slumped under a bus shelter. Fuck it. Anna clicked on 'add friend' and looked up to the kitchen. She should put the kettle on. By the time she looked back at the computer there was a message in her inbox, 'I think I know who you are. Are you my sister? What do you want to know?'

4

EIGHT WEEKS GONE

'By the time you're eight weeks pregnant, your baby is called a foetus, which means offspring. You may be feeling very tired. Fatigue is extremely common at this stage of your pregnancy.'

A brand-new species of joy had nested in Anna's chest. She had a sister.

'Start Small' said the white book with the silver writing. 'Get To Know Each Other Slowly,' so they did. *What are you having for lunch?* Hebe would text Anna. *Do you like these boots? What's your favourite font?* Anna would send her a photo of a young man in a poncho on a train platform, *Train bro ready for shoot-out*, or a badly rhymed advert, *pure poetry*. And Hebe would reply with a long series of laugh emojis which were exactly at odds with her serious photo. Anna and Dermot had never done the messaging thing. But now Anna had someone to share inconsequential things with. It was exhilarating.

Something physical seemed to have changed, too, which Anna, constantly checking her pulse, attributed to the new relationship. She was endlessly sleepy. As a rule, she was bad at sleeping, but these days she fell asleep wherever she was. When she lay down on the sofa in the evening, she nodded off within a few minutes as if warmed by some inner fire. Perhaps this was what it felt like to be part of a family.

'Meeting Your Birth Family Can Feel Romantic' said the book, as Anna filled 'Hebe' in the empty box.

As if on a first date, Anna tried as hard as she could to counter Hebe's questions with pertinent and entertaining, uncomplicated questions of her own, 'Do you speak any other languages? What's your favourite sitcom? Do you have any pets?'

Hebe wished fervently that she hadn't brought the empty pushchair on the train. It made her look like a crazy person, as if she was out searching for some random baby to fill it. The man in the seat across from her kept looking at her. She tried to smile at him in a way that indicated she wasn't insane.

'Don't worry,' she volunteered, pointing at the pushchair cheerfully, 'it's for my cat!' The man looked out of the train window. Hebe had thought she could strap the cat basket in the pushchair and make it easier to move but the thing kept falling off. The man was now avoiding her gaze. She needed to reassure him further that she was normal.

'My cat's real!' she said. 'He's not an imaginary cat! He's called Ziggy Stardust. I almost called him the Thin White Duke, but I didn't think it would be good to shout out of the front door at night!' The man gave her a half-smile. 'Plus, he's actually tortoiseshell.'

Hebe hoped she'd done enough to convince him. People liked talking about cats. It was a normal conversational topic. He definitely looked more friendly. She'd done OK. She had not said: 'I had to leave my cat because my mother walked in on me having sex with her boyfriend.' That was the sort of thing she shouldn't volunteer in conversation. It was inappropriate. She was glad she hadn't said it.

When Tristan had first come to dinner, a short, twenty-six-year-old French vet, Hebe had thought her mother was trying to give her some sort of boyfriend-present, but that she'd made an error because there was no way Tristan was straight. He didn't even seem bi. He seemed gay. He couldn't really have seemed any more gay, but then, unexpectedly, they'd ended up having sex, twice. The sex was strange: not disgusting, but just sex without any sex in it. It was more like having a lukewarm bath in a slightly grubby hotel bathtub. Hebe only found out that he was already having sex with her mother when she walked in on them. She thought she should just go away, at the time. But afterwards, she felt terrible for leaving like that. He couldn't really be a very nice man, could he? It was only after she was on the train that she got the text message from her mother. *I've survived far worse. And I have another daughter.*

Hebe didn't want to go back to her mother's house. But she needed to get Ziggy. It wasn't that he wasn't safe there. It just wasn't fair to expect them to take care of him. The man was looking at her again. His eyebrows appeared to have been coloured in by a young child. Her mother always said, 'Ask questions! People love talking about themselves.' Hebe leaned forward, 'Do you have a cat?' she hazarded.

'No,' he said, 'but I like pussy', and he stuck out his tongue and flapped it rhythmically against his top lip in a way that made Hebe cry.

It took ages to get her stuff together to move down the carriage, away from the pussy guy. By the time she got to Woldingham, Hebe was bruised and exhausted. The basket had proved incredibly unwieldy and banged her shin every time she took a step. And she had to wheel the pushchair with her spare hand. The journey down the long gravel drive had been surreal. As she let herself into the front door, she pushed back a pile of post.

She paused in the hall, looking at the wooden teeth of the parquet chomping away to the far end. It was perhaps forty or fifty feet long. The heavy velvet landing curtains were drawn.

'Ma?' said Hebe, but there was no response. She put down the cat basket and pushchair and wandered through the rooms calling 'Ziggy! Ziggy!' but there was no sound. She stopped at the door of her mother's bedroom, unwilling to cross the lintel. 'Ma?'

The bed was unmade, the duvet dragged halfway across the room. There were streaks of something across the sheets.

'Ma?' Hebe's voice went up a key.

Hebe sped up as she went downstairs into the kitchen, where two glasses sat on the side with the remains of a meal, mould growing on the plates. Hebe recognised one of her mother's signature dishes: rabbit stew. She looked under the sink for the cat food, reassured by the squeaking of the cupboard door. There was a good stock there. Hebe peeled back the silver paper on the top of the Whiskas tin, and the smell of chicken liver filled the room. She got out a spoon and dinged it against the side of the tin.

Suddenly, in the wall, came the noise of something falling over and, in a strong French accent, a distinct, '*Putain!*'

'Tristan?' Hebe dropped the cat food and was across the kitchen, raising the old-fashioned latch which lay across the heavy oak pantry doors. As she opened the narrow doors towards her, her cat, Ziggy Stardust, launched directly at her, scratching and screaming.

Hebe fell back hard against the kitchen table, her arms smarting from where the cat had ripped her skin open, and from this position, sitting on the kitchen floor, came eye to eye with her mother's boyfriend, tied up in the cupboard, naked and covered with crap.

Hebe was so good at asking questions it took some time for Anna to notice she didn't answer them.

. . . *What was it like*, Anna asked . . . *having your mother bring you up?*

It was . . . . (Typing, typing . . .) Anna waited for the reply . . . *never dull. What was it like growing up without a mother?* Hebe would reply.

Fine, Anna would text.

No, really? Hebe would say.

In some ways it was useful to Anna that her motherlessness was absorbed into the greater motherlessness of the school. She stood out less. Though other girls called their teachers 'mummy' by mistake, Anna never did. And when Anna met her schoolfriends' real mothers at Sports Days and exeats she didn't feel like she was missing much. They were often brittle, nervous women, stretched between the need to succeed at work (my mother's the youngest cardiologist at King's), and the need to remain desirable to their ugly, blustery men. They were stretched thin, so very, very thin.

Didn't you miss your dad? Hebe would ask.

Not really, Anna would reply.

She had spent school holidays at her dad's house in Peckham, or, twice, excitingly, in Whitstable. He had brought her up as if he was trying to follow an incredibly difficult recipe in a hot kitchen to a terrifying deadline. Even though she had been a textbook child (maybe that was why she was a textbook child), he was sweating with the effort of it all until he could send her back to school and was released from the obligation to keep her alive.

What about your dad? Anna would ask Hebe, as she watched the dots.

Ah there's a story! Did you always want to work with refugees?

Anna hadn't. In her twenties she'd fallen into a niche area of administration at a mental health charity, which was simultaneously emotionally demanding and appallingly paid. She had hoped, in the end, to work with autistic children, but her plans to train as a clinical or educational psychologist got pushed back. Higher ambitions were subsumed by the business of paying a London rent. She'd always been drawn to clever, artistic men: men with no money. Then she was with Dermot, huge, hilarious Dermot. Dermot was telling her his stories, Dermot was singing her his songs. Dermot showing her stuff: hilarious, huge Dermot, so easy with himself it had seemed, the first person to say, 'Fuck it, stay on the couch! Play that again! Harmonise with this! Ah, we could all do with another bottle, couldn't we?', so that by the time she realised he wasn't easy at all, it was far too late, and he'd become her home.

Besides, Dermot was brilliant. His music was brilliant. His band was brilliant, he was always on the verge of somebody noticing just how brilliant he was. And the work itself was necessary. The urgency of the charity's various calls: the need of the clients was always greater than her own needs and she was helping people, wasn't she, psychologically? Even though it was by aligning databases and cataloguing symptoms. Without her, the place would, well, not fall apart, but they'd definitely have to get someone else in. She was a part of something important, wasn't she? The importance of the charity's work and then the importance of Dermot's talent, and so eight years, the eight years that separated her and Hebe, had just slipped away.

But now Hebe was asking her what she wanted, how she felt, and the light of this attention upon the facts of her existence cast new shadows. So it was only later, after she had put the phone under the sofa cushion and started scrolling down the listings, that she asked herself: what did that mean, *there's a story*? It had told her, Anna, precisely nothing.

Hebe had told her no facts at all. That was not quite true. She had told her that her hair was short despite Marlene wanting her to grow it long. Whenever she referred to Marlene it was as 'Marlene' or 'Ma'. Anna's job, part of it, consisted of piecing together case reports: the life stories of the charity's 'clients', people who had suffered unspeakably, fact by fact. 'Fatiha was held by the Iranian religious authorities in a cell so small she could not sit up. She was flogged every day. She was raped and impregnated. While pregnant the beating was limited to the soles of her feet. When the baby was born it was taken away from her and she experienced a septic fever. She now suffers infertility and incontinence, as well as being unable to bear weight on her left leg, and limited eyesight after nine years in the dark.'

Anna knew these case studies never told the whole story, other facts were available. 'Tell them I loved to read,' Fatiha begged her, 'don't put just all these bad things. It's depressing! Tell them I can still read a little if I just have my special glasses. Tell them my father had the best bookshop in Shiraz. Tell them I chose to help him there! I volunteered! That's why they beat me.'

Anna grasped that we are all much more than the things that have happened to us. She also knew most people wanted to tell you why: why, from where they are now standing, their lives took the direction they did. She knew that even those who had suffered most attributed that suffering to their own choices, or at least the survivors did. Anna sometimes wondered if the dead also imagined that they had power over their fates. Surely we all need to believe we steer our own lives, even if all the evidence is to the contrary. She knew that's why the women always blamed themselves for being raped. Blaming oneself is a profoundly optimistic thing to do. It assumes you had something to do with your own tragedy. The alternative: that someone else took every last scrap of self-determination, is worse, far worse, than believing it's all your fault. The survivors blamed themselves, and in doing so, wrested back the wheel from the arseholes who'd taken it away, even as they also libelled themselves.

But Hebe didn't want to claim ownership of anything, or not to Anna. She had no rehearsed story of why she'd taken this path or that, she only had more questions. Since asking Anna, 'What do you want to know?' she'd behaved as if these late-night text conversations were taking place in a court room, and anything she might say could be ripped to shreds by opposing counsel. Or had she? Anna had settled on *Law & Order*. It was playing now. She was getting carried away. Hebe was just polite. Dermot was right. She, Anna, was unnaturally suspicious. Her work, documenting the worst of humanity, had warped her. She hoped it was that. If you anticipated people being kind and open, they would be. People were always nice to Dermot – wherever he went people bought him rounds. She'd once asked Dermot if he'd got pocket money when he was a kid and Dermot had said, 'No, just the normal money.'

'What normal money?' Anna had asked.

'You know, when grown-ups come up to you in the street and give you some money to go and buy sweets.' Anna didn't know. 'Perhaps it's an Irish thing.' Anna suspected it wasn't an Irish thing, but a Dermot thing. People just gave him money for being Dermot. Anna was probably too suspicious of Hebe. Wasn't she?

'Where's my mother?' Hebe demanded. 'What did you do to her?'

But Tristan couldn't speak, or not in English, or not so that Hebe could understand.

She put Tristan in front of the wood-burning stove in her mother's 'snug'. Tristan couldn't stop shivering. Hebe noticed her own tremor had gone. Her hand, taking the fire-lighter to the pile of kindling, was suddenly steady as a rock. She found crackers and cheese then set Tristan up with a little pile of food on a plate, on the rug in front of the fiery window.

'Don't!' he said. 'I'll get crumbs on the carpet!' He was now dressed in one of Marlene's expensive quilted house-coats, a quasi-Japanese affair with delicate cherry blossoms on. It contrasted his sturdy dark features. The black hair that was visible on all the uncovered parts of him was drying into little whorls, like a goat. She'd helped him shower, leading him trembling and stinking into the William Morris guest bathroom. She'd held what she'd heard plumbers refer to as a 'bum hose' over his head as he squatted in the bath. He had his own share of cat scratches and bites, and some of them were now livid and raised, clearly infected, and she'd watched him, over the space of two short minutes, change from beast to man. As she washed him, she made out the words, 'Why did you leave me so long?' in his powerful French accent. Or thought she did. Is that what he said? Now he squirmed in front of the fire.

'What day is it?' he asked.

'It's Friday. How long were you in there?' Hebe said.

'Very funny!' said Tristan. 'That's not very nice!'

Hebe was deeply confused.

'Who locked you in the cupboard?' she asked. 'Why were you there?'

Tristan looked at her with absolute incredulity. 'You did it!' he said. 'It was you!'

'First things first; are you having an affair?' Layla sounded upbeat.

'What?' Anna said, her stomach turning over.

'Dermot thinks you are having an affair.'

'He said that?' Anna said warily.

'No, he implied it.'

'What?' Anna said again.

'He wants me to take you out and pump you for information in a professional capacity and check, and I quote "if she's happy with everything".'

'Why is he suddenly concerned about my happiness?'

'He strongly implied if you *were* having an affair, that would be all right.'

This was a surprise. 'How did he imply that?' asked Anna.

'He said, "If you find out something's going on, whatever's going on is fine."'

'Wow! So, I'm allowed to cheat!' Anna declared. 'It sounds like that's what you are telling me. Dermot's giving me permission to bang hot guys!'

Layla snorted but added, 'But seriously, is something going on?'

'Like what?' Anna was defensive.

'He said you were acting "different". I think he's worried about you. My guess is he thinks you are going nuts. He wants me to ascertain if you are going nuts, but subtly so you wouldn't work out what was going on. I believe he used the phrase "girl talk",' Layla said.

'Christ!' Anna, unusually, swore.

'Yes,' said Layla. 'Hence, he thinks you're banging someone else. He wants my professional opinion as to exactly how mad you are, and whether this madness has manifested in aforementioned banging.'

'Right. Are you going to take me out?' Anna asked.

'Who has the time?' Layla replied airily. 'I just thought I'd ask you instead.'

'This is so weird. He's never shown the slightest jealousy. He's the most confident guy in the world.' Dermot really was confident. She was such a horrible slut. Dermot never looked at another woman – had never looked, had never spoken to. She had not for a moment seen his eyes wander. 'Why would he suddenly think this?' Anna said.

'He says you've stopped coming on to him,' Layla told her.

'He turns me down every time!'

'I know that! Plus, he says you spend all night texting someone and hiding the phone under your pillow.'

'I didn't realise he'd noticed.'

'Oh my God!' Layla was excited. 'You are texting someone! Who are you texting?'

Anna took a deep breath, 'My sister.'

There was a moment as Layla absorbed this. 'Plot twist!'

'I found her two weeks ago. I haven't told Dermot yet.'

'Is your mum alive?' Layla got straight to it.

'My mother,' Anna corrected her, 'yes, she's alive.'

'Oh my God, Anna!' Layla started crying. 'You're going to meet your mother!'

'I don't know that,' said Anna.

'Why wouldn't you?' Layla asked.

There was a pause. 'I'm . . .' Anna began, 'I'm not sure my sister wants me to.'

'Fuck your sister!' said Layla. 'What's her problem? Is she jealous?'

'I haven't even met her yet.'

'Well, it sounds like you should. And for shit's sake, tell Dermot it's your sister you're texting and not some mysterious stranger.'

'She's kind of both,' said Anna.

Hebe wondered what Tristan meant. How could she have locked him in the cupboard? She hadn't been here for days. She would have remembered if she'd done that, wouldn't she? But she'd done things before, hadn't she, that she didn't remember afterwards.

'I didn't lock you in the pantry!' Hebe declared. That sounded pretty definitive. That sounded true.

'You have to tell your mother you made me do it!' pleaded Tristan.

'What?' Hebe said.

'Sex!' said Tristan.

'I just came for my cat,' said Hebe, and went off to find him.

Tristan, to her surprise, helped her look for Ziggy.

'He won't go in there,' said Tristan when he saw the cat basket.

They found Ziggy in Hebe's sometime bedroom, what her mother called 'the tower room'. All the windows were open, the drawers out, the wardrobe emptied onto the floor. Ziggy was hiding in a pile of clothes. He was obviously spooked, his fur rising on the arch of his back.

'This cat is crazy,' said Tristan. 'It should be sent to sleep.'

'Put to sleep,' corrected Hebe.

'Yes,' said Tristan.

'No!' said Hebe. 'It's "put to sleep" not "sent to sleep". Please don't put my cat to sleep!'

'I know what sent to sleep is! I'm a vet,' grumbled Tristan. For all his irritation, Tristan was very gentle with Ziggy and coaxed him out with some treats and calmed him down, gradually handling his head until the fur lay down flat again.

'He doesn't normally like strangers,' said Hebe.

'I'm not a stranger. I look after him. He's my cat!' Tristan snapped.

'He's not your cat,' Hebe said.

'Why does this cat belong to you? Because you say so? We look after him,' Tristan stood up and flexed his unexpectedly large arm muscles. 'We love him. It's our cat!'

He picked up Ziggy with his right hand, walked over to the window, and as if punching the air, extended his arm out vertically, with Ziggy on the end of it.

Hebe expected Ziggy to wriggle and yowl, but he just slumped, hanging over Tristan's hand like some extravagant trapper's glove.

'You tell your mother you made me do it!' Tristan said.

Hebe felt grief wash over her in advance. Surely he wouldn't throw the cat out of the window? He was bluffing. She should just agree. She should just agree that she made him do it. But it wasn't true.

'Don't hurt him,' she said.

'Say it!' said Tristan.

Hebe tried to form the words, but instead she gagged. She felt like she had a fur ball coming herself.

Tristan gave Ziggy a tiny shake.

Hebe coughed again. She desperately wanted to lie to save Ziggy, but the lie wouldn't come out of her. Nor could she sacrifice the cat. But some sacrifice needed to be made. She must not tell Tristan about Anna. It wasn't fair to Anna. She should give her the chance to find her own mother herself. She must not tell Tristan about Anna. She must not tell Tristan about Anna.

'I've found her daughter,' said Hebe. 'You can give her that.'

Tristan looked deeply suspicious. 'But you are her daughter!' he said.

'Her other daughter,' said Hebe.

Tristan considered this, visibly calculating the value of this information.

'She'll be pleased,' Hebe assured him. 'You'll be in her good books.'

Tristan seemed to believe her. Ziggy twisted out of his hands and dropped like a stone.

Anna found it impossible to pin Dermot down. She texted him. *Let's have dinner tonight. I'll cook liver for you!* Anna was vegetarian, and Dermot wasn't, so this kind of offer was usually accepted rapidly. But Dermot was out, *Sorry. Band practice. Neil's being a real dick!* and the next night and the next. In the end, at two o'clock on Saturday afternoon, having woken to find him already out, and then spent the day resolutely not texting and clearing out the cupboards, Anna finally texted, *Are you in the pub?*

I don't want to have some big talk! he replied. 'Dear God,' Anna thought, 'he thinks I'm going to break it to him that I'm having an affair. He's hoping to avoid the news with band practice and drinking.' She texted, *I'm not having an affair. Come home*. That was true. She wasn't.

As if you would! and a HAHA emoticon. But he was home in twenty minutes, the kind of drunk that was just on the turn, anxious and easily offended. Anna guessed he'd been wandering around the parks of London since early morning, drinking lager from supermarket bags. He was not in the best state to have a complex conversation about finding her biological family, but if she waited for him to be sober they might both be dead of old age.

Anna had vaguely assumed that as their relationship became established and he got more comfortable, Dermot would rein in the booze. But it had seemed to have the opposite effect on him. He'd come home each night with the bottle of wine he used to get for the two of them, and a spare, and would polish off most of the first bottle before they ate.

'Drinking for two?' Anna would joke, patting his pot belly. She suspected that some of the bottles were coming, not from the local offie, but from the pub he did shifts in.

Now, in the evenings, Dermot would take the wine outside on to their tiny balcony, so he could smoke endless cigarettes as he polished it off. Sometimes he'd do a kind of charades through the glass door, miming lifts or complex obscene scenarios. He'd moved his favourite chair out there, as well as a little collapsible table, and his sleeping bag to keep his legs warm, so that by now there was a little 'shadow' front room outside, or, more accurately, the kind of station that homeless people set up in doorways. She realised he'd taken a favourite cooking pot of hers and filled it with cigarette butts. Looking out at the horrible nest on the balcony, Anna was acutely aware he was going through something. His mother had been ill for a long time. It was a recurring cancer, which made it almost impossible to know if she was going to last as long as everyone else her age or if she was close to death. Anna didn't know why he didn't go home, despite his father. Dermot's father was an alcoholic, one of those loved-by-the-whole-village alcoholics in rural Sligo, charming, popular and casually violent. Even though he was close to a foot shorter than his six-foot-five son, Dermot had been terrified of him. Perhaps he still was. But his parents were split up now. Surely, he could see his mum without having to go through it all with his dad? Dermot said she didn't understand Ireland. Anna was aware that Dermot felt uncomfortable with his own massive size. He was always a target for any angry drunk who felt threatened in their own masculinity at quarter to eleven. At that time of night, Dermot was to be found outside the pub, hunkered down on the ground, smoking, making himself as small as possible, or offering to buy whoever might threaten him – 'All right, big man?' – a pint.

He'd been out a lot, and strange and distant when at home. But she was going to have to talk to him now without making him angry or sad.

'Layla said you asked her to talk to me,' Anna began.

'No!' Dermot was belligerent. 'Why would she say that?'

'Because you did. It's all right! I don't mind!'

'Why would you?' Dermot was heading for the fridge. He opened the door and stared at the shelves, as if willing Kronenbourg to appear.

'Layla says you're scared I'm cheating.'

Suddenly the desire to confess about whatever had happened with Neil overcame her and she knew she was going to tell him.

Dermot slammed the fridge door and turned to her with eyes full of tears.

'Please! Just don't say anything more. We can just carry on! You can do what you like. Just don't say anything and don't leave me!'

'Christ,' Anna thought. 'He'd rather I had sex with someone else than that he stop drinking.'

'I have been texting someone,' she said.

Dermot actually put his hands over his ears and Anna pulled them down.

'It's my sister, Dermot. It's my sister I'm texting. I've found my family!'

Dermot blinked at her through his tears.

'You've found your family?'

'Yes, sweetie,' Anna said.

'You aren't going to leave me? Please don't leave me now.'

'I won't leave you now,' Anna promised.

'I can't lose you and my mam at the same time,' Dermot sobbed.

'It's all right, love. I'm going to stay with you and I'm going to look after you.'

Dermot crumpled on to the floor.

'No!' He thumped his heart. 'I'll look after you!'

'We can look after each other then.' Dermot nodded tearfully. 'My sister, Dermot! She's called Hebe! And she looks just like me, only prettier.'

'Impossible!' Dermot declared gallantly. 'Although I should definitely meet her, to check!' he grinned.

Anna thumped Dermot's arm, 'Let me meet her first!'

Hebe returned to her friend Becky's flat with a new bundle of clothes inside the cat basket. She dumped them behind the sofa, next to her sleeping bag.

'Where's the cat?' Becky asked.

Hebe was enervated and excited. By the time she had made it to the window, Ziggy was disappearing round the side of the house into the neighbour's garden, not a scratch on him.

'I couldn't get him. My mum's driven him mad,' she said.

Becky levelled a solid Scottish stare at her, 'Uh-huh.'

'I found my mum's boyfriend locked in the pantry in a pile of shit.'

'What?' Becky looked startled.

'Yeah! He'd been locked there for days. Then he threw the cat out the window. But he survived!' Hebe shook her head. 'Crazy!'

'What?' Becky said again.

'I know! Even though he said he loved the cat! No wonder the cat's gone mad.'

'The cat's gone mad?' Becky asked doubtfully.

'Yeah.'

Becky turned to go into the kitchenette to put the kettle on. She wasn't looking at Hebe when she said, 'So, have you thought at all about maybe . . .'

Hebe was squashing herself into the sofa and didn't hear the end of the sentence. 'What?'

Becky burst into tears. 'Please don't make me say it again! It's not fair! It's so not fair to make all this my problem!'

Hebe went to hug her. 'Are you OK?' she asked.

'Honestly?' said Becky. 'I don't think I am. I just . . . I don't mind you staying here and all that but I can't deal with the lies.'

'What lies?' Hebe was bemused.

Becky sat Hebe down and squeezed her knee. She enunciated carefully.

'I understand that from your viewpoint you aren't lying. You're just finding stories to express how you feel. I'm no psychologist, but maybe you're the mad cat?'

'What?' said Hebe.

'Maybe, like, you think the cat's mad because you're . . . not well? Have you ever thought that?'

Hebe was starting to understand. Becky thought she was making it up. She should offer specifics so that Becky would believe her. 'When he held the cat out of the window it looked like a fur glove.'

Becky exploded. 'Oh my God! Please stop! Your mum's boyfriend wasn't "locked in the pantry", OK? Nobody threw a cat out of a window! I don't blame you. I know you've had this diagnosis and you . . . think things that aren't real, are, but I can't cope . . . I just . . . I can't have you on the sofa any more. I need to care for myself right now.'

Hebe fought the sense of unfairness rising within her. He had definitely been locked in the pantry. She just didn't know if she'd locked him there. She looked at her forearms which were covered with scratches. They were weirdly neat.

'What do you think these are?' she said.

'Honestly, Hebe! I don't know. Maybe you are cutting yourself. I don't want to know.'

Hebe realised she hadn't eaten in at least a day. She felt faint, despite sitting down.

'Listen, Ian's got a spare room in his house for the next couple of months – at least, it's spare all week, there's just a guy there at the weekends. But you need to see a doctor.' Becky swallowed, 'It's my flat. I've got a right to say who stays here.'

Hebe nodded, 'Of course you do. I'm really sorry. I'll go now.'

Becky was contrite, 'I don't mean now. You can stay tonight.'

'It's fine. Not to worry. I've got somewhere else I can go. Can I just go to the loo first?'

'Yes, Hebe! Of course you can go to the toilet. I'm not some monster. You see! This is what's upsetting me!' Becky said.

In the quiet of the bathroom, Hebe took a razor and traced a line between the cat scratches on her wrist, lightly and swiftly. The endorphins helped her rise above her growing panic. If people thought she was doing that, she might as well get the benefit. It gave her the brief surge of power needed to get her shit together.

'I think this'll be best for everyone,' Becky told her as she hoisted her rucksack on. 'Where are you going to go?'

The morning after their row, Anna and Dermot were having coffee. Dermot was in a lovely mood, tactile and sweet. He came up and cuddled Anna from behind. Anna turned around to wrap her arms around him, slipping her hand into the chub under his armpit.

Anna said, 'I think I might talk to Hebe about next weekend. What do you think?'

'Who's Hebe?'

Anna turned to search Dermot's eyes to see if he was joking.

'My sister?' Anna waited. 'Who I found on Facebook?'

There was not a shred of recognition on Dermot's face.

'You don't remember! Jesus! How much did you drink? You were crying. You were fucking crying and promising me you'd take care of me! And you don't remember? That I found my sister. I can't . . .'

'I didn't forget!' Dermot was styling it out. 'Your sister! I know you found your sister. Hebe? Right?'

Anna grabbed her wallet and put it in the orange handbag, which she was now using every day.

'I *will* take care of you,' Dermot promised.

'How? How are you going to take care of me when you spend all your time in some booze cocoon? What does that even mean? It's just words, Dermot.'

'Tell me off!' Dermot raised his voice.

'What?'

'Tell me I'm a shit! Tell me I'm useless! I'm a piece of shit!'

'I'm not going to tell you off!'

'I want to make you happy. Whatever you want, I'll get it for you,' Dermot had started to weep.

'Dermot, you can't even get me a fucking pickled onion!' Anna picked up her parka.

'Where are you going?' Dermot asked.

'I don't know. To Layla's probably. I just . . . need to be somewhere else,' and she was out of the flat.

Dermot didn't text her. When Anna let herself back into the flat it had been carefully cleaned. On every, now polished, surface were jars and jars and jars of pickled onions. Pickles on the coffee table, pickles ranged along the bookshelves, pickles piled on the kitchen counters. The flat looked like the den of some mad Victorian scientist, forever preserving the testicles of ghosts.

'What's all this?' Anna's bag fell to the floor.

Dermot's beard was freshly trimmed, and his clothes were clean.

'It's to show you, instead of words. Whatever you want.'

'Where did you get the pickles?' Anna asked.

5

NINE WEEKS GONE

'You might have pregnancy cravings for unusual foods. Remember that what your baby really needs is a healthy balanced diet.'

Anna had changed her outfit three times.

'She's not going to care what you wear!' Dermot's gorgeous torso was parcelled in an ancient hoodie which said, 'Mid-Western Univrsitty'. His huge arms were attempting an escape.

'You don't know that. She's kind of fashion-y. She looks amazing. I don't want to be some troglodyte next to her.' Since most of Anna's clothes came from charity shops, she couldn't do the all-black thing. It didn't really work when the blacks were all different shades of washed-out grey. In the end she wore a short green dress and her red boots. It was more dressed up than she ever was – more dressed up than she was comfortable with. Dermot was freaked out.

'You look . . . different,' he said.

'Good, different?'

'I just don't see why you are getting all fancy. It's not you.'

'I'm not that fancy! It's just a dress!'

'Are you sure that's how you're meant to put make-up on? It's sort of leaking at the sides.'

Anna bolted back into their tiny bathroom and scrubbed the make-up off with a wet flannel. It was probably better that way.

'There!' said Dermot when she came out of the bathroom. 'That's more you! Are you sure you don't want me there?'

'I think it's better if it's just the two of us: one relationship at a time. I'll meet her and if it goes OK . . . then I can ask about meeting Marlene.'

'Marlene is your mother, right?' Dermot said. Anna gave him a look. 'I'm kidding! I'm kidding!'

Anna picked up the orange handbag.

Dermot looked at her with keen understanding. 'Are you scared of meeting your mum?'

'I just . . . I hope I'm the daughter she's been dreaming of all these years.'

Dermot affected a cheesy American accent. 'Well, you're the woman of MY dreams.' He picked Anna up and swung her round like a seven-year-old. 'Cheer up! It's your sister! It might be fun!'

Shortly after, Anna neared the coffee shop where they'd agreed to meet. She adjusted the bag under her arm and scanned the chairs outside for Hebe's distinctive black bob and short fringe. Just as she recognised her silhouette a few steps away, an older woman barrelled into her and wrapped her in her arms.

'Let me look at you!' she said. 'My darling girl! My little Pickle!' Anna stumbled; the unaccustomed heels on her boots made it hard to balance.

'I'm sorry!' said Hebe. 'She wanted it to be a surprise.'

'Don't apologise!' The woman who had hugged Anna, slapped Hebe playfully on the arm. 'Don't apologise for bringing her her mummy!'

The woman held Anna's face in both her hands.

'Well, thank God you're not fat!' she said. 'Now I don't have to pretend it doesn't matter!'

Anna looked into the face of her mother. It was an amazing face, lively and handsome, strangely ageless. Marlene could have been anything from about forty-five to sixty-five. Her hair was . . . expensive – that shiny silver which could be blonde. Her teeth were preternaturally perfect. And her clothes were downright crazy. Anna was faintly aware of fringes and heavy silver jewellery. She was looking at her with unalloyed love.

Marlene suddenly screamed, 'Look! Twinsies!'

'Sorry?' said Anna.

'Twinsies! We've got the same bag!' They had, indeed, got exactly the same bag. 'We're birds of a feather!'

'Yes,' Anna was confused, 'it's the bag you . . . it's the bag I was left in.'

Marlene absorbed this seamlessly. 'Of course it was! Look at your hair! Have you ever cut it?'

'I cut it all the time.' Why did she say that? 'It just . . . grows.'

'You see, Hebe? Look how pretty it'd look long! You'd be like two little dolls together!'

Marlene had undone Anna's hairbands and was unplaiting her hair. Her fingers were combing out the twisted cord. Now they were on her scalp, rubbing her head, scratching at a small scab behind her ear. 'Look at you! Just look at you! You're perfect. Perfect! Do you ever wear it up?'

'I tried . . . I didn't . . .' but Anna stopped. It was overwhelming. Against her will, and in front of these two strangers who were not strangers, Anna began to well up.

'Don't worry!' Marlene wiped away Anna's tears and embraced her, hard. She whispered in Anna's ear, 'Don't cry, darling! Now I've found you I'll never let you go!'

'Hello,' said Hebe, reaching forward, her sleeves so long they covered half her hand as she extended it. 'I'm your sister.' Anna shook the hand offered. The sleeve caught between their palms, and only their fingers touched. 'Sorry,' said Hebe, and Anna glanced up into eyes just exactly like her own.

'Don't mind her!' Marlene winked. 'She's always been frigid. Right! What do you want to know? You must have so many questions about me. I'm all yours!'

Marlene leaned in, cupping her face in her hands.

Anna tried to catch her breath. She felt her lips, without her will, form a 'w'.

But Marlene's eyes had shifted back to Anna's long dark hair. 'You should have been washed in the pot!'

'I'm sorry?' said Anna.

'From the old music hall song,' said her mother. 'You know!' she insisted.

'I don't think I do,' said Anna.

Marlene stood up and held one arm out – a troubadour – and began singing, as if to a little kid, but with a broad Cock-er-ney accent.

'If your smalls are dark then you must be discreet
Wash 'em in the pot and not aht on the street!'

Marlene's voice was a confident vibrato. Other customers were turning to stare. Hebe caught Anna's eye and flashed her a rueful smile.

'You *must* know it,' Marlene said.

'I don't think so,' Anna replied.

'About the baby so little and dark that it turns out to be a ball of dirt!' Marlene continued singing, making circular motions with her hands as if expecting Anna to join in any moment.

'Now that you've washed it there ain't nothing there
But a dirty old tub, full of mud, dust and hair
Yes, your baby was nothing but mud, dust and hair!'

Marlene looked at Anna enquiringly, 'No?'

'Sorry,' Anna answered weakly.

'Oh well! Let's feed you up, shall we, Pickle?' Marlene looked around airily for a waiter. 'You know why I call you Pickle, don't you?'

Anna realised as she answered 'Why?' that no actual sound came out.

'Because that's all I could eat when I was pregnant with you!' Marlene said.

Anna tried very hard to keep her face still, while a series of electrical nodes lit up like traffic lights and her life screeched around a corner.

'Pickle? Are you all right?'

Marlene was blissfully happy. She was perfect. It was perfect: the meeting. It couldn't have gone better. It made it all worthwhile, all the heartache. She loved her so much it hurt. She always had, of course, but now the fuzzy pictures in her head had crystallised into this incandescent image. It was amazing how much she looked like Hebe. Hebe had done the right thing in the end. And her daughter was, of course, utterly beautiful. The internet was wonderful. She could not have believed what it had given her. Who could have predicted it would bring back her baby? If she had known she would have paid attention years ago.

'You don't look old enough to have a thirty-five-year-old daughter!' Tristan complimented her. Marlene gave him a level look.

'Oh Tristan! I don't go in for all that flannel! I've always looked my age. How old is your mother?'

'What?'

'How old is your mother?' Marlene repeated.

'She's fifty-six.'

'So, I'm older than her. Were you a good baby?'

'I don't know. What is a good baby?' Tristan asked.

'You know, a good baby. One who isn't always crying! Hebe was such a good baby. She barely ever cried. She could be sitting in a pile of shit and she wouldn't cry. But then girls are dirtier than boys. Boys like to be kept clean. She hardly ever fed. She used to sleep all the time. I would have to wake her up to play with her. She was such a lovely baby! But all babies are lovely, of course. I tell you what: therapists have a lot to answer for. I don't think any jury would convict if you murdered a therapist.'

Marlene caught Tristan's guilty expression.

'You don't see a therapist, do you?'

'I used to.'

'Oh Tristan, no! Therapists are just there to blame the mother! It's always the mother's fault.'

Marlene looked alluringly back over a naked shoulder. 'What about like this?'

Tristan had helped Marlene set up an Instagram account under the name CallMeMa, and they were taking photos for it.

Marlene lifted her chin, twinkling her eyes at the camera. But Tristan was looking at the last photo on the phone. It was of the two orange handbags on the floor of the cafe. Marlene's bag was closer to the camera and seemed bigger than Anna's. They looked, for all the world, like little mother and baby bag creatures.

'I took that by mistake. Beth turned up with the same bag as me,' Marlene said airily.

'You should post this,' said Tristan decisively. 'People will love it.'

Marlene didn't know why she didn't want the thirty-five-year-old orange bag to be displayed but she didn't. She had completely forgotten what she'd left in it. And yet she'd moved hell and high water to get a replacement. Funny how our minds worked. Still, that was all water under the bridge now.

'*Met my #longlostdaughter today and she had the exact same bag as me! #firstmotherslove #familyreunion #bloodwillout.*'

'Don't say "exact same",' said Marlene, 'it's not grammatical.'

'People don't care!' said Tristan.

'Look,' Marlene was delighted, 'lots of people are liking it! I've got thirty-eight new followers. They love me!' She fished at the spectacles dangling on her breasts to read the comments. '"Congratulations on finding your baby!" Look! Someone called @birthmom1982 has said, "Looks like you bagged a good one!" Clever. Let's post again.'

Marlene gestured across the room for Tristan to bring her some wine, but he didn't understand the gesture and started undoing his trousers.

Marlene covered what she thought was the microphone on her mobile before remembering the internet couldn't hear her. 'Not wanking, for goodness' sake! Wine! Wine!'

As Tristan trotted out Marlene wondered if her house was big enough. At the moment Tristan had his own room, there was the spare bedroom, set up as her weaving room, Hebe's bedroom, and Ben's. But perhaps she should move, so there was a room for Beth and her partner to stay. She knew she wasn't called that now, but Marlene had thought of her as Beth for thirty-five years and she wasn't about to stop now. Perhaps she'd change her name. That would be a nice gesture. Then, she could always use Hebe's room. Hebe had left of her own accord, and the decoration already suited a little girl: a forest. She'd pack up Hebe's spare things and deliver them to her London address tomorrow.

A dim memory surfaced of the bed she had slept in during her own childhood, first with her sister, then her brother, then her mother. Tristan handed her the glass, but it tasted disgusting. Disgusting! '*Dégoûtant!* It's corked!' she told Tristan. 'Open another!' The wine certainly tasted horrible, like fear and mould.

She called through to Tristan, 'How do I google everything about her?'

When Tristan had brought her a new glass of wine he asked her, 'What happened?'

'What do you mean, what happened?' Marlene said.

'With your daughter? Why did you give her away?'

Marlene felt rage engulf her, and then, just as quickly, leave. She said gently, 'I didn't give her away. I saved her.'

'Who from?' asked Tristan.

'What in God's name are you wearing?' Dermot was open-mouthed.

'Do you like them?' Anna asked anxiously.

'Sure!' said Dermot. 'They're great! Because it's 1984 and you are about to release "Like A Virgin"!' Anna was wearing fingerless lace gloves.

'They were a hundred and eighty quid,' Anna said.

'You're fucking with me!' Dermot's face creased with worry.

'Don't worry!' Anna prepared to deliver her line: 'My mother bought them for me!' And then, as if she were someone else entirely, she did a little scream.

'What? I mean . . . WHAAAT? You met her? What's she like?'

'She's . . . flamboyant, very affectionate. She kept kissing me,' Anna told him.

'Well, she sounds horrible!' Dermot said.

Anna laughed. 'She wants me to call her Ma!'

'Ma? Is she Irish? Don't tell me you're an undercover Irishwoman!'

'No, no, she's English. It's kind of short for Marlene – like Marlene Dietrich.'

'Everyone calls me Ma!' she'd said. 'Not just my kids! Or Mummy! Just not Mum, so common! And what do I call you? I can't call you Pickle,' Marlene had said.

'I'm Anna,' she'd said.

'Oh!' Marlene's face had fallen. 'I was going to call you Beth. Can I call you Beth?'

Hebe had interrupted, 'She's called Anna now, Ma!'

'What about Anna-Beth? Just sometimes . . . I'll call you Anna-Beth sometimes! It'll be our special name,' Marlene paused, 'but I won't if it makes you at all uncomfortable. I just want you to be happy. It's all I've ever wanted.'

'She's rich, by the sound of it,' said Dermot.

'Yeah, I think she's rich,' Anna replied.

'Really?' Dermot was jubilant. 'Are we rich then? She's *actually* a gajillionaire?!'

Anna laughed. 'It looks like it!'

Dermot started to dance around the flat, singing Jessie J and pretending to shit money. The mime got derailed when he also wiped his arse with the imaginary cash.

'Let's celebrate! Have a drink with me,' said Dermot.

Anna was just so tired of saying no. Why couldn't they have a drink together? She could take a test in the morning. She could think about all that tomorrow.

That night Anna got a text from Hebe, *So sorry for springing her on you.* Anna texted back, *No need to be sorry. It's what we were aiming for anyway. It's all worked out!* The three dots appeared and seemed to scroll forever, *It's probably best to assume if you're talking to me, you're talking to her.* What did that mean? Anna showed the text to Dermot.

'I don't know what she's implying,' Dermot said. 'That your mum is reading her texts? How could she?'

'She's not my mum,' snapped Anna, then, affecting a super-posh accent, 'she's my mother.'

'Well, when am I going to meet her?' said Dermot.

Anna had cleaned the flat for the second time. Usually, it was a stinking mess. Neither Dermot nor Anna was naturally tidy. They always said that they wouldn't even notice if it was burgled. But lately she'd found it almost impossible to tolerate dirt. The gum stuck on the streets made her gag, the rubbish left by the side of the road, Dermot's ashtray. So, inside the flat she had started to take comfort in the smell of bleach. Didn't pregnant women like everything clean? She knew she should pee on a stick today. But she just didn't have the headspace this week if the worst was true. When was the last time they'd had sex? She just needed to get past today. If she was pregnant, it was only a few days. She had time to deal with it.

She'd made some snacks for the occasion. Dermot had suggested a packet of Pringles.

'There is literally nothing on earth you can make that's as good as a packet of Pringles,' but Anna felt strongly that Marlene – Ma – would not be the Pringles type. Dermot was now cramming posh toast covered in a pea and garlic dip into his wide mouth.

'This is actually really good!' he declared.

'Please don't eat all that before she gets here.'

'Do you want me to put it back?' Dermot offered jokily.

'No!' Anna was properly irritated. 'Could you get the wine out?' Dermot's hand stopped halfway to his mouth.

'Were we saving that wine?'

Of course. Of course, he'd drunk the wine. She'd bought it two hours ago and now it was gone. But now was not a good time to have an argument.

'If I go and buy some more, will you leave some of the food?'

'Sure! No need to be huffy!'

How was she going to get to the Brasso cash without him seeing? Anna decided to just brazen it out. She opened the cupboard under the sink as if getting out a cloth and then dropped the brass tin whole into her handbag. She checked it as soon as she was out of the house and pulled out the last tenner.

The first shop she went to was boarded up, the front window clearly smashed in by a rogue car veering off the road – or possibly, a sledgehammer – so it was a fifteen-minute round trip by the time she opened her front door again. Anna found Dermot sitting on the sofa with her mother, both of them holding cans of Stella and laughing. Marlene had her hand on Dermot's leg.

'Oh Pickle! You didn't tell me he was such a humourist!' Marlene turned to Anna with delight. Anna felt a stab of jealousy she was instantly ashamed of. And who was she jealous of?

'I'm glad to see you are being looked after!' she said.

'Yes,' Marlene raised her lager, 'I'm drinking straight out of the can!'

'I'll get you a glass.' Anna rushed to the kitchen cupboard.

'No!' Marlene demurred. 'When in Rome! I think it's fun. Dermot here has been telling me all about his band. I hear the lead singer has a crush on you!'

'What? I don't think so.' Anna blushed with her head in the cupboard.

'Don't be embarrassed, sweetheart. Who wouldn't have a crush on you? With that hair!'

'She's gorgeous, isn't she?' Dermot grinned with satisfaction.

'Are you sure nobody wants tea?' Anna asked. The kettle had been dead for weeks so she tried to turn on the back gas hob, but it wasn't working.

'Is it not working?' Marlene was over in an instant.

'It keeps going off. It's just the ignition thing. I'm sure it's fixable.' Anna lit the ring from a match.

'Once they're gone, they're gone. Much better to replace the lot.' Marlene put her head on one side and looked at Anna. 'It must be a terribly high-stress job, being a writer!'

'Who said I was a writer?' Anna looked towards Dermot.

'You did! You write things, don't you?'

'Yes, I write reports. I don't make anything up! In fact, it's important I don't.'

'Well, what do you call yourself?' said Marlene comfortably.

'A Grants Officer? Knowledge Management if I'm feeling fancy.'

'Oh no! That doesn't sound right. You do charity work! That sounds perfect. You do charity work!'

'I think if you "do charity work" you do work for charity for free. I work *at* a charity.'

'I'm sure concentrating on ugly things like wars must be very stressful. You should quit.'

'What? I can't stop working!' Anna laughed.

'Why not?' asked Marlene.

'Well, apart from anything else, we need to pay rent.'

'Do you not own this?' Marlene enquired.

Dermot properly laughed, and then swallowed rapidly in an effort not to lose even a mouthful of beer, which resulted in a coughing fit.

'No,' Anna said. 'We don't want to end up on the streets!'

'Don't be ridiculous! People like us don't end up on the streets! What is it, a one-bed?' Marlene's eyes were darting around. 'Well, you'll need to move anyway when you have a family.'

Anna and Dermot's eyes met.

'I think you need money for all that,' Dermot said. Anna was grateful really, that Dermot was such a good talker. It meant she could keep quiet and stop her brain from floating off. There was something profoundly unsettling about the whole situation. The things Marlene said seemed . . . odd. She was, Anna realised, an odd woman. Anna was thinking this thought when the doorbell rang.

'I'll get it,' she said.

A man and a woman stood on the doorstep, dressed in police uniforms.

'We'd like to speak to Dermot Dwyer.' Anna felt the air thicken.

'Dermot? It's someone for you,' she said. She should tell him, warn him it's the police. But her mouth didn't form the words. Dermot came to the door.

'Dermot Dwyer?'

'Yup, what's all this then?' Dermot leaned one big arm against the door frame.

'Are you the Dermot Dwyer who's barman at the Black Lion in Kilburn?'

'Yup.'

'We'd like you to come with us.'

'Oh, come on now! Is this a joke?'

'It's not a joke. We'd like you to come and answer some questions.'

Dermot planted his feet against the skirting, and Anna knew with absolute certainty he was about to get himself arrested.

'Please, Dermot! Just go with them,' she entreated.

Marlene had appeared in their tiny hallway.

'Who *are* these people?' she said, although it was blindingly obvious who they were.

'Is this about the fucking pickles?' said Dermot. Anna felt like she was at sea, in a small boat. 'You can tell Ian that I'm bringing them back. No, wait! I'll tell him myself. Just wait!' Dermot held up one hand to the male policeman to 'wait' in a gesture so rude it looked illegal, and fumbled out his mobile with the other. It rang just once. 'Ian! Mate! Have you sent the fucking police round? Well, tell them it's all right.' Dermot handed the mobile to the male officer. 'He'll tell you!'

The officer spoke to Ian, and Anna could tell that it

wasn't all right. The officer handed the phone back to Dermot.

'I'm sorry, mate, we really need you to come with us.'

'Mate! Don't fucking call me mate! I'm not your fucking mate! How old are you anyway? I'm not being arrested by some teenager who calls me mate!'

Anna could see the fear in the policeman's eyes. Dermot was swaying, all six foot five of him. 'Shit!' Anna thought. 'He's going to assault a police officer.' She felt the need to sit down, but before she could the linoleum floor tilted and came up to meet her face, and as it did she thought, 'Not again.'

For a few seconds she felt the wings of a bird beating against her cheeks.

When her eyes opened the officer was gently pressing Marlene aside and using some discarded mail to fan her. She was propped up against the wall in their tiny hallway.

'Are you OK?' The officer turned to Dermot. 'Does she often faint?'

'Only if she sees blood,' said Dermot.

There was an expression on Marlene's face, like she was doing long multiplication without a calculator. 'She looks like Gollum,' Anna thought, 'she looks hungry.'

Two hours later, Anna was sitting on a chair designed to induce arthritis at a police station trying to make small talk with the mother she'd met two days before while they waited for Dermot to be released.

'I'm so sorry,' Anna apologised for the fifth time. 'I'm sure it's a mistake. Dermot has never been in any trouble.'

'It's no problem at all. You just rest. You keep your strength up!'

A woman covered with tattoos approached them. Anna was confused. Was this a policewoman?

'You should go home,' the tattooed woman was saying. Anna was mesmerised by her arm, where her shirt was pushed up to reveal the name JADE in a heart.

'Is he coming out now?'

'No, he's been charged. He'll be remanded in custody till he appears in court tomorrow.'

'Tomorrow?' Anna was confused. 'Sunday?'

'Sorry,' the tattooed lady smiled charmingly, 'it'll be Monday now.'

'You mean . . .' Anna felt a rising panic. 'He'll be in prison until Monday?'

'He'll be in the cells here. He's been charged on three counts of theft.'

'Three? This is insane. Dermot's not a thief!'

'It's all right, darling! I told you he shouldn't have spoken to them without a lawyer!' Marlene said.

'I don't think you did,' Anna replied tautly.

'Didn't I? Well, I thought it!'

'What do I do?' Anna felt wiped out. 'How do I apply for legal aid?'

'Legal aid! Don't be ridiculous!' Marlene put her arms around Anna. 'She doesn't need this stress!' she explained to the tattooed policewoman. Marlene zipped up Anna's coat. 'We'll get him the best lawyer in London. I'll pay for everything.'

'Am I allowed to text him?' Anna looked at Marlene. 'He'll be so scared.'

'My poor little baby!' Marlene kissed Anna as if she were eight years old. 'Mummy's here now. You leave it all to me.'

This would have been the perfect time to take a test, but by the time Anna got home on Saturday night she had no money left. A search of the sofa revealed two pounds eighty and Anna bought milk and bread. She spent the weekend not thinking about being pregnant. Then she didn't think about Dermot being in a police cell and then she went back to not thinking about being pregnant again. On Sunday evening she realised that some part of her brain believed that if she didn't take the test, she actually wouldn't be pregnant. Then she threw up.

The lawyer Marlene found turned out to be an ex-lover of Marlene's, a tall man with the paper-thin skin of the highest deck of the upper classes, and a mouth which looked like his insides were escaping through his lips, like the mouth itself had piles.

'There's no reason,' Marlene opined, 'why a pretty woman should pay for anything. Though of course I've always paid my way – I'm no prostitute!'

Anna was getting used to these sudden about-turns of Marlene's. She seemed to have no trouble holding exactly contradictory views at the same time. Anna still didn't quite understand where Marlene's money had actually come from – her Home Counties accent would slip occasionally to reveal Midland working-class roots. The reports that Anna had found in the orange bag were apparently from a grammar school in the Birmingham area.

Anna had no idea if the lawyer was any good.

'Of course he's good!' Marlene was irritated. 'He's my friend. He's the best!'

But the hearing at the magistrates' court on Monday morning started badly. Marlene was flamboyantly taking photos. The lead magistrate snapped at her that unless she stopped, she'd be removed.

'It's only for my Instagram!' Marlene replied.

'It's only contempt of court!' the magistrate snapped back.

'Put it away, Ma,' the posh lawyer murmured at her.

Anna found it hard to follow the lawyer's argument, but it seemed to be that Dermot hadn't actually stolen anything. The 'thefts' were informal loans Dermot's boss was making to him, and the only reason Ian suddenly started accusing him of theft was because he had been stealing from the brewery himself.

The three magistrates left the court room after the lawyers had spoken. They imposed a surety of six thousand pounds.

'What does that mean?' asked Anna.

'It means you have to come up with six thousand now, to get him out,' explained John Darling – Marlene's lawyer friend.

'Six thousand! Is that normal?'

'It's extremely unusual. The magistrate thinks he's a flight risk. He's of no fixed abode.'

'What are you talking about? He lives with me,' Anna explained.

'He's changed address multiple times in the last two years. And he's stolen from his employer, allegedly. Magistrates tend not to like that.'

Anna was at a loss. Marlene chimed in, 'It's because he's Irish.'

'Marlene!' John chided her.

'Well, it is, John! You and I both know. But you mustn't worry, Pickle! We're taking it to Crown Court anyway.'

'Why?' asked Anna.

'Just trying to keep him out of custody!' John said cheerfully.

'Custody?'

Looking at Dermot in the courtroom, his stubble growing out ginger, his pale blue eyes red from crying behind his greasy hair, Anna could understand why the court thought he might disappear.

'Even if the worst comes to the worst, he's unlikely to get more than nine months,' said the lawyer.

The length of time echoed around Anna's brain.

She couldn't stop looking at the lawyer's bursting lips. 'I can't afford to pay you for a trial.'

'Don't be silly, Pickle!' Marlene chimed in. 'You're my daughter. You can pay anything.'

Anna imagined Dermot in prison, the target for every fool with masculinity issues, and felt rising panic. At the beginning of the hearing the lead magistrate had asked, 'Has the defendant been examined by a doctor? He appears to be in some state of withdrawal.'

'Withdrawal from what?' Dermot was disbelieving.

Anna could smell the alcohol sweating out of his clothes across the court room.

'Don't worry,' said the lawyer, 'we'll take care of him.'

'I'll have to pay you back,' Anna said.

Marlene put her head on one side and looked at Anna

with huge indulgence. 'Ah!' she said. 'Proud!' Anna didn't know if she was proud of Anna or if she was saying Anna was proud.

'Thank you, Mr Darling,' said Anna.

The lawyer barked with laughter. 'I'm Mr Samson,' he said. 'John Darling is what your mother calls me.'

But, since Marlene paid the surety, Dermot was allowed to come home with her. He refused to talk about any of it.

'It's all bullshit! I haven't nicked anything. I borrowed some stuff. I'm going to put it back!'

'What did you borrow?'

'Just some money and that! I can't believe Ian's making such a fuss about it.'

'Where are you going?' Anna watched him put on his long-sleeved black work shirt.

'To work!'

This was a new level of denial. 'I don't think you should go into work. I think you're fired.'

'What?' Dermot scoffed. 'I don't think so! Ian hasn't said anything!'

'He's got you arrested and charged you with theft!'

'That'll blow over! He won't be able to cope without me on shift.'

Dermot actually left the house and got halfway down the road before he phoned Ian 'just to check' and then came home, with a bottle of wine.

When Anna woke up in the morning she was forced to remind herself of the new facts of her existence: I have a mother. I have a sister. My boyfriend is being charged with theft and may go to prison. I might be knocked up. Then she'd get up, leaving Dermot asleep (what did he have to get up for?). She'd go to the kitchen, where the jars of pickles eyeballed her reproachfully while she made coffee. Her stomach turned. Why had it not occurred to her that she could be pregnant? Because they never had sex. When was the last time? She couldn't remember. 'I defy the magpie I defy the magpie I defy the magpie!' Anna said suddenly aloud.

That night, after work, she asked Dermot, 'Where are we going to get six grand?'

'Your mother's good for it. You don't need to pay her back.'

'I've just met her!'

'So?'

'So – I don't want to start our relationship owing her,' Anna said.

'I think that ship has sailed,' muttered Dermot.

'What?'

'She's your mam. You already owe her your fucking life!'

'Dermot, I am not owing someone I don't even know six grand.'

'Maybe you could get to know her then?'

Marlene knew it was here somewhere. The last few days had been quite an education. The important thing was to be totally authentic. People responded to authenticity. She'd had no idea there were so many people out there just desperate to connect with a real story. Of course, the whole court room drama had been a godsend follower-wise. Not everybody got hundreds of people hanging on their every word within a few days. Tristan had been trying to get her to use Stories, but she liked to be able to look at her posts afterwards. Marlene lifted Hebe's sweaters out of the dresser but couldn't resist checking back. Three new followers just in the last half-hour!

But Hebe was calling her. Marlene sighed and answered.

'Yes, Hebe? Why would you think I've still got your cat? It's nearly two months since you left. I'm not in the business of looking after other people's animals.' Marlene hung up.

The cat! What had Tristan said? 'Titties and kitties!' That's what the internet was for. He could be very droll.

Where was the cat? She hadn't seen it in about three days. It wouldn't answer to the name she'd given it, and yesterday she'd found a shit outside the cat box. Even before it had disappeared it was always yowling and had taken to skulking. And it had different colour eyes. It made it very hard to imagine it was Malfeasance. Malfeasance had been a beautiful cat. Hebe's little creature wasn't a patch on Malfeasance, really, especially in the face. It was nice when it was asleep. When it was asleep you couldn't see the eyes.

Marlene looked at the pile of clothes she'd moved from Hebe's dresser. It's not as if Hebe wanted any of it. Quality will out. And everything Beth owned seemed to be shoddy. All this could be put to good use. And she could be guided – to have good taste. She didn't like to picture her little pickle in that horrible little flat – God knows how long since it had been decorated. In the 'kitchen', such as it was, the flooring had been that sort of vinyl with a picture of wood on it. There were probably real floorboards underneath, for crying out loud! Why didn't they just strip and sand back? Well, if she was introduced to beautiful things perhaps she would start to get a feel for them. After all, Marlene had grown up in the dullest possible surroundings – she recalled the horrible doormat against her cheek, where it dipped in the middle: the bit of light leaking to her outside. Despite this, she had the best taste of anyone she knew. Beth wouldn't stay in the flat once the baby came, surely? She would need another bedroom.

It was clear as day she was expecting. The pickles and then the fainting. Marlene had been just the same! It didn't look like the relationship was exactly stable. Though she could quite see the appeal – Dermot was a proper man's man. A real man. The kind who could lie on top of you and stop you getting away. Perhaps he wasn't the father of Beth's baby – that might help. Poor little petal, if he was the father. The baby will run right through her. She'll be incontinent before she's forty! Perhaps it's this other chap, the lead singer of the band.

She still hadn't found what she was looking for. It had to be here somewhere. All these clothes of Hebe's – completely untouched. She never wore what would suit her. She was very creative, of course. The stories she told about people trying to find her. Entirely convincing. She'd actually contacted a friend in MI6 to try to help her. Told him all about it over coffee; the people who Hebe was convinced were following her. He'd said, 'Are you sure these aren't delusions?' It had been so humiliating. She'd told Hebe, 'Nobody's looking for you! Nobody cares.' But the clothes were still lovely. Perhaps Beth might fit them after she'd had the baby. By then she might be living here properly.

Marlene could help her through the first bit. Girls these days didn't know anything about looking after babies, and it wasn't as easy as it looked. Here it was! Thank God! She recognised the shoebox. But as she moved the box Marlene discovered where the cat had been hiding.

'Is it you?' she crooned. 'It is! Isn't it? It is you!' On a sweater of Hebe's in the corner of the chest of drawers was Hebe's tortoiseshell cat, Ziggy Stardust, and four multi-coloured kittens. That explained why he'd been acting so strange lately. He was a she! Well, at least Marlene would get to name these herself with proper names for a cat. Maybe Méchant for the darkest one and Saboteur – she'd always wanted a cat called Saboteur.

And Insta-wise, these kittens might be even better than what was in the shoebox. She could post pictures of these little kittens and save the other thing until Beth had seen it.

Marlene took four or five perfect photos, posted them on Instagram and then went down to the kitchen to get the Victorian barrel. It was a very nice antique, with original brass hoops, and it would be big enough. It was surprisingly heavy, but she could carry it empty. Would it be watertight though? Marlene poured a jug of water in from the kitchen sink – it didn't seem to be leaking out. She let out the water by the little spigot. She'd take it upstairs. She nipped out the back pantry to fetch a hose and wound it over her shoulder. Then put the barrel on its side. A little dribble came out, but she could clean that later. Marlene started to roll the barrel up the main staircase. The hose was long enough to reach from her bathroom.

People who weren't country people would be horrified, of course. But they didn't understand. It was a baptism, in a way. Ziggy didn't make a sound as she lifted up the kittens. Well, if she gave them up that easily she wasn't cut out to be a mother.

Anna was already wishing she hadn't taken the test in the GP toilet. There were two locks, one on the door to the waiting room and one on the inner area with the toilet, but she didn't trust the lock to the waiting room, so she had to pee on the stick incredibly carefully, since she couldn't wash her hands. She set her mobile alarm to two minutes but a few seconds in there was a loud bashing at the door and she dropped the stick on to the filthy floor.

'There's someone in here!' she called out.

An angry London voice came from the washbasin, 'This is a doctor's, you know!'

Anna did know. The GP was wearing opaque green contact lenses. Anna had asked her for a pregnancy test.

'Have you had a positive test?' she had asked.

'No,' said Anna, 'why would I need one if I'd already had one?'

'You can buy just as accurate a test over the counter,' she'd said.

'Yes,' Anna had replied, 'but I can't get one of those.'

'You can get them at any pharmacy,' insisted the GP.

'I'm sure you can,' Anna had said, 'if you have any money.'

Then the doctor offered 'options' on the NHS, if she was 'having problems conceiving', all behind the green wall of her contact lenses, heavily implying any referral needed to be made before Anna's last remaining egg turned to dust and blew away. 'It's later than you think,' she'd said, 'did you want to have a family?'

Anna looked at the stick. Was she going to pick it up? She had to. The urine had soaked into the hem of her jeans. They were darkened up to six inches off the floor. The angry woman banged again.

'I'm sorry!' yelled Anna. She glanced at the phone: thirty seconds to go. She couldn't not know for another thirty seconds. But, looking down, she confirmed what she had secretly known for the last week. She was pregnant. But 'Ten Weeks Pregnant'. Ten Weeks! That was impossible. She desperately thumbed back through her calendar on her phone. Ten weeks would take her back to . . . her birthday. Her birthday. She'd had a period since then, hadn't she? She bent over to look at the little window again with its LCD wording. Her dad always gave the same lecture about the discovery of liquid crystals, how all his fellow scientists thought holograms would be the thing to change the world, but it wasn't, it was the humble LCD. Ten Weeks Pregnant. And she had no idea who had made her that way.

The woman outside beat on the door. 'What in Christ's name are you doing?'

'Well, it's a valid question,' the shrink purred at her.

Yanni had sent her through the appointment, and 'popped his head round' to make sure she went. It was only when she'd got to the door that Anna had seen the name plaque in its slot: Dr Alec Higham. The brother's shrink. He had the easy air of a man whose life had been one long lunch at YO! Sushi, a conveyor belt of opportunities leisurely sweeping past him as he decided which delicious healthy snack to pick next. Anna hated him on sight. He was in his fifties with silver hair but clearly did eight hours of martial arts a week, comfortable in his own skin.

'Do you have to keep what we say confidential?'

'Yes,' the psychiatrist couldn't speak without it sounding like flirting. 'Unless you're planning to commit a crime. Are you planning to commit a crime?'

'No.'

He looked at her through his white eyelashes like he was going to ask her out. Had Anna met him before? She couldn't have done. She'd only left a voice-note about the reunion.

'I understand your line manager referred you.'

'That's right,' Anna said.

'Because he's worried about you,' prompted the shrink.

'I think he referred me to cover his back in case I have a breakdown and kill myself like that girl last year,' Anna replied.

'Girl?' The shrink raised an eyebrow. Oh shit. This was the guy Layla had reported. Anna considered standing up and walking out.

'And have there been any major changes in your life recently?' he asked.

'Major changes? Like what?'

'A move? Or . . .'

Anna was overcome with the desire to tell this prick the truth.

'Well, I'm pregnant,' she said, 'I found out yesterday. And I got mugged. And found my mum, my biological mum – I'm adopted – and she seems pretty weird, and my boyfriend got arrested for stealing pickles. It sounds insane now I say it out loud. He got charged with theft because he's committed theft. We don't have any money to have a baby. And I'm not a hundred percent certain Dermot's the father. Something happened with his best friend, but I can't remember what because I was completely arse-holed. How can I be pregnant when Dermot used a condom? And then I got this insane sense of smell. I could smell my mother in this bag, and I found her after wanting to find her my whole life and it turns out I have a sister. But I think she's kind of cagey. But my mother isn't. She gave me all this money. And she doesn't even want it back. And I don't know if I should keep the baby. I keep seeing . . . It doesn't matter. This is probably my only chance. There aren't a lifetime's harvests left. What, I'm going to have a baby who might starve to death with the last people on earth? What kind of life is that to give a kid? But only the GP knows – I haven't even told my boyfriend. He'd tell everyone. And he's always drunk. I mean, always, all day all night he's drunk. I can't have a family with an alcoholic. But he might be against an abortion. He's Catholic – lapsed Catholic. I don't know if you can be a lapsed Jew. I can't keep the baby, can I?'

The suave psychiatrist looked up sharply.

'You're Jewish?'

'Emphasis on the "ish",' said Anna.

'What do you mean?'

'My mum was Jewish – my real mum. I mean, my adoptive mum. My biological mother is . . . I don't know. So, I don't know what I am. Are you Jewish?'

'Yes,' the psychiatrist replied. Anna looked at him more closely. He was a completely different person from who she had judged him to be, not Higham: Hyam. His family must have Anglicised the name. 'Shanah tovah!' said the shrink.

'Yeah, you too,' said Anna.

'Seems apt!' said the psychiatrist.

'Why?' Anna asked.

The psychiatrist shrugged. 'It's Rosh Hashanah. Some Jews believe you have ten days before your fate is sealed for the next year.'

'You think if I abort the baby my name won't be written in the Book of Life?'

'What do you think?' the psychiatrist asked.

'Are you a shrink or a rabbi?' Anna looked at him.

He looked right back. 'Is ending the pregnancy the only option?'

'How do you mean?'

'Well, you could have the baby and let someone else bring them up.'

'You mean, give her up for adoption?'

'Her?'

'I mean . . . I don't know if it's a boy or a girl. You think I should give away my baby?'

6

ELEVEN WEEKS GONE

'As your first trimester progresses you may find that your emotions vary – you'll feel happy one moment and sad the next.'

Anna spent a couple of days baking bread and making a pros and cons list for abortion in her notes app. On the pros side it said: 'no money, no family'. She consciously stopped herself from writing 'father?' in case Dermot saw it. There was nothing on the cons list. She made challah, but she also made sourdough, and then posted a picture of it on Facebook, like some twat. The challah she did not post, although it was beautiful, a round plaited loaf, from a recipe on some American website, for the Jewish New Year. Dermot ate it before she could turn around.

'This is amazing!' he said, his mouth full.

Anna had made her first loaf of bread when she was ten with the twins' mother. The twins invited her to their house for the weekends when going 'home' was mandatory, where the food was considerably better than at school. Huge roasts were served while dachshunds padded around under the table, being snuck slivers of lamb by Anna and the twins. Their mother was old and hearty and negligent.

She let them 'have their heads'. 'Children are like dogs!' she used to say. 'You just need to let them run around in the fresh air every day and feed them!' She turned and narrowed her eyes at Anna, 'You aren't a Jew, are you?'

Anna shook her head. After all, now she went to the chapel on Sundays. She was allowed to skip it, but her father suggested she keep quiet about her Jewishness – 'After all, Anna, you are only Jewish by adoption' – so she filled out 'C of E' on the form. Slowly, the memories of late-night Passover feasts and almond macaroons for breakfast faded. When they learnt about the Holocaust, she pretended it was news. She dressed up for chapel in tights and the Sunday dress uniform just as she had dressed up for synagogue on the few occasions she'd had to go, sitting stiff and hungry, waiting to eat – it wasn't so different. The Hanukkah song drifted apart in her memory until it was a string of syllables: 'my atsu ya shoe are tea' which floated into her mind every time they lit the chapel candles. 'Shoe are tea,' she thought, trying to make it meaningful, trying with the wreckage of the sacred words, to conjure her mother's face, 'Shoe are tea.'

Anna learnt not to feel her mother's absence. Her mum had never lived here. Slowly the home and love leaked out of her. The only time she noticed the egg in her chest was when she got sick. At school sickness resulted in a stay in what was still called 'the san'. Anna was afraid of the place, ever since a kid had gone there and died of TB. When she was a little girl, before she'd reached the grand old age of eight, sickness meant chicken soup with lokshen and staying under the special blanket her mum's mum had made, the 'Granny blanket' crocheted from squares of wool in oranges and browns. It meant being allowed to watch cartoons all day while her mother marked exercise books. It almost made being ill something to look forward to. Sometimes, if you were lucky, in the san, there was another kid's phone to play Tetris on, but the blankets were even thinner than in the dormitories and the windows were always open. The windows, like prison windows, were slits, which showed tiny slices of the sea. The cold got into her. It was too much, the contrast, so just like her father had stopped feeling things, Anna solved her problem by never being ill.

And she joined the choir. Anna began to sing. It gave the boring hours in chapel some purpose. At the beginning she pretended to know the notes and droned along with whatever the girl next to her sang. But when it came to the high notes, as the cold wind blew through her hollowed-out frame, something came out of her which did not belong to her: a strange pure sound, as if she were a flute, or a guitar, a girl-shaped musical instrument being played by the universe.

In the half-light, Marlene put the car into reverse. She looked over her shoulder. She couldn't see anything. Was he even behind her? 'No!' The little prick was slapping her car. Her car! Well, fuck him! Marlene engaged the engine and tried to run backwards towards him, just to make him think twice, but she wasn't in reverse. She was in first. Her BMW crunched forward into the stone ball that marked the end of the drive. And now he'd made her crash the bloody car.

'You've made me crash the car!' Marlene yelled out of the window. 'You've made me crash the CAR now! You've RUINED the verge!' Where was he? He kept darting around. She tried to put it into reverse again, making sure the gear had clunked in, and drove backwards, as intended. There was a satisfying crunch as his guitar splintered on the gravel. She'd got the guitar! Not him, but the bloody guitar at least.

'My guitar!' Tristan was crying. He was actually crying. Was he? Marlene stepped out of the BMW.

'I don't know what you're crying for. It isn't your guitar. It's mine. I paid for it! Am I crying?' Kids always made such a fuss about things – well, other people's kids certainly. And men were the worst for tears. 'I'm the one who's been rejected! You're the one having the tantrum!'

'I'm NOT having a tantrum!' Tristan balled his hands into fists and stamped his foot. 'What's a tantrum?'

Marlene felt the rage recede as she looked at his tear-streaked face. After all he was French. French people were crazy. 'Oh, come and have a cuddle,' she opened her arms wide. 'Come on!' Tristan looked up at her in bewilderment. 'It's not your fault, is it? You're jealous! I'd do the same for you. Come on. Come to Ma!' He looked petulant now.

'I don't want to come to Ma. You ruined my guitar!'

'Come on!' She pulled open her long dress to reveal one breast. It was a good breast, for anyone, let alone a fifty-eight-year-old woman. 'I'll buy you another guitar.' Tristan eyed the breast. 'Ma's waiting. Don't sulk!' Tristan looked up at the manor house, his eyes wide – he looked younger than twenty-six.

'What if the gardener sees?' he asked.

'Lucky gardener!' She searched next-door's windows for the neighbour. Tristan was now on his knees on the gravel in the twilight, sucking her breast. 'Oh poppet!' she moaned. 'Do your knees hurt?'

'Yes,' said Tristan, his mouth full.

'Good!' she thought. She looked out over the gloaming garden. From here, in the shadow of the beeches edging the drive, she could glimpse some of the outbuildings and the woods where some of her many babies were. They were rooting in the undergrowth. It was the boar that had brought her Tristan in the first place.

Marlene thought it might be time to let Tristan go home to his aristocratic French mother. It had lasted longer than she'd hoped. But at that moment she spotted the neighbour's wife in the window. Better, in a way. She was something double-barrelled, too. We all need a witness. Marlene extended her arm and raised her right middle finger. She stood there, stock still, finger upraised as Tristan's dark goaty head bobbed and butted at her nipple. At the window, the woman closed the curtains. Had she seen them? Marlene felt the first thrill since his lips had closed on her breast – perhaps she had.

Anna felt a sense of peace descend as soon as the decision was made. On Monday morning she called the British Pregnancy Advisory Service and made an appointment for the next week. The woman on the end of the phone was kind, the language was all pleasant. They couldn't give her the 'treatment' without a 'consultation'. They would contact her GP with her permission. At the consultation, which she did over the phone, they asked her reasonable, measured questions and made a lot of sounds to indicate they were listening to her answers.

They did not ask her if she had been visited by babies in danger: babies burning, babies choking, babies drowning. They did not ask her if she thought her decision meant she would be written in the Book of Death, or even in the third book, the book for those who are not all bad or all good. They did not ask her if she had spent three days trying to pray. They did not ask her what she had to atone for.

It was twenty past five on Monday and she was thinking about packing up early at work when she got the message from Dermot: *GOOD NEWS!*

Have they dropped the charges? she texted back.

No! Better! Come to Neil's!

Neil lived about twenty minutes from Anna's work in a house he shared with two blokes and an unfeasibly good-looking woman he apparently wasn't sleeping with. Neil and Dermot were in the front room, with the inevitable cans.

'Here she is!' Dermot got up and greeted her with a hug. She hadn't seen him this animated in a long time.

'What's all this then?' Anna asked.

Neil glanced at Dermot. 'We're just celebrating,' he said, 'it's a big deal!'

'It's for "Fly High"!' Dermot was grinning broadly.

'What?' Anna was beginning to get that floating feeling, like she was no longer tied to her own life.

'We've sold "Fly High",' yelled Dermot, waving his arms, as Neil ducked out to the kitchen.

'Fly High' was a song Neil and Dermot had written after their friend Tara had died, just before Anna had met them. Tara had grown up with Dermot, was close to Neil, sang with them, struggled for many years to come out, and just when she'd finally done it, falling in love with their bandmate Brede, died suddenly at the age of thirty-three. It was a folk/pop hybrid with a chorus that sounded like it had been discovered chiselled on to the stone in front of the grave of some mythical queen. Dermot said it was a simple trick, saying the word high, while lowering the note, but it cracked Anna's heart open every time she heard it, and was part of the pure sorcery of music-making which made her feel so far away from Dermot and so much like she wanted to be part of him. Anna didn't like to admit to herself just how much of her attraction to Dermot came from his undeniable musical skill. She didn't want to be one of those women, trailing talented men from room to room, but he had been singing 'Fly High' the first time she'd seen him, an enormous, beautiful man. It was only on stage he didn't try to make himself look smaller. He looked around the crowd, such as it was, and he'd smiled straight at her. Of course, later she'd learnt he wasn't wearing his contacts, but it didn't take away from the way she'd felt that moment.

Often Neil sang solo, but they both sang on 'Fly High', Dermot joining for the chorus. You didn't know straight away what it was about. It was so damn joyous. The verses of the song listed the banal details of Tara's life, her likes and dislikes, almost as described by a child, to a thumping upbeat rhythm, ending in the deeply sentimental lyric . . .

'And we should have known you were never earthbound
'Cause your heart was too light to stay here on the ground
So, fly high, little starling
Fly high, my kindest friend
Fly high, pretty darling
Your soul's taking flight and you're free in the end.'

After the show she'd ended up in a group with three of Dermot's siblings, all talking about Tara and the song with tears in their eyes. She'd never felt so warmed by any bodies.

'You've sold it?' Anna asked. 'What have you sold it for?'

Dermot looked her right in the eye, 'Twelve K.'

'Jesus!' Anna sat down on the collapsed sofa.

'Yep, some guy emailed Neil. Trying to find out who owned it. He wants to use it for an ad, so . . .'

'An ad? An ad for what?' Anna asked.

'You don't want to know,' Dermot gave a sideways smile as he flopped next to her.

'Let me guess. An airline?' Anna said.

'Yes,' Dermot was delighted, rolling around, 'a fucking airline!'

Neil came back in with a can but also handed her a mug. It said, 'World's Greatest Dad'. Anna decided to ignore the fact it hadn't been properly washed from whoever had last used it.

'Have I got this right? You're going to sell Tara's song for an airline ad?' Anna said to Neil, but Dermot chipped in . . .

'It's like, a sad ad, you know, everyone flying back for a funeral, so it'll be tasteful, like.'

'Fuck it!' Neil interrupted. 'It's what she would have wanted! She always wanted the band to make some cash!'

'Too fucking right,' said Dermot. 'Tara was always asking us why we wanted to keep the band such a secret!' Anna felt her spirits lift as they chinked mugs and cans together.

'Here's to twelve K!' Dermot said.

Neil raised his can. 'Here's to Tara!'

It had to be true. It was too weird. And Dermot wouldn't lie about this song, not this song. Anna's mind was whirring.

'So will there be more money to come?' she asked.

'Oh yes!' said Dermot. Neil was clearly not expecting that.

'Really?' Anna asked.

Dermot nodded enthusiastically, 'Absolutely!'

Yanni had refused point blank to give her the time off, even when Anna had said it was for a hospital appointment. The day of the procedure was the day Anna was meant, with her entire department, to be on some hellish team-building exercise.

'Can't you re-schedule?' asked Yanni.

As was often the case, a reply surfaced unbidden in her brain: 'Not really – because every day that passes the foetus inside me grows bigger and gets more and more difficult to get rid of.' But she didn't say it. She said, 'I can try.'

'I've already lost a couple of people to Yom Kippur,' Yanni added.

'Yeah, Yom Kippur starts at sundown,' said Anna.

'Does it?' said Yanni, visibly making a mental note to force some people back in.

'But I might not be able to swap,' Anna replied.

'I'd appreciate it,' said Yanni, as if she'd just agreed to it. 'It's taken me forever to schedule this and I just don't know what it says about you that this day of all days you want to pull a sickie.'

Anna told herself not to panic. The appointment was at four thirty. She could just do the training and then fake a migraine after lunch. The clinic was only about a twenty-minute tube ride from work.

But when she got to the office that morning finance, IT and fundraising were all milling around on the street outside. It was beautiful weather and there was a real party atmosphere.

'What's all this?' she asked.

'The training day!' said Darius.

And a coach pulled up. The highly specialised employees of a human rights charity, doctors, lawyers, data experts, immediately reverted to twelve-year-olds as they trooped on: keen ones at the front, rebels at the back.

Anna found herself about three seats back from the driver, next to the fragrant Darius.

Yanni had taken a position at the front of the coach with a microphone like he was about to do a tour: 'Why You Aren't As Good As You Think' maybe. 'Stuff You Thought You Got Right But You Didn't'.

'Who's running the training?'

Darius jerked his head at Yanni.

'On *team-building*?'

Yanni was now handing out questionnaires on strengths and weaknesses.

'There's no need to waste the journey time,' Yanni added sternly.

But every time Anna tried to look at the paper her stomach turned ominously. Even picking up a biro made it threaten to rebel. She started looking out of the window and then glanced down, trying to read question one as fast as possible before looking out of the window again.

Darius leaned over, 'Do you want me to fill it in for you?' Anna looked at him with puppy-like gratitude.

Her mobile buzzed: a text from UCLH. 'Don't forget your twelve-week scan has been booked in at our pre-natal service.' Her heart lurched. Of course, the scan had been booked. The other path continued, and as the coach sped along Anna had a powerful sense of the miles she was diverging from it.

'First question,' read Darius aloud, 'what do you YEARN to do?'

'Can you put "rip up this questionnaire"?' Anna replied.

Darius grinned. 'I don't think that's what Yanni was thinking of.'

'What are you putting?' Anna glanced at the sheet.

'What does yearn mean?' said Darius.

'It's longing for,' said Anna.

'I thought so!' said Darius, 'I knew that! Why are they asking us what we yearn for?'

'I'm sure they've got some master plan,' said Anna. 'Maybe they're going to probe us with questions which will subtly reveal our flaws.' But it wasn't quite as sophisticated as that.

'Do you find it hard to ask for help?' Darius started writing. 'I'm putting "yes".'

'I don't find it hard to ask for help,' said Anna.

Darius looked at her. 'You didn't even ask for help filling in this questionnaire. What are some unusual skills that you have? Are you good at saving your files in an orderly way? Do other people describe you as aggressive?' He helped her fill the answers.

'Perhaps,' thought Anna, 'Yanni isn't as stupid as he looks.'

'Now let's do mine!' Darius said, but Yanni interrupted them.

By the time they got to the conference centre in St Albans the day's earlier hysteria had fizzled into a general caffeinated buzz. They were all wearing name labels, despite having worked together, in some cases, for thirty years. And Yanni had 'collated their results'.

'We're all going to work on our own special challenges,' he intoned pompously. 'There's actually a lot of evidence to suggest that focussing training to the individual is a lot more effective than a "one size fits all" approach.'

He was really enjoying himself now. 'Please introduce yourself to the person next to you.'

'Hello,' said Darius to Anna, 'I'm Darius.'

'Hello,' said Anna, 'I'm Steve!'

Darius laughed. Anna didn't know why she felt so giddy.

'Darius,' said Yanni, 'let's start with you. It looks like you have trouble completing things . . .'

At lunchtime a plate of sad vegetarian sandwiches was brought in, along with some more people from Clinical Psychology, including Layla.

'Did you have to do the questionnaire?' Anna asked Layla.

'Yup,' confirmed Layla. 'Apparently, I'm fucking aggressive! Yanni can fuck off!'

It was after lunch by the time he got round to Anna's group.

'What we've identified from your questionnaire,' he said to Anna, 'is that you find it hard to ask for help.'

'Right,' said Anna, 'was that because in answer to the question, "Do you find it hard to ask for help?" I answered, "Yes"?'

'No!' said Yanni. 'But we are going to focus on that challenge. I'd like you to do an exercise. Could you ask your colleagues for help now?'

'OK,' said Anna. 'Layla, could you give me a lift to the station? I've got a migraine.'

Layla had Anna's back. 'Absolutely!' said Layla. 'I'd be happy to offer a helping hand to my colleague: in a completely non-aggressive way.'

'That's not what I meant,' Yanni whined. But he had to let them go.

They were both giggly as they piled into Layla's car – a beautiful vintage MG that Layla was inordinately proud of.

'So where are you going in such a hurry?' Layla asked.

'Clinic.' It seemed insane to keep it quiet from Layla. Anna blurted out, 'I'm pregnant.'

Layla appeared to be struggling to keep her face still.

'Congratulations!' she replied evenly.

'Don't say that! I'm so sorry, Layla!' Anna pleaded.

'Don't be sorry,' Layla tried desperately to straighten her face, taking in great gulps of air. 'I'm happy for you. Honestly. When's it due?'

'No! It's not like that. I'm only around eleven weeks. So . . .'

'So what?'

'So, I can still . . . stop it.'

Layla swerved over on to the verge. The man in the car behind her leaned on the horn. 'Cock off!' she shouted at the other driver. She turned towards Anna.

'You don't need to stop the car,' Anna said.

'Oh, I think I fucking do,' said Layla dangerously. 'When did you find out?'

'A week ago?'

'Why's it taken so long? You're more paranoid about getting pregnant than anyone I know.'

'I don't know. I had breakthrough bleeding. And then I met my mother.'

'What's that got to do with it?'

'Everything's gone crazy. Dermot got arrested.'

'What?'

'Yeah. He's been stealing booze from the pub.'

'That's because he's an alcoholic.'

'Yes. Which is one reason why I shouldn't have it. I don't think he can help look after the baby.'

Layla exploded, 'Of course he can't look after the baby! He's a fucking mess!'

'Yes! That's what I'm saying! So, I'm thinking . . . I shouldn't have it. He's drinking like a maniac!'

'Of course he is! He was drinking before. He's never stopped drinking.' Layla took a breath, 'Look, I get Dermot's drinking must break your heart.'

'It does. It breaks my heart to watch him wasting himself.'

'Don't you think he might feel the same way about you?' Layla eyeballed Anna.

'What?' Anna felt the tops of her ears begin to warm up.

'You're a clever woman, Anna. You could do anything. What do you do? Nothing!'

'I work!' Anna defended herself.

'You work in a job that's way beneath you. You accept terrible behaviour from your boyfriend.'

'I'm trying to be patient with him.'

'You're a doormat! You're too chickenshit to tell him how you feel! You second-guess everything! And now you're going to abort a baby I know you want?'

'I'm not you, Layla! I don't know how to do stuff. I don't have a family!'

'You don't have a family?' Layla was suddenly furious. 'What the fuck am I? What the fuck is your dad? What the fuck is your boyfriend?'

'Why are you so angry with me?' Anna asked.

Layla was physically struggling to control her rage. She took long breaths through her nose and out of her mouth. She started massaging a stress point on her palm.

'Just give me a second,' she said. She crossed her arms on the wheel and dropped her head on to them.

'I don't think I should talk about it with you,' Anna said. 'I'm sorry, I shouldn't have told you.'

'Why not?'

'Because, you know, the IVF. This must feel like a slap in the face.'

'Because?' Layla goaded her.

'Because you . . . can't get pregnant.'

Layla's head jerked back against the head rest. 'Fuck's sake! I am pregnant!'

'What?'

'I am pregnant,' said Layla, 'last round was successful. I'll be having a baby in March.'

Anna was unable to hide her surprise. 'Congratulations!'

'Cheers!'

'You'll be a brilliant mother.'

'You don't know that. Perhaps I'll be a shitty one. Who fucking knows!'

'What?'

'Oh my God! Do you think anyone who gets pregnant thinks, "I've got this?" Who the fuck knows how to be a mother? Get out!'

'What?'

'Get the fuck out of the fucking car. I'm not driving you to an abortion you don't want.' Anna got out of the car and stood on the verge. Layla leaned out of the window. 'You might be lucky enough to be given a family, but you have to fight to keep it.' And she roared off.

Anna had to walk to the station. On the way it started raining. And when she got on to the platform, having used the last of her Oyster to get into the station, she discovered the trains were cancelled.

Anna was soaked in St Albans. She took out her mobile. It had taken to randomly disappearing bars of energy. It was now at the bottom of the red. She called up her contacts, and Marlene Mather.

Marlene answered after a single ring.

'Hello, Pickle!'

'Hello . . . Ma . . . rlene!' she said. 'Could you come and pick me up?'

Marlene's BMW was fantastically cosy, after the storm outside. It was already four.

'My God, you're dripping! Just reach over the back,' said Marlene, 'there's a sweater on the seat.'

The sweater was huge, a chessboard of russet and caramel crocheted from some soft wool . . . Merino? Was that a word? Or Cashmere? It seemed too good to wear. And it reminded Anna powerfully of something, but she couldn't remember what.

'Are you sure?'

'Of course!' said Marlene. She affected a Cockney accent, 'Where to, guv?'

'Goodge Street,' said Anna. 'Can I plug in my phone?'

So she plugged her ratty charger, with the wires poking out of its white rubber casing, into Marlene's BMW, and struggled out of her black work hoodie and into the gorgeous jumper.

'You must keep that.' Marlene darted sideways glances at Anna. 'It looks like it was made for you.'

'I can't take your sweater!' said Anna.

'Of course you can!' Marlene smiled. 'What's mine is yours!'

The phone blinked into life. Anna tapped the location of the clinic into Maps. She was late. Even if there were no delays, she'd still be twenty minutes behind schedule. What would they do? Let her be seen, or make her come back? It was only meant to take ten minutes.

'I'm so sorry to bother you. I hope I haven't ruined your afternoon,' she said.

'What's more important than picking up my daughter? Shall we put the radio on? I think we might catch the end of *Gardeners' Question Time*.'

Marlene turned on the radio. A woman's voice, very Radio 4, was saying, 'If you want to know who you are, become a mother.'

It was just a matter of perception, thought Anna. Just as when you were in love, the whole world seemed to be talking about romance, so now, when she was about to end her pregnancy, everything seemed to be about babies – mothers and babies. It was a filter, that was all – as if the world had applied a baby filter on its feed and she saw the whole world through it. It was not that the world was telling her to have the baby. She was not important enough for the world to tell her anything. We are pattern-seeking creatures. We look for intention where none exists.

Now another woman, one with a Sunderland accent, was talking about having hallucinations of babies being hurt.

Anna literally felt her ears burning.

The posh woman was talking again. 'These thoughts can be very vivid. Many pregnant women who experience this fear they'll be a bad parent, but in fact, it's *just your body's way of preparing you to keep your baby safe.*'

'Oh,' said Marlene, 'it's not on.' And she tuned the channel to Radio 3 where Dolly Parton's paean to a mother's love 'Coat of Many Colours' was banging out.

'You've got to be kidding me,' Anna thought, but Marlene sang along gamely and very loudly.

'Ooh! I *love* Dolly!' she cried.

'You really do know the words . . .' Anna said.

Marlene suddenly swung into a service station with total confidence. Anna braced herself against the door.

'I know you're in a rush, but I have to stop for petrol.'

Anna was left alone with the lyrics, sitting in the car in the jumper of at least seven colours that her mother had given her. When Marlene came back, she had two polystyrene cups.

'Hot chocolate!'

The BMW was purring again and almost too warm when Marlene said, 'I'm glad we got this time together. I wanted to give you something. Look at your feet!'

Anna leaned down to discover a smart Selfridges shopping bag in the footwell, with a shoebox in it.

'Really! You mustn't buy me anything else!'

'It's not bought,' said Marlene.

Anna opened the shoebox. Nestled inside, carefully wrapped in white tissue paper, was a beautiful Victorian white christening gown, with tiny mother-of-pearl buttons. It had clearly been created by hand. There were little lace cut-outs, and each tiny hole had been carefully edged with miniature stitches. Across the bottom of the dress were names embroidered in different coloured silks: 'Florence',

'Bertha', 'Jack', 'Sidney', the roll call of working-class life over the last century, then, the names visibly leap-frogging a class, 'Lilith' and 'Hebe' and before Hebe, 'Edward'.

'Who's Edward?' Anna asked, but Marlene just smiled.

'That's me there!' Marlene replied, pointing at 'Lilith'. 'That's my first name,' she said airily. 'Can't stand it. I found this when I was having a clear-out. I thought you might like to have it. My mother gave it to me, and now I'm giving it to you. For when you have a baby.'

Anna could hardly breathe. She felt like she'd been running for a long time. Something about the engineered curvy, plasticised confines of the BMW made the delicate handmade fabric unbearably human.

'So, you are a Christian?' Anna said.

'All the babies in our family have worn it for their christenings. Not you, of course. I never got a chance to christen you. But I embroidered your name on it when I lost you. And I added your new name last week.'

And there, at the bottom of the dress, in tiny, tiny gold writing was her name: Anna. And next to it, embroidered in white on white, was the name Beth. Anna ran her thumb over it. It was so silky.

'I know I've been a bit much,' Marlene said, 'but it's because I love you, you see. You're everything, everything I could have ever dreamt of.' She looked at Anna, her eyes huge and dark, and whispered, 'You can let me love you, you know. Now, I'm being silly, aren't I? Let's go!' and she gunned the engine like a boy racer.

'Here we are!' Marlene called out, pulling up in the pouring rain on Goodge Street. The rain drummed on the BMW's roof. Marlene had driven so fast she was hardly late. It was quarter to five. The sun was setting. It was the Day of Atonement.

'Actually,' said Anna, 'could you just go around the corner to UCH?'

'Of course!'

And so, Anna didn't go to her appointment. It flitted across her mind that there might be other people who'd decided not to go ahead with an abortion because their mum had given them a Christian baby dress on Yom Kippur. She wondered who they were. She went for her twelve-week scan instead, and when she had her twelve-week scan it was her mother who was with her. When the little picture of the ghost baby got printed out, her mother asked for a copy, and Anna gave her one. It was her mother who held Anna's hand when the image first appeared on the screen, and it was her mother who listened with her as the tiny galloping hooves of the baby's heartbeat were heard, galloping up the riverbed, galloping towards her.

Anna took one ragged in-breath and the sonographer handed her a ridged plastic cup filled with water. 'Got to keep Mum happy,' she said, winking.

'Mum'll be happy when this little one is in my arms,' said Marlene.

Anna thought about correcting her, but it seemed churlish to say, 'She meant me. I'm the mum.' Marlene leaned forward and slipped her hand into Anna's, holding it in a special way, hooked around her little finger, and Anna gasped.

'I didn't want to have a baby without my mother there,' Anna said, in a small voice.

Marlene whispered, 'You don't have to, darling!' She leaned in to look at the foetus's face, and said, 'Who does he look like? Is it me?'

SECOND TRIMESTER

7

THIRTEEN WEEKS GONE

'You'll notice a small bump developing as your womb grows and moves upwards. If you've been feeling the urge to pee more often over the last few months, it's because your womb was pressing on your bladder. This should ease off now.'

'Is this it?' Dermot was leaning forward in the dappled light from the trees lining the drive. 'Oh my God! Would you look at this place?'

'I think it is.' Anna was looking at her mother's handwritten instructions. '"Three miles south of Woldingham. When you see the owl corbel, you're home!" What's a corbel?'

'No idea! Why don't you text her?'

As Anna reached for her phone, she saw her pre-natal vitamins and realised she hadn't taken them today. If she snuck one into her mouth fast enough Dermot might not notice.

'Give us one!' said Dermot.

'What?' said Anna.

'Of those painkillers,' Dermot nodded.

'Sorry!' said Anna. 'Last one! Oh look! That stone pillar is carved into an owl.'

Dermot pulled up on the gravel in front of a beautiful square brick house with carved, curled eaves. The garden was immaculate. It looked pricey.

'It looks like a video game!' said Dermot. Anna knew what he meant. The garden was Japanese 'inspired': all sweeping lines and acer trees rising out of a mist of white flowers. They sat for a moment together.

'Ready to eat the fatted calf?' Dermot asked.

'Well, the fatted tofu,' Anna said.

When she got to the front door, she stepped back. 'You ring!' she pushed Dermot.

'It's your mam!' he protested.

'I'm too nervous!'

So Dermot rang the doorbell, and he was already raising his arms to greet Marlene with a hug when the door opened to a tiny grey-haired man, who visibly shrank back at the sight of Dermot.

Anna took the lead. 'We're looking for Marlene Mather?' The old man's eyes were on Dermot, and he didn't acknowledge Anna at all. Dermot repeated it.

'You want the big house,' said the little old man, and as he turned Anna noticed he had a hearing aid. 'This is the Lodge. Just carry on down the drive.'

'Thanks!' Anna smiled desperately at the little old man as the door closed in her face. She looked at Dermot. 'Christ! How big is the big house?'

The wheels crunched on the gravel as the band's van rolled to a stop.

'Where should I leave the van? Is that a garage?' Dermot asked.

'I think that might be a . . . stables?'

Dermot looked at the various outbuildings, the garden, disappearing into a wood. 'Fuck me!' he said. 'She does have a castle.' Anna wished she'd worn something smarter than her green cardigan. They sat in silence for about a minute. Dermot did his old Sligo lady voice, the voice of his mother. 'But think of the bills!'

And a steady crunching, like a giant chewing rock, heralded the arrival of Marlene, opening Anna's passenger door and screaming . . .

'I can't believe you're really here! Welcome to Prescott House! Welcome home!'

'And Hebe you know, of course. And this is Tristan – he's mine! And this is Benedict.' Marlene gestured to a rangy young East Asian man in a three-piece suit, who was better dressed than any human Anna had yet met. 'And Tom and Sophie from next door, and these are their little darlings. It doesn't feel like a house without the sound of children running around!'

'Next door? It feels like we're quite a long way away from anyone.'

'No, Dermot. The house is split down the middle, or not quite. I think I've got two-thirds, haven't I, Sophie? The East Wing! It's practically a semi. Really! Come outside! Charmaine, will you bring the bits and pieces through the drawing room? Don't ask Charmaine anything, Dermot! It's such unseasonably nice weather, why don't we eat on the veranda?' Anna's coat was taken by a woman with the face of a lifelong smoker: baked skin and the hair dyed a single solid colour gelled into a 'pixie' cut, if the pixie were made of Lego.

'Hello!' Anna said.

'That's Charmaine,' Marlene added, 'she's from the Lodge.' Charmaine was scanning their faces. Anna realised she was also deaf and handed her coat over to get her attention.

'I think we might have met your dad,' Anna said.

'What's this?' Marlene was agog.

'We stopped at the Lodge on the way down. We thought it was your house.'

'Oh marvellous!' Marlene was delighted. 'You thought I lived in the Lodge!'

'And a man answered the door. Was that your dad?'

'Was he deaf?' Marlene asked. She raised her voice to a shout, 'Charmaine, they stopped at the Lodge!'

'My dad lives at the Lodge,' Charmaine confirmed.

'It might not have been,' Marlene interjected. 'It might have been your boyfriend, mightn't it? You shouldn't make assumptions!' Marlene squeezed Tristan's shoulder.

'He's my dad,' Charmaine repeated.

'Now, phones in the basket.' Marlene waved a wicker basket with several phones already in it under their noses.

'What?' Dermot was shocked.

'My house, my rules! I do not allow my guests to be constantly staring at their phones like zombies. In the basket, please! You'll be given them back when you leave.' Marlene winked. 'Like prison.'

Anna and Dermot surrendered their phones.

'This way,' Marlene was leading them through the 'drawing room' outside on to a brick walkway which appeared to surround the house on two sides. As Anna stepped through the French doors, she saw, smashed on the Georgian brick, several bodies of tiny birds.

'Don't mind them,' Marlene said, as if it were a personal campaign against her, 'they *will* nest in the eaves! And look who's here . . .'

Sitting on the wall, curled around a glass of stout, was Neil Byrne.

'Neil!' Dermot seemed genuinely happy to see him. 'What the hell are you doing here?'

'I invited him.' Marlene was overjoyed. Anna couldn't understand why she was so pleased, unless it was just visceral delight at having a man who looked like Neil on her wall. Neil, in the September sun, was an illustration in a child's book of flower fairies.

Benedict, who appeared to have been dropped on the terrace from the nineteen-thirties, whooshed camply up to Neil with his hand out. 'And whooooo is this?' At the last minute turning his hand and offering the back of it to be kissed. Neil, surprised, obliged.

'Neil's my boyfriend's bandmate.'

'I think he's a little more than that!' Marlene cried. How had she even got in touch with Neil? And why? 'Couldn't have a "Welcome Home Anna-Beth" party without your best friend!' Marlene winked broadly at Anna, 'Now, who's for a drink?'

'Sorry about Ma!' Benedict was close to Anna's ear. 'You might not have gathered from the way she introduced me but I'm your brother. Hello!'

Anna was tripped up. She took a deep breath. 'Oh! Who's Tristan?'

'That's her boyfriend. I know! Oedipal!'

'Marlene's your mother?'

'Please! My dad's wife! Couple of husbands ago. I'm your brother – step-brother really. So you are absolutely allowed to want to bang me!'

Anna half-laughed, half-coughed. 'No, you're all right,' she said, and he looked authentically delighted at this rejection.

'We're going to get along.'

'Are you . . .?' Anna wanted to say Edward, but something stopped her.

'I'm Ben. Heebs! Heebs!' Benedict hissed at his sister, and she came over. She was looking beautiful, though thinner than when Anna had last seen her and, if possible, even more bloodless. She was dressed in black. Benedict gave her a cigarette. 'Heebs was waiting to tell you about me so we didn't spring everything on you all at once, but Ma got in there first. She's the family vault, I'm the loudhailer! Anything you want to know, ask me!' Ben tucked a piece of paper into her cardigan pocket, with a significant look. 'Ciggie?'

'What are you lot plotting?' Marlene descended on them. 'I haven't had a picture! Tom! Tom! Could you take a picture of me with my beautiful, beautiful children? Now, someone's missing. Who's missing?' Anna caught Hebe and Benedict exchange a guarded glance. Marlene visibly shook herself. 'No one, that's who! Come on, Neil. Get over here!' She turned to Anna. 'Tom's allowed a camera! He's a photographer, you know.'

Neil had uncoiled and was backing off the walkway.

'You too, Neil! You're family too!'

Anna caught this. What did Marlene mean? Did she think Neil was related to her? She sought out Dermot in the moving bodies. He was happily sipping beer on the wall that Neil had just vacated. He hadn't been invited into the picture. She gave him a little wave and he raised his can as if to say, 'Continue!'

Neil was now on Anna's left, with Benedict on her right. Marlene was arranging everyone.

'Neil, put your hand on Anna's shoulder.'

Neil respectfully placed his hand on Anna's right shoulder. Anna could feel the individual pads of his fingers.

Benedict leaned into Anna's ear, 'Tom's a builder! Hebe actually is a photographer,' he added quickly. 'Best to take anything Ma says with a pinch of salt!'

'What are you saying?' Marlene was immediately between the two of them.

Ben brazened it out. 'I was just advising Anna it's best to take everything you say with a pinch of salt!'

'Oh Ben!' Marlene's eyes glittered. 'Sometimes I wish I'd given you away instead of Anna!'

Anna met Dermot's eyes just as he spat out his beer, then travelled to Benedict, whose face was set in an ironic eye-roll.

'You can't give away what you never had!' Ben shot back.

'I'm joking! It's just my wicked sense of humour. Everyone!' Marlene was now in the middle and beaming at Tom, the neighbour with the camera. 'Well, smile, darling! It's not every day you come home. Raise your glasses, please. To my new daughter! To Anna-Beth!'

Tom's camera actually clicked.

'And to her baby!'

Neil's hand withdrew from Anna's shoulder. Anna couldn't breathe. The air was heavy smoke. Her ears were ringing. Tears pricked at her eyes. But she willed them to the spot on the brickwork where Dermot had sat. There was no one there. Maybe he hadn't heard. Maybe she had time to take him aside and tell him herself.

'Oops!' said Marlene, slapping her own wrist theatrically. 'Have I put my foot in it?'

Ben was hugging Anna, 'Congratulations!'

'Yes, congratulations!' said Hebe, putting her thin arms around Anna.

Tom, the photographer, had moved forward to hug her too, with his yoga-thin wife Sophie.

Where was Dermot? What had happened to Dermot?

'I'm so happy for you, Anna!' Neil stuttered out. 'And you, Dermot! Congratulations, man!' and Neil stuck out his hand to shake Dermot's, who was suddenly beside her.

Anna looked up to catch Dermot's eye, but he was hugging Neil. It lasted a long time. When she finally saw his face, his expression was stone.

'I should have . . .' she whispered, but Dermot stopped her.

'I'm so happy!' he whispered back to her. 'I'm so fucking happy!' Then he desperately patted his pockets, shouted, 'Oh my God! I have to tell Mam!' and loped off to find his phone. Anna did her best not to look at Neil.

'Excuse me!' Marlene was standing with her arms outstretched, Jesus-like. 'Isn't there someone else you should be congratulating?'

The group turned to look at her.

'Me,' said Marlene. 'I'm the grandmother! Don't *I* get some love too?'

Another round of drinks had been poured. Marlene hung over Tom's shoulder, scrolling through the photos. 'Now, Tom. You'll have to help me post this on Instagram. I'm officially a mommy blogger now. Pretty soon I'll be a grandmother blogger, whatever those are called!'

'I'm not sure that's a thing,' murmured Hebe.

'Mirror, Mirror on the wall, who's the greatest mother of all?' Benedict muttered.

'Not that one, Tom!' Marlene slapped him playfully. 'I look enormous!'

Anna sought out Dermot in the hall. He was on the phone but hung up when he saw her and wrapped her up like some mad Santa. Anna was preparing to apologise, but Dermot stopped her.

'Don't you dare. Don't you fucking dare! You can't make this anything but the best thing ever. Now, let's find me a drink!'

The food was good, and Marlene was constantly filling glasses. By four in the afternoon, with them all except Anna at least slightly drunk, Marlene had demanded a song – 'something Irish' – of Dermot and Neil, who, with the lack of self-consciousness of professional musicians, obliged with a complex harmonic arrangement of the magpie rhyme which Anna had never heard before. Their lovely voices intertwined and floated over the lawn. 'How did you know that is my favourite song? And now the children,' demanded Marlene.

'Oh, Anna doesn't sing,' Dermot informed her.

'Nonsense,' Marlene protested, 'all my children sing! Ben! Do the honours.'

Ben started, po-faced, singing in a falsetto, like a choirboy, the Song of Ascents, Psalm 121, 'I will lift up mine eyes . . .', the note on 'eyes' lifting to F.

'He thinks he's funny!' Marlene shouted.

But Hebe joined in, slipping her hand into Anna's, 'unto the hills from whence cometh my help'. And Anna found herself, for the first time, singing in front of Dermot, and in front of Neil, her voice exactly matching Hebe's top soprano, note for note, a clean, sweet sound that floated out across the lawn. Anna couldn't look at Dermot, who she just knew would be mugging and grinning, but when she did allow herself to catch his eye, he was sitting, eyes closed, enjoying the music.

Marlene repeated, 'All my children sing! You see?' Tristan swung a bargain basement acoustic guitar on to his knee.

'Not now, Tristan!' Marlene said firmly. 'Lunch is over!'

'Thank you!' said Anna. 'It's been a lovely party.'

'Oh, this isn't the party!' said Marlene. 'Aren't you sweet?' The doorbell rang. 'That'll be the first guests!'

Anna couldn't sleep. Dermot lay next to her in 'Hebe's room'. The wallpaper was an incredibly complex repeated pattern of some woodland scene, the deer and badgers and owls appearing again and again in formation just like the woodland outside. Hebe herself had been put in 'the spare' (the bed was smaller – much had been made of Dermot's height). After the big announcement it was inevitable they'd stay. The last of Marlene's guests had only left at one in the morning, but Dermot and Anna had been allowed to give up and go to bed earlier, 'on account of the baby'. Anna could see from her phone, which she had rescued from its wicker holding cell, that it was now four. She had a craving for milk.

Anna crept down the stairs, trying to keep her bare feet on the uncarpeted edges of the steps, away from any creaks, so she didn't wake everybody up. Since she was a little girl, she'd found herself waking whenever she stayed in strange houses. At school, if you woke at night, there was no fetching something to drink.

On the second landing her left foot caught on something, some cord; she heard the unmistakable sound of something scraping across wood, and her left hand shot out reflexively to catch whatever it was. A landline phone, in its little cradle. Anna turned on her mobile torch to replace the phone on the precarious mahogany occasional table, which wobbled a little. It was nearly as tall as she was and on it, next to the red cradle, was a small porcelain statuette. The figure was self-evidently Marlene, naked and incredibly beautiful. She was reclining, leaning on one elbow which was also supporting the head of a baby, who suckled at her breast. At her feet another tiny child sat up, playing. The statuette was the most beautiful, idealised portrait of motherhood. Anna turned off the torch and it disappeared.

Anna wondered if Neil had gone home. It seemed unlikely. He was on the bike and wouldn't ride after even a single drink. She went through the abandoned 'drawing room', now cleared of party detritus, the furniture pushed back against the walls, to the French windows which gave on to the garden, and the woods beyond.

She tried the French window and it opened on to the 'veranda' they had sat on earlier in the day. From here a short flight of brick steps went down to a lawn.

Anna stepped down on to the damp grass. There was so much space. She started running, sprinting silently across the sodden lawn. At the far right-hand corner was a short path made of flagstones which led through to a wooded area. Over a wall Anna could see a field. As she got closer, she heard a soft whinny. Somewhere deep in the woodland she could hear some creature snuffling in the undergrowth. She had come too far – she ought to go back.

As Anna quietly let herself back into the drawing room, she saw a light coming from the hall on the left. At the end of the parqueted hall was the arch leading to the kitchen and standing under it was Marlene, dressed in a quilted kimono. It was printed with a repeating design, what could have been feathers, or possibly eyes. Marlene stretched both her arms upwards so that her body made a Y shape in the archway, the sleeves falling away from her like wings. On her hands Anna could just see her huge silver rings glinting.

'Is someone there?' Marlene's voice sang out.

Anna stepped out. 'It's only me! I was just after some milk.'

'Oh! Are you a night owl, like me?'

'I am,' said Anna.

Marlene busied herself in the kitchen boiling the kettle.

'Isn't this cosy?' Anna decided it was private enough to try to broach the unexpected announcement. She took a deep breath.

'I was a bit surprised today. I wasn't expecting to tell everybody about the baby.'

'Well, you'll understand when you're a grandmother. You just can't imagine the love until you've experienced it. It's like nothing you've ever felt before.'

'Do you have grandchildren then?' Anna asked.

'I'm sorry?' Marlene was nonplussed.

'I didn't know you had grandchildren. Do you . . . have other kids?'

'No. Just yours. Yours is the first!'

'Oh!' said Anna.

She tried to unpack the last thing Marlene had said. So Marlene had never experienced love for her own children like she felt for Anna's unborn child? And Anna had not experienced love for anybody like Marlene experienced for Anna's unborn child? Motherhood was confusing.

'Dermot didn't actually know.'

'I gathered as much!' Marlene said. 'He seemed *very* pleased.'

She got down the paraphernalia to make real coffee.

'Actually, could I just have milk?' Anna asked. 'I won't sleep at all if I drink that.'

'Oh! Do you have trouble sleeping?' Marlene was still at the kettle.

'Not usually.' Suddenly Anna longed for her messy little flat. 'Your house is beautiful. It's a real rabbit warren.'

'Yes!' said Marlene, getting out boxes from the cupboard. 'Parts of it are over nine hundred years old. Prescott means priest's hole! Though I've cleaned every inch of it and never found one.'

'What's a priest's hole?'

'It's where the priests hid during the Elizabethan raids.'

'Of course,' Anna said. 'Well, we don't have any of those at mine.'

'No!' said Marlene.

'Do you know where Neil got to?'

'Oh!' said Marlene, managing to fit a lot into a single syllable. 'Is that why you are flitting around in the middle of the night?' She raised her eyebrows at Anna.

'No! I just didn't know if he stayed over.'

'I'm just teasing you, darling. Though I wouldn't blame you one bit! He's out in the stables.'

'The stables?'

'Yes, there's a very comfortable room above the horse box.' Marlene handed Anna her tea and went over to a kitchen drawer and took out a brand-new iPhone.

'Do you want this?'

'I can't accept that!'

'Don't be silly! I got an extra on my tariff. I don't understand these things. They just sent me this.'

'Thank you.' Anna was touched. 'That's very kind.'

As Marlene was fiddling about with the phone, inputting the password, Anna tried to work up the courage to ask her mother something real.

'I've put my birthday, so you won't forget,' Marlene said, waving the phone.

'I don't know your birthday,' Anna said.

'It's exactly one month before yours.'

Anna could feel the muscles in her face clenching.

'I don't know when that is either.'

'Oh, I forgot! Mine is the first of June!' So, the first of July was her birthday. Her real birthday.

'Marlene . . .' Anna began.

'Call me Ma!' said Marlene.

'Ma,' Marlene beamed at Anna using the name, 'can you tell me who my father was?'

Marlene dropped the phone. Her face twisted, then straightened, then contorted again. She covered her face with her hands and shuddered.

'I'm sorry!' said Anna. 'I'm so sorry!'

A low keening came out of Marlene, like a dog that's been kicked. She stood up groggily, and pushed past Anna to the kitchen sink, where she began to retch over and over again. Anna crossed to her and reached out to pat her back, rubbing her shoulder as she made rhythmic movements like a cat coughing up a fur ball.

'I shouldn't have asked.'

'No, you shouldn't,' said Marlene, her voice thin with irritation. And just as suddenly, she softened. 'But I forgive you. You weren't to know.' Marlene turned and grasped Anna's neck, pulling her head forward until they were eyeball to eyeball. Marlene's hand was strong and faintly bumpy with arthritis. 'You are *nothing* like him. Do you understand? Nothing. You are *all me*. Now, do you think you can go back to sleep?'

Hebe, in the study, was having trouble sleeping herself. The ceiling seemed too low. After Becky had kicked her out she'd gone to stay at Ian's – he was in a three-bedroom shared house in Kennington. In one bedroom were Ian and his girlfriend, in another a guy called Will who she didn't know, and she was in the third bedroom during the week, but the guy who was sub-letting his room, Marcus, came home every weekend, which turned out to be Friday to Sunday. At first, she'd moved on to the sofa those nights but Will stayed up late, smoking dope endlessly and playing *Call Of Duty* as her head bobbed on her neck, unable to turn out the light. Then Marcus had started staying up too, pushing his legs up against her in the flickering light from the game. She washed the sheets every Friday morning, sneaking them out with her and doing them in the washing machine of one of the houses she cleaned, but Marcus started making weird comments about the smell of the room. 'Mmm,' he would say. 'Smells like mackerel! I love mackerel!' He was generally perfectly pleasant, even courteous, to her. Then she had dozed off, her head on the arm of the sofa, and had woken to find he'd lifted her skirt and was staring at her arse and wanking vigorously in the light from the video game as Will continued playing. As she woke up Will had glanced round and then looked straight back at the screen.

She got up and went into the kitchen to sleep on the floor, where Ian tripped over her in the morning. 'Shit! Heebs! What are you doing?'

After that she'd started making sure she was out on weekend nights. Since she didn't have the money to go 'out' out, she'd either sleep on Ben's sofa or ride the night bus until three or four to make sure everyone was asleep by the time she got home. And she no longer spoke to Will. For some reason his decision to ignore what was happening bothered her even more than Marcus's public masturbation. When she closed her eyes at night it was Will's eyes shifting back to the screen that she saw.

Marcus had approached her with a cup of tea and told her he felt just terrible about what had happened and wanted to make it up to her, after all she was contributing to the rent, so why didn't she sleep on an airbed in his room if he promised to keep his hands to himself? She'd walked in to find him wearing only a rugby shirt with the collar turned up, his hands by his sides. Then he moved sideways to show her the profile of his erection, like he was doing shadow-puppetry of the penis. She'd got her rucksack together and left.

That had been six days ago.

The next spot Hebe had found to sleep had been unusual. 'Is this mad?' she had asked herself. On the surface of things it seemed like it might be. Everyone seemed to think she was mad, but it had been raining the night Marcus's penis silhouette had been burned on her retinas and there didn't seem to be anywhere else to go. The lorry wheels were quite tall. It wouldn't be that bad, would it? Surely the engine starting would wake her up if she fell asleep, and she could scoot out from under it then.

She had been under the lorry when she got the party invite. Marlene had a habit of texting at odd hours of the day and night. 'You are cordially invited to a party to celebrate the news that I have a daughter!' Not 'a new daughter', not 'two daughters', not 'a daughter I thought I'd lost and have now found': just 'a daughter'. Marlene had actually forgotten that Hebe existed, so pleased and excited was she with her new plaything. It was strange. It didn't even hurt. In fact, Hebe had felt . . . what was it? Lying under the lorry she felt light as air: a surging, powerful relief.

Hebe pulled her mother's spare blankets up over her shoulders and went to her mother's Insta feed and found the picture of the kittens. It was a clue. She could see the resemblance. Ma had definitely lied to her, and if she had lied about this it was entirely possible that she'd lied about other things. Now Hebe began to imagine that the ceiling was the underside of the engine, and her breathing got longer and slower. The images: Will's face turning away from her, Marcus's penis framed against the curtain, his hands dangling, the white letters 'I have a daughter!' started to fade under the conjured belly of the lorry.

Tomorrow would be the time. After that, she would have to make it up.

Anna woke in a vast bedroom, with windows which looked out over beautiful lawns and woods beyond. She felt like she'd never slept so deeply. She had a metallic taste in her mouth she attributed to a disturbed night and an unfamiliar bed. Dermot did take up most of it. He was staring at her with a goofy expression she'd never seen before.

'Why are you looking at me like I'm all magical and female?'

'Is this our baby?' he said, waving his phone at her.

It was. It was the ultrasound scan. It was on Marlene's Instagram feed, under the handle 'CallMeMa'.

'I'm so sorry,' Anna said. 'I didn't know she was posting that.'

'It's fine.' Dermot was still looking at her, head cocked, like she was a precious and delicate porcelain figurine. 'She's got loads of you.'

Anna took Dermot's phone. Marlene's feed was photo after photo of Anna. Some she recognised – but some she had never seen before. The latest post was from yesterday, when Marlene had asked them all to raise their glasses. The picture was of Marlene with Hebe, Ben, Anna and Neil on the 'veranda'. Neil was next to Anna, his hand resting lightly on her shoulder, the light shining through his curls, and through hers. They seemed like a couple, without a shadow of a doubt, except Neil's mouth was open in shock. He looked like he'd been punched in the gut.

The bedroom door opened and Marlene paused, framed in the doorway, dressed in an entirely transparent nightgown and full jewellery. 'Room for a little one?' And she was under the covers.

Dermot sprang out of the bed with the speed of a much smaller man and bolted for the en suite shouting 'Need a piss!' and Anna found herself in the bed with her near-naked mother.

'So, you're on Instagram?' Anna said.

'And I have a blog,' said Marlene. 'I know. How nineties of me! But I'm trying to be an inspiration for other mothers who've been separated from their babies, to say, "There! Is! Hope!"' She formed fists and jangled her bracelets, punching the air. 'I'll see you downstairs for croissants.' She turned back, 'I'm so happy!'

Neil and Ben were at the breakfast table, which was laid out like a boutique hotel with baked goods and fruit salad. Anna tried to catch Neil's eye but he kept his gaze resolutely on the pastries. Tom, the builder/photographer, appeared at the back door.

'Sorry to intrude,' he called out cheerfully, 'has the cat wandered back here?'

'What's wrong?' Marlene asked.

'Nothing,' Tom reassured her, blinking slightly as he tried to keep his eyes from drifting nipple-wards, 'we've just mislaid the cat and Sophie's worried because we're trying to get him settled in. Buttered his paws, but he's gone walkabout!'

Marlene dropped the tray she was holding on to the side and pushed past Anna, sprinting along the hall.

'What was all that about?' Anna asked Ben.

Ben looked sheepish. 'No idea! D'you want some little bits of granola mixed with frozen blueberries?'

But Marlene was back, spitting fire. 'Ben? Do you know where Hebe is?'

Ben picked up his plate and started piling it with food, so he was in motion when he said, 'She left this morning.'

'Did she have a cat?' Marlene's voice was terrifyingly steady.

'I believe she was carrying a cat basket, yes,' Ben added lightly. 'I mean, it was her cat!'

Tom looked thoroughly confused. He said to Marlene, 'You gave us your daughter's cat?'

'Excuse me, Tom – could you give us some family time?' Marlene grabbed Ben's arm and marched him out of the kitchen. Tom, Anna and Neil looked at each other awkwardly as they could hear the bollocking coming from the 'drawing room': '. . . such an insult – thought I could trust you – who walks four miles – today of all days . . .'

'I'll, er, come back later,' Tom muttered courteously.

And Neil and Anna were alone.

'I'm really sorry, Neil. I didn't know that was going to happen.'

Neil saw something fascinating in the butter dish.

'What was going to happen?' he asked.

'That she was going to tell everyone about the baby.'

'Who's she? The Cat's Mother?' Neil was suddenly all Dublin.

'Apparently not,' said Anna. Neil grinned and allowed himself to meet Anna's eye.

'I'm really pleased for you both. Well, at least he'll shut up about it now.'

'About what?'

'Having a baby! It's all he talks about.'

'Is it?'

Dermot had seemed extremely happy. For the first time the thought invaded Anna's head, unbidden, that Dermot could have done something to the condom. She immediately suppressed it. Of course he hadn't done something to the condom. That would be horrendous, horrible, immoral, the act of a criminal.

Dermot banged his head on the arch to the kitchen. 'Jesus! What are we discussing?'

They took the coach out from Victoria Station late and crossed over from Holyhead to Dublin and then took another bus to Sligo bus station, then another bus out to Ballymote. Anna and Dermot were sitting behind a woman taking her father's ashes home who sobbed throughout the trip. At Sligo they were relieved to see she left the bus, but then she got right on the next bus with them. By the time they got to Cathy's bungalow Anna's nerves were shredded.

It was the first time Anna had stayed at Dermot's mum's place. She'd met Cathy twice before. The last time was in London a year ago, when she'd looked completely different. Dermot was staying in the garden in a tent, as his eldest sister Caroline and her husband Noel had been in the second bedroom ever since the diagnosis. But Anna, in deference to her condition, was given the couch.

'I can sleep outside with you.'

'I don't think so,' Dermot had snorted, 'I mean, we can't share a bed till we're married, even if you were pregnant with twins.' Dermot paused. 'You aren't, are you?'

The couch in front of the gas fire was unbelievably comfortable, and the first night she slept as well as she did at Marlene's.

She was woken by Cathy, her face, now round with steroids, beaming with happiness. She had brought her a cup of tea.

'So, when's the wedding?' Cathy asked. Anna's eyes darted to Dermot. 'It's all right, I'm messing with you! We're not some backwater, you know! I'm not going to force a shotgun wedding. You'll do it when you're ready.'

That evening Dermot went to the pub and Anna and Cathy were left alone together.

'He'll not be back tonight,' said Cathy, 'hanging around with the big boys hoping to join in.'

'What's that?' said Anna.

'He's taken his fiddle,' said Cathy, 'he'll be waiting to play with the real players. He'll be waiting a long time.'

'The real players?'

'There's a load of them hang around Shoot The Crows. I wish he'd learn.'

'I don't understand. Isn't Dermot a real player?'

'He used to be. But now he plays all that other stuff, isn't it?'

'What other stuff?'

'All the bastardised stuff with that Neil.' Cathy spat the name Neil.

'You don't like Dermot's music?'

'That's not Dermot's music! Dermot's music is his father's music! It's his grandfather's music! That's Neil's music.'

'I'm sorry.'

'It's all right,' Cathy's moon face softened, 'you're English.' She sighed. 'We all had such high hopes.'

Anna, driven by some impulse to defend Dermot, blurted out, 'He just got twelve grand for a song!'

'He what?' Cathy's voice was shaking.

'He sold a song.' Cathy's mouth was folded in a straight line, her lips turned in, and the space around them so white it was blue. 'I'll let him tell you about it.'

'I'll get you another cup.' The banality of the words contrasted sharply with the unidentifiable passion behind them. Anna had no idea what she'd said wrong.

'Please, let me,' she said, standing up.

'No. Sit yourself down!' snapped Cathy.

'It's no trouble!' Anna protested.

Cathy turned around and shouted full in Anna's face.

'I can still make a cup of tea in my own house!' Anna sat down.

It seemed the music Dermot played that Anna thought was so brilliant was a source of shame to his mother, at least. And she'd never be a part of his family.

It was later that Cathy volunteered, 'It's exciting about the baby.'

'Yes,' said Anna.

'He always loved babies. He was wonderful with the younger ones when he was a lad. It's a pity it's taken you so long.'

'Sorry?' Anna didn't understand.

'It's a pity it's taken you so long to get pregnant.' Cathy patted Anna's knee. 'I know you've had the most terrible trouble. It must have been tough.'

Anna went out to the garden. Why had Dermot told his mam they were trying for a baby? She was overcome by the need for a cigarette. 'Not a need,' she told herself, 'you just want one. You want a cigarette, but you shouldn't have one.' Surely one couldn't do any harm. She ducked her head into the tent in search of them. The place smelt strongly of Dermot. Over the last eighteen months his smell had changed from what she thought of vaguely as 'fields' to something worse. He smelt like a micro-brewery that hadn't passed its hygiene certificate. And somewhere in the brewery was a pile of teeth. And now the tent smelt the same. Dermot's rucksack was lying on the ground. Why hadn't he put it in the bungalow? Feeling faintly guilty she flipped through the stuff in the top searching for a smoke. Maybe she could have one puff and throw the rest of the cigarette away? But in amongst Dermot's worn T-shirts was his box of condoms. Dermot had bought a jumbo box of fifty in the early days of their relationship and they were, as he put it, 'working their way through them'. Anna was gripped with suspicion. They didn't seem to have been messed around with. The little purple packets were unopened. Maybe he'd spiked them? He could have pushed a pin through them, couldn't he? She started holding them up to the last of the light slanting through the tent opening, but she couldn't see properly. She got out her phone and turned the torch on, shining it on the condom packets against her hand to see if light leaked through the pinpricks – not that one, but maybe the next.

A shadow blocked out the light. Dermot's head was poking in the tent.

'I thought you wouldn't be back till late,' said Anna.

Dermot took in the condoms and the torch. 'What the fuck are you doing?'

On the bus on the way back they sat side by side. It had never bothered Anna that Dermot was so huge; she was so small the overspill didn't bother her. But now she was bigger all over; her hips were bulging over the waistband of her jeans and Dermot's size was just another inconvenience. He dug into her in unexpected places. They hadn't actually spoken to each other in two hours. Anna knew better than to approach the subject before Dermot was ready. He could nurse a grievance for days, feeding it soup and tucking it up into bed at night.

'I almost miss the woman with the ashes now,' she deadpanned. And Dermot laughed. 'I'm sorry,' she confessed.

'What were you thinking?' Dermot pressed her.

'Maybe it's the . . .' Anna volunteered, but suddenly the word was missing. 'The . . . you know, you get them when you're pregnant, but everybody has them.'

'Kids?' Dermot hazarded.

'They're like pheromones but not smelly.'

'Hormones?' Dermot said, and as Anna looked relieved he asked, 'Are you drunk?'

'No!' Anna said. 'Your mum seemed to think we'd been trying for a baby and it freaked me out.'

'So, you thought I'd stealthed you?'

'I don't think it's stealthing if you keep the condom on,' Anna demurred.

'You know what I mean.'

'Everything's changing so quickly,' Anna mumbled. 'Please don't hate me.' Dermot shifted his long legs. 'Why did you tell your mother we were trying for a baby?'

'Do you have an Irish mother?' Dermot asked Anna.

'No.'

'Well, don't fucking judge me then.'

'I didn't know she was iffy about Neil,' Anna added.

'She's not iffy about him,' Dermot contradicted her, 'she fucking hates him.'

'Why?'

'He charmed me from the one true path, didn't he? With his magical pipe!' Dermot waggled his eyebrows and Anna noticed he had a couple of old man hairs making a break for his forehead. 'If he hadn't come along, I'd be playing the fiddle in the grand tradition and I'd never have gone to England and I'd be living in her spare bedroom, sandwiched between Caroline and Noel, presumably. And

I wouldn't have fallen out with my dad. Neil's everything she hates. Except English.'

'I told your mum about the ad.'

'Jesus, Anna! Are you trying to kill her?'

'I thought she'd be pleased.'

'Fuck!' Dermot exclaimed, wiping his long hair out of his eyes.

'I don't know about your world!' Anna declared.

'It's not a world, Anna! It's just a country,' Dermot exhaled. 'They aren't going to air it anyway,' he added.

'What?'

'The ad.'

'When did you find that out?'

'Last week. I still get the money though. It's just my mam won't have to, you know, listen to me betray hundreds of years of Irish musical tradition. She'll just know I've done it. Fuck, Anna! You shouldn't have told her!'

'Oh my God!' Anna exploded. 'You got fucking arrested! How did I end up in the wrong?'

'I don't know,' said Dermot, 'but you did.'

Anna and Dermot sat for a while, as the bus churned along, and the low houses and pubs trundled past. Anna glanced at her phone. There was a text from Marlene: *Were they VERY Irish?* Anna felt a hole in her stomach. Her pulse was thudding in her ears. She had done a terrible thing. She had broken a sacred trust and Dermot would never forgive her.

She stood up and squeezed out past Dermot so she was in the aisle, flapping her green parka around her, and got down on her knees on the bobbled black lino of the coach floor.

'Dermot Dwyer, will you do me the honour of becoming . . .'

'Fucking hell!' yelled Dermot. Out of the side of her left eye Anna could see the people in the seats behind her standing up to look.

'Let me finish, will you?' Anna croaked. She cleared her throat. 'Will you do me the honour of becoming my husband?'

Dermot grinned, 'Where's my fucking ring?'

Anna felt in her parka pocket and took out her keys – they were on a metal keyring. It was quite large, but then, so was Dermot's finger. She rapidly twisted it, pulling the keys which accessed the different parts of her life off the metal circle: her flat front door key, her flat front door lock, her desk drawer at work, the door to the balcony, the van The Byrnes used for gigs. The keys snapped off one by one and dropped into her pocket. She lifted up the metal ring, and Dermot, grinning, pulled it on to his ring finger.

'All right then!' he said. Anna realised she hadn't seen a baby under threat for weeks – not since she'd decided to keep it. Maybe that meant this was right. Maybe this was the right road after all. The bus rumbled on, carrying her back, back to where she'd started from. Then Dermot stood up, stooping low under the overhanging roof, and turned towards the back of the coach to bow and show off the ring, to scattered applause.

8

SIXTEEN WEEKS GONE

'The muscles of the baby's face can now move, and the beginnings of facial expressions appear. Your baby cannot control these yet.'

Anna and Dermot were, much to Anna's surprise, having sex for the second time in a month, practically a record for them. Dermot had woken up at seven in order to make it to work and had come on to her by pressing his erection against her back. Marlene had found him the job with another of her ex-lovers. Since the job, and the engagement, Dermot's drinking seemed to be in some sort of holding pattern. Anna told Dermot she was going to be late for work herself. She needed to leave by seven fifteen, which would leave her, like, nine minutes, post-coitally, to get ready. They were both laughing and physically connected when the doorbell went. Anna disengaged and wrapped herself in Dermot's massive Jedi dressing gown. She opened the door to find her mother, particularly strangely dressed today in some sort of visor.

'Are you tired, Pickle? You look tired.'

'I'm fine,' Anna tried to keep the frustration out of her voice, 'but I'm sorry. I've got to go to work.'

'I don't know why you're still working.' Marlene shook her head. 'It can't be good for the baby. All that stress!'

'I haven't really got much stress. Not important enough,' Anna objected.

'You work all the time, don't you?' Marlene persisted.

'Just Monday to Friday!' Marlene looked genuinely startled. 'So, now's not a great time to visit.'

'I'm not a visitor!' exclaimed Marlene. She held up a paint tin in one hand. In the other she held up a wrench, 'I'm a handyman! And this is my crew!' Behind Marlene was an old man and a young boy – he looked about fourteen. 'I don't want you worrying about any of this!' Marlene turned to the old man and shouted: 'Just put those over in the corner!' She turned back to Anna. 'You said you didn't like your flat!'

'Did I?'

'Do you like the colour?' Marlene grabbed a screwdriver and deftly levered off the top of the paint tin. It was a remorseless orange. 'The future's bright!' Marlene was pleased with herself. 'I thought . . . since you liked the bag . . .'

'Gosh! It'll be like living inside it!' Anna stuttered.

'Exactly!' said Marlene. The fourteen-year-old took her painting off the wall: the one Sammy had given Anna.

'I don't think the landlord will be keen on us decorating,' Anna warned.

'Where did you get this?' Marlene was peering at the roots painting.

'A client at work painted it,' said Anna.

'What client? An asylum seeker?' Marlene queried.

'Refugee,' Anna corrected her.

'I've contacted the landlord,' Marlene asserted, 'and he told me, and I quote, to "fill me boots"!'

'How did you contact the landlord?' Anna asked.

'All that info is held on the land registry,' Marlene explained, as if it were the most normal thing in the world. 'So the artist is a foreigner?' Marlene had put on her specs to look at the signature. 'Is that Arabic?'

'She's new to the country,' said Anna.

'I bet this'd sell,' Marlene declared, 'it's *very* good. Plus, dealers love all that, a tragic story.'

'I don't want to sell it,' replied Anna, smiling. 'I love it. We can't afford to re-decorate.'

'I'm paying! Do you not want it re-decorated?' Marlene spoke as if she were about to back off, as Anna hesitated. 'Just say the word. If you don't want it done, I'll just send these men home.'

'It's not that,' Anna stammered. 'It's not just up to me . . .'

'Since when do men care about decor? I'll need a key!' asserted Marlene confidently.

'What?'

Marlene spoke slowly as if explaining to a small child. 'I need a key for the builders so I can let them get on with it. I'll replace the hob. And possibly, put in a dishwasher. You can't have a baby without a dishwasher!'

'A dishwasher? Really?' Anna looked around at the flat. Despite her best efforts Dermot's balcony-nest had reappeared, and she was acutely aware the balcony door was the only thing between them and the world's wettest ashtray.

'You aren't still fighting me, are you?'

Marlene looked up and down the road. Bloody London. There was never anywhere to park. She had the address on a piece of paper – and she was just putting on her glasses when she saw it on the wall.

It was unmistakably one of hers, a carved box she'd sent on to Hebe at this address, along with some of her other bits and pieces, a couple of months ago. The girl had left it outside the house: no respect for nice things. It had a sign on it 'Free – please take'. So this was how she treated her gifts! Marlene pulled up and left the car in front of the house, rescuing the box. If they wanted to give her a ticket, they were welcome to.

Marlene pressed the doorbell and counted to ten but there was no answer, so she went around the side of the house, where there was an entrance to the garden. She pounded on the bedroom window, at least it looked like a bedroom curtain, lined, but no one stirred. There was a trowel lying on the paving stones, which clearly hadn't been touched as the garden was completely unloved. So Marlene picked up the trowel, pushed it into the doorjamb, and sprung open the back door. Inside the flat she saw lots of the things she had sent to Hebe, many of them ruined. A particularly beautiful Chinese lacquer table was riddled with rings.

In the kitchen, which came off the front room, Marlene found a series of plates of Hebe's, just mixed in with all the rest of the tat. She was going through the cutlery drawer, (she'd found a silver butter curler) when Hebe's dumpy little Scottish friend came through the front door.

'What do you think you're doing?' she asked, in that accent.

'I could ask you the same thing!' Marlene replied.

The girl was fantastically obtuse, but Marlene managed to gather that some sort of alarm had been triggered and that Hebe hadn't lived there for some time. 'You just thought you'd steal my things, did you?' Marlene challenged her. Of course, she had no answer for that. But she still made the most appalling fuss about Marlene taking home Hebe's items, and in the end Marlene was obliged to take her down a peg or two. She'd hardly said a word, had merely offered a few thoughts about her own upbringing and the likely cause of her dishonesty, but the girl started crying like a baby. Girls were so wet these days.

Still, Marlene got a phone number for Hebe out of it, as well as some of her bits and pieces back. She almost felt bad for misjudging Hebe, for putting things out on the wall. Hebe had taste, after all, even if she was hostage to this cult of victimhood they all seemed to go for these days. Still, while it was Marlene's duty to remind Hebe about her so-called prescription, it was very much up to Hebe to pick it up.

When Anna got home that evening there was no electricity. Whatever the plumbers had done trying to put the dishwasher in had uncovered a world of unsafe jerry-rigged wiring. The majority of the tiny flat now apparently needed to be 'chased out' and re-plastered. 'I'll chase *him* out,' Dermot had said, but he'd packed a bag and they'd trooped off to Layla's for the night.

'It's no problem,' Marlene had said, 'you can stay with me!'

But Anna had explained she needed to be at work in the morning and Layla's place was twenty minutes away on the tube. Plus she had an actual spare room with a sofa bed.

'It's not a spare room. It's a cocking office!' Layla protested.

When they got to Layla's Anna offered to cook, to thank her for letting them stay, so Layla joined her in the kitchen while Dermot stretched out on the sofa in the front room, humming, his long legs dangling off the end of it. Anna had not only worked in kitchens but put some effort into learning to cook, partly because good food was so deeply associated with her mum, but also because she took a contrarian delight in messing with meat-eaters' expectations of crap vegetarian food.

Anna had seen less of Layla recently – they'd both stopped going to the pub, and Dermot's drinking and nesting habits had made the flat untenable as a venue for fun. They had quickly returned to their old easiness at work after what they now called 'Training Day'. 'Sorry I chucked you out of the car,' Layla had mumbled. 'You were right anyway,' Anna had mumbled back, and they'd been back to complaining about co-workers and the plotting of TV shows. 'A short fuse' – that was what her father had always said about her mum, and that was how Anna thought about Layla.

Layla poured herself a glass of wine, which made Anna blink a bit, and over the chopping of onions they talked about the errant wiring; over the squashing of garlic, about Darius's distracting forearms; over the grating of ginger (and in lowered voices), about Cathy's unexpected hatred of Dermot's music; over the simmering of tomatoes, about

Layla's mother's opinion of Layla's haircut. Layla poured herself a second and then a third glass of wine.

'When's your scan?' Anna asked Layla, glancing at the half-full bottle, 'I mean, the twenty-week one.' But Layla just quit the kitchen to 'find Dermot', taking the bottle with her.

They all ate Anna's aubergine curry around the kitchen table. Once Dermot joined them the conversation turned to his new boss, another of Marlene's ex-lovers, for whom Dermot was writing websites: a job he was profoundly unqualified for. The boss, Hamish, sold DNA tests online, and business was booming. The company was called Gee-Gnome! Its icon was a gnome with a fishing rod, fishing in the gene pool, presumably, and it claimed to be able to sequence your entire DNA and predict, among other things, your vulnerability to depression, susceptibility to addiction, even personality 'traits' like 'loneliness'. It also claimed to be able to predict if you had the potential to become 'a psychopath'.

'It's basically a massive fucking scam,' Dermot said.

'For fuck's sake!' Layla banged her glass on the table. 'This shit makes me so fucking angry!'

'What's wrong with DNA tests?' Anna asked.

'Are you pissing around?' Layla asked. 'You are twelve percent African. Please go directly to jail. Do not pass go. Do not collect two hundred pounds. They aren't just wildly unscientific, they could be used for all sorts of terrifying shit. You might as well read some racist horoscopes. You haven't done them, have you?'

'Years ago, when they promised to find your parents,' Anna said.

'Well, you're fucking white, aren't you?' Layla said.

'Jesus, Layla!' Anna protested.

'Well, if you weren't white, you wouldn't be so happy to be on some database,' Layla declared, gulping back her wine.

'Nice!' said Anna. 'It's the white guys who find out they are twelve percent African and start rapping you want to be worried about.' Layla almost smiled. 'Yes. In part I was trying to find out how Jewish I am.'

'Really?' Dermot was gobsmacked. 'Why did you think you might be Jewish?'

'I . . . hoped,' said Anna. 'I suppose, I hoped I might be.'

'What did you find out?' Layla poured another glass of Pinot.

'I thought it was all bullshit?' Anna raised her eyebrows.

'It is,' Layla insisted.

'I just . . . I've never known what my status is. Adoption can be tricky. I thought if I found out I was from Jewish heritage *and* my adoptive mum was Jewish it might be enough to find a rabbi and convert.'

'Can't you convert anyway?' Dermot asked. 'What are we going to bring up the kid as? Fuck knows I'm not bringing it up Catholic!'

Anna felt lost. These were questions which had been nibbling at the edges of her consciousness and she felt breathless to have them asked directly.

'What are *you* going to do?' she asked Layla. 'Religion-wise? About your baby?'

Layla swiped up the bottle again. 'I'm going to have another drink.' Anna didn't know why exactly she reached out to hold the bottle away from Layla. 'Fuck off!' said

Layla. 'I'm not having a fucking baby any more. So, fuck off.'

That was the Tuesday night. The next night Dermot and Neil had a gig which traditionally went on into the small hours. So Anna stayed at Marlene's.

'Don't worry!' said Marlene. 'Women friends will always let you down. Women just don't support each other. Not me, of course. I'm your mother.'

'She's just sad about the miscarriage,' Anna said. 'I wouldn't want me around either.' She gestured to her belly.

'Are you going to wear that to work?' Marlene asked.

Anna looked down at her jeans and jumper, both carefully chosen to hide her shape. Now, it was more important than ever that nobody at work worked out she was pregnant, and she was beginning to look different. She'd googled the rules on maternity pay several times. She needed to be in 'continuous employment', an employee rather than a worker, so Yanni's insanely capricious management style could jeopardise it. For the first time it occurred to Anna that that was what it was designed to do. She hadn't had a full year's employment at any point in the last decade. The clothes were starting to smell unsavoury.

'You could try on some of Hebe's? You have to dress for the job you want, you know!'

Ten minutes later Anna was regarding her bloated profile in her mother's full-length mirror.

'It looks like the job I want is "beached whale".'

'What are you talking about? You can hardly see the bump. This looks very glamorous! I wish I had the figure to wear body-con! Everybody will be green with envy,' Marlene trilled.

'I just think it might be too glam for work?' Anna offered.

'Oh God, you must always ignore any and all dress codes. They are there to make ugly women feel comfortable. You are beautiful so you can wear what you like! Ooh! How about this cape? To go with?'

'A . . . cape? You mean, like a superhero?'

Marlene's voice was suddenly steely, 'There's no need to be sarcastic.'

'Sorry! I'm just joking!'

Marlene's voice immediately switched to deeply indulgent, 'Of course you are! We're still getting used to each other, aren't we?'

Anna looked at the outfit, which would have been unflattering on a teenager. 'I'm happy to wear my jumper.'

'Well, if you don't want a tight dress, how about this?'

Marlene held out a dress in green and blue tartan. The fabric was exactly the kind of thing that Anna liked, but she was always too scared to wear a pattern. Patterns were for other people.

'That's nice.' Ten minutes later, having struggled out of the sheath dress, so named for looking like a giant condom, she was in front of the bedroom mirror wondering if it was in fact nice. The dress had a lace collar, like for a Victorian child, and a flat panel at the front that drew attention to her always big and now swollen breasts. She usually chose clothes based on: a) Is it plain? b) Is it V-necked? and c) Does it hide my tits? This had an expensive zip which was hidden in the clothing. Anna struggled to find it, but before she could her mother had jumped into the bedroom.

'Oh, that's perfect!' Anna automatically covered her chest, even though she was clothed.

'Put your arms down!'

'What are you doing?' Anna asked.

'I had no idea you were so prudish! I thought since I'm giving you the clothes, I might get a say in what you wear.' Marlene's hands were suddenly under the dress and on her bra, hauling at the straps, hoiking her breasts higher and flatter. 'We'll have to get you a decent bra.' She looked at Anna in the mirror. 'You know what would finish this off? Those gloves I bought you!'

Anna thought of the fingerless gloves on her chest of drawers.

'They're at home,' she said. Marlene's hands tightened on her bra straps.

'You know you don't have to keep them!' Marlene's voice was brimming with hurt. 'I'll have them back if you don't like them.' Her eyes narrowed. 'Have you lost them?'

'I haven't lost the gloves,' Anna reassured her. 'I love them! I've just not got them with me.'

'Well,' said Marlene. 'We'll have to sew them onto a little string round your neck, won't we?' Her eyes misted with tears. 'Don't you look perfect?'

It was over an hour and a half driving in, but Marlene said she was coming to London anyway and gave Anna a lift to work. As she pulled up outside the charity she pointed at her cheek, and Anna kissed it.

At lunchtime Anna came back from a meeting with legal. She checked to see whether Hebe had texted back if it was okay to borrow the dress. It seemed rude considering Anna was already wearing it, but she felt a need for her blessing. *Go for your life!* Hebe had texted. *My tits are too small for it.* And two pea emojis. *Help yourself to anything!* Anna was about to dump her handbag on the desk, but there, in the place she usually put it, was another just the same. So she opened the bottom drawer of the desk, which had a key, and dropped her bag in there instead, and some instinct made her turn the key and put it in her pocket.

She went into the little kitchen at the end of the floor. Leaning against the kitchen cabinets, dressed in an extraordinary designer boiler suit that made her look like a runaway from the *Star Wars* canteen, was her mother. She was talking to Yanni.

'Well, we'll see what happens when the baby comes! Everybody thinks their lives won't change and then they actually have the child!' Anna's heart slowed to a sickening thud. Yanni's eyes met hers, and then immediately dropped to her waist to appraise just how pregnant she was. Well, that was one conversation she didn't need to worry about any more.

'Hello, Pickle!' Marlene beamed at Anna with her incredible teeth. 'I'm here to take you out to lunch! Where shall we go?' She turned to Yanni. 'Is there a good Indian? I *love* Indian food!'

'Oh shit,' thought Anna, 'she thinks he's Indian.'

'London is so wonderfully diverse, isn't it?' Marlene said.

Anna interrupted. 'There's a great Indian restaurant next to the tube. You'll have gone past it on the way here.'

'Or there's a Middle Eastern place at the end of the road,' Yanni added.

'Oh God, no. I can't stand all that oil!'

'Come on!' Anna was desperate to get Marlene out of her workplace, somewhere she couldn't make any glaring errors about people's ethnicity or insult any more cuisines. But Darius came in, wearing a white shirt with rolled up sleeves. There was no way she was going to get her out now.

But Marlene went one better than Anna could have imagined. She managed to get Darius to agree to come to lunch with them, along with pretty much the whole department, and Anna found herself outside the front door looking round wildly for her mother. She caught up with her along the pavement. 'I wish you hadn't told Yanni I was pregnant. He's going to fire me.'

'He can't do that!' Marlene was aghast.

'Yes, he can! I'm a temp. He doesn't have to hire me next week!'

'You told me you've worked here eight years!'

'I have!'

Marlene was immediately reassured. 'Well, you're fine then!' She slapped Anna playfully. 'You had me worried there! You leave it to me!'

Hebe had been around this block before. She knew the GP's surgery was somewhere nearby. She'd seen it one night when she'd been waiting for Ben to get home and she'd tried to walk out a star pattern around his flat. She'd been searching for the surgery for at least ninety minutes and she still hadn't found it. Her phone was fucked. There was nobody else about except a man waiting for a bus. Hebe started whistling. It was weird to just be standing around on the street, but it was OK if you were whistling. She tried to work out if he was all right or a bad man. He had a cardigan on, which seemed like a good sign. Bad men don't wear knits. But on the other hand, he had one of those beards which looked like a drawn-on jawline. Would a bad man have a drawn-on jawline?

Hebe considered giving up but she needed her pills. She'd been stringing them out, taking one every other day to make them last. Her mother had sent her a reminder. It was touching, surely, that she was trying to understand what Hebe was going through. But once she'd re-ordered her meds, she realised she couldn't afford the train to pick them up.

She approached the cardigan and tried to sound casual.

'Any chance you know of a doctor round here?'

That sounded stupid. But the guy seemed to know immediately. 'You're looking for the place round the corner.' He gave her directions succinctly, and then patted his pockets and gave her an apple. Hebe was surprised but she didn't turn it down. He was clearly all right.

The GP was, simply, the best she'd ever been to. They did a thorough check, weighing her, measuring her, giving her meds, cream for a horrible skin infection she couldn't seem to shake and an eye check-up. Her glasses had broken a few weeks ago and were stuck together with electrical tape. The place was brimming with beards, but apart from that it was perfect. Hebe sipped free soup as she waited for the optician. They gave her a new prescription (her eyes had deteriorated further), and an address for where to pick up her new glasses.

A few days later Hebe was on her way to collect the specs when she ran straight into a man with a knife in his skull. 'Oh,' she thought, 'of course, it's Halloween.' The man wasn't angry with her. He sounded drunk.

'What are you?' he said. 'A sexy witch?'

'These are just my clothes,' Hebe said.

The address was in the back of a church somewhere near Victoria, and as she stood in line the church bells started ringing for Evensong. There was a long queue. She looked at the people in front and behind her to raise her eyebrows about the deafening noise, and she couldn't help noticing a lot of them were dressed up as homeless people: the girl in front of her and the boy behind. Why were they wearing homeless costumes? Hebe worried about the ethics of this. It seemed wrong. After all, it's not like the homeless people could help it. The queue moved forward as the bells rang out, and Hebe found herself at the front of the queue, before a kind of booth set up in the crypt. She fished out the chitty they'd given her at the GP for her glasses and presented it to the middle-aged white guy in the booth, who was gamely wearing a pair of devil's horns with his dreadlocks.

The dreadlocked devil was incredibly friendly and handed over her new specs, which were indistinguishable from her old ones, except they were free. She settled them on her nose with satisfaction when the guy said, 'And do you have somewhere to stay tonight?' Why was he asking that? As it happened, Hebe didn't have anywhere to stay tonight because Ben was having a girlfriend over, but she had planned to ride the night bus until the girlfriend had gone home.

'I'll be OK,' she responded. 'Thanks for asking.'

'It's just we've still got a bed left,' offered the guy, 'if you need it.'

As Hebe's eyes adjusted to their new lenses she saw herself reflected in the open glass door which proclaimed the name of a charity. The reflection showed a filthy and skinny woman with red sores on her face. The realisations cascaded down on her: this was a homeless shelter; the doctor's office she'd been to was a doctor for homeless people; and she herself was homeless.

'I'm fine,' she said. 'I'm just between flats. I don't think I qualify.'

The devil man looked at her with infinite kindness.

'I think you do,' he said. Again, Hebe thought about riding the bus all night.

'That would be very kind,' she said.

The guy squinted at the chitty.

'Oh shit,' he apologised, and he appeared sincere, 'you're over twenty-five. Our charity only works with youth. I can give you some other numbers, if that would help?'

'Yes, please,' Hebe replied.

The door to the shelter closed, and the homeless woman disappeared. She wasn't a witch – she was a ghost.

Anna was working on a particularly tricky bit of data-wrangling when Yanni dropped by the office she shared with three others. They were all in Halloween costumes. Anna had a pair of vampire teeth sitting next to her keyboard.

Historically, on the intake forms, sexual violence had been recorded separately from rape. Therefore clients who were being treated for some of the most violent rapes were, for database purposes, recorded as 'experienced no sexual violence' which was clearly insane. Some clinicians, filling in the form, had informally used the 'sexual violence' tick-box to differentiate between vaginal rape and other forms of sexual violence, like rape with an object (a bayonet perhaps), and some had filled both fields automatically. It was a mess, and Anna was trying to create new fields on the database which wouldn't mess up the historical data. The work was made more complicated by the fact that she had read many of the case files which the data represented and she was acutely aware that the violence recorded at intake bore no relation to what had actually happened, which often came out during therapy. There were names on the database of people whose harrowing accounts she had heard first-hand, whose rape babies she had met, whose data reflected a more pristine life experience. There had to be some way to record the data without making them live through it all again.

The room was quite dark. Anna looked out of the window, directly at the light. Then she closed her eyes. On her eyelids she could see the wiggly lines of her blood vessels. She remembered the keloid scars which crisscrossed Sammy's back, forming a root system as vivid as the one she had painted.

'Got a minute?' Yanni was clutching some papers, and

dressed in black tie; the traditional Halloween costume cheat. 'Ah!' he said, gesturing at Anna's plait. 'Rapunzel!'

Anna put in the fake teeth she kept in her desk drawer. 'I'm a vampire,' she said. 'Shall I come to your office?'

'No!' Yanni said quickly. 'No need! I just wanted to drop off your contract!' he announced.

'My contract?' Anna said.

'Yes, as discussed!' said Yanni. 'It's much better if you're on a contract. Much better reflects the fact you've worked for us for eight years! Doing skilled work, I might add.' Anna's office buddies: Mo, the data entry guy (head-cleaver), Constanta, the Argentinian event organiser (virgin sacrifice) and Heather, the marketing person (random *Star Trek*) looked up from their computers. Yanni had never knowingly praised anyone.

'So, I've already signed it. You just need to sign it and hand it back to me. And, of course, you'll be able to claim statutory maternity pay. We can claim it back off the government, in case that helps.'

'Th-thank you.'

'Just check the contract. I've made it out in the name we've got on the database. Just let me know if you'd prefer to use another name.'

'Another name?'

'I think someone mentioned your real name is Elizabeth?' Yanni's voice was a good four notes higher than usual. 'So do let me know if you'd like the contract in that name.'

'The date on this is three months ago.'

'Yes,' Yanni smiled, showing all his teeth. 'You can start your maternity leave whenever you like. If you are pregnant! Which I haven't asked!' And he scuttled out.

'What the hell did you say to him?' Anna asked Marlene as she scooped herself into the passenger seat and pulled the belt across her swollen stomach. She was enormous. How could she possibly have thought she was hiding it successfully?'

'Nothing!' said Marlene. 'I simply told him I knew what he was doing.'

'How do you mean?' asked Anna. 'Like,' she lowered her voice to a threatening whisper, '"I know what you are doing . . ." or,' she affected a cheery, upbeat tone, '"I know what you're doing!"?'

'You are a silly sausage,' said Marlene. Her tone darkened, 'But men like that are always doing something.' She pulled out into the road with total confidence. 'You're welcome. I'm taking you to Neil's, is that right?' Marlene managed to imbue this with heavy sexual significance.

Anna looked at her.

Marlene added, with crazy cheeriness, 'I'm taking you to Neil's, right? You see? I can do it too! Are you beginning to find out . . .' She now adopted her own dramatic tone, '*who you are*? Are you, for example, somebody who accepts the promotion?'

'I think so,' said Anna, 'I mean, what else would I do with my life?'

Marlene actually threw her head back and laughed. 'Anna-Beth! You're my daughter! You can do *whatever* the hell you like.'

Anna was hiding out in Layla's office the next day, avoiding Yanni, when her friend came in.

'I'll go,' said Anna.

'It's OK,' Layla sat at her desk. 'Eat your sandwich here if you want.' Anna got out her brown paper bag. 'Why are you hiding from Yanni, other than that he's Yanni?'

'He's being nice to me,' said Anna.

'Fuck a brick!' said Layla. They were both silent as Layla opened her box of salad. 'I'm not going to apologise,' Layla said.

'I don't expect you to!' said Anna. 'I can't imagine how hard it's been. You can talk to me, or not. I'd understand why not.'

'I just can't think about it any more,' Layla said. 'How's it going with your mum?'

Anna felt heavy; she searched for the word to describe how she was feeling. Lately she'd found a number of these holes in her memory. She could look at the place where the word should be, but there was nothing there . . .

Wait: guilty. She felt guilty for wanting to speak ill of her.

'It's a bit overwhelming,' she said. 'I'm sure she means well. She's just quite a big personal—'

But Layla was screaming and screaming and screaming: a high-pitched scream that went on and on, not pausing for breath. She pushed back from her desk, standing with her back against the wall, her shoulders hunched, in an attitude from a horror movie.

Anna's sandwich fell out of her hand.

'What is it?'

Anna speaking broke the spell. Layla stopped screaming. She made a small sound, an 'uh', like she'd been punched in the solar plexus, and nodded towards the desk drawer, which was open a crack.

Mo and Constanta appeared at the office door with faces registering blind panic.

Screaming was not unknown in the building. Every now and then one of the therapy rooms erupted into an insistent keening as a torture survivor could no longer hold up the walls of normality. But there were few clinical staff on this floor. And the sound Layla had made was otherworldly.

Anna's gaze moved from her colleagues' terrified faces to the top of Layla's desk. The drawer was only open a few inches. And from where Anna was standing she couldn't see much. She edged around the desk to get a better view. As the contents of the desk drawer came into focus her stomach turned – she shifted her eyes on to the blue carpet but it tilted alarmingly, one way, the other and, inevitably, as it always did, hit her in the face.

Anna woke up to Layla's wry expression. Layla looked just as she usually did, but a little greyer. 'Way to make it all about you.'

'I'm so sorry,' Anna said.

The drawer had been taken out of the desk and was sitting on the floor of the office in the far corner. Someone had scattered A4 paper over the contents.

'Is it a . . .'

'No,' Layla's mouth was drawn, 'it's a tumour. It's a cancer.'

'From a human?'

'We have no idea,' said Layla. 'I doubt it.'

Constanta crossed to Layla's desk and picked up the landline, pressing nine for an outside line.

'What are you doing?' Layla asked.

'I'm calling the police,' Constanta replied.

Layla and Mo exchanged looks. 'Are we sure that's the best move?' Layla asked.

Anna was catching up. 'You think it's a client? Are you treating anyone who's really disturbed at the moment?'

'When aren't I?' Layla answered. 'If we report it, it might affect their legal position.'

Constanta was outraged, 'It should!'

'Calm down!' said Layla. 'There's no harm done.' She walked over to the drawer, and using a pencil, pulled the paper away from the mess of flesh beneath. 'This might be pig.'

'That's Islamophobic . . . probably. They can't get away with this!' Constanta protested.

The faces of Mo and Layla closed, drawing the wagons around the survivors. 'We're not calling the police!' Layla said. Mo shrugged and opened his arms in an expansive gesture, taking in the lost of the world, the tortured, the persecuted, the beaten. 'We're their family.'

Constanta protested, 'Anna fainted! She could have hurt herself! You want to call the police, right?' And they all looked at Anna.

9

TWENTY WEEKS GONE

'The twenty-week screening scan looks in detail at the baby's bones, heart, brain, spinal cord, face, kidneys and abdomen.'

Anna went back to Neil's that night, to sleep on the sofa with Dermot. It was one that folded out, three pieces of thin foam, and it was stunningly uncomfortable. Dermot was still awake. Every time he so much as scratched his arse, the whole bed caved in. Whenever Anna closed her eyes, she saw the tumour in the drawer, so she kept her eyes open.

'What do you think of my mum?' she asked.

'No,' Dermot replied, firmly. 'I'm not opening that can of worms.'

'What do you mean?'

'You are allowed to slag your own mam off. Nobody else's. That's the rule!'

'I'm not asking you to slag her off.'

'You see? It's contentious already!'

'Do you think she's OK?'

'What do you mean, "OK"?' Dermot eyed Anna warily.

'She's quite . . . dramatic,' Anna ventured.

'Yeah,' said Dermot, sighing, 'she's a bit two shits.'

'What's that?'

'You know, if you've had one shit, she's had two. If you've painted the Forth Bridge, she's painted the Fifth.'

Anna laughed. 'I know what you mean.'

'But if you ever bring this up again – I never said that.'

'You think that's what it is? You don't think she's . . . a bit crazy?'

Dermot's phone rang. Anna looked at her own. It was past midnight.

'Yes, yes, of course!' said Dermot into his mobile. 'What do the doctors say?' He turned to Anna. 'It's Mam. I need to go home.'

Anna felt weird and scratchy about staying at Neil's without Dermot, and didn't want to stay with Layla, rubbing her big belly in her face, as it were, so when Marlene texted offering a bed for the weekend 'just until my men have finished your flat' Anna accepted straight away.

At about six Marlene 'shooed' Anna into the bedroom she had stayed in last time, the tower room with the huge fireplace, saying she was sick of seeing her in 'those rags'. Anna was confused, considering 'those rags' were Hebe's clothes that Marlene had given her two days ago, but she obliged. Laid out on the bed was a white dress. It was a ridiculous romantic white dress. It would have looked silly on somebody who wasn't pregnant, but on her it looked like something a medieval princess would wear, cut under the breast to skim her pregnant belly.

As Anna came down the stairs, Neil walked up the hall.

'Neil? What are you doing here?'

'Your mum said you needed the bag you left at mine.' He lifted Anna's duffel bag.

'Oh shit,' said Anna. 'I really don't. I'm sorry you had a wasted journey.'

Marlene scurried forward from the door.

'Well, you're here now,' she purred, 'why don't you stay for supper?' Marlene looked at Neil's impassive face. 'Well, don't you look like the cat that's got the cream!'

Marlene's supper was fish.

'I made it for you, Beth!' she said. 'Since you're vegetarian! What do you call vegetarians who don't eat fish?'

'Vegetarians,' said Anna as Neil hid a smile, 'but it really doesn't matter.'

'Who's Beth?' Neil whispered to her as they followed Marlene across the parquet.

'That'd be me,' said Anna. The conversation over supper was perfectly pleasant. Anna and Neil had always got along. He was much more serious than Dermot, but it made it satisfying to make him laugh. Anna found that her mind was always looking for the next joke when she was in his company and she was intensely aware of whether his lips were closed or open over those wonky canines.

During the meal Marlene kept trying to point out how much they had in common, although she knew next to nothing about either of them. If there was the shortest lull in conversation, she'd re-introduce them with thoughtful details. 'I bought a wonderful recording of Montserrat Caballé – but what am I talking about? Of course you're both musical!'

'Oh! Are you musical, Neil?' Anna would say.

'Yes,' Neil would say. 'I'm in a band with your fiancé.'

'You're teasing me!' Marlene hooted. Every time she spoke they were thrown closer together in silent amusement at Marlene's strange behaviour. It occurred to Anna that Marlene was acting like they were on a date, but she dismissed this insane idea. Why would Marlene be setting them up with all the subtlety of a forklift?

When Anna went up to bed it was chilly, so she dove straight under the covers before taking off the ridiculous princess dress and chucking it out of bed. Immediately, she inhaled deeper – the dress had been cutting into her bump. She put her head under the covers, hoping that her breath would warm her up. So she was completely submerged in what Dermot called 'the downy' when she felt the weight of someone sit on the bed. Anna squawked, and whoever it was stood up again rapidly.

'Sorry! I didn't know you were there!' It was Neil, wrapped in a woman's housecoat.

'This is my room – our room.' Anna corrected herself. 'It's the room we stay in.'

Neil shrugged, 'She put me in here.'

'What?'

'Your mum told me this was my room.' Neil gestured at the door. It was shut and someone had hung his bag on the back of it.

'Could you just pass me my clothes?' And Anna gestured, not to the dress but to the crumpled clothes she'd been wearing before. Neil went to pick up Anna's trousers and she felt a fast flash of shame: the only time she'd been trouser-free with Neil Byrne, it had not featured an elasticated waist. Neil chucked her the jeans and then stood waiting before remembering himself.

'I'll just go into the bathroom,' he mumbled, heading for what Marlene had called, as if it were one word, 'then-suite'.

'Thanks,' said Anna. As soon as she'd struggled into decency, she went to the bedroom door, calling out, 'Apologies again!' But the door was locked.

'It's locked!' Anna said.

'What?' Neil was out in a second. Anna rattled the door. It was massive, a heavy Georgian oak with a huge lock. A lock which had a large key in it, usually. But now there was no key.

'She's fucking locked us in!' Anna swore.

'Maybe it's stuck?' Neil's voice was eminently reasonable. He put his shoulder against the door, but it didn't budge. 'Maybe she locked it by mistake?'

'Should we shout?' Anna said.

'I think she's gone to bed,' Neil answered.

'Should we break it down?'

Neil raised an eyebrow. 'You want to break down the door?' he asked. 'You're so worried about being stuck with me you want to smash up your mum's house?' Neil looked at her and his eyes were the colour of life. When Anna looked into them, she felt as if she were already outside – as if she had only to meet his eyes for the door, the walls to vanish and the roof to fly off, and she would be alone with him, in the green. She dropped her gaze.

'Better not let her hear you calling her my mum . . . it's Ma, thank you!' Anna said.

'So sorry!' Neil said. 'Ma!'

Anna could feel the conversation rolling towards her.

'Christ, it's freezing. It's never been this cold before.' Anna looked at the bed. Neil followed her gaze. Anna's eyes dropped and then found the only chair in the room, in front of the fire. 'There's a fire!' Anna looked at it doubtfully. 'Is that wood decorative?'

It took Neil ten minutes to get the fire going. He had a lighter, of course he did, and he ripped up a copy of *The Lady* magazine which sat on a small mahogany table in the corner, and set fire to it, to check the chimney was drawing the air, before using the rest as kindling. On the hearth a huge iron ring was sunk into the stone.

'What's that for?' Anna said, and Neil flipped the ring with his feet.

'Livestock, I guess. They'd be tied up to this before they slaughtered them and put them on the spit. This place is old.'

He found a blanket and Anna covered herself in the easy chair in front of the fire while they were waiting for it to get going.

'Are you warm enough now?' he said.

'I'm fine,' said Anna.

The deer and badgers and owls gambolled across the walls again and again in endless repetition just like the woodland outside. They both looked at the fire.

'So, are you going to take his name?' Neil asked.

'Whose name?' said Anna.

'Dermot's.'

'Probably.'

'You used to be Anna Rampion. And now you'll be Beth

Dwyer,' Neil mused. Anna didn't say anything. She leaned forward and gripped the metal ring.

'It's Dermot's baby,' she said suddenly. 'I'm sure.'

Neil turned to look at her and incredulity spread across his face.

'We didn't fuck!' Neil said.

'What?'

'Did you think we had sex?' Neil asked.

'No!' Anna lied, now blushing purple. 'I mean, I didn't know. There was a lot of drink and . . . coats.'

Neil started laughing but stopped when he saw how ashamed Anna was.

'There was some, you know, digital action but we stopped. If you thought that was my dick, you're going to lose it when we actually do it,' Neil's eyes travelled to Anna's breasts.

'We can't ever do it,' said Anna, and she meant it.

Neil looked like he'd absorbed this. 'I can sleep on the chair,' he offered.

'It's all right,' said Anna, 'we can both sleep in the bed.'

Neil took off the padded kimono and put on the thermal leggings and top he wore under his bike leathers. Anna looked resolutely into the flames when he did so, so she didn't see his beautiful arms in the firelight.

In bed, she tucked the duvet around herself. Neil propped his head up on the pillow so he could see the hearth as it died down. Anna felt suddenly relaxed. He wasn't going to try anything. It would be too terrible, to take advantage of a pregnant woman. Neil wasn't the type to let his hands wander in the night. He was an honourable guy. And she wasn't exactly appealing. She felt suddenly sleepy, so she didn't quite know if the voice was real, or from a dream, which said, 'You know you don't have to marry Dermot. You could marry me instead.'

Anna dragged herself awake and lay tense in the fire-glow thinking, 'Did you really say that?'

Neil answered her aloud. 'I said you could marry me.'

'Don't!' Anna said. 'You're joking, right? Say you're joking!'

'No, I think I'd be better for you.'

'You think WHAT?'

'I think I'd be better for you than Dermot. He's an alcoholic. I don't know if you've noticed.'

'I'm about to have Dermot's baby.'

'I don't care. I could love the baby. We could be a family.'

Anna sat up, pulling the covers around her. 'I've got a family.'

'No, you don't. You've got a fiancé. And you're pregnant. You're not married. You could still choose me.'

'Where the hell is this coming from?' Anna's voice was fierce with rage.

'What? You're not angry if I ask you to fuck, but you're livid if I say I love you? I've always liked you. You know that.'

'I don't know that!'

'Don't you? Why d'you think I've not had a girlfriend?'

'Because you're a . . . you know.'

'A what?' Neil asked.

'A player.'

'A player? I'm not. I never have been, I'm just pretty.' Neil gestured ruefully to his beautiful curls. 'I haven't had a girlfriend because of you.' Anna got out of bed. She couldn't say anything. Any response would be wrong. She imagined relaying any of this conversation to Dermot and hit a wall.

'I love you,' he said.

'I shouldn't even be listening to this,' Anna was now sitting up straight.

'Why? Why can't you marry me?'

'Dermot is the father.'

'So what? He can still be the kid's daddy.'

'The baby won't . . . be yours. The baby won't look like you.'

'Why? Because he's white? My mum's white!'

'Not 'cause he's white – or she, for that matter. Oh my God! It's hard for a kid if they don't know where they come from!'

'Fuck off, Anna!' Neil said. 'You think I don't know that? Your family isn't just blood. It's who you'll fight for. You want to be with Dermot, that's OK. But it's your choice. You can choose him. Or you can choose me. Or you can fuck off and live in the Maldives till they're under water. But I'm not going to let you pretend it isn't a choice.'

Anna looked at the door. 'Did you lock that door?' she asked.

'What?'

'Did you lock that door, so I'd have to stay and listen to this shit?'

Neil just snorted.

'What am I supposed to do now?' Anna said. 'You've put me in a completely impossible position. Do I tell Dermot, or do I keep quiet and . . . and . . .'

'What? I didn't think you'd have a problem keeping quiet. You keep quiet about everything else.' Neil went to the chair and picked up the blanket. 'I didn't lock the door. Tell him or not. It's up to you. I'll sleep in the bath.'

But after he had gone into the bathroom, some part of Anna's internal mechanism split off and floated free. She started to cry properly, really cry, as she hadn't since that first night at school when she was eight years old. She couldn't keep it quiet. She wrapped her arms around her face, her elbows jutting out to protect her as her chest heaved and she sobbed. She heard Neil pad in softly and felt his hand cup her elbow respectfully.

'Why did she leave me? Why?'

'Who?' Neil's voice was gentle, kind.

'My mum!'

'Which one?'

'Both of them!'

'There, there,' said Neil.

'What's wrong with me?' Anna wailed.

'Nothing,' Neil said, 'not a damn thing. You're no worse than anyone else. You don't have to turn yourself inside out to deserve a family.'

The phone lit up. 'What's that?' said Neil.

It was a text message from Dermot saying *Goodnight Dickhead*.

'It's from Dermot. It's private.'

'Not that,' said Neil, 'your wallpaper, on the phone.'

On Anna's phone was the painting Sammy had given her. Anna had photographed it and set it as the background.

'It's a painting from this girl. I . . . She found her family. And she gave me this painting. It's beautiful, isn't it?' Anna called up the original photo to show Neil. 'It's a blossom growing from these massive roots.' She handed over the phone. 'Isn't it amazing?'

Neil turned the phone around.

'Yes,' he said. 'But it's a tree.'

Anna looked at the picture from Neil's side. Viewed upside down the meaning of the painting was utterly transformed. Now a towering tree grew from a pool of blood. The trunk was still framed against the blue sky, but the earth and the clouds were inverted. 'Look!' it seemed to say. 'From my pain I grow!' Viewed from one side the painting said: 'All beautiful things only grow from deep roots.' From the other it said: 'I, impossibly, stand upon this ground. From my pain I reach the sky.'

Anna felt her neck get hot. 'That's not the way you're meant to look at it,' she said, 'she's signed it at the bottom.'

'She's signed it at the top,' said Neil, 'that's Arabic. This is the way up it's meant to be.'

And that night Anna dreamt the roof came off and the room's wallpaper came alive, and in the middle of the forest was Sammy's tree, and she was one of the creatures of the wood, and she ran along the riverbed with the sheepdog that was Neil Byrne, but all the time an owl flew overhead, beating its wings, chasing them.

The door opened easily in the morning. The key was in the lock outside. Anna stayed in the room after Neil had gone downstairs. She examined the door again, opening and closing it to see if it stuck. She took a moment to practise a few openers, 'Hi Ma! Did you imprison me last night?' No good. 'Morning, Ma! So, was it you or someone else who locked me in with him?' Not ideal. 'Good morning. Is there something wrong with the door?' That was better. But the moment she entered the kitchen Marlene blind-sided her, 'You don't have to call me Ma if you think it's funny.'

'What?' Anna said.

Marlene scrubbed a plate. She had the sort of expensive rubber washing-up bowl that does a significantly worse job than the plastic ones.

'You don't have to call me Ma if it's such a funny word.' Marlene's mouth was twisted in a rage. Even her back looked angry.

'I don't think it's funny.'

Marlene was silent. She turned around, wiping her hands dry on the dishcloth, and immediately moisturised her hands, rubbing in the white goo.

'I heard you, Beth. Last night.'

'How?'

'Oh, for God's sake! You were making enough noise to wake up the whole house!'

'We got locked in. I'm sorry if we disturbed you.'

Marlene's hands twisted rhythmically, slapping the cream around. 'Crying and crying!'

'I . . . sorry . . .' said Anna.

'Do you see me crying?'

'What?'

'Your father treated me like a piñata every night of my life and do you see me crying?'

'I . . .' Anna was hot. She was boiling. She must say the right thing. 'I'm so sorry that happened to you.'

'Your generation! Always complaining! It never occurs

to you that perhaps bad things happen because you aren't a very good person!'

'I . . .' Anna didn't know what to address first, 'I know women can blame themselv—'

'Not *me*,' Marlene snorted. 'There's nothing wrong with *me*! I'm talking about *you*, Beth!' Marlene slapped the dish-cloth against the edge of the Butler sink. 'You're the one who's making a fuss!'

Anna backed out of the kitchen and went back upstairs. The lock on her bedroom door now had a key on the inside of the lock. She scanned the room. The only thing that looked out of place was a pile of unopened baby stuff. One of the boxes in the pile was for a baby monitor. A cord led to the wall plug, where the monitor's plug blinked. As if in a dream, Anna went into Marlene's room opposite and, inevitably, next to her mother's bed, with some paracetamol and a heavy-bottomed green drinking glass, was the other end of the monitor. Marlene had been listening in.

Anna felt a strange sensation, as if a belt had been tied around her swollen stomach and suddenly yanked, and she knew, with a cold certainty, that there would be blood.

She heard crunching on the gravel. It was Neil, carrying his motorcycle helmet, loping along the front drive towards his bike. Anna tried to open the window, but it had a strange brass lock on the sash, a complicated pulley mechanism, and it wouldn't budge. Why did nothing in this ancient house actually work? She banged on the window, hoping beyond hope that the skinny man half-dancing towards his motorbike would hear her. He must. But he didn't.

'Neil! Neil!' Anna palmed the window as he crunched further up the drive.

She turned and ran down the main flight of stairs. As she reached the bottom, she glimpsed Marlene, still holding her dishcloth, at the far end of the hall leading into the kitchen. Anna ignored her and bolted towards the front door.

She stopped on the porch, a gabled entrance outside the front door, and shouted as loud as she could.

'Neil!'

Neil stopped. And turned, putting his helmet under one arm and shielding his eyes as he looked at her.

'Are you going back to London?' He was nodding. Was he? 'Can you give me a lift?'

Neil answered by pointing to the spare helmet. He began to walk back towards her. The squeezing around her womb slackened a little. With every step he took towards her the belt loosened.

'I think there might be something wrong with the baby.'

Neil rocked on to his toes. 'Shouldn't we go to the nearest hospital?'

Anna shook her head. 'I need to go to London.'

She held on to Neil all the way back up the A25 to London, the baby sandwiched between their bodies. By the time she got to the hospital her mother had called twenty-seven times.

'Mum not with you today?' the sonographer asked.

'No,' Anna replied.

'Well, you've got Dad instead.'

'The father is in Ireland. This is my friend Neil,' Anna said.

'And are we happy discussing things in front of Neil?'

Anna nodded. Her phone lit up and buzzed on the table next to the bed: Marlene.

'Sorry about that,' she said. She flipped the mobile on to the bed she was lying on to muffle the vibrations, but she could still feel them, travelling across the mattress and shaking the taut flesh of her belly.

'So, you've had some bleeding?' *Buzz, buzz, buzz.*

'Not much but it feels really weird,' Anna replied. *Buzz, buzz . . .*

'Don't worry. Bleeding can be for any number of reasons. It doesn't necessarily mean there's anything wrong with baby.' The little wand was scanning her stomach. Her phone finally stopped buzzing. So there was complete silence when the technician said, 'And is there any history of kidney problems in the family?'

'What? Why?' Anna asked.

'Do you or the dad have any kidney disease?'

'I just have one. I was born that way. I just have one kidney.'

'And your husband?'

'Fiancé. No, I mean, he drinks a lot, so I can't imagine they are in great shape. Is there something wrong with the baby's kidneys?'

'The kidneys do look large. Have you been drinking water?'

'Yes,' Anna confirmed.

'It's just that the placental fluid is scarce.'

The phone began to vibrate again. Anna's face must have registered blind fear.

'Please don't panic. The kidneys could be large for any number of—'

'But what could it be?' Anna interrupted.

'It could be a problem with the valves coming out of

your baby's bladder. Or it might be just a normal development and the baby will grow out of it. There's a slim chance it could be something called ARPKD. I'll need to book you in for a scan next week. There's a genetic test but we don't tend to do it. I don't want you to worry. Even if the baby does have kidney problems there are treatments.'

Anna felt the string that had been connecting her to the earth had been cut.

'A gene? You think I've got a genetic disorder?'

'What sort of treatments?' Neil asked.

'Let's wait to see what it is first – or if it's anything.'

Anna's mobile lit up again. *Buzz, buzz, buzz.* She glanced at the phone. It was an unknown number. She turned to the technician. 'I'm so sorry. I've got to take this.'

'Is this the daughter of Marlene Mather?' The voice was male, warm, Australian.

'One of them,' Anna answered.

'Are you sitting down?'

'Yes, why? I'm sitting down.'

'I'm with your mother. It looks like she's had a bit of an accident. Can you tell me if her mouth normally pulls down to the left?'

Stroke. He thinks she's had a stroke. 'Um – no, not really,' Anna said.

'OK. I'm a triage nurse and luckily I was at the scene when she drove into the wall.'

'She drove into a wall?'

'I've called an ambulance and they should be here any minute. I'm just a bit concerned that she might have had a stroke and that's why she blanked out. She says she doesn't remember the last fifteen minutes.'

'What's the last thing you remember, Marlene?' The Australian's voice was incredibly reasonable.

Anna could hear Marlene's voice, slurred, like she was drunk.

'I was looking for Beth! Is that Beth? Tell her I love her! I wanted to find where she was!'

The technician interjected. 'I think it might be a good idea to resume that call later. Your blood pressure is *way* up. It's not good for baby.'

On the other end of the phone a weird keening started up. From far away Anna heard Marlene scream, 'I can't lose the baby!'

'Tell her it's OK!' Anna almost shouted down the phone at the nurse. 'Tell her she's not losing the baby! I mean, I'm not losing the baby!'

'Let me talk to her!' Marlene was desperate, terrified.

The Australian voice was speaking away from the phone, 'She wants to talk to you.'

'Not her!' Marlene was sobbing as her voice came into clarity. 'The baby!'

'What?' Anna couldn't keep up.

'Let me talk to the baby! Hold the phone to your stomach!' Marlene ordered her.

Anna, feeling like a fool, did so. She had never spoken to the baby, not in her most private moments.

'Sorry,' Anna mouthed at the technician, who shrugged angrily.

'What's she doing?' Neil whispered. 'Is she singing?'

Marlene was indeed singing, crooning at the baby, and the tune was familiar. Neil leant forward to make out the song . . .

'Shut up!' he yelled. 'Shut the fuck up!'

Anna looked at Neil in confusion. 'It's "Fly High"!' he said. 'She's fucking singing "Fly High" to the baby! She's cursing it!' Anna lifted the mobile to her ear to confirm that yes, Marlene was warbling at the child in her womb the words written for dead Tara to send her on her way to the afterlife.

'How does she even know that song?' Anna asked.

Neil's usually unperturbed beauty was marred by defensiveness. 'Don't ask me! What are you asking me for?'

The tech was visibly annoyed. 'Could you calm down, please?' she snapped at Neil. 'You'll upset your baby!'

'It's NOT MY BABY!' Neil snarled and stalked out.

From her mobile still came the mad sounds of Marlene singing. Anna held the phone at a distance, as if it might bite her, and then, overwhelmed, hung up.

She was only off the phone for sixty seconds, but by the time she called Marlene back, the nurse answered, 'She doesn't want to speak to you. I think she might be having another stroke.'

'Which hospital is she going to?' Anna asked. 'Just tell me where they're taking her!'

On the train Anna googled polycystic kidneys. There were so many 'ifs' and none of them good. 'If both parents carry a faulty version of this gene, there's a one in four chance of each child they have developing ARPKD.' The treatment, if the baby had it, was a transplant. If Anna was a match, she could give the baby a kidney – except she couldn't, obviously. If Dermot was a match, he could. Anna suspected that Dermot's kidneys would be in no state to donate. If neither of them could donate, they would look first at immediate relations, like Anna's mother. Anna's mother might be the only chance for her baby's survival: Anna's mother, who she had just put in the hospital.

Anna walked down St Thomas' hospital corridor. Marlene had found herself a private room. Anna expected to find her sitting up in bed, ordering around the nursing staff and taking selfies. But the room was silent. As she came in a nurse in her forties was silently putting away a blood pressure cuff. The nurse raised a finger to her lips.

Marlene was asleep, propped up on the bed. Her face, with no make-up, was so pale it looked like old paper; in fact, she looked a lot like Hebe. Her eyelids were translucent. Anna could see the blood vessels branching under the skin and the glasses which she usually used to punctuate her flamboyant gestures were hanging on a chain around her neck.

The nurse gestured for Anna to speak outside the room.

'Are you Beth?' she said.

'I'm . . .' It was all too much to explain. 'Yes, I'm Beth. What's wrong with her? Has she had a stroke?'

'Maybe,' said the nurse. 'The MRI looked good but sometimes the holes don't show up. She was very confused. Sometimes old people get like this.' Her accent was heavy Filipino and her English was pristine.

'She's only . . .' Anna realised she did not know Marlene's age, but she couldn't be more than, what? 'Fifty-two?'

'You should talk to the doctors. Maybe it's a temporary confusion, it's not always dementia.'

'Dementia?'

'She was very confused. And distressed. She was very lucky.'

'How's that?' Anna asked.

'The guy who found her was a triage nurse. As she said: she's got the devil's luck!'

When the nurse left Anna pulled a chair up to Marlene's bed and sat and read a newspaper she'd bought on the train. After an hour or so Marlene's foot began to twitch under the hospital blanket so Anna stroked it. It seemed to calm her down, so she just held on to it for another forty-five minutes while Marlene slept, the arm of her spectacles pushing into her cheek.

She snorted awake, and immediately started crying.

'It's all right!' Anna found herself murmuring. 'There's nothing to worry about, it's all right.'

'Are you OK?' Marlene questioned Anna querulously. 'Is the baby OK?'

'Shh! Everything's fine!'

Marlene had the searching, fearful look of a child who's woken after a nightmare.

'I hurt myself!'

'I'm sorry!' Anna blurted out. 'It's all my fault you're here.'

Marlene's tawny eyes were filled with tears. She didn't seem more than seven years old.

'Why did you run away?' Marlene asked.

'I just went to the hospital,' said Anna. 'I had some bleeding. But everything's OK now. You sleep.'

As Marlene fell back to sleep, Anna felt profoundly cold, bone cold. Despite the stifling NHS heat of the room, she began to shiver. She pulled the thin blanket further over her mother. How could she ask her now about the baby monitor and if she had locked her in with Neil? Suddenly, Marlene spoke, in a much more normal voice, as if confessing.

'I thought Neil was the father and you didn't tell me because he's black.' Anna gasped. Though she didn't know why she was surprised – Marlene made a habit of gasp-worthy statements. 'I don't blame you! Not everyone's as open-minded as me. My stepson's half-Vietnamese, for God's sake!' Anna attempted to marshal an appropriate response. 'You aren't cross, are you? I'm just curious about my grandchild! Prince Philip was the same about Archie! Or was it Charles?' Anna laughed suddenly.

'Well, you sound better!' she said.

'And what would you say to Dermot if the baby's black? I've been worrying,' Marlene's voice cracked. 'It's only because I care. I didn't lock you in on purpose, it was just habit.'

'The baby's Dermot's,' said Anna, 'so I'm guessing it'll be very white.'

'Unless your own father was black,' Marlene corrected her.

Anna was aware her face must have read: buffering, please wait.

'Don't ask!' said Marlene shakily. 'You said you wouldn't ask about him.'

'Something's happened,' said Anna, slowly. 'The baby might have a genetic problem. It looks like there's a problem with the kidneys, and I haven't got a spare. It would be very helpful to know about . . . any close relatives.'

'Does the baby need a kidney?' Marlene asked. 'I'll give

him a kidney!' she said earnestly. 'It's the least I could do! You don't need your father!' Marlene looked terrified.

'What did he do to you?' Anna asked gently.

'It's not that,' Marlene was plucking at her spectacles on their chain. 'It's what he did to you.'

10

TWENTY-ONE WEEKS GONE

'You may notice a dark vertical line between your pubic bone and your belly button. This is the linea nigra or pregnancy line. It was always there, it just gets darker when you're expecting. Some experts theorise that a more visible "dark line" helps new-borns, who can't yet see very clearly, find their way to the breast to nurse.'

Anna looked at the picture of roots. The decorators had re-hung it as Anna had, roots to blossom, not as Neil had seen it: blood to tree, but now her mind automatically reversed the painting as she looked at it. Hadn't that been in biology at school? Didn't young babies, when they were born, reach for things in the wrong place because their brains had not yet learnt to flip the picture provided by their retinas? Didn't they see the whole world upside down? Anna wondered if until yesterday she had been a baby herself.

The flat, now it was re-painted, was a deeply disquieting place to wait for medical news. The colour of the walls was the colour of amniotic fluid – no, Anna corrected herself, of a Chinese Lantern . . . or a beautiful autumn flower . . . or a pumpkin. She couldn't shake the sensation that she was suspended in something fleshy, something with veins. Normally she would clean, to take her mind off things, but with Dermot absent, the whole place was already spotless.

So Anna went to stay at her dad's, where she could reliably be needed to clear up. The house she'd lived in as a young child in Peckham, and then moved back to after her mum died, was full of unnecessary objects: half a cafetière, a bamboo umbrella stand, a pile of silver spoons, boxes of the *New Scientist* from thirty years ago. Her childhood bedroom had become another storeroom. There was still a bed there, but it could only be reached via a pathway through the junk. The junk made him feel safe. And, if Anna was honest, it made her feel safe too. After the tumultuous events of the last few days, the dusty, undisturbed smell of her dad's house, as if a small animal had died several years ago and had been allowed to desiccate in peace, was deeply comforting.

She happily started scrubbing the sink.

'My goodness, Anna!' said Nicholas, looking at her large belly. 'You look like someone else entirely. It's only a few weeks since you called.'

'Yes,' said Anna, 'but I was already twelve weeks then.'

'I hope they are looking after you,' Nicholas said.

Anna felt like she'd spent days googling medical conditions: her mother's, her own, Cathy's. She had decided to wait for the next scan before telling Dermot. If she wasn't a carrier there was no need to tell him at all, not about the kidneys, not about the trip to the hospital and not about who had been with her. He had enough to contend with. Like every time he went back to Ireland, Dermot's text messages had turned from effusive and charming to tense and cryptic: *Mam worse. Caroline a bastard.*

Dermot was incapable of answering her questions about Cathy's treatment. 'What has she been prescribed?' Anna would ask him. 'How long will chemo last?' She could almost see Dermot shrugging. 'Do I look like a fucking doctor? I'm not a doctor, Anna!' And if he was really irritated: 'Neither are you!' It had always been assumed, by both Anna and her father, that Anna would become a doctor, but in her final year at school her physics teacher had pointed out that Anna fainted at the sight of blood, and she switched to psychology. Dermot had said more than once, 'In my family we just die when the middle classes tell us to.' Anna found Dermot's unwillingness to question the medical profession fantastically frustrating. 'What good does it do?' Dermot would ask. 'It's not going to change anything.' But Anna was sure it could change everything. People lived or died based on whether the doctors believed them, whether they pursued symptoms, whether they were tired or hungry or grumpy or wanting to show off to a good-looking superior. Any change in circumstance might take you down another branch, another line of life that might continue to yet another capillary or lead to a dead end.

'On that,' said Anna, 'it looks like there's a possible genetic kidney problem with the baby.'

'You mean the foetus,' said Nicholas. 'Oh, dear! Well, keep me informed.'

Her father was the first person she had said it out loud to, though she had texted Hebe.

'You know I promised to tell you,' Anna said, 'if I found my biological mother.'

'I'd have thought you'd be a bit busy for all that,' Nicholas gestured at her belly.

'Actually,' she said, 'the possible kidney condition has made it all a bit more pressing.'

When Anna was with her father, she spoke like him: cautious, conditional. She wondered why.

'Was the book helpful?' he asked.

Anna remembered the white book with the silver writing, sitting abandoned after the second chapter in her flat.

'Thank you, yes. I found her, my mother.'

Nicholas sighed heavily. He cleared his throat several times, making an odd reaching movement with his neck. 'Really? And is she as you expected?' he asked.

Marlene's texts, unlike Dermot's, had got longer and longer. They were sometimes cogent and, occasionally, bizarre. Anna was finding them complex to manage. She feared she had not been effusive enough in thanking her for the new dishwasher and over-corrected to the point where, she was pretty sure, Marlene thought she was being sarcastic. *I'm sorry I bothered decorating it then!* Marlene had messaged, and it had taken two days to sort it out. The messages, Marlene's doctors assured her, were no doubt evidence of her continued 'delirium', which they were now attributing to a petit-mal seizure, rather than a mini-stroke. That was why she'd driven into the wall.

'Um . . . She's . . . She's my mother, so . . .'

'Excuse me,' Nicholas said, and patted his pockets, where he took out a pill, going over to the sink and filling a mug with water. 'Beta-blockers!' he said. 'Old age!' He swallowed the pill. 'And have all your questions been answered?'

'Some of them: I've got a sister, and a step-brother. She won't tell me anything about my father.' Nicholas started nodding rapidly, and carried on nodding, as if he were a toy with an elasticated neck. He sat down on one of the many kitchen chairs. Anna reached forward and patted his knee.

'You know that if she does tell me who my father is, he won't replace you. He can't. You'll always be my dad.'

Nicholas's bright blue eyes crinkled at the edges. He hung on to her hand.

'That is very reassuring, Anna. Thank you. Now, I know you're itching to clean up.'

Anna caught sight of her father's odd collection of silver spoons. She could polish them, one by one. That would be both manageable and satisfying. But she saw her dad frown at her bump. A segment was now exposed between her top and her cords – the segment with the dark line on it. She pulled her green cardigan across the naked flesh and buttoned it, and as she did, felt the piece of paper in her pocket. It had a phone number on it. Anna looked at it stupidly for several seconds. The last time she'd worn this cardigan had been for the party. Next to the number was written, in a clear, curly script: 'Loudhailer!' It took a further six or seven seconds until she remembered where it had come from. She took out the new iPhone 8 her mother had given her, and keyed in the digits. *Hey Ben! It's Anna* . . . and she hesitated before adding *-Beth*. He texted back immediately. *Thank God you texted. Meet me asap.*

Ben had chosen the place. Anna knew she'd been to the cafe before but she couldn't pin down when. It was a nice place with lots of buttery French pastries piled high in the window and actual chairs, instead of those high uncomfortable stools and thin wooden shelves for tables which so many central cafes seem to go for. It also served food on plates, instead of flowerpots or discontinued medical supplies.

Benedict was dressed in another glamorous outfit, black trousers and a black wraparound jacket, with strange slipper/espadrilles which made him look like an extra from *Narcos*. His hair was now cut in a bowl and his specs were completely different from the last time they'd met. Anna realised he was younger than she'd thought. He couldn't be older than about twenty.

'I've brought you here under mysterious circumstances,' Ben began, miming opening a book as if at the beginning of an episode of some fifties TV mystery. 'Because I have news regarding your father.'

'Fuck off, Ben,' said Anna, standing up.

'Sorry! I thought that would be funnier than it was.' Ben slid a photograph across the table. Anna glanced down, faintly aware of a group picture.

'What's this?'

'It's a picture of your biological father.'

Anna crossed her forearms across the photograph, covering it, and tried to still her thumping heart. The blood was thudding in her ears so hard she feared it might make the table shake. She pictured the coffees on the table toppling in slo-mo and wished Ben would pick his up.

'Where did you get this?' Her jaw felt stiff. Her mouth wasn't working properly.

'From the witch! Night of your party,' Benedict replied.

'She's currently in hospital,' Anna chided Ben with a shaky voice, 'after having a stroke.' She corrected herself, 'Suspected stroke.'

'Sorry!' Ben was all contrition. 'Suspected? Sorry!' He almost winked. 'You knew who I meant though.'

The skin on Anna's stomach was hurting. The photograph was exerting a pull on her. She forced her eyes up to Ben's face. He was looking at her arms.

'Aren't you going to look at it?' he asked.

'Does she know you're showing me?'

'Christ, no! She'd be furious. This kidney thing is a fucking gift for her. I bet she's overjoyed!'

'I don't think she's overjoyed her grandchild might have a life-threatening illness!'

'What? And she's the *only* one who can help. Oh, I think she is. But she won't give you a kidney, so you might as well see if your father will.'

'Why are you being so horrible about her? I thought you guys were close?'

'Is that what she told you?' Ben was instantly muscles and teeth.

'You seemed close at that party.'

'I came for you!' Ben swiped off his specs, which were so fashionable they looked like the kind you wear at an optician's to test your eyesight. Without them he looked serious.

'What?' Anna said.

'I came to that party to meet you. Because you were about to get hit by the Marlene train.'

'So you don't get on with her?'

'I get on with her just fine!' Ben bristled. 'It's Heebs you want to worry about!'

The people at the table to Anna's left glanced at them. Anna lowered her voice, and Ben leaned in too.

'What are you talking about?'

'You know Heebs has serious mental health issues?' Ben launched in.

'She does?'

'Yeah, and Ma's been a real cunt to her about it: basically shunning her.'

'I find that hard to believe. I don't think she'd shun someone for having mental illness,' Anna said.

'She wants grandchildren. You get that, right? You get that's why she's so into you? Because you're a human pram?' Ben's voice was clear and carrying and Anna was starting to feel prickly and hot.

'I don't think that's the only reason!' Anna protested.

'She thinks it's some sort of terrible reflection on her that Heebs gets ill. And it fucking is. She told Ma she doesn't want kids. Big mistake! Ma brought Tristan home for her, put him in Heebs' bedroom, the whole bit.'

Anna thought of what had happened with Neil. Yes, she could believe that.

'So Heebs and Tristan banged but then it turned out Ma was already banging him. Heebs scarpers covered with guilt, for no reason! Like Ma gives a shit if she's sloppy seconds! Probably set it up so that she could steal Heebs' man. But Heebs is donning the hair shirt, obvs.'

'Is Hebe OK?'

Ben shrugged, 'I don't know. I think she's got some new guy. I haven't seen her for weeks.'

'Hebe hasn't said anything to me about any of this,' Anna said.

'That's because she wants you to have a chance with Lilith!'

'She doesn't like that name,' Anna said.

'I know. That's exactly why I use it!' Ben was not quite shouting.

They both waited for a moment, to let the anger subside. The couple next to them glanced over again. She didn't want to do this here.

'I'm going to take this home and look at it there,' she said, pulling the photo towards her.

'Don't leave!' said Ben. 'Your dad'll be here in a minute.'

'What?'

'Your biological father. He has lunch here once a week.'

'How do you know that?'

'I don't know if you've ever heard of something called a . . .' Ben's long fingers did elaborate air quotes, 'search engine?'

Anna lifted her arms. It was an old coloured photograph of a group of seven people. One was instantly recognisable as Marlene, in a huge hat and a tiny dress. Standing next to her, his face shadowed by her hat, was a lanky, handsome youth, in a light suit. And standing next to him was the Queen of England.

'Is that the Queen?'

'Yes,' said Ben, 'I think that's why she kept it. But it meant I could look up the occasion; official visit.'

Beyond the Queen were another four people, three of them men. But Anna's eyes were pulled back to the tall figure next to Marlene. There was something profoundly familiar about him. Anna leaned closer. Something was stuck on the photograph, some tiny crumb, and Anna's forefinger wiped it away, resting on the dark figure next to her mother. She looked up. Standing by the door, adjusting the bag on his shoulder, was her father, Nicholas.

'That's my dad.'

Ben's eyes were on the photograph. 'How did you know?'

Anna stood up slowly and crossed the cafe.

Nicholas's face creased into a delighted smile. 'Anna! What are you doing here?' He looked into Anna's eyes. 'Would you like a tea?'

'Am I your daughter?' Anna asked. 'I mean, your biological . . . Are you my biological father?'

Nicholas's handsome old face collapsed as if the bones had been caved in with a hammer.

'She told you!'

'No!' Anna said. 'But why didn't you?'

Half an hour later Anna was perched outside the cafe on a metal chair, with a cup of tea. Ben had made a rapid exit. 'You must have a lot to discuss.' They did. She had never noticed before how Nicholas's skin hung off his jowls. Wind chimes were tinkling at the edge of hearing, annoying the crap out of her.

'Why do all the significant moments in my life happen in shitty cafes?'

Nicholas tutted. 'There's no need to swear!'

'There's no need to swear! Are you serious?' Anna felt rage thumping through her. 'I'll swear if I fucking want! Why the fuck did you tell me I'm adopted?'

Nicholas blinked.

'You *were* adopted, by your mum and by me.'

'All these years I've wanted to know who my family

were! All these years I've dreamed of finding them! And all this time you could have told me! At any point!'

Nicholas was nonplussed. 'I had no idea you felt so strongly about it.'

'What? You had no idea I . . . what?'

Nicholas ran his hands through his still thick salt-and-pepper hair. 'It wasn't so easy to tell you. Technically, I was guilty of quite a serious crime.'

'You stole me from my mother.'

'No!' Nicholas suddenly shouted. 'No, Anna! I rescued you!'

Nicholas said he'd had a brief relationship with Lilith . . . as she was known then, which Nicholas did not know had resulted in a child.

'What?' said Anna. 'A relationship! Wasn't Marlene still at school?'

Nicholas was stunned. 'Dear God, no!' he said. 'She was in her twenties.' Anna struggled to follow.

By the time Anna was born, Nicholas claimed, he had met and married Anna's mum and they had already put their name down for fostering in Golders Hill in 1985. But Nicholas had got a call, out of the blue, from Marlene to come and help with 'your bloody baby' as she put it. He'd found her in a terrible way, with a new-born. She'd given birth at home, an experience which appeared to put Lilith's mental health, always fragile, over the edge. By the time Nicholas saw her she was 'behaving very oddly'.

'What do you mean?'

'She kept trying to throw you away.'

'She did what?'

'I would turn around and you'd have gone.'

'And you let her?'

Nicholas looked astonished. 'What was I supposed to do?'

Anna briefly considered if her father's bemusement was fake, but no, he really didn't know what she meant. 'You were supposed to take her to the doctor! You were supposed to take care of her! Why didn't you take her to hospital, for God's sake?'

Nicholas faltered, 'Please don't raise your voice, Anna. She didn't want to go!'

Anna wished she'd put sugar in the tea.

'So, the handbag? The traffic island? That whole origin story? That's all a lie?'

'Oh, no! She left you on a traffic island. It just wasn't the first time. I'd found you twice before – in the bin at the front of the house and hidden in the tins at a local shop. She'd told me to fuck off and kill myself! She was always very violent in her language. And I thought she might try to throw you away again. So I followed her in the car.' A muscle next to Nicholas's eye was twitching. 'I could see where she'd stopped, and I got out of the car and I could hear you crying. It was horrible rain. I was looking all along the verges. And the crying kept on and on through the traffic noise. And then I found you, in the middle of the road, in the bag. You were soaked through. And I thought I could take you back again to Lilith and let her throw you away again. Or I could take you somewhere safe. And I looked up and I saw the synagogue.'

'The synagogue?'

'Yes, they called the police. And I phoned Sarah; I telephoned your mum to come, and she came straight away.'

'I thought the synagogue called Mum.' Anna was drowning.

'They did. I mean, I did, from the synagogue. I was going to tell her. I'd meant to tell her.'

'You mean,' Anna was incredulous, 'she didn't know you had a baby?'

'Oh no! I thought it might upset her. And the moment she held you, Anna. The moment she touched you, you stopped crying. You looked at her and it was like you recognised her – like you knew her and she knew you. Like . . .' Nicholas struggled with unfamiliar sentiment, 'she was already your mum.'

The police had let them have her the first night, since they were on the fostering register. Another family looked after Anna for weeks but returned her to social services, fearing pre-natal drug addiction. Eventually Nicholas and Sarah were allowed to foster her, since 'we had shown a natural interest' and, Nicholas added, 'they were looking for a Jewish family, because you'd been left outside the synagogue. And your mum, of course, was Jewish.'

'Didn't they suspect you were the father?' Anna interrupted.

'I'm sure the police considered it but, after all, I was not exactly the playboy type.' Nicholas was massaging his temples. Anna knew how he felt.

'And Marlene never tried to find me?'

'She didn't know I'd taken you. But no. They advertised it across London, for the mother to come forward. And she didn't.'

'What do you mean? Didn't you see her again?'

For the first time Nicholas had the grace to look ashamed.

'Yes, I did go to see her and I asked where the baby was.'

'Fuck! That's cold!'

'Yes. By then we hoped to keep you. She said, "What baby?" She seemed very pleased with herself. After that of course I changed my name.'

The wind chimes were suddenly deafening. Anna stood up and pulled them off the wall. She dropped them on the floor and stamped on them.

'What do you think you are doing?' Nicholas was shocked, shaken.

Anna ground the split bamboo under her heel, ignoring the question.

'Is Rampion not my name? What's my name, Dad?' She was aware she was shouting. 'What's my name?'

'It's Rampion . . . now. I changed it. It was a sort of joke. Because Rampion means Rapunzel.'

'What? What was your name before?'

Nicholas looked tired. 'Goodfellow. My real name is Goodfellow.'

'Well, there's an irony!' Anna laughed bitterly. She took a deep breath. 'I thought it was because I was adopted.'

'What?'

'I thought that was why you could just send me away without giving a shit. Because I was adopted.' Twenty-five years of suppressed bitterness washed over Anna in an instant: the nights trying to warm up on the lukewarm water pipe, the other girls' tears, running down the corridors trying to get from one half-arsed radiator to the next, the wind, the endless wind. And now she was outside again, again, in the fucking cold.

'I didn't send you away!' Nicholas protested.

'To school! You sent me away to school.'

Nicholas had clearly never considered this. 'Be reasonable, Anna! How could I work and take care of you?'

'The same way millions of single parents do? I'd just lost my mother! And you sent me away!' Anna's rage was now filling her lungs, inflating her, making her feel huge and dangerous. 'You sent me away!'

'You've turned out all right, haven't you?'

'Have I?' Anna thought of the parade of babies – babies hurt, babies dying.

'Where's all this coming from?' Nicholas said, bewildered.

'Did you hit her?' Anna glared at her father. Nicholas's mouth formed a strange triangle.

'It . . . Marlene and I, it wasn't like that.' Anna looked at her father levelly. Tears began to run down his cheeks. 'I'm sorry that . . . it . . . wasn't what I wanted.' The tears were falling off the loops of skin on his jaw. 'Your mum and I were going to tell you. When you got older. It just . . . never seemed . . . she died.'

'You mean,' Anna's rage left her. 'Mum found out that . . . that . . .'

'That I'm your real father,' Nicholas supplied.

Her father stood up and took a step forward, opening his arms to try to hug her. She couldn't let him touch her. If she did, she was complicit. She pushed her chair back, crunching the dead wind chimes on the floor.

'I'm your father!' he said. 'I'm still your father!' But he wasn't. And she didn't know if he ever would be again.

Anna was profoundly nervous waiting for her scan. It was about forty minutes past the appointed time, and she was just trying to reassure Hebe by text when a heavily pregnant woman came out of the room. She walked unsteadily through the door, paused in front of Anna, swaying, and fell on her knees, pulling off her headscarf to pluck at her hair, howling. Her face was contorted in pain. Anna gasped and spontaneously moved towards her but her husband held up his hand: stop. He helped her to her feet and wrapped his arm around her shoulders as she made for the lift, still sobbing.

'Ms Rampion?'

Anna shook herself and followed the technician into her second scan in as many weeks.

The foetus wriggled and stretched, lifting one hand and almost waving at the camera. Anna couldn't help noticing the profile looked like her father and not, as at the twelve-week scan, like her mother. She wondered if the baby had changed, or she had.

'Ah! Isn't that cute?' The technician smiled at Anna. 'Everything looks fine.'

'What do you mean?' Anna asked.

'Clean as a whistle.'

'Isn't the placental fluid low? Are the kidneys large?'

The technician checked the screen and squinted at the image.

'I don't think so.'

The jelly on her stomach was cooling and drying, pulling the skin. When she was a kid at school, in her mum's classroom, she had painted Copydex on her hand to enjoy the feeling of peeling it off.

'A week ago, they said the baby might have ARPKD.'

'What?' The technician started flicking through Anna's notes. 'I'd be amazed. There aren't any blisters in the kidney. She looks totally fine.'

'She? It's a girl?'

The technician looked startled. 'Did you not want to know?'

'It's fine! It's fine!' Anna said. 'The kidney thing's just . . . gone away?'

'Maybe you were dehydrated? Are you taking any medication you aren't telling us about?'

'No, just pre-natal vitamins,' said Anna, 'my mother gave them to me.'

'It all looks OK now.'

Anna sat, stunned. She saw the look on the face of the woman who had been scanned before her.

'Was the woman before me . . .' but the technician's face shut down the question.

The shadow which had fallen across the baby had lifted as quickly as it fell, as if a flock of birds had passed overhead.

The kidneys cleaned the blood. Her baby would be able to clean her blood. Or would she? The weather had changed, as the birds passed. The sky had darkened. And at the edges of it, humming, lowering, Marlene's dark intimations about her father. Anna tried to look at the threat directly. She didn't believe it. She didn't have to believe it.

She couldn't separate it out. Her mother was either lying to destroy her, or utterly insane, or it was . . .

'Oh look,' said the technician, 'she's sucking her thumb!'

Was this the blood her child was to clean? 'I think if I was going to turn out to be a cold-hearted killer it'd have happened by now, don't you?' Her dad had said that, when they discussed his own father. She saw Nicholas's face cave in and the tears falling off his chin. They used to call Stella 'wife-beater'. 'A pint of wife-beater', that was how men had ordered from her when she tended bar as a teenager. Whatever the truth of the other thing, he had as good as admitted to beating Marlene, and that he had taken Anna. He was the child of a killer. He'd lied to her all her life. Everything she had ever believed was a lie. And he had sent her away more than Marlene had, who was clearly suffering from something, and he was what she was made of. Both things could not be true, surely – her father couldn't be such a bad man, and her mother a bad woman? One of them must be good.

The technician was talking on, issuing vague warnings; they should keep a close eye on Anna because of her one kidney and the baby was, indeed, sucking her thumb. The liquid rhythmic squeezing of her heartbeat filled Anna's ears. Now she thought the baby might be safe, the possibility that something might take it – her – away was almost insupportable. She saw the face of the woman in the headscarf. How must Marlene have felt when her own baby disappeared? How frightened must she have been? Marlene was clearly pretty crazy, but what had made her that way? She'd had post-natal depression. Marlene needed care, and instead, all her worst fears had been realised. The threat to her own baby had sent her to Marlene and then to Ben and then to her father. And here was the baby with her father's face. 'We are all blood vessels,' she thought. She was a vessel, and she had a profound sense of herself being pulled down-river with her cargo, by unseen currents, under the gathering storm.

The technician touched Anna's shoulder quite roughly.

'Anna? Please don't cry! It's good news! There's nothing wrong with the baby! You can go home!'

'Home?' Anna thought. 'To what? To who?' She could almost hear her father correcting her grammar.

'To whom, Anna! To whom!'

As Anna touched the flat's front door it swung open. The first thing she saw was the pile of her clothes cut to ribbons. Whoever had broken in had turned the whole place upside down. In the middle of the room the burglar had created a circle made of shredded hoodies and tracksuit bottoms; it looked like all Anna's pyjamas and some of her comfort clothes had been cut up. As Anna approached the pile, she realised the edges were little triangles, as if they'd been cut with serrated scissors, like they have in nursery schools. The painting was no longer on the wall. Anna went into her bedroom. Her bras had all been pulled out. Her tiny box of jewellery, and the lace gloves which lay on top of it, was missing. She went back into the front room. There was a terrible smell. She reached into the back pocket of her jeans where she kept her mobile phone and tried to raise it to her face. She looked at her hand and realised it was violently shaking. Still, she managed to call up Dermot's number.

'Yes?' Anna could tell just from the one word that Dermot was drunk.

'Where are you?'

'I'm at the pub. It's a family thing.'

'Do you think you could come home?'

'I can't come home, Anna! My mam's dying. Don't ask me to come home!'

Anna wondered briefly what she might say if she were someone else. 'Please! I need you.' But instead she said, 'OK.'

She googled 'what to do if you are burgled'. It said not to clean up in case evidence gets disturbed. So, Anna called the police and then sat down on the sofa waiting for them, and looking at the tattered remains of her life. Nothing had been real.

She was still there, four hours later, staring at her phone. She must not text Neil. She must not text Neil. She texted Neil: *Can you come over?*

He was there in twenty minutes.

'I'm really glad you texted,' he said. 'I really wanted to . . . What the hell happened here?'

He took one look at Anna's face. 'I'll get you some sweet tea.'

Neil went into the kitchen, where he stepped in the shit on the floor.

'Fuck!' he said. He took his shoe off, opened the tiny door to the balcony and threw the shoe directly off it.

'What are you doing?'

'That's human shit on my shoe!'

'So now you've thrown it on to someone's head?'

'Why didn't you clean it up?' Neil asked.

'I'm waiting for the police.'

'Jesus!' Neil said. 'The police aren't coming!'

'You were the one who always wants me to report stuff!'

'The police don't come for stuff like this! Trust me. I've been burgled a *lot*.' Neil was opening the door to the balcony – airing the place out. 'What have they taken?'

'Not much that I can see, just the Switch, and my jewellery, and the painting.'

Neil suddenly whirled around.

'It's OK,' said Anna, 'they didn't touch his seventy-eights.'

'Thank God for that!' He looked around. 'And they left the TV!' Neil regarded Anna's stance, hunched on the sofa. 'Maybe you should turn it on?' he suggested gently.

'I was worried they've touched the remote. Fingerprints?'

'Fingerprints?' Neil squatted in front of her. 'Anna, the police aren't going to dust the place or test the dump for DNA. Are you OK?'

'I'm OK,' Anna said, 'the baby hasn't got it – the kidney thing.'

'That's good, isn't it?' Neil asked. Anna didn't respond. What was she supposed to say? The baby isn't sick, except she has my blood, and my blood is the blood of my father. Then she tried to stand up, but Neil stopped her.

'I'll clean up. You don't want to touch that, not in your condition.' So Neil cleaned up and brought Anna a cup of tea. He put the tea down and squatted in front of her. He put his thumb into the centre of her palm and pressed it.

'I don't need you to rescue me, you know,' said Anna.

'Don't fucking text me then,' said Neil.

'Knock, knock!' a female voice said. 'Don't worry, it's not the beginning of a joke!' A ridiculously cheery policewoman was popping her head into the front room. 'Ooh! Any chance of one of those for me?'

Ten minutes later the policewoman was perched on Anna's armchair.

'And there were no signs of forced entry?'

'No,' Anna thought back. 'The door was already open when I got home. It was on the latch.'

'Why had you left it on the latch?'

'I hadn't!'

The officer put her head on one side. 'Are you sure?'

Anna was not sure.

'What do you reckon?' Neil was hanging back. 'Meth-heads?'

'This isn't *Breaking Bad*!' Anna snapped.

'In all likelihood,' the policewoman offered, 'it was meth-heads, or heroin addicts.' She looked at Neil's feet. 'Why are you wearing one shoe?' Her eyes travelled up to his face. 'Are you a resident?'

'Neil's just a . . . mate,' said Anna. Neil looked at her.

'Just a mate?' Neil said, and he looked her right in the eye.

'I'd better go,' he said, and the door closed with a horrible finality behind him.

It occurred to Anna she could tell the policewoman about her father. She could say, 'My father stole me from my mother. I've just found out. You should go and arrest him.'

'Well, that's me, then,' said the policewoman. 'Unless there's anything else?'

When the policewoman left, the flat felt emptier than it had ever been before. The smell of new paint mixed with crap and bleach was unbearable. Anna went out on to the tiny balcony and looked up at the night sky. Huge flakes of snow, almost the size of ten-pence pieces, were floating on to the freezing metal railing which stopped you from jumping. Anna heard the familiar sound of the owl screaming.

She took her phone out of her pocket and dialled Marlene.

Marlene answered with a voice that was at least a half-octave lower than her normal speaking voice, 'Hello, Marlene Meunier?'

'The baby's OK,' Anna said. On the other end of the phone there was silence. Anna shook with cold. 'Are you OK?'

'I'm just waiting for a cab at the hospital. Bloody Tristan's gone AWOL.'

'Are they sending you home?'

'They say it's fine if I have someone with me for twenty-four hours.'

'Is anyone with you?'

'I'm managing!' Marlene said. 'I always pull through!'

'Wait right there,' said Anna, her teeth chattering. 'I'm coming to take care of you. I'm coming now.'

11

TWENTY-SIX WEEKS GONE

'The baby may move about a lot and respond to touch and sound. A very loud noise may make them jump and kick, and you'll be able to feel this.'

Twenty-four hours turned into forty-eight, and forty-eight into a week, and suddenly it was Christmas. Anna had always been fascinated by other people's Christmases. Most years she spent it with Layla's family. Layla's dad was a fierce atheist and her mother was Muslim, so the December celebration was almost exclusively about food, though Layla's nieces and nephews all got presents, usually with some spurious justification unrelated to the holiday: 'you came second in your swimming meeting' or 'you've learnt to be much tidier'.

Dermot's mam was still at death's door. No one knew if she would make it past the week, so he didn't want to come home. 'You don't give a shit about Christmas, anyway, do you?' Dermot had said. Anna had not told him about the burglary. It seemed another thing for him to worry about.

Growing up, Anna had spent the day with her father, coming downstairs from whatever homework she was doing to watch the Queen's Speech at three and disappearing upstairs again to work. There had never been Christmas, of course, when her mum was alive; in fact, Anna had a vague sense that her mother had always got more Jewish around Christmas time, the menorah displayed on the front windowsill in their tiny Peckham terrace flat, so it seemed odd to start alternative traditions after she left them. Anna's father would give her a single present on Christmas morning, a textbook she needed so she 'wouldn't feel left out'. These days he always called her at six.

So Anna was only faintly surprised that, at Marlene's house, no accommodation appeared to be made for the coming festivities. Marlene spoke disparagingly of the 'village decorations – honestly, why not put them up in July?' and Anna began to grasp that Marlene believed the posher you were the later you decorated. It was only on the 23rd that Marlene began weaving great handfuls of holly and ivy up the oak banisters of the 'main staircase', so called despite the fact that it was the only staircase. Marlene kept going outside to check the neighbour's windows for Christmas lights, playing some personal game of decorations-chicken. Then, on Christmas Eve, she abruptly rushed in, shouting at Charmaine, 'They've gone up!' With astonishing speed, the house morphed into a Dickensian Christmas card. Mistletoe hung above the front door, along with beautiful lanterns for candles. Each mantelpiece was covered with tiny porcelain houses, their windows glowing invitingly, and in the 'drawing room', the large reception room underneath Hebe's bedroom, was a vast Christmas tree, decorated exclusively in silver and white. It was an Instagrammer's wet dream.

'Come and help me decorate the tree!' Marlene had said, as the fire roared in the grate, and Tristan's expensive speakers pumped out Christmas music at a higher spec than it had been recorded at. 'Here!' said Marlene, taking out a carefully wrapped egg box. 'Here are the children's letters!' Wrapped in tissue were the letter 'H' and the letter 'B' delicately carved out of wood and painted silver, with tiny silver ribbon loops so they could be hung. 'Oh!' she said. 'There isn't one for you! We MUST remedy that!' Marlene surveyed the beautiful tree. 'It's going to be perfect this year, just perfect!'

Anna was nervous. Would the other children resent her presence? She didn't want to elbow into family traditions. 'Don't be ridiculous!' Marlene reassured her. 'You're the mother of my grandchild!'

Was she expected to buy presents for everyone? 'Oh, no! We only do joke gifts. Don't spend more than fifty quid!' Anna tried to remember a time she had spent more than fifty quid on anything and came up with her sofa ten years ago, the Ikea job which had cost two hundred. Anna thought long and hard about the gifts, and her finances, and ended up finding Hebe an old camera with, she was told, undeveloped film still in it. And for Ben she got a tweed *Peaky Blinders* hat from a charity shop. But Marlene and Tristan stumped her, until she was struck with the inspiration to buy them something jointly for the house. She found sheet music for 'The Magpie', her mother's favourite song, which Dermot and Neil had sung on her first visit. She put it in a charity shop frame, bought some wrapping paper from a posh bookshop and was secretly very pleased with the result.

It was a 'family tradition' that they 'all' went to church on Christmas Eve. 'It's so beautiful with the lights,' Marlene had said. 'I'm sure even an atheist wouldn't object!' and Anna had agreed to come. She was waiting in Marlene's polished hallway, dressed in Marlene's old red coat, when Marlene herself appeared.

'Get in the car!' she said, and Anna found herself crunching out on to the gravel before she'd even consciously heard the words. She got into the back seat and tried to pull the seat belt across her pronounced belly, but it jammed. Marlene sat in the driver's seat and slammed the door, turning on the engine.

'Is Tristan coming?' Anna asked tentatively.

Marlene leaned on the car horn for a full twelve seconds: once, twice, three times, until Tristan appeared on the 'porch' in a grey coat.

'You look like an estate agent!' Marlene snapped.

She stamped on the accelerator and roared up the drive. Tristan craned around in his seat to look at Anna, who did the universal gesture for 'beats me', shrugging her shoulders and widening her eyes.

'Is something the matter?' Tristan asked.

Marlene savagely chugged the gears into third, 'Why don't you ask Beth?'

Anna tried to hold her travel sickness at bay as the BMW roared along the 'country' lanes. She moved into the middle of the back seat so she could see the speedometer, which was over fifty, before clicking in her seat belt.

'I'm really sorry,' she said. 'I don't know what you mean.'

'Did you or did you not know that Ben wasn't coming to church?'

'Is he not coming?' Anna asked.

'No, he's bloody not! What did you say to him?' Marlene asked. 'You must have said something!'

'I didn't say anything,' said Anna, 'just that I was looking forward to seeing him.'

Marlene stayed quiet. Anna could see Tristan's head looking down at his lap. Marlene's voice took on the sharp tone Anna was beginning to recognise as a warning sign.

'Why isn't Dermot staying for Christmas?' Marlene asked.

'He has to stay in Ireland,' said Anna.

'You aren't trying to keep him from me, are you?' Marlene's eyes narrowed. 'You aren't trying to keep him to yourself?'

'No . . . his mum's ill.'

'Honestly, darling! You'd think you were jealous! What am I going to do if he's here? Reach over and wank him off?' Anna blinked. 'Am I just going to reach across the Christmas tablecloth and wank him?' Marlene twisted in the driving seat to look directly at Anna and do a wanking gesture, towards Anna, as if Anna had a penis, but as if it were a tiny penis, the penis of a small boy. It was profoundly disgusting. And terrifying, since Marlene continued to drive at great speed. 'Is that what you expect of me?'

Marlene faced forward again, and Anna could see her darting looks in the driving mirror. 'What are you doing? Catching flies?' she asked.

Anna realised her mouth was hanging open. She closed it. 'I don't . . . Dermot's just looking after his mother who has cancer.'

'Is that why he can't accept me? Because he's losing his own mother?'

'What do you mean? He does accept you!' Anna said.

Suddenly Marlene smiled. 'I understand!' She cocked her head to one side. 'You want me all to yourself!'

'I'm not . . .' Anna began.

'Not another word!' said Marlene. 'My daughter wants me to herself!'

She swung off the road and pulled up outside a tiny, picturesque village church.

'Stay in the car, Tristan. Beth needs some time alone with me.'

It was freezing. As the car door slammed Anna suddenly thought, 'What would happen if she doesn't let me back in? How will I survive the winter?' She caught herself. She was being irrational. Marlene was upset about Ben's no-show. It must be a significant thing for her, Anna reasoned, enough to transmute into this idea that Dermot was rejecting her too. There was a logic there somewhere. If she could just catch her breath, Anna felt sure she could untangle it. They walked towards the church and Anna turned back to see Tristan, hunched in the passenger seat, blowing on his hands. He looked like he was sheltering against a storm.

Anna found herself standing next to Marlene through the Nine Lessons and Carols. Marlene was right. It was pretty. Candles were lit all around, and the church was decorated in great swathes of greenery. Anna was very familiar with the nine lessons, having listened to them each year through the decade of her schooling.

It started, of course, with Adam and Eve. 'Who told thee thou wast naked?' and what Layla called 'the first slut-shaming'. Eve, with her female body and her baby-making ways bringing down the man-boy Adam, ending his innocence. So many other religions had creation myths in which female gods birthed men from mud, but this one had a grown man at the beginning, and a woman ruining him. Anna had never really understood why it wasn't a move into the garden of plenty rather than out of it: this discovery of the way to make more humans. Was it a simple substitute for adolescence? Or was it a population warning: too many babies and there'll be nothing but dust bowls?

But next Abraham was willing to sacrifice his child. Then he was rewarded with many, many descendants 'as the stars of heaven and as the sand which is upon the seashore'. Marlene grasped Anna's hand. What did she mean by that? That she, Marlene, had been willing to sacrifice her child, Anna, for a greater good? But what greater good? Anna gave her enough of a squeeze back to be released.

With the baby flipping in her belly, Anna's mind was alive to new possibilities in the Christmas story. She'd always thought of the biblical stories as metaphors; complex, confused metaphors retold over centuries. But now, for the first time, she seriously considered the idea that some element might be true. When the fourth lesson began, and the angel Gabriel came to Mary telling her she was 'with child' and Mary replied, 'How shall this be, seeing I know not a man?' it occurred to Anna that Mary might have been a real teenager saying she was a virgin to protect her baby. What teenage girl, on being brought the news that she was pregnant and faced with being stoned to death, with losing not just her own life but her unborn child's, what teenager would not say, 'How shall this be, seeing I know not a man?' Even assuming the very best, that she had understood what it was to 'know a man' and had done so willingly. What if Mary, the refugee, had got knocked up, and come up with this story and then had been forced to stick to it?

And then that story, thirty-three years later, resulted in her child's death. The stories we tell about our children become their reality. The word was made flesh. Prophesies are fulfilled. Anna shook herself. It was just the usual bullshit: Eve and Mary, the woman who would and the woman who wouldn't.

At the Sign of the Peace, Marlene introduced Anna to everyone she clasped hands with.

'Peace Be With You,' she'd say. 'This Is My Daughter. Peace Be With You! This Is My Daughter! I'm very proud of her!' she said, to anybody who would listen, and many who were trying not to.

'This Is My Daughter! I'm Very Proud Of Her!' she shouted across the aisle. 'My other children are coming tomorrow!'

Marlene was cooking from six in the morning. By the time Anna went into the kitchen at seven there were already multiple dishes on the go: roast potatoes, sausages wrapped in bacon, turkey, stuffing, bread sauce, cranberry sauce.

Since Anna had been responsible for most of the meals since Marlene had come home from hospital, she tentatively asked if she could help.

'No!' Marlene said. 'It's all in hand!'

'I know it can be a pain in the neck,' Anna replied, 'cooking for a vegetarian.'

'Oh God!' Marlene exclaimed. 'You're vegetarian, aren't you?' She thought for a moment. 'You can eat the potatoes! They're cooked in goose fat, delicious! Or you could pick the bacon out of the sprouts? We've also got oysters!'

'Lovely,' said Anna. 'I hope you like your present.'

'Oh, have you got me something?' Marlene asked.

'Yes,' said Anna.

'I'm sorry I hadn't thought,' said Marlene. Her brow furrowed. 'Actually, there is something that might suit!'

'Oh!' said Anna. 'There's no need. All this is present enough.'

'No!' said Marlene. 'There is something. But if I give it to you, what are you going to do with it?'

'What do you mean?'

'If I give it to you, you aren't going to give it to someone else, are you?' Marlene asked. 'Or ruin it? Are you going to appreciate it?'

'I don't really know. If it's something special to you, perhaps you should keep it?' said Anna.

'I don't want to *keep* it. I want to give it to *you*, as a present. I want you to have it! But I only want to give it to you if I know you'll look after it. Anybody can be given something. But not everyone can keep it! If you aren't going to look after it, I'll give it to someone who will.'

'Sorry, what are we talking about?' said Anna.

'The present,' Marlene persisted.

'I mean . . . it depends what it is?'

'I'm not going to tell you what it is! It's a present, for

goodness' sake! I don't go around telling people what present I'm going to give them. Just promise you'll take care of it the way I'd like.'

'I . . . I . . . don't know, of course . . . if I can . . . I don't know what we're talking about . . .'

'Oh, for God's sake!' Marlene banged the pan containing the bread sauce. 'Forget it!'

At two, Marlene descended the main staircase in a velvet trouser suit in forest green. There was, as promised, a Christmas tablecloth. Tristan and Anna sat in front of the fully set table. The only things not laid out were the plates, which were piled next to the turkey. The turkey had sat under foil for two hours but was now uncovered so that Marlene could take photos for Insta. Beautiful dishes held glowing Christmas food: the bright orange of the sweet potato mash offset the livid green of the sprouts. In the centre of the table was a bonsai tree decorated with tiny baubles. Marlene had taken pictures of the vase, then the napkin rings, the cushions, the little tree, the serving forks . . . there was nothing else to photograph. By three Hebe and Ben had still not arrived and Marlene had called Ben fourteen times. At three minutes past three Ben picked up.

'Where are you?' Marlene demanded.

Anna couldn't hear the other end of the conversation.

'I've been cooking since six a.m.!' There was a pause as Ben said something on the other end. 'Not to *church* . . . you said you weren't coming to church. Of course you're coming to Prescott for Christmas dinner!' Another pause. 'Nonsense! Let me speak to Hebe.' Tristan and Anna glanced at each other. 'She's not here!' Marlene said. 'She's not with me! I'm sure there's a perfectly simple explanation. She'll be with one of her silly boyfriends.' Anna could make out the alarm in Ben's voice on the other end. Marlene responded, 'Oh, but you're not worried about *me*. For her you'll go shooting off at a moment's notice but I'm to be . . . Ben? Ben?'

Ben had clearly hung up. Marlene's face was entirely set, like a mask had been made of herself and then she'd put it on. The hairs on the back of Anna's neck rose.

Marlene turned and took the first plate off the pile, pulled her wrist back as if the plate was a frisbee and skimmed it across the room directly over Anna's head. The plate smashed on the wall behind her, the pieces ricocheting towards her.

'Get down!' Tristan muttered urgently.

Anna slid off her chair and manoeuvred her pregnant belly under the kitchen table as another plate smashed on the wall behind her. A broken piece of the plate skidded towards her and she stopped it with her hand. She shuffled further under the table and ducked her head down until she could see Marlene, face still frozen, taking plate after plate off the pile and skimming them around the kitchen. When she finished with the ones on the side, she moved on to the wooden plate rack. Pieces of broken crockery were landing in the potatoes, the gravy. Tristan whispered to Anna, 'Don't say anything!' They sat together under the table for what felt like a long time until the crockery went quiet. They both heard Marlene stalk out of the kitchen. Tristan scuttled out from under the table and Anna looked up at him. They were looking at each other when they heard the crash.

'Is that the tree?' Anna asked, and the baby kicked her so hard in the ribs she gasped aloud. When they went into the 'drawing room', Marlene had felled the tree like some crazed lumberjack. With the handle of an umbrella, she was smashing the presents one by one.

Marlene looked at the wreckage of her perfect Christmas.

Tristan had brought her a whisky.

'Come on, Ma,' he said. 'You should sit down.' Marlene's hand was shaking violently, and her glass clattered against her beautiful teeth as she downed it. She perched on the edge of the brown leather sofa, and then stood up.

'I've changed my mind about your present!' she said. 'I'm going to give you the gift of my time!' Marlene knocked back the last of the whisky. 'I'm going to teach you to drive!' She left the drawing room, then stuck her head back round the door, 'Come on!'

'Now?' Anna asked.

'Yes, now!' Marlene barked.

In the BMW Anna pulled the seat belt across her swollen belly and clicked it in. The baby was going nuts. She must be flooded with adrenaline. Anna could feel her tumbling and kicking against the seat belt.

'How much driving have you done?' Marlene asked.

'I learned when I was seventeen,' said Anna.

'Then why didn't you take your test?'

'The guy was pretty creepy,' Anna explained breathlessly, 'you know.'

'No?' Marlene's face was alive, animated. 'Tell me more!'

'He would talk about wet T-shirt competitions and how well I would do in them. This was a while ago.'

'I'm sure you'd still do well!' said Marlene.

'I just meant . . . wet T-shirt is a bit . . . nineties. He kept leaning over me.'

'Well, he probably had to do that to keep you safe.'

'What?' said Anna. 'Talk about my tits?'

Marlene cocked an eyebrow. 'Very smart,' she said. 'You see, we're getting to know each other better already! Why don't you find the bite?'

Anna depressed the clutch, eased up a little and opened up the gas.

'You didn't check your mirror!' Marlene chided her.

'We're at the end of a long drive,' Anna said. Then, 'Don't you think we should eat first?'

'No!' said Marlene. 'Take her away!'

Anna released the handbrake and crawled up the drive.

'Faster!' ordered Marlene. 'Faster!' She leaned forward. 'Left at the end!' Anna stopped where the drive merged on to the road.

'Go!' screamed Marlene. 'Go now before anything comes!'

Anna obeyed again before her mind was able to consciously process the words. How did Marlene do that? As she pulled out a car came round the bend too fast and swerved to avoid her, beeping hard.

'Keep going!' Marlene yelled. 'Don't stall!' Anna was finding the combination of remembering where her feet went and managing her emotions about Marlene's response to the creepy guy story difficult, no, impossible. She couldn't catch her breath. But Marlene seemed to be cheered up by the excitement and was launching into one of her monologues – the Marlene Lilith Mather Williamson McHugh Meunier Show: Drive Time with Marlene! – Men Who Drive Penis Extensions – What Was Great About Beauty Contests – Men Who've Paid Me The Compliment Of Sexual Harassment. Anna stopped at the first lay-by and pulled in, taking great gulping breaths at first, and then trying to count her breaths to calm down.

'Oh no!' wailed Marlene. 'We were just getting your confidence up!'

The conviction began to fill Anna that it was essential that Marlene know something about her. Even the basic facts like vegetarianism hadn't, as they say in political circles, 'cut through'. Anna took another breath.

'My mum was killed on the road,' she said. 'A lorry hit her. I was there. I saw her die. She wouldn't have been there if she wasn't taking me home. So, that's why I've never learnt to drive.'

'Oh, my poor darling Beth!' said Marlene, leaning across to hug Anna. 'Don't worry! You've got me now!'

Once Anna had started confessing, she couldn't stop. 'I talked to my father,' she said, 'he's the one who adopted me.'

This was clearly news to Marlene. Her face cycled through emotions as if she were demonstrating emojis. Anna didn't know what she would settle on, but when her face stopped moving, it projected a profound concern.

'Did he hurt you?' she asked.

'No,' said Anna, 'I mean, only in the usual way parents hurt their children.'

'My poor darling!' Marlene said. 'Parents don't hurt

their children!' Marlene was studying her face, searching into its corners for some evidence of damage.

'He did his best.' Anna felt it was now vital she defended her father.

'I wish I'd put ground glass in his food when I had the chance,' Marlene declared.

Anna exhaled, exhausted.

'Well, I think you owe me thirty-five Christmases,' said Marlene brightly. 'Do you want me to drive home?'

Back at the house Tristan had already got the tree propped up again and the crockery cleared and was squeezing sweet potato mash through a sieve to get rid of the shards for Anna. He sliced up the chestnut stuffing and toasted it, spooning cranberry sauce as a dip, while Marlene piled up the sausages wrapped in bacon on to a plate. All three of them began to get a little silly, as if expected to stay solemn at a funeral, taking their plates through and eating in front of the fire in the drawing room.

Marlene offered her a drink and Anna thought, 'One glass of wine can't hurt.' She was sipping white wine by the blazing logs and wondering if she could manage a third slice of stuffing, when Marlene handed her Ben's 'B' ornament from the tree, coming up close.

'This can be yours now,' she breathed, 'for Beth.'

'Thank you,' said Anna. And Marlene snapped the H in half and threw it in the fire.

'Have you got a name for the baby yet?' Marlene asked. 'What about Barnaby, then he could inherit this?'

'It's a girl,' Anna said.

Marlene looked disappointed, but perked up immediately. 'Never mind,' she said, 'that means you'll be the mother of daughters, like me!'

They looked at the rest of the trashed presents like naughty schoolchildren.

Then Tristan picked up a piece of broken cup – was it, or part of Hebe's camera? – from the wreckage. 'It's a monocle!' he said. 'Thank you so much! I always wanted one!'

Anna found a book which had had a great chunk of pages ripped out of the spine. 'A Choose Your Own Adventure Story! Put the pages in whatever order suits you! That was on my Christmas list!' She grinned at Tristan.

'Look!' said Tristan. 'This one's OK!' The present Anna had so carefully bought and wrapped for Marlene was unscathed, and Marlene opened it eagerly. Her eyes filled with tears when she saw the musical notes in their black frame.

'Oh look,' she said, 'it's gorgeous! I'm going to put it up over the fireplace!' and she propped it up on the mantelpiece behind the little glowing houses, where it looked absolutely in place.

'It's very cool,' said Tristan, with his pronounced French accent. 'It's banging!'

For some reason, 'It's banging!' in a strong French accent became the funniest thing Anna had ever heard.

'What about the tree, Tristan?' she asked. 'Is that banging too?'

'It's banging!' said Tristan, delighted that they found it so funny.

'And the sausages?'

'They are banging! They are banging bangers!'

After that the three of them pronounced everything 'banging' for forty-five minutes. They were still being deeply silly when Anna's phone rang, and Nicholas's Memoji came up with the title 'Dad'. Marlene glanced at it, then at Anna with an unspoken appeal in her eyes.

'Are you going to answer that?'

THIRD TRIMESTER

12

THIRTY-FIVE WEEKS GONE

'You may get some swelling in pregnancy, particularly in your legs, ankles, feet and fingers. It's often worse at the end of the day and further into your pregnancy.'

Marlene assured her it was normal to feel this tired. 'Some women,' she said, 'just aren't very good at carrying a baby. It never bothered me! But I've been told some women find it incredibly tiring and it looks like you're one of them.'

Anna was now, a month before the baby was due, unfeasibly large. She would look at the insane bulge of her belly, with its blue veins. How was it possible? It seemed so unlikely that there was a baby in there and that it would come out. But then a tiny foot would push hard outwards and she'd see the bump of a little sole on the smooth surface of her stomach skin.

The days had settled into a rhythm. First thing in the morning she'd take her pre-natal vitamins. Then she'd make breakfast. She'd started by making meals for Marlene and taking them to her on a tray, and that hadn't really stopped. Anna didn't know exactly when it had become fully clear there had been no stroke and Marlene was returned to full health and strength, but it had been soon, perhaps two weeks after she'd moved in. When had she moved in? Two months ago? It was before she started her maternity leave. When Layla took a sabbatical, work had become a lonelier place to be.

And there was plenty to do here. Tristan would leave for work at the vet practice most days after breakfast, and Anna would help around the house. There seemed to be an unending to-do list, even though most of the physical work was completed by Charmaine and her father, who lived at the Lodge. But there was always something else: the hydrangeas needed cutting back. The parquet needed polishing. The wood for the stove needed to be taken into the outhouse to dry out. Anna did some cleaning chores – Marlene liked everything pristine – and then started work on Marlene's property business. Marlene owned a lot of flats, most of them in London, all run chaotically by different agencies. She'd owned most of them for twenty years. Anna had discovered this when Marlene had said, 'Could you be a sweetie and sort out my desk?' Marlene had literally no idea how many properties she owned, and since her accountant had died four years ago she didn't appear to have paid any taxes.

'Why would I pay tax?' asked Marlene.

'So you don't go to prison?' Anna had replied. Anna spent the weeks making a filing system for the properties, diarising when their gas safety certificates were due, making sure they were insured, and chasing agencies for rent.

'You're so good at that!' Marlene would say. 'I'm not able to concentrate long enough to do all that boring work – the consequence of having a creative mind, I'm afraid.

But you can put numbers into the computer till the cows come home!'

Anna sent emails from Marlene's Gmail 'office' account, which Marlene gave her the password to and which was, in other ways, almost completely unused, working on Marlene's laptop. 'What's mine is yours!' she'd say. Marlene did not give her a credit card, however; she wrote cheques instead, signing the whole cheque book and handing it over to Anna.

'You see how much I trust you, don't you?'

Anna would make lunch for Marlene, though many days she drove off 'To London!' (for what purpose was never quite clear). If Marlene was around they ate soup with crusty bread and cheese, and Anna was allowed to share. In the evening they ate separate meals. Anna would cook Marlene roasts: sides of beef or venison, and Anna would eat 'the vegetarian option'. Marlene had started to buy ready meals for Anna, calorie-counted mushroom pies and low-fat macaroni cheese.

'You do seem to be gaining a *lot* of weight. Nobody could ever tell I was pregnant, from behind. When I'd turn around, they'd gasp because, of course, my figure was just as good as it had always been.'

Anna did wonder about these tales of Marlene's: just exactly who it was who was viewing her surreptitiously from behind and then, as she swung round, presumably silhouetted in a warm golden light, gasping with amazement that such a pregnant woman could also have such a perfect arse.

But then she felt unworthy for having such thoughts.

Tristan sometimes ate late in the 'snug', watching TV, and Anna started to look forward to these occasions, when she'd take in a tray of boiled eggs and soldiers after work. It reminded her of her dad, who she hadn't spoken to since the cafe. Anna would push off her red boots with gratitude and lie down on the bean bag. One day she couldn't get them back on. She'd struggle to stay awake past half past nine.

Anna ordered a delivery once. She planned to bake a loaf of bread. Marlene kept in plain flour but not strong white flour. Marlene loved bread and ate it all the time and Anna thought perhaps this was something she would like, but Marlene turned away the van.

'I haven't ordered anything.'

The Ocado guy, a chubby black guy in his fifties, had already put three bags on the step. 'It's for an Anna Rampion.'

Marlene's voice chilled. 'There's nobody of that name here,' she said. 'Do I not feed you?' She rounded on Anna, livid, 'I suppose I've been starving you all these months? I suppose all these meals I prepare for you are imaginary!' It didn't seem the time to mention it was Anna who prepared the meals. 'And to use that name! The name the man who stole you gave you! You're just throwing it in my face!'

'It's the name on my debit card,' said Anna. 'I wasn't trying to insult you.'

'Let me see!' said Marlene.

'You want to see my card?' asked Anna.

'Not if it's a terrible inconvenience!' Marlene said. 'Not if it's too much trouble!' Anna fumbled out her wallet.

Marlene took the debit card and snapped it. 'There! Now I won't have to see that horrid name again!'

Anna tried to call Layla, but she kept getting the same message: 'The person you are calling is not accepting calls right now.'

In the evening sometimes Anna would have text conversations with Dermot, in Ireland. The reception was notoriously terrible, so they'd long ago given up speaking, and as the weeks passed the text conversations had got shorter and shorter.

Her mother would say, 'Why don't you text your fiancé? Marriages mean work, you know.' She would hover over Anna for the first five minutes. 'Why don't you tell Dermot about the irises? They are so beautiful today. There's so little colour in February.'

But when she left Anna was seized with self-consciousness. What could she possibly tell Dermot that would interest him? Anything which occurred to Anna that Dermot would find funny – her mother's crazy outfits, Tristan's malapropisms – seemed incredibly disloyal to bring up. So, what Anna and Dermot had always been good at – messing about with each other, finding the jokes, joining together against the stupidity of the rest of the world – seemed to have evaporated.

The irises are coming out, she texted.

Whose fucking irises? Dermot texted back.

My mother's, she replied.

Has she got cataracts? Dermot asked.

The flowers: irises. How's your mum doing? she'd text.

Still dying, said Dermot. *How's the baby?*

The baby's fine, Anna texted, *the baby's good.*

It wasn't as if she couldn't get out. 'Feel free to borrow the car any time!' Marlene would say. 'Oh! You really must have driving lessons!'

Anna could leave any time she liked.

There was nothing to indicate today would be any different from yesterday. Anna was on the first landing dusting the eggs with a make-up brush. Marlene had a collection of eggshells. The eggs had been hollowed years ago: a pin-prick put in each end and the insides blown out, leaving just the shell. The shells were painted to look like owls and displayed together in a wicker nest. Marlene's eggs were painted in gold and teal, the tiny eyes picked out in gold leaf, along with the little beaks. Staring back at you, they appeared to be made of money.

Marlene had been dressing in her bedroom for quite some time. She emerged a couple of times in different outfits, huffed and disappeared into her room again. In the end she manifested in a Sherlock Holmes tweed cape and beret. Her hands were heavy with huge designer rings, her enormous bunch of keys in hand. As Marlene passed Anna on the landing she noticed the Hoover sitting at the top of the stairs.

'Who left this here?' she asked.

'You did earlier,' Anna said.

'I . . . what?' Marlene narrowed her eyes. 'What did you say?'

'You left it here?' Anna offered tentatively.

'I *think* I would remember if I'd left a Hoover on the stairs, Beth! I think that's the sort of thing that *might* stick in my memory. Or perhaps you think I've gone gaga, do you? You think I'm a little old lady and I'm quite, quite gone?'

'N-no,' stuttered Anna. 'Are you OK?'

'No! I'm not OK when people start accusing me of being demented! Lazy and dirty and demented. Is that what you think of me?'

'I don't!' said Anna, really confused now. 'I don't think you are lazy. I don't think you are dirty.'

'I am the cleanest person I have ever met! I am not the sort of person to leave a Hoover on the stairs!'

At the top of the banister, where the stairs met the landing, was a post, which Anna had heard Marlene refer to as a 'newel' post. The post was perhaps nine inches in diameter, with a carved round head. As Marlene reached her, Anna still held the eggshell cupped in her hands.

'Honestly,' said Marlene. 'I give and I give and I give!'

As Marlene passed Anna, the tension in Anna's hands must have transferred to the eggshell. It crumpled into pieces.

'I'm sorry!' said Anna, and she looked up into Marlene's impassive face. Her expression was beautiful, patient, pained.

Marlene regarded Anna's cupped hands filled with broken eggshells and smashed them sideways into the post with her own ringed hands. Anna's right ring finger, which took the full force of the keys, dislocated and snapped. After a few seconds, Anna noticed that she was screaming.

'Oh, don't make such a fuss!' said Marlene.

'I think . . .' Anna gasped, 'you broke my finger.'

'*You* broke your finger. I rapped you on the knuckles!'

And Marlene walked down the stairs and out of the front door.

Anna looked down at her hand. The pieces of painted eggshell were white on the inside and for a moment she thought her bone was sticking through the skin. But it wasn't. As the finger swelled and turned purple in front of her eyes, Anna's thoughts ran clean like a mountain stream. They had been muddy but now they were sparkling, iridescent. A voice bubbled up from inside her. 'I told you so,' it said. 'This pain is good. This pain is the truth.'

She was propelled towards the kitchen, like a marionette. At the bottom of the stairs she passed Charmaine, who was carrying clean towels. Charmaine nodded at Anna.

'Charmaine!' she called to Charmaine's back, but she walked on. 'The tap!' said the voice, and Anna held it under the cold water. 'Now,' said the voice, and Anna pushed the bone back into place.

As Anna felt the finger slide into its correct position, she regained control. She immediately felt a sense of loss. She missed the clarity. On her own, the thoughts in her head were murky. Her hand hurt like fuck. She needed to make some sort of splint. She rifled through the drawers with her left hand, finding an old children's spoon, and she looked for Micropore tape in the medicine cupboard.

Anna found paracetamol in the cupboard – not enough – there was a packet of co-dydramol. The packet was open. Her finger was now throbbing: a dull, heavy *boom, boom, boom*. How the hell would she even get them out of the packet one-handed? But they popped out, skidding across the counter top. Anna gulped two pills down.

As she put the packet back she jogged the shelf and a brand-new prescription bag tumbled down. It was a glorious white. It was exerting a force over her. Anna had a strong presentiment that Marlene would not want her to open this bag. But Marlene was not here. Anna looked at the label. It was made out to Hebe Williamson. The prescription was for quetiapine. Anna knew this drug. She'd seen it in the files. Sammy's brother had been prescribed it. He'd experienced terrifying nightmares when he got to the UK. He thought people were following him, trying to bite him, and the drug was an anti-psychotic: it stopped hallucinations and made you sleep.

Anna was touched by a terrible suspicion. The meds were sealed. She needed to look at the pills themselves, but if she opened the packet Marlene would know she'd seen them. Climbing on to a kitchen stool, she searched the cupboard for an open packet and found one. Backed on to silver foil, on a packet marked 'quetiapine 400mg' were what were, without a shadow of a doubt, her pre-natal vitamins.

'Anna?'

Anna fumbled the packet and it fell down on to the counter.

'What are you doing?' It was Charmaine.

As Anna turned round she noticed that she couldn't feel her feet. 'It's my finger! I hurt it.' But it didn't hurt any more. Her hand was freezing cold, but it wasn't throbbing. 'I'm getting some painkillers.'

Charmaine crossed the room and looked at the packet.

'That's not painkillers, that's your sleep medicine.'

'My sleep medicine?' asked Anna.

'Yeah,' Charmaine looked sympathetic. 'Your mum told me about your trouble.'

'Did she?'

'Yeah, my brother's got the same. Well, his is depression. Oh my God!' said Charmaine, looking at Anna's hand. 'That looks bad!'

It did. Charmaine began to bandage Anna's right hand. She found a real splint and got to work attaching it to her middle finger.

Anna got out the phone Marlene had given her. She sent a text to her dad, which she hadn't done since their fight. *Hi!* But an error message came up. She looked up his number, but it wouldn't connect. It wasn't the same as when she tried to call Layla, the phone just wouldn't connect. It kept blinking back to the address book. Next she opened settings with her left hand. Her feet were blocks of ice, and the cold was creeping up her legs. Location Services were enabled, but she knew she'd turned them off. What was going on?

Charmaine touched her finger wrong and Anna flinched as feeling returned momentarily.

'Sorry!' Charmaine said, and her eyes fastened on Anna's face. 'You don't look good,' she said. 'You look pale.'

Layla! Anna went back to their last text message conversation. It was completely normal. Layla had sent her a link to a stupid meme which featured an angry American throwing something in a radio station. Maybe there'd be texts on Messenger.

As Charmaine wound the bandage round and round, Anna downloaded Facebook. She'd deleted it ages ago but when she tried to log on, she couldn't remember her Facebook password. On her old phone it had always just remembered her.

Charmaine connected the bandages with a little silver clip with jagged teeth. Anna stood up.

'You should probably stay sitting,' said Charmaine.

But Anna walked slowly into the snug. The fact that she couldn't feel her feet gave her a strange sensation, as if she were floating – just a big pregnant belly floating to her mother's laptop, which was lying abandoned on Marlene's desk. Anna tapped awkwardly with her left hand, trying the same password her mother had for her Gmail, and it worked. Her mother had both Facebook and Instagram open on her laptop. Anna didn't know what she was looking for. She clicked on Insta and called up Marlene's feed CallMeMa, a succession of sentimental but well-shot posts. But when she clicked on Facebook it was not her mother's feed. It was hers. It was her picture. Marlene was posting on her profile. There were several posts she hadn't put up, amazingly intimate updates on the pregnancy. 'Felt the baby flip today!' She found it hard to read them, or even understand what they were. She didn't understand. She just didn't understand anything. She clicked on the messages.

Layla was about ten people down the messages list: the ones at the top were all people with A and B surnames, like someone had started going through her friends list alphabetically and then given up. The messages said, *Hi! I'm leaving the big smoke and quitting Facebook so if you need to contact me, please text . . .* and a number she didn't recognise.

When she got to Layla their last message conversation came up, except it wasn't a conversation. It was one side of a conversation. Anna's side had been deleted. But Layla's was getting increasingly enraged.

Are you OK? – You don't seem well – How fucking dare you? – A slut! A slut? Nice Anna! Classy! Feminist! – You're welcome to it! – Why would you say that? – She's not good for you – Fuck you, Anna! Fuck you to hell! I hope you fucking choke! – Don't ever speak like that about my mum again! Well, you are a fucking psycho. Dermot's too good for you! – Go to a doctor! Anna's right hand was throbbing as if it was trying to tell her something.

No wonder Layla had blocked her. Marlene was fucking with her phone. Anna started to sweat. She felt clammy. Marlene was tracking her and giving her medicine without telling her. Anna knew there was a word for that, but the hole was in her head again: drugging. Marlene was drugging her. And her dad had been blocked. Who else was? Had she said anything to Dermot? To Neil? Anna's stomach turned. She was dizzy. She was four miles from the station, heavily pregnant, unable to drive, with a broken hand. Suddenly Anna looked down at her freezing feet. She was barefoot. She couldn't remember the last time she had worn shoes.

Should she call 999? What would she say? She just needed to get out. She could call a cab. Anna opened the cab app that was still on her home screen. The card it was linked to had been snapped by Marlene but that shouldn't matter. She pressed the home screen. The nearest cab was thirty-five minutes away.

Fuck it, she could walk. Where was her bag? It had been so long since she'd left the house she couldn't immediately remember where she'd left it. She went into her bedroom. It was relatively hard to get down on the floor, manoeuvring her big belly, but she did it, leaning on the heel of her purple hand and lying down on her side to peer under the bed, and there it was. Nothing else mattered. Shoes. Where were her shoes? Her red boots.

As Anna scanned 'her' bedroom, then the upstairs hallway, the shoes started to take on a heavy significance. Wasn't that a perception experiment, you tune your brain into 'red' and then suddenly, red is all you can see? Red object after red object presented itself to her: the cover of a book, the pattern in the hallway rug, a cardigan folded up and waiting on the stairs. But not her round-toed red boots. On the second landing was the red landline and Marlene's 'mother' statuette, depicting Marlene naked and beautiful, feeding one child while another played at her feet. Anna scanned the area under the pedestal it sat on for her shoes, nothing.

She decided to abandon the shoes. She just needed to get next door, where Tom's yoga wife, Sophie, would be at home. What would she say to her? It didn't matter. She would work it out when she got there.

Anna let herself out of the front door, clutching her handbag, and on to the gravel. The stones cut into her feet. Her feet had hardened over the last weeks, but her weight was much greater. With each step she winced. It was a matter of just thirty or forty steps to the neighbour's front door.

'Sophie!' she called, weakly. 'Sophie!'

Anna saw Marlene's BMW at the top of the drive.

She was coming. Anna tried desperately to speed up as she hobbled towards the neighbour's door, but Marlene's car swooshed silently in front of her, fast, so fast, cutting her off.

'Hello!' Marlene trilled. 'I'm home!' Immediately she launched into a monologue. 'God, these people! Some bloody turd – flipped him off – had to pull over – won't be making love to his wife in the near future . . .'

Marlene looked at her bag on Anna's shoulder, and down to her bandaged hand and her bare feet.

'Going somewhere?'

'I was just . . . no,' said Anna, 'not going anywhere.'

The next-door neighbour appeared at her front door.

'Hello, Sophie!' said Marlene. 'I think I might stay home today, instead.' And she lifted Anna's bag off Anna's shoulder.

'It looks like I've got a sick little girl to look after!'

It occurred to Anna, later, that she could have made greater efforts to get her phone back, after Marlene 'confiscated' it. After all, by then she knew she was in danger and the cab was just thirty-five minutes away. What would Marlene have done if she had yelled out to Sophie for help? What if she had told Charmaine, 'I don't need sleeping tablets.' What if she had told Sophie, 'I want to leave.' What would Marlene have done? Anna didn't know. Anna didn't know, and that was the spell Marlene cast. Anna did not know from which direction she might hear the beating of wings, from which direction she might feel claws upon her neck. Why had she not shouted? Why had she not run? Yes, she was afraid of her. But something more powerful than fear kept her in thrall. She still wanted her mother to love her.

That night Marlene demanded Anna wash her hair.

'You look like a servant!' she said. 'Not my daughter!'

As a rule, Anna carefully detangled her hair every three days, washing it and then combing through conditioner while the hair was still wet. It was a war of attrition against her hair's natural tendency to turn into a bird's nest. Even trying to brush it dry was a recipe for disaster, creating matted locks. But she'd been busy, and the constant naps had left her hair starting to tangle. But with her finger in a splint, it would be tricky to comb it out.

'I don't think I can do that . . . with my hand,' Anna said carefully.

'Don't worry!' Marlene piped. 'I'll help you.'

'I need to do it in the bath.'

'Yes?' Anna realised Marlene intended to watch her. Marlene's eyes were shining. Anna had never noticed how much yellow surrounded the iris. When they fastened on her, Anna froze.

'I'm just . . . shy.'

'Don't be ridiculous!' Marlene said. 'I'm your mother!'

Marlene ran a bath. Anna took her clothes off with her left hand. She wrapped a towel around herself, but with the pregnant belly, it hardly covered her. Her hair, which hung down to her thighs, provided a natural veil. Marlene had laid out new nightclothes on the bed.

'Is that a nightdress?' Anna asked.

'It's a onesie!' Marlene was pleased with herself. 'They're very glamorous now!'

Anna went into the bathroom and Marlene let her get into the bath, following her every movement.

After Anna had shampooed her hair and rinsed it Marlene began trying to comb it. She combed from the top, and the hair got even more tangled.

Anna kept her voice gentle, 'Do you want me to try?'

'I *think* I know how to brush my own child's hair!' Marlene was on a knife edge.

'It's my fault,' Anna said quickly. 'I've got this crazy curly hair. You have to comb it from the ends. Or I could do it?'

'I'll do it!' shot back Marlene. 'I'll do it!'

'If you put conditioner on it, it makes it easier,' Anna suggested tentatively.

'Oh all right!' Marlene squeezed out a tiny gob of white conditioner on to her palm.

'I think you might need a bit more,' Anna said. Marlene irritably squeezed half a tub on to her hair and started trying to tease out the snarls.

'I'm getting the hang of it now!' said Marlene, slapping the conditioner around. As she combed out Anna's hair, she began to sing in a Mockney accent.

'A father come home to his baby one night . . .'

Anna recognised the tune. It was the song Marlene had sung in the cafe when they first met. At first, Anna wasn't really listening to the words; the combing was quite painful and she was trying not to make it worse. It was a story song, something about a dad who demanded his wife bath their youngest child – 'so small and so black' – in public. When Marlene sang 'That don't look like dirt that will ever wash off!' Anna snapped to attention. What the hell was this song?

'Ma started to scrub, but to her great surprise
The baby turned white right in front of her eyes'

So the mother was expecting the baby to be black? Anna was open-mouthed. But it got worse . . .

'She held the babe high, she sang Rub-a-dub-dub
But it slipped from her hands and fell into the tub . . .'

Marlene combed as she sang. She was now really hurting Anna. Almost every time the comb touched her hair it pulled out a hair or two, and much as she tried, Anna couldn't help flinching. But Marlene ignored it. Her voice soared.

'She searched 'neath the water, she moaned and she cried
"Oh! Please Save My Baby!" The neighbours replied,
"You really must be at the end of your rope
We didn't see no babe – just a bit of old soap."'

Marlene tugged on the comb, hard.

"There wasn't no baby! Mud sticks and mud stuck
What you've been loving weren't nothing but muck.
Now that you've washed it there ain't nothing there
But a dirty old tub, full of mud, dust and hair."'

'Jesus Christ!' Anna said.
'What?' said Marlene, 'It's a lovely song!'
'Isn't it about . . .'
'What?' said Marlene. Anna took a breath.

'About drowning a baby because the mother thought it might be black?'

Marlene sat back on her heels. 'How on *earth* can you think that? It's about finding out the baby was a ball of dirt. It's comical! Why do your generation see ugliness everywhere?' And she set about her combing again, furiously.

Anna was freezing cold. She tried hard not to shiver as she kept her right hand, with its splint, out of the water. Marlene's lips were set.

'I'm sorry,' Anna said. 'I didn't mean to stop you singing.' Marlene was silent.

'Please,' Anna said. 'Sing me something.'

Very slowly, in a much lower register, Marlene began to sing the chorus from Tara's song. 'We should have known you were never earthbound . . .'

Anna couldn't help herself, 'How do you know that?'

'I know all sorts of things,' replied Marlene dangerously. 'Don't look so surprised. It's my song.'

Anna was confused. 'It's Tara's song.'

'Who is Tara?' asked Marlene.

'She's Dermot's friend. He wrote it for her when she died.'

'Well, it's my song now!' said Marlene. 'I paid for it!'

'What?'

'I paid for it.' Marlene pulled a large hank of curls through the comb. 'I bought it, and now it belongs to me.'

'Dermot sold that song for an airline ad.'

'An airline. Silly girl! I'm the airline!' Marlene pointed at herself wildly. 'I was happy to do it. After that publican overreacted to a simple enquiry! I simply asked if he was *quite* sure Dermot's behaviour was above reproach. Had he *checked*?' Marlene squeezed out another gob of conditioner and slathered it on Anna's hair, sighing, 'This is a lot of work, isn't it?'

Anna realised how stupid she had been. Had Marlene got Dermot arrested? Did Dermot know it was Marlene's money? Had he lied to her? She tried to dip her head under the water.

'No!' said Marlene. 'I'll do it!'

Marlene pulled the comb again and it got stuck. 'Oh, for God's sake!' she snapped. And pulled harder.

'Ow!' Anna let out involuntarily.

'It's completely stuck!' said Marlene. 'I can't get it out!'

'Don't worry!' Anna protested, her panic rising. 'I'll do it!'

Marlene kept hold of the comb with her right hand and, with her left, reached across to a cabinet above the bath, where she grabbed a pair of scissors.

'No!' yelled Anna, as Marlene cut off the offending hank of hair right at the scalp. It made a noise like someone preparing to spit.

'There!'

The hair came away. It was about three foot long. Anna watched it float away from her head, as Marlene held it at arm's length, as if it were trash, and then dropped it on the bathroom floor. Marlene was a little breathless.

'Well, it's done now! We'll have to take the lot off!'

She was waving the scissors close to Anna's face.

'Snip, Snip!'

Anna followed Marlene's scissors with her eyes as she began to hack off Anna's hair at the root, dropping each wet ringlet on the pile on the floor.

'Tristan!' she yelled, excited. 'We're cutting Anna's hair! Bring me the clippers!'

Tristan left the clippers at the door, carefully averting his eyes from Anna's pregnant nakedness, and that moment of discretion was worth everything to Anna. She tried as hard as she could to hold the image of Tristan looking away in her mind as the clippers buzzed, and the lengths of hair fell away.

'You know they did this to the collaborators after the war?' Marlene sounded dreamy.

'Did they?'

'Yes, to punish them for sleeping with the enemy. So unfair!'

'Keep it neutral,' thought Anna, 'don't make her angry.' 'Do you think?'

'Of course! But the really clever ones, they shaved their own heads, before anybody could humiliate them. And they stuck their hair into a hat, and then, when the mob came to get them, they just whipped off the hat,' Marlene whisked away a handful of hair, 'and revealed themselves, head held high! Because, after all, we are all collaborators, aren't we? We are all guilty of sleeping with the enemy.'

'Just keep asking questions,' thought Anna. 'Are we?' she said. 'Who is the enemy?'

'Men,' said Marlene.

Anna stepped out of the bath, shorn. She no longer tried to hide her nakedness. She was so much more naked than she'd ever been before. Marlene had taken away the clothes she'd taken off, so she had to put on the onesie. As she did so she noticed Marlene scooping up all the scissors into one of the bathroom baskets and taking them away. 'I could leave now,' Anna thought, and she tried to command her unwilling body. 'Just walk out of the door.'

Marlene returned.

'Come on then!' she said, leading her by the hand to the bed, and tucking the covers in around her like she was four years old. 'I think it should be bed rest from now on.' Marlene inclined her head to the side. 'We don't want to hurt the baby, do we?'

Anna saw that the bedroom lock was now missing its key. It must be on the other side of the door.

Marlene did not bring her food that night. Anna went to sleep hungry. But she was woken at about three a.m. by Marlene switching on her bedside lamp, carrying a 'supper tray'. Anna instantly, despite her grogginess, recognised this technique from her case histories. The intention was to create a time distortion, to make Anna confused as to which way was up, and to make her grateful to her captor. Sometimes there would be food, sometimes not. A rat that is rewarded intermittently will keep pressing the button until they die. She understood all this intellectually, but she was both hungry and tired.

'What is it?' said Anna.

'Bacon sandwich!' sparkled Marlene.

Anna fought off the fog of sleep. Did Marlene know where her distaste for meat came from? Anna had never eaten pork. At school she claimed to be 'allergic', in case anyone connected this peculiarity to Jewishness. The no-pork rule had extended, as she grew older, into vegetarianism, a vegetarianism that had lasted twelve years, until her 'stay' here. So far, however, the food Marlene had provided for her had included chicken and fish but not pork.

'Eat it!' said Marlene. 'It's not good for the baby to be vegetarian. It's very selfish of you.'

Anna was so hungry. And she was sure that this could be the only food for quite some time. She looked at the bacon sandwich. There was a spoonful of apple puree on the plate, and next to it, a weird burnt nodule.

'It's all organic,' said Marlene. 'Tristan gets it for me.' She pointed at Anna's belly. 'Bacon in the drawer!' she said.

'What?' Anna asked.

'Isn't it marvellous! It's a French idiom: "*un lardon dans la tiroir*"! Means pregnant!' She swiped the nodule and dipped it in the apple sauce, crunching it between her perfect teeth. 'Malignancy!' she said. 'Best bit!' Anna did not throw up. But she could not eat it: not now. 'I'll leave it with you,' said Marlene. 'I want that gone when I get back.'

In the lamplight, Anna considered all the places she could hide the bacon. If she threw it out of the window Marlene would find it. Could she burn it? She'd smell it. Would it flush down the toilet?

Anna heard a scuffling at the bottom of her door, and the key turning in the lock. It was too soon, surely, for Marlene to return. But it was Tristan.

'Give it to me!' he said urgently, taking the sandwich from her. He was holding the jar of apple puree. He shoved it at Anna and stuffed the bacon sandwich into his face, chewing rapidly, the bread clearly clagging up his mouth.

'Tristan!' Marlene called, and Tristan put his finger to his lips and locked Anna in again.

Anna ate the jar of apple puree with the fingers of her left hand. 'She's turning me into a baby,' she thought. 'She wants me to be a baby.' The onesie was a babygro. She had as much hair as a day-old child. Even her ears were still covered with the fuzz from her head, like a new-born. Her hair! She had no hair. She was shorn, shaved.

A baby, was that what she was? Was that what Marlene had intended, if, indeed, she had intended anything? Maybe she had no intentions. Anna was beginning to understand that while Marlene clearly planned some things, it wasn't exactly clear to her why. Had Anna asked her, 'Did you begin this evening meaning to denude me of my hair, because this long hair of mine had become a symbol of all the years you missed, yet another recrimination, yet another piece of evidence that you are, in fact, a terrible mother?' Marlene would have been shocked, would have thought that only someone sick could even have considered such a possibility. If she had said, 'You have tried to turn me into the baby who was taken from you, Marlene,' Marlene would have laughed that self-conscious laugh of hers. Marlene really didn't have a clue what she was doing.

Well, Anna had had the conversation with herself many times: maybe I should cut a fringe, maybe I should dye it, and now, the decision was made for her. Despite the late hour Anna felt like she was waking up. Marlene had shaved her head very, very close. She had not eaten the bacon. She noticed how thin she now was. Her belly had grown while the rest of her had shrunk. In the bathroom light Anna looked at herself. Her jaw and cheekbones jutted out from the rest of her face and her head had patches of hair and patches of baldness. She reminded herself of something. Now that she had seen it, she couldn't unsee it. Had Marlene done this on purpose? No, Anna thought, this was entirely an accident. She wanted a baby and instead she got . . . Anna laughed. Anna saw someone looking back at her in the mirror. She saw what she used to be a long time ago, when she'd had a real mother, a mother who'd taken care of her. A mother who'd told her she was strong and good, and that although she had no family, she had the biggest family in the world. She did not see a baby. She remembered the twins' mother, who had taught her to bake, 'You aren't a Jew, are you?' Anna wished from her very depths that she'd said, 'yes'. And it occurred to her now that perhaps the next time Marlene tried to hurt her, she could resist. She could resist.

13

THIRTY-EIGHT WEEKS GONE

'Most women go into labour between thirty-eight and forty-two weeks of pregnancy. Your midwife or doctor should give you information about what to expect if your baby is overdue.'

Anna's life was now restricted to the four walls of the room, and the little bathroom which led off it. At least her head was clear, though the drug withdrawal had been intense.

Anna's main worry was that the baby would be born addicted to the quetiapine – or be hurt by it. Even though she knew people usually came off anti-psychotic medication slowly, she just stopped dead. She pretended to take it and her mother didn't check. 'Too bloody lazy,' Anna thought. Rebellious thoughts returned as the drug slowly left her system, along with anxiety. Suddenly she was worrying about everything. 'Quite right,' she thought. For too long she'd not had any worries. She had not been awake in any sense of the word. But now, strange electrical pulses ran through her. She fidgeted constantly – the restlessness of her legs, which had been growing throughout the pregnancy, went into overdrive.

Anna paced the thick green carpet in her bare feet. Although she'd asked for them, no shoes had been forthcoming. 'What do you need shoes for?' Marlene had replied.

Marlene had emptied her room of sharp objects, and she wasn't allowed a laptop to watch TV on, since she could also use it to contact the outside world. But Marlene had arrived with something in a pillowcase.

'I've got a present for you!' she said, delighted with herself. She took out scraps of material.

'What are they?' Anna asked.

Marlene's face was animated. 'They're patches! To sew into a quilt.'

'For the baby?' Anna asked.

'I suppose so,' Marlene agreed irritably. 'Or whoever you'd like to give it to. Look! You can spell out "Mother". Don't you think it's darling? The time will fly by!' she said. Each little patch of fabric had a zig-zagged edge, like it had been cut with serrated scissors.

There were also lots of children's books, and these proved Anna's salvation. She could read and re-read the children's classics, many of which were about children orphaned and alone. It was necessary, she told herself, that she did not go mad over the next few weeks, for the sake of the baby. In between her reading she examined the room.

Marlene kept the key to the massive door. Anna was fairly sure the wall in the tiny bathroom was just two by four and plasterboard construction. If she could find a way to smash it down, she might be able to get through to the next bedroom along, but she didn't see how she could do it in time. The first crash would give the game away. That left the windows. They were sash, a modern make but in the

Victorian style. The room itself was in the older part of the house. The fireplace appeared to be, perhaps, Elizabethan? Anna didn't know. The windows were now triple-glazed, with little brass 'locks' made of sunken stoppers so the windows could open, but not wide enough to let a burglar in – or, crucially, an eight-month pregnant woman out. The stoppers had a 'key' shaped like a hexagon, an Allen key would have opened them in an instant, but Marlene was not exactly likely to give her one. If she smashed the window she would be heard. Below the window was a brick wall, and a drop: too far to jump on to a little portico which covered the French windows of the drawing room below. From the portico it was only about seven feet to the ground.

Anna began by working on the quilt. Her right hand was still painful, but by swapping the splint from her middle to her baby finger she was able to grasp the needle. She put together the 'M', then the 'O' and the 'T', getting it wrong twice and laboriously unpicking the seams. By the time she'd completed the word she hated the charming, flowered cotton. She showed it to Marlene one morning when she'd brought her breakfast, and then asked for what she wanted.

'I thought I might do some sketching,' she said, 'perhaps I might have a pencil? And a sharpener?'

Marlene nearly clapped her hands. The use of the word 'sketching' had been judicious. 'Oh yes!' she said. 'Are you good? Of course you are! All my children sketch!'

As it happened, Anna was good at drawing, or had been at school. Marlene brought her the pencil, and the paper, but no sharpener, and Anna was obliged to produce a good likeness of Marlene herself before she relented.

'I thought you might have been trying to pull a fast one!' Marlene confided, as she handed over the little plastic sharpener.

'Really?' Anna asked. 'What could I possibly do with this?'

Marlene had been expecting something much more downmarket and was pleasantly surprised.

'It's so kind of your daughter to give you her hair!' The woman seemed sincere, as she settled Marlene in front of the mirror.

'I know!' Marlene welled up a little. 'I'm sorry! She's a very special girl!'

'Don't apologise! I always say if you can't cry here where can you cry?' She had Essex vowels.

The mirror was surrounded by light bulbs, as if in a star's dressing room, and the light they cast was golden rose, which showed up her eyes to advantage. The woman, though, was not exactly what Marlene had been hoping for. Marlene could see nicotine stains between her fingers and around her front teeth, although she only smelt of toothpaste, thank God. Her foundation was chalky and drew attention to the light orange fur sprouting from her jaw. Her own 'hair' though, was wonderful, thick copper and cut straight to the shoulder. The woman caught her looking at it.

'This is one of mine.'

'Is it?' Marlene spoke clearly to show her how to speak. 'I did wonder! It suits you.' It didn't, but everyone benefits from a little butter.

'Now! Let's see what looks best on you.' The woman started pulling down wigs and fussing about, flashing her yellow rabbit teeth, trying to make her own suggestions. Sometimes it's best to give in to the process.

'All right!' Marlene leaned back. 'Pamper me!'

'We all need some of that, don't we?' The woman cocked her head to one side. She gestured to Marlene's own silver blonde do, 'Can I take it off?'

'Of course!'

Marlene closed her eyes as the wig woman removed the pale crop and revealed Marlene's close-shaven scalp.

'Have you had a go at this yourself?' She sounded critical.

'I confess I have!' Marlene looked coyly up at her. 'I won't wink,' she thought.

'When did you get diagnosed, if you don't mind me asking?'

Marlene did mind. After all, what if she had had cancer? Would she want to discuss it with all and sundry? 'Seven months,' she replied shortly.

'The chemo can really take it out of you.'

'Yes,' Marlene allowed. 'It certainly can.'

'I had cancer myself. That's why I decided to . . .' God, the woman couldn't stop talking about herself. Just once, Marlene would like to meet a woman who could keep her mouth shut. Now she was alluding to famous people who'd been in front of the mirror, a certain daytime TV host who came every six months. It was hardly discrete to be dropping such bald hints. Marlene snorted at her own silent pun. But the woman was giving her the look – like she was a child who'd just wet herself.

'You know, they say a woman is only truly beautiful if she's beautiful bald!' Marlene shared grandly.

'I haven't heard that,' the wig lady joined in. 'I know most of my ladies, and men of course, don't feel beautiful unless they've got hair.'

'I don't have that problem!' Marlene rejoined. 'I think I'm gorgeous!'

'Quite right too!' the woman placated her, settling a red bob on her scalp. Marlene was surprised how deft she was and rested her head for a moment in her hands, but she was afraid the woman would break her neck, so she leaned forward again.

'Now this is quite chic!' As the wig woman lowered her head to get the measure of the wig, her eye bags sprung out – two purple shadows like she'd been punched twice. It was awful.

'But that's nothing like the colour!'

'Oh, we can dye the hair any colour. And cut it any length.'

'But I want it as it is!' Marlene protested. 'There's not much point in my daughter giving me her hair if I don't keep it as it is.'

Marlene picked up handfuls of Anna's hair and held it against her head, lowering her chin, and batting her eyelashes. It looked very fitting. But this woman was being slow.

'You mean you want the hair natural?'

'Yes!'

'You can't want it that long, surely!'

'Yes,' Marlene insisted. 'I want it just as it is! Can. You. Do. That?' she asked, as if speaking to a mentally deficient teenager.

'I don't see why not!' The woman was now concentrating on gathering up all the strands, trying not to lose any. 'Your daughter didn't mind going without it?'

'Oh no!' Marlene replied airily. 'She's gay! I think it was liberating for her to cut it off! She said to me, "Ma!" – everyone calls me Ma – "Ma!" she said, "I'm gay!" So of course I said, "I'll love you whatever you are, and I'm happy to accept this beautiful hair, as a symbol of your love for me!"'

'What a nice story!'

'Isn't it?' Marlene smiled.

Anna dismantled the cheap plastic sharpener and released its tiny blade. The only way was to hide in plain sight.

She carved the end of the pencil, creating a tiny hexagon. It took her a while to get the space right to fit the tiny lock, but she got it. As she inserted it into the brass stopper and turned it gently the pencil groaned, and for a second she thought the wood would split. But it eased, the stopper unscrewed and came away in her hand. She could open the window. Now she just had to decide when to go.

She was pretty sure Marlene had gone out. It had been quiet for a while.

Anna pushed up the sash as high as it would go. She threw the spare blanket from the bottom of the wardrobe down on to the shelf of the portico. It was by no means directly underneath the window, but to the right at least four feet.

She got her bag, packed with her useless wallet, which Marlene had left her (though she'd taken her keys), and chucked it out on to the brick shelf. Even had she not been pregnant, the drop would have seemed impossible. She couldn't lean on her stomach as she usually would, so she sat precariously on the windowsill. She jammed her left, unbroken hand behind her and her right was tucked round the edge of the frame.

Anna half fell off the window, swinging round and lurching to the right. The baby squashed against the wall but not too hard, and her toes, unexpectedly, found some tiny purchase on the brick. For a microsecond she hung on the wall like a big pregnant crab, and then she fell on to the blanket at the edge of the brick portico. Would it hold? Under her weight, the old pointing crumbled and Anna, along with a lump of bricks, the blanket and the bag, fell the seven feet or so to the ground. Her ankle turned and she felt a stabbing pain in her foot. Yelling out in pain she looked up, through the French windows and straight into the eyes of Tristan.

'Anna!' She could hear him clearly through the old glass. 'No! Anna!'

Tristan went directly to the door to open it as Anna staggered to her feet, but stopped at the handle, rattling it from the inside. 'He'll go to the next window to get out,' thought Anna, so, out of instinct, she loped off in the other direction, towards the side of the neighbours' house. If she could just get within sight of their back windows . . . Surely they wouldn't ignore a pregnant woman in a babygro with a shaved head? But as she reached the boundary between the two houses, she saw a thick hedgerow that met with a jutting garden wall. She heard Tristan behind her and knew she'd never outrun him. Anna changed direction and began to pelt straight towards Tristan. It worked. Tristan seemed amazed. Rooted to the spot. Anna stopped too, and they looked at each other. They were in a 'wildflower meadow' next to the lawn. Anna could see across the lawn, up a bank to the drive. Tristan had stopped a few metres away from her next to an iron stake, sunk into the ground, which presumably had been used for livestock back in the day. A loop of nylon rope was threaded in the eye of the stake at the top, trailing out across the long grass. Tristan kept his eyes on Anna as he picked up the rope on the ground. Anna started moving again, veering around him, as if she were the goat or whatever poor animal would've been tied up here. She kept her distance, her eyes fastened on him as she swung closer to the lawn, and the drive, and freedom.

'Please, Anna!' Tristan pleaded. 'Please! She'll kill me!'

Anna paused. She turned her head towards the driveway. Marlene's BMW was missing, but the neighbours' Toyota SUV was sitting there. She might get there.

The rope landed around her neck.

'I'm sorry!' Tristan was sobbing. 'I'm so sorry.' Anna reflexively put her hands up to push the rope off her neck and flip it off her head, but Tristan pulled the rope at the same time and the noose tightened around her hands, bashing her broken right hand against her left. It hurt like hell.

'Don't do this, Tristan,' she said.

'I have to,' he said.

Dermot was banging on the door. It was ten at night. Marlene opened it to find him swaying on the doorstep, the porch providing some protection from the driving rain, looking like a particularly large Weeble.

'Is she here?' Dermot said.

'Is who here?' Marlene feigned ignorance.

'Anna!' For a moment it looked like Dermot was just going to come in, but some force held him back.

'Beth's not here,' Marlene corrected him.

Dermot looked absolutely crestfallen. The Prius on the drive double-flashed its headlights.

'Well, I suppose I'll go then.'

'Oh, for crying out loud,' Marlene took pity on him. 'Come in!'

'Really?' Dermot searched Marlene's face. 'Have you got any money for the cab?'

'Just wait there!' Marlene went to her coat in the hall to get her wallet.

'Here,' she said, pressing a couple of twenties on him. Dermot trooped back in, trailing water over the waxed floor, ducking under the door lintel.

'Let's get you out of those wet clothes!' she said. 'Now, have you eaten?'

'Oh, my goodness what an appetite! No wonder Beth has to work so hard. You'll be eating her out of house and home! Whisky?' Marlene flashed a full bottle of Glenfiddich.

'I'm trying not to . . .'

'Nonsense! You can't turn down a single malt. You'll stay here tonight.'

'I don't want to put you to trouble.'

'No trouble,' said Marlene, 'no trouble at all!'

Dermot put his plate on the hearthstone as Marlene poured him a few fingers of whisky.

'I'm actually not great with spirits,' he excused himself.

'My house, my rules!' Marlene handed him the nearly full glass. 'What's going on?'

Dermot's head hung limply, and he wiped the hair out of his eyes. 'She won't reply to my texts.'

Marlene cursed herself for missing them. 'Have you had a tiff?'

'I don't know! I don't know if I've upset her! I haven't been in touch as much, with my mam.'

'Of course! How is your mother?'

'She died.' Dermot's eyes filled. 'She died.' He was sobbing deeply. 'I just . . . I wanted her to see the baby. But she didn't.' He slid off the sofa and curled up on the floor, pulling up his knees.

Marlene pulled an embroidered scarf which lay along the back of the sofa as decoration over Dermot, and let him cry, patting his shoulder as he rocked.

'You cry,' she said, 'you've lost your mummy, haven't you? There, there! You can tell me about her, if you like.'

Two hours later Marlene dumped the bottle in the recycling. It might be hard to move him after all that booze, but Dermot responded to instructions like a little lamb, climbing the stairs and getting into the day bed in the study on the mezzanine. That augured well. Marlene could hear Beth still slapping on the door with something, but she'd stopped crashing around.

Marlene surveyed herself in the full-length mirror on her mahogany wardrobe. She was wearing Anna's oversized T-shirt, which she hadn't washed, and the wig was just wonderful. In the moonlight from the sash to her left all she could see was the huge hair and her bare legs, which, while they weren't Beth's legs, were very good. The plan had only come to her when he'd come to the door. He'd looked so vulnerable and attractive. This would show Beth he wasn't worth her. She was saving her little girl from a gold-digger – a gold-digger and a cheat. And it would be nice to be full. Maybe he'd fall in love with her? A lot of people did. That might be complicated. She'd have to let him down gently. Tell him she'd love to be with him, but she was too good a mother; she couldn't do that to Beth. She was about to turn away from the mirror when she caught a glimpse of her pubic hair, from under the edge of the T-shirt. That would be a giveaway. All the young people shaved their genitals these days, didn't they? If he felt pubic hair, would that alert him to something wrong? She had seen Beth's vagina in the bath, and it hadn't been bald, but when had she baby-proofed Beth's room? Perhaps, if she had the means, Beth would ordinarily de-fuzz. She would have to guess. Marlene went into her en suite and sat in the bath, shaving her privates with a slightly blunt razor. Usually, she didn't even shave her legs so she found the whole thing hard work. She started to resent Dermot. Really, men demanded such ridiculous things of one these days. She hoped he was worth it.

Marlene crept into the study. Dermot was lying on his back on top of the covers, fully clothed. It would be easy. But she hadn't counted on Dermot's boots. He was wearing huge, high-topped leather boots and it took a massive amount of force to try to get them off. But, to her surprise, Dermot did not wake up. Forget the boots, she thought. She pulled down Dermot's jeans and boxers. Then she let Beth's hair drag across his thighs for a couple of minutes, and when he shifted slightly towards her, she climbed on top of him. Her newly bald vulva felt especially naked. But as it contacted Dermot's upper thighs, he shoved her away hard.

'No,' he uttered gruffly. He didn't wake up. He just pushed her off. Marlene was startled by the speed and violence of his response. She tried again, and once again he shoved her away. Marlene was starting to get angry. She put both hands on his right arm to hold it down and put her face on his penis. Dermot's hand whacked her in the head and into the iron bedstead. All her excitement disappeared. Poor Beth, if this was what he was like! She had done the right thing to find this out. They had a terrible sex life. He was basically a wife-beater! It was all right. She had another idea.

Dermot woke from some terrible dreams. He'd been in that horror story about the guy banging on the roof of your car. Someone had been banging on the roof of the Prius he had been in last night. A Prius! Why had he been in a Prius? Slowly the information filtered into Dermot's brain that he had come down to find Anna at her mum's house. He was covered in a duvet. And on top of that some sort of patchwork quilt. His mouth felt revolting. And there was someone in bed with him.

'Good morning!' Marlene looked up at him with loving eyes. Dermot froze. 'Did you sleep well?' Dermot realised first that he was naked from the waist down, except for his boots, and then that the weird feeling he had like a wet sink scrubber pressed against his leg was his girlfriend's mother's prickly vagina.

'No,' Dermot said. Marlene had a black eye. 'What happened to your eye?'

'You got a little bit cross with me.' Marlene saw the horror on Dermot's face. 'Don't worry! I enjoyed it!'

Despite Dermot's hangover he managed to move fast. As he lurched out of bed, steadying himself on anything within reach, he knocked over a fiddly little chest of drawers next to it.

'Sorry!' he shouted. 'Fuck!' He pulled on his jeans and ran down the stairs three at a time.

'Well, at least stay for breakfast!' Marlene said, trailing Dermot to the front door, in her T-shirt.

'Would you put some trousers on?' yelled Dermot, his eyes darting about the front hall, looking for his coat and rucksack.

There was a distinct crash from upstairs.

'What the fuck was that?'

'It's the birds in the chimneys!' Marlene said. 'They knock the bricks out!'

Dermot opened one of three cupboard doors.

'Do you know where she went?'

'Do you not remember talking about this last night? Before we made love?'

'What?' Dermot exploded.

'Before we made love!' Marlene repeated.

'I don't believe you!'

'What don't you believe?' Marlene raised an eyebrow.

'I don't believe that I fucked you!'

Marlene appeared shocked. She drew herself up proudly in her short T-shirt, revealing her crotch. Dermot flinched and covered his eyes.

'Why not?'

Dermot leaned forward and raised his voice, shouting into her face, 'Because I'm not into mad old bitches!'

Marlene's mouth screwed up further. She gestured down her excellent body.

'This is what your precious Beth will look like in twenty years!'

Dermot furiously pulled on his bomber. 'She's called Anna! ANNA! And no, it fucking isn't! What kind of mother would try to fuck her kid's fiancé?'

'A good mother! A wonderful mother!'

'You're fucking deluded! Do you know that? You are completely insane!'

'I'll tell Anna you hit me! You used me and you hit me!'

'So, you know where she is?'

Marlene suddenly looked cunning. 'If you want to know where she is, I suggest you ask your friend Neil.'

Anna found it hard to open her eyes. Tristan had given her three or four of the 'vitamins', saying, 'it will help with the pain' and it had. If she kept her ankle still it didn't hurt. It wasn't as bad as it could have been. She thought she'd knocked over the wardrobe but it was standing up now. She'd been asleep for . . . how long? She reached automatically for her phone before she remembered it had been confiscated. Not confiscated: stolen. Taken! It had been taken. Anna thought with sudden longing of her old phone with its cracked screen and plastic case and no one spying on it. The rope around her wrists had been replaced by a pair of weird cuffs and a chain. The chain looked like part of some piece of agricultural machinery and led to the fireplace, the iron ring sunk into the stone on the left-hand side. The same ring that Neil had flicked at with his feet. She needed to think, but she soon drifted under again.

When she woke up Tristan was sitting by the fire, and it was lit.

'Are you meant to be here?' she asked. 'Does Marlene know you are here?'

'She knows.' Tristan was shaking.

'Are you sick?' Anna asked.

'No,' said Tristan. 'Do you think you might have the baby soon?' There was something in his voice that made Anna sit up.

'I'm not due for . . .' She realised she didn't know how long – a couple of weeks at least.

'She said we can't wait,' Tristan was twisting his phone in his hands, 'we can't wait.' Anna didn't understand.

'She'll come when she comes,' she said.

'She wants me to make it come.' Tristan's mouth was a lopsided triangle. Anna could feel something thudding towards her. All she knew was that something was very, very wrong. 'She says the old-fashioned way.' And the realisation clicked into place. She'd seen enough sitcoms.

'You don't have to do that, Tristan.'

Tristan was twisting and twisting, 'I don't want to!'

'You don't have to,' Anna insisted.

'But she wants me to do it. Otherwise . . .'

'Otherwise, what?'

'Otherwise she wants to do,' Tristan lowered his voice and came to perch on Anna's bed, 'a "Sea".'

'A "Sea"? What's a "Sea"?' Anna's brain felt rusty, clogged.

'A Caesarean!' Tristan exclaimed.

Once again, Anna couldn't understand. 'I'm not booked. I'll go home when it gets closer.'

'No,' said Tristan.

'I'm going home,' Anna began.

'No.'

It sounded like a final no. The air had thickened as Anna got her drugged brain around what Tristan was saying.

'I don't want to do a Caesarean,' Tristan cried. 'I'm not very good.' Anna could feel sleep clawing at her. If only she could think clearly. 'She's your mother,' Tristan was saying. 'Why don't you ask her? Ask if I don't have to do the operation.'

'Have you done them before?'

'Yes, on the animals,' Tristan shrugged.

'The animals?' she said.

'We have to do the other,' said Tristan, and he came to stand by Anna's bed. He was standing very close to her, with a look of abject terror on his face.

'You know, Tristan, that if you have sex with me that will be rape, because I don't want you to. I don't give you my consent.'

'But if I don't . . .' Tears were falling now, his face screwing up and unscrewing as he tried to make the decision. He turned his phone around and around in his hands. 'She'll make me! She'll make me do it!' He began to mutter in French but Anna couldn't follow it. She dredged her brain for her GCSE French.

'Tristan! Look at me! *Regardez-moi!*' Anna grasped his two hands in hers. 'Tristan! You don't have to do either! OK?' Tristan was still chewing his lip. 'Go and wash your face!' said Anna, in a voice like Marlene's. Tristan looked up, surprised by the instruction. He had never heard that tone come out of Anna's mouth before, and neither had Anna. Her voice betrayed total confidence in her own decision-making. It was a mother's voice, her mother's voice. 'You look a sight!' she said. 'Go and wash your face!'

Tristan turned on his heel and went into the bathroom.

Anna fumbled the phone. It was still alive. Unlocked. It was only three seconds since it left Tristan's little paws. She must not drop it. Her hands were sweating, but she pressed the messages button before it went dark. Any second now he'd come back in. Texts. Texts are silent. She switched the button on the side on to silent mode. She pressed the little pen. What should she say? Suddenly her mind was blank.

Tristan was running the water. Dermot's number! It was the only one she remembered. Was he in Ireland? With trembling thumbs she tapped in his digits. The water stopped. Anna texted, *It's Anna police SOS I'm at Ma's* and pressed send.

She put the phone on the floor next to the bed and skidded it across to the doorway as Tristan came in from the bathroom. He was much calmer.

'I'll tell her you don't want to have the sex,' he said. As he walked out of the door he saw his phone on the floor and stopped to scoop it up.

'That was nearly bad!' he said, waving the phone at her.

Marlene came in ten minutes later. Her voice was gentle.

'What's all this about not wanting to have the baby?'

'I want to have the baby! I just don't want to have sex with your boyfriend.'

'He's very nice. I wouldn't want you to have sex with anyone nasty. He's a sweetheart.' Marlene put her head on one side and stroked Anna's shaved and bumpy scalp.

'But do you understand . . .' Anna's voice was rising against her will. 'Do you understand that I don't want to have sex with him? So that would be assault.'

Marlene tutted, 'I'm not going to make him assault you. Assault! You girls are so silly about all this! We just had sex when we were asked. We didn't make all this fuss. And we're fine! You don't have to have sex with him if you're going to make me feel bad about it!'

'If I make you feel bad about it?'

'But you're very silly. Why don't you just leave?'

'What are you talking about? I can't leave. You've tied me up.'

'No! I mean when he's inside you. Just go away, in your head! That's what I do!' Marlene said.

'What do you mean?'

'If you are having sex and you don't want to . . .'

'You mean if you are being raped . . .'

'That! Well, just go away in your head.' Marlene snapped her fingers. 'Like that! I was lucky. The very first time for me was like that, so I've had that ability ever since.'

'I'm sorry . . .' The first crossbeams of understanding fell into place in Anna's brain, shaky foundations for the weird gingerbread house of Marlene's reasoning.

'Do you mean that the first time you had sex you were raped?'

'Yes!' Marlene looked delighted that, finally, Anna had understood.

'I'm so sorry that happened to you.'

'Don't be!' Marlene smiled brightly. 'He went in – I went out! I've been able to do it ever since.' She continued to beam at Anna.

Anna wondered whether to say it. Many torture survivors described something similar . . .

'Psychiatrists call that dissociation.'

'Psychiatrists! Trust them to have a silly word for it!' Marlene snorted. 'I call it flying. It's a gift. I'm not tethered like so many women. Tethered to their children. Their homes. The rules. I've found it very useful in my life, because I can have sex with the most horrible men and not feel a thing! And of course, I can fly anywhere, anywhere at all.' Marlene leaned in confidentially.

The hairs on Anna's arms rose up. They shone golden in the firelight, each one a little soldier ready to defend her: useless, useless soldiers.

'I flew all over! I watched you, growing up. And I watched you make that little baby.' She prodded Anna's stomach playfully. 'Wouldn't you like to fly too?'

The next morning Marlene brought in a rubber sheet for Beth. If that's what she wanted that's what she wanted.

'Oops-a-daisy! Up you get!' she said. She knew she'd been right to keep it. You couldn't get them any more.

They just had those fiddly little soft things that would let anything through. This was the real thing.

Tristan was dragging his feet as usual. And when he did turn up, he'd wrapped all his stuff in the wrong towel.

'I'm not ruining the good towels!' said Marlene. 'Get a beach towel!'

She sat down on the bed, on top of Beth's legs.

'Now, I know you don't want to, darling, but we're going to do the operation.'

Beth was being silly. 'What do you mean?' she said.

Marlene was quite sure she knew exactly what she meant. But she needed reassurance. That was natural. 'Tristan can do the Caesarean. He's very good, you know. He's done it with pigs many times!'

'No,' Beth started fussing. Marlene was obliged to give her a light tap and restrain her. She was getting hysterical like a child. The cuff fitted perfectly around the bedpost, as if it were made for it.

'Can't we wait,' said Beth, 'until the baby wants to come?'

'And I suppose we'll just let her eat chocolate for breakfast and play in the street with the street urchins too!' Marlene replied. 'Today's best! Because you know what today is, don't you?'

Many times, Anna had fantasised about how she would react if put in mortal danger. Many times, when she read the case studies, the testimonies of the tortured, she asked herself, why didn't they fight? When the soldiers came, why didn't they run? And the answer is, of course, that at that moment, the moment the soldiers enter your house, it is far from clear that it is now, as they break down the door, that you choose life or death – that now is the moment to risk everything. It is now, right now: the time to fight or die. The very next moment, it will be too late. Will it?

'She can't be awake!' Marlene protested.

'I have a spinal! It will take away the pain,' Tristan replied.

'Why can't you send her to sleep?'

'No!' Tristan was stunned. 'Of course not. I can't do that here!'

'Why not?' Marlene was outraged. 'When I gave birth to Hebe, I had a general!'

'This isn't a hospital.' Tristan thought for a moment. 'I could give her morphine.'

Anna struggled on to her elbows.

'You can't give me that. What if it drugs the baby?'

'They give you heroin in hospital,' Marlene said. 'What do you think diamorphine is?'

Tristan swigged directly from a whisky bottle.

'Please don't drink that,' said Anna, 'if you are giving me an injection in my spine.'

'With pigs we put their head in a vice,' said Tristan.

'You'll just have to stay still,' Marlene instructed her. 'Do you think you can do that?'

Anna nodded. She could do that. Where was Dermot? How long since she had sent the message? She saw her message as a bird, flying directly into a closed window. Had it even been sent? Could anybody hear her?

14

MOTHER'S DAY

'You can give birth at home, in a unit run by midwives, or in hospital. If you're healthy and have no complications, you could consider any of these birth locations. If you have a medical condition, it's safest to give birth in hospital, where specialists are available, in case you need treatment during labour.'

By the time Dermot got to Neil's flat he was in a foul temper. He had no memory of where he'd spent the previous night. He remembered waking up in that horrible house and then he'd called up a couple of mates from the old days and got pretty drunk. When had he stopped drinking? He wasn't drunk now. He stood outside Neil's flimsy front door. It was still raining but the rain wasn't so heavy. Dermot took a few little runs, limbering up for hitting Neil. He was going to have to hit him. It was the law. He even threw a few punches into the air. Neil couldn't steal his girlfriend while his mum was dying and expect to get away with it. They were probably in there now, watching *Homes Under the Hammer*, Neil stroking Anna's stomach as it stretched and bulged with *his* baby. Dermot lit a cigarette. He'd just have this one. There was no point going in there to fight

Neil if he hadn't had a smoke. He looked at his phone, but it had died. Maybe it was Neil's baby. Maybe he, Dermot, was the arsehole coming in to try to take Neil's baby away from *him*. This was a bad thought.

He pressed Neil's doorbell for far too long and checked his watch. It was half ten in the morning. Fuck, he needed a drink. Neil came to the door in his motorcycle leggings, took one look at Dermot and tousled Dermot's hair like he'd been out late playing in the street and was home for his tea.

'Fuck, man! What happened?'

'Mam died. She died!' Dermot stumbled into his oldest friend's arms, and Neil enclosed him in a tight hug as he broke down into tears. They stood together for a full minute. 'Can I come in?' Dermot asked.

Dermot suspected Neil had poured pity whisky into the tea. The dirty fingernails stopped scratching at his brainstem.

'I'm sorry to just turn up like this.' Dermot sniffed, ripping off a massive piece of kitchen towel and blowing his nose on it.

'That's OK! You know you are always welcome here.' Neil put his arm around Dermot's shoulders and patted him gently.

'I didn't know where else to go. I don't want to disturb you and Anna.'

'What?'

'I'm not trying to crash in on you and Anna.'

'Anna's not here,' Neil sounded bewildered.

'It's OK.' Dermot's face crumpled up again. 'I'm not going to hit you.'

'Anna's not here, man. I thought she was with you.'

'I haven't seen her for weeks,' Dermot told him.

'What?'

'I've been in Sligo.'

'So has she!'

Dermot shook his head. 'Are you two not together?' he asked Neil.

'No!' Neil looked confused. 'Have you split up?'

'I don't know!' Dermot stood up and started pacing. 'She just stopped answering me. You know what the reception's like. We were texting for a while. But then I left her a message that Mam had gone. And she didn't get back to me. So she can't have got it. I Facebooked her but sometimes she doesn't have it on her phone and I thought she might be staying with her mum.'

'She definitely was staying there,' Neil offered, 'until the scan.'

'What scan?'

That was how Dermot learnt that his unborn child's life was threatened and his home had been burgled. 'She didn't tell you?' Neil asked.

Dermot was now unable to sit still. He kept running his hands through his long hair and scratching his beard.

'What if she's left me, Neil? I can't manage without her.'

'It's OK.' Neil did his best to calm Dermot, but Dermot was weeping again. He put his arms round Neil and Neil embraced him back.

'Shh!' said Neil. 'It's OK. It'll be OK.'

Their faces were close together. Dermot's unkempt beard was catching on Neil's twists. Dermot looked down at Neil's green irises. They were ringed with a darker green.

His teeth were slightly yellow and uneven. His incisor was long and had formed a tiny dent in his lower lip. In a sudden movement, Dermot leaned in to kiss Neil on the mouth. But Neil drew back.

'No, man!'

'Sorry!' Dermot swung away, his head in his hands. 'I'm so sorry.'

'It's all right, Dermot.' Neil patted his back. 'It's just not a good idea. You've just lost your mam.'

'So what?' Dermot shrugged wildly with his long arms. 'We can't do it 'cause my mam died?'

'Jesus, Dermot!'

'We used to,' said Dermot wildly. 'We used to do it all the time!'

'We did it four times! Years ago!'

'And now I've got a baby on the way,' Dermot muttered bitterly.

'No! It's not that.' Neil looped his hand around the back of Dermot's neck. 'I'm so sorry, man,' said Neil. 'I shouldn't have strung you along like I did. I was a prick. It's just . . . you were so brilliant and nobody had ever been in love with me before.'

'Well, someone thinks a lot of himself!' said Dermot, shoving Neil. 'I was never in love with you!'

Then his eyes came up to meet Neil's. Neil held his gaze. Dermot's head swung down on his long neck.

'Come on, Dermot!' Neil appealed to him softly. 'She's gone now. You don't have to bullshit any more.'

'Who? Anna?'

'Your mam! You don't have to bring home a woman. You did it. You told her you were having a baby before she died. You made her happy. Now you can make yourself happy.'

'What?' Dermot's voice was camp, almost mocking, 'Find myself a lovely fella?'

'Yeah!' said Neil. 'Preferably one who's gay,' he deadpanned. Dermot started laughing but the laugh turned into a cry. He shook his head.

'I'm fucked. I've fucked myself, haven't I? I've got to take care of the baby.'

'You couldn't take care of a fucking tortoise! You're not well, Dermot. You're not doing well. What's the plan? Drink yourself to death? Marry Anna and then cheat on her with every fan-boy who offers you a handy?' Neil said.

'I wouldn't cheat on her!' Dermot protested.

'You were literally just about to try and bang me.'

He was a shit. He was a massive cheating shit. But Neil was looking at him like he wasn't. Neil was looking at him like he was all right. Dermot started to grin.

'I mean, I definitely would have!'

Neil smiled back. 'And who'd blame you?'

'I do love her though,' Dermot said fiercely.

'I know you do! But you aren't meant to try to fuck other people.'

'That mother of hers tried to fuck me,' Dermot offered.

'She WHAT?' Neil gulped.

'She tried to fuck me!' Dermot exclaimed.

'Jesus! Where is Anna?' Neil bit his bottom lip with his dogtooth. 'Have you been home?'

But Anna wasn't at the flat and hadn't been for some time. It stank of wet dead cigarettes and something else.

'It's the cat!' Neil pointed to the corner of the living room, which had turned into a cat's toilet. Old dry cat shit piled up under newer shits in a kind of shit installation piece.

'We don't have a cat,' Dermot replied.

'I think you do now,' said Neil, peering out to the balcony where a mangy tortoiseshell cat with two different coloured eyes skulked.

'Where have you come from?' Neil asked, in the voice people reserve for talking to cats and babies. He put some water in a bowl and put it down for the moggy, who swiped at him with one piebald paw.

'Ow!' Neil said.

The blood-orange that Marlene had painted the flat was overpowering. It was giving Dermot a headache.

'Who's the landlord?' said Neil, looking at the livid walls. 'Maybe she's told him where she's gone?'

'I don't know. Anna always deals with all that.'

But in the post piled up in piss-soaked snowdrifts against the front door they soon found out who the landlord was and just how much was owing.

'I don't think she has dealt with it,' said Dermot.

'Do you need money?' asked Neil.

'No, you're grand,' said Dermot. 'Mam left me some.'

'Doesn't it take ages to come through?' Neil asked.

'Not really,' said Dermot, pulling out a roll of notes, 'it was in the biscuit tin. She had to hide it from the Pillock.' 'The Pillock' was how Dermot referred to his dad. 'I can't think in this shit-hole,' he said.

So Neil took some of Dermot's mam's hidden cash and went out to buy some black bin bags and cat food and beer.

'There's fucking flowers everywhere,' said Neil, as he returned.

'It's Mother's Day,' said Dermot.

They cleaned up the cat shit together, looking under the sink for cleaning fluids. There, Dermot found Anna's Brasso tin with its hidden twenties, just like his mother's.

And when Neil silently passed him a can of Kronenbourg, even though dehydration was clawing at Dermot's brain and he wanted nothing so much as to feel the tiny gobs of condensation forming into tears on the side of the tin, Dermot thought, 'I don't have to drink that,' and said: 'No, you're grand.'

Neil checked his phone again. 'Has she left you a message?'

'Shit!' said Dermot. 'It's been off a couple of days!'

And Dermot, at last, plugged in his mobile to charge.

The woman with the bald head had refused to leave Caffè Nero when she was asked, according to the barista. The young police officer noted that the barista had told her repeatedly to leave. When the woman had pretended not to hear and hid behind the counter, that's when he had called them. The police officer decided to call the Mental Health Team himself.

'Is there anybody we can call for you?' the constable asked the woman.

'I lost them,' the woman explained. 'I lost my family.'

'I'm so sorry.' That made sense. The young policeman turned to his partner, 'She says she's lost her family.' His partner clucked sympathetically. 'How did you lose them, sweetheart? Did they pass away?'

'No!' said the woman. 'I did.'

'What's that?' The police constable was a few weeks into the job, and this was exactly the kind of thing he didn't want to do.

'I died recently,' the shaved woman said. 'I know I'm not supposed to know that!' she said. 'Don't tell anyone! I don't want to frighten them.'

'Why would you frighten them?' asked the police constable, swallowing.

'It's scary when dead people talk to you.' She bit her bottom lip. 'I'm not scaring you, am I?'

'No,' said the constable, 'you aren't scaring me.' He was lying. She was freaking him the fuck out. Her skin was so pale it was almost translucent, and the few tufts on her head were greasy and the smell was of someone who hadn't washed for a while. Maybe she was dead, or talking to the dead, at least. She smelled dead.

'I smell dead,' she whispered.

'Fuck!' he swore. She could read his thoughts. He caught his partner's disapproving glance and ignored it.

'What's your name, sweetheart?'

The cat turned down the food that Neil had bought. Someone must be feeding it.

Dermot went through Anna's things to, as Neil put it, find out what's missing.

'I mean, it isn't there,' said Dermot, 'how will I know what's not there?'

'What about her star jumper? The grey one with the white star on it?' Neil asked.

'Yeah, that's here,' said Dermot.

'What about her red hoodie? That's her favourite. And it's massive. She could keep on wearing it however pregnant she gets.'

'Found it!' Dermot held up a ragged red hoodie. Neil nodded curtly. He took a step back from the hoodie abruptly. As if it would burn his skin to be near the fabric that had touched hers.

'It's not poison!' Dermot said.

Dermot looked at Neil in the late afternoon light, unable to touch Anna's clothes, and a little row of dominoes fell over on top of each other in his poor desiccated brain: Neil, thumping the pub table, Neil, jumping away from Anna's shoulder when he heard about the baby, Neil, biting his bottom lip, asking, 'Where is Anna?'

'Oh,' Dermot said.

'What?' said Neil.

'Nothing,' said Dermot, pausing. 'She's left everything.'

'I don't see her green jacket,' said Neil, 'you know, the parka one.'

'I know!' said Dermot.

'What about her books?' asked Neil. 'Did she take her comfort books?'

'What books?'

'She re-reads kids' books when she's sad. She wouldn't have gone anywhere without *Northern Lights*.'

Which is how they found Anna's laptop. It was filed on the shelf as if it were a book, next to a dog-eared copy of the *Northern Lights* Trilogy.

'Why would she leave this here? If she was going away?' Neil asked.

'You're shitting me up now!' said Dermot. 'Do you know her password?'

'Why would I know that?' said Neil.

Dermot shrugged. 'You know everything else about her.'

Dermot was opening Anna's laptop when he heard the little musical noise of a text coming through to his charging phone.

The place she was now could be a waiting room. But it could also be a cell. It was definitely a cell. Now there was someone else asking her questions. He seemed like a psychiatrist but he looked barely eighteen. Maybe she should text someone. Who could she text? She looked at the screen, with its network of cracks.

'Is that your phone?' asked the eighteen-year-old. 'Are you texting someone?'

'I was going to,' said the woman.

'Who?'

'I can't remember,' she said.

'Can I look?'

'Yes.' The woman handed over the phone. The psychiatrist looked at the apps.

'Is it OK if I look at your Facebook?' She was scratching at a sore patch on her wrist. She nodded.

The baby psychiatrist touched the little blue square with the white f. And then the tiny photo in the bottom right-hand corner to call up the profile. It brought up a photograph of a woman with waist-length hair. She touched her head. There was not much hair there.

'Is this you?' asked the psychiatrist, turning his face on an angle.

She took the phone off the baby man and touched the camera icon, and then turned it around. Was this her? The lady in the mirror didn't look very well. She looked at the profile photo. That looked a lot like the lady in the mirror, if she were cleaned up. She wished someone would clean her up. She passed the phone back to the young person.

'Are you Anna?' he asked. 'Anna Rampion? It's OK.'

'Are you going to take me to hospital?' She was trying to keep her voice steady.

'Would you like me to take you to hospital?'

'Yes.' She looked into his kind, kind face. 'Yes, I would.'

'What the fuck does that mean?' Dermot showed the message to Neil.

It was from an unknown number: *It's Anna police So's inatmss*

Neil felt as if an invisible hand had closed around his throat.

'I think So's is SOS,' he said.

'Jesus!' Dermot was overwhelmed. 'Should I call it?'

But it went through to a standard recorded message.

Neil looked at her favourite book on the shelf.

'Try Pantalaimon . . . the password.'

'Try what?'

Neil took the laptop out of Dermot's hands. Pantalaimon didn't work.

'What does it mean anyway?' Dermot fretted.

'Just shut up, will you? Just shut up!' Neil thought. He tried it again but with the 'a' as @. P@nt@l@imon. The home screen blinked into life.

'You beauty!' Dermot celebrated. 'What are you doing?'

'I'm finding her iPhone,' Neil said. He breathed in through his nose on a count of three and out through his mouth. The app had gone green. A blue circle in a green circle, and the light was spinning clockwise, seeking her out.

'It's the name of the main character's daemon, in the book. In the world everyone has a soul in the shape of an animal. Witches have souls that are birds.'

Spinning. Spinning.

'Servants have souls that are dogs.'

'That's fucked up,' said Dermot.

'I dunno,' said Neil. 'I think my soul would be a dog.' The icon landed. 'Where is that?' He zoomed in to see Anna's location on the map.

It was in Shepherd's Bush.

'She's there!' Dermot yelled excitedly. 'We've found her! Look! It's a police station. She's with the police. They've got her!'

Dermot and Neil piled downstairs into the van they used for gigs. But when they got to the van it wouldn't start.

'Battery's gone,' said Neil.

'There's a jump lead in the back,' said Dermot.

Neil opened the van doors. 'What the fuck is that?' In the back of the van amongst the amps were the pickles Dermot had stashed, rows of accusatory eyeballs.

They settled in the van as they always did, with Neil in the driver's seat. Only this time Dermot had Anna's laptop open on his knee.

'Why didn't she text us from her phone if she's got it?' Neil asked.

'Maybe she ran out of juice,' Dermot suggested.

But Neil had a bad feeling in his gut like he hadn't eaten for three days. 'Let's phone the place.'

Dermot called the police station. 'Is it her?' Neil asked.

'Yes,' Dermot nodded. 'Anna Rampion.'

'Ask them what she looks like. Make sure it's her,' said Neil.

'Who else is it going to be?' said Dermot. 'Does she have crazy long hair?' he asked into the phone. Dermot turned to Neil. 'They say her hair's all cut off. But it's her all right. She's wearing her green parka!'

Neil nodded silently. Dermot was still listening.

'But she's being moved. They're taking her to hospital.'

'To hospital! Why? What's wrong with her?' asked Neil.

'Just to make sure she's OK. They said she wanted to go.'

'Which hospital?' Neil quizzed Dermot.

'Lambeth.'

Neil glanced across at the laptop. 'We're only ten minutes

away from the station. Ask them not to move her till we get there. If she's OK . . .'

'She's OK,' Dermot said, 'she's OK.' And their eyes met and they both smiled at each other in relief. Then something occurred to Neil.

'What about the baby? Ask about the baby!'

Dermot asked breathlessly, 'What about the baby? Is the baby doing OK?' He listened attentively, and then slowly, the arm holding the phone dropped, as if he were a weightlifter, the phone were an iron ball, and the weight had become too much to bear.

'What?' asked Neil, his eyes darting from the road to Dermot's devastated face.

'They say she's not pregnant,' Dermot said, 'there's no baby.'

When Neil pulled up outside Shepherd's Bush Police Station Dermot was about six hours sober. His beard, which came in part ginger, part grey, was an inch long even where he usually cut it, and it met his chest hair. His eyes were bloodshot. He looked like he'd just disembarked from his Viking longship after some three-day pillage-party. Dermot swung out of the van and loped towards the entrance, and Neil parked, badly.

By the time Neil made it to the front desk Dermot was being booked for missing his court date.

'My mum died,' Dermot yelled, 'she really did die. She died!' he yelled in the impassive face of the young police officer. 'She fucking died!'

'Call your lawyer!' Neil told Dermot.

As Dermot was taken into custody he pleaded with Neil, 'Take care of her! Please!' But they wouldn't let Neil see her. He watched the little bleeping dot that was Anna float away from him towards Lambeth.

Neil went back out to the van, but it was clamped. She was going away. She was going away from him. He had failed to act and now she was on her way to hospital, and she was going away from him. With each moment that passed she got further away, and Neil felt as if his heart were a plug in a dam and the little dot on the laptop was pulling on it, threatening to let the ocean through, drowning him.

The landline rang in the kitchen, and Marlene cursed it. She spilled her coffee. She had no idea why she was so jittery.

'Hello? Marlene Meunier!' She wasn't actually married to Tristan but 'Meunier' sounded marvellous. It was her friend John.

'John Darling! How lovely to hear from you!' John had always been drawn to her.

'I just thought I should let you know that the lad's surfaced, your daughter's boyfriend. He called me. He's been arrested. You still happy to pay his fees?'

'No,' said Marlene, 'he's turned out to be a bad sort. He doesn't deserve a penny.'

'He did sound quite disturbed. Very upset he'd just missed your daughter at the police station. Wanted me to make enquiries. How about that? Shall I check she's all right?' the lawyer offered.

'What do you mean, at the police station?'

'He seemed to think your daughter had been arrested too, or taken in by the police.'

Marlene dropped the phone and sprinted up the stairs three at a time, the wallpaper flashing past her. 'Please let her baby be there,' she prayed. 'Let her not have lost the baby. Please.'

Neil went to Lambeth hospital on the tube. After an excruciating wait, he was taken up to Nelson Ward, 'Acute Care', his heart thumping, and went into a tiny, dirty waiting room, with two clearly ill people on the municipal chairs.

One woman was sitting silent, in a Lithium haze. She was about sixty-five and black, with natural hair which had greyed in beautiful streaks. The hair reminded Neil of his Oma – his father's mother. The other woman's hair was cut short, and she had shaved patches with raised, crusty red sores on them. She was moving constantly, her arms shooting out forward and down towards her legs, then up to scratch her scalp. She kept chewing her cheeks, then moving her jaw from side to side in little staccato bursts. She didn't recognise him. But he recognised her.

'Hebe?' said Neil.

Beth was there, thank God, lying on her side, facing the door, her wrist no longer connected to the bedpost. Tristan's back was blocking Beth's lower half so it took Marlene coming into the room properly to see that he'd cut a hole about two inches long into her belly. Was that all he'd managed?

Marlene leaned over Beth and looked at her back. There was a small puncture wound where Tristan had spiked her spine. Tristan's phone was poking out of his back pocket and Marlene took it out, tapped in the passcode and looked at the last message. It was a message to her about the morphine, so she scrolled back a few messages and found one to an unknown number: *It's Anna police So's inatmss*. She'd been trying to send an SOS. Marlene slapped Tristan's back.

'Stop!' said Tristan. 'I'm trying to cut her.' Marlene slapped him again, and he dropped the scalpel.

'You silly boy! I'll have to sterilise it!' she said.

But the spell was broken.

'I can't do it,' Anna heard Tristan say. 'I won't do it.'

'I'll do it then,' said Marlene. But not so Anna believed her.

Tristan put his foot on the scalpel.

'She should go to the hospital!' Tristan's accent had thickened. '*C'est complètement dingue! Ce n'est pas ton bébé!*' and Marlene was screaming at him in French.

Anna could make out very little of the row, just some swear words – '*Putain*!' and that word over and over '*bébé*' which she knew was 'baby'. Tristan stalked out of the room and Marlene followed him, the two of them shouting at each other. They left the door open.

Anna looked on the floor, where they had left the scalpel. Her legs felt completely numb. Tristan had been competent at anaesthetising her. Her fears on that score had been groundless. She rolled off the bed to the right. Her legs buckled under her and she ended up lying on the rug over the polished floorboards. She started to push with her legs, trying to shuffle like a caterpillar around the bed. She could still see the scalpel, glinting on the polished wood. If she could make it to the scalpel, she could make it to the door. It was only about four feet away.

Anna pulled herself across the floor on her elbows, trying desperately to cover the wound with her nightie so it didn't get infected. She reached the scalpel and her hands closed around the handle. Marlene's legs appeared in the door frame and thudded across the floor. She was standing over Anna.

'Give that to me!' she said. She held out her hand, palm flat.

Not knowing why, and with a sense that it could only ever have been this way, Anna gave it to her. Marlene turned on her heel, locking the door behind her.

Anna held the wound together with her fingers for as long as she could. She could hear them fighting. Then everything went quiet. By the time Marlene returned she judged several hours had passed, maybe even a day. A crust had started to form over the cut. Anna was in the bathroom, trying to fill her empty belly with water from the tap, when she heard the bedroom door open.

'What are you doing in there?' Marlene's voice was irritable.

'Just getting some water,' said Anna.

'Well, come here and help me with something.'

Anna came out of the bathroom. 'What . . .'

Lying on her floor was Marlene's boyfriend Tristan. He was tied in the kind of plastic netting which covers a Christmas tree, with knots at both ends.

'This,' said Marlene, 'what are we going to do about it?'

'Is he . . .'

'Don't be ridiculous!' Marlene snapped. 'Of course he's bloody dead! Look at his face, for God's sake!'

'Call the police?'

'I'd *love* to call the police!' said Marlene. 'But I can't because of madam here!' She gestured towards Anna and her belly and the chain which led to the ring buried in the hearthstone. 'Can I?'

'What did you do to him?'

'Me?' Marlene was outraged. 'I didn't do a thing! I just found him like that. He did it to spite me! He knew my first husband did it like that.'

'Your first husband killed himself?' Anna asked tentatively.

'They all did! As he well knew! I refuse to feel sorry for him!'

Anna didn't know if she was faint from hunger, the sight of the corpse, or the revelation that Marlene's three husbands had all killed themselves, but for a moment the room swam.

'Well, what are we going to do? Girls who make messes need to clean them up.'

And at that moment, the cord tying Anna to Marlene, keeping her close, snapped.

'How is it my mess?'

'Don't you talk down to me! If you'd just said yes to the natural childbirth, we wouldn't be in this pickle.'

'Natural childbirth?'

'Yes, girls these days! All too posh to push! It's laziness really. But birth is so medicalised. That's why I wanted you at least to have a home birth.'

Anna looked at Tristan's corpse and remembered him pushing a needle into her back. 'Is that what you thought that was?'

Marlene's voice became dreamy. 'I gave birth at home with you. And it was wonderful! Until your father came,' Marlene's voice turned vicious and bitter, 'he gave you *my* birth stone – can you imagine? Waltzes up with a pearl necklace, if you please! Well, we all know what that means! Disgusting! He never gave me pearls. So I knew he had designs. I put aside my own pain and did what was best for you. And I was proved right!'

'What are you talking about?' Anna said. 'How were you proved right?'

'You said,' Marlene nodded at Anna, as if they had the most perfect understanding, '*he did his best*.'

'To look after me,' Anna said. 'He did his best to look after me! Not to hurt me!'

Marlene didn't miss a beat.

'You'll learn! As a mother you need to be selfless! But you've always been selfish.' Anna's face must have betrayed total bewilderment. 'You had a twin. Did you know that? Edward. I lost him at five months. You kicked him out.' Marlene affected a Texan accent, 'This womb ain't big enough for the both of us!' She looked at Anna over her spectacles. 'Selfish, right from the start. You took his life, and what have you done with it?'

What had she done with it?

No accusation could have hit Anna deeper. She wondered if this was some trick of Marlene's – if she had invented this twin. But Marlene seemed to read her mind.

'Thank you!' Marlene said. 'They tried to give me a D and C. After I lost him. But I knew I was pregnant. I begged them to do a pregnancy test. But they never listen to women. They thought it was the grief from the miscarriage but I told them – I don't have any grief! I feel nothing. I was heading under, from the anaesthetic. Then when I woke up, you were still there.'

'Jesus Christ!' said Anna. 'I'm sorry. I'm so sorry.'

'You're sorry? YOU are sorry? You're the one who got rid of him! And now,' Marlene pointed at Tristan, 'you're going to get rid of *him*.'

Anna looked at Tristan's corpse. He was completely stiff. But, otherwise, he looked like himself, only melted. His face was curiously pale, his normally olive skin a shade of grey, and all his features seemed less sharp somehow, a little smudged. He had a purple neck. He also appeared to have wet himself.

'He's wet himself,' Anna said.

'Don't you know anything about death?' Marlene was annoyed. 'They all do. We've got a day before he starts to smell. Right, I'm making lunch!'

And Marlene vanished.

Anna spent the night with Tristan's corpse. At first, she thought that her mother was coming back, and listened out. By night-time she became convinced no one was coming. There was no food, but she didn't have much of an appetite. She turned on a lamp for company and shifted so the corpse was obscured by her own pregnant stomach. The mound of her belly was bisected by the dark line. Wasn't the evolutionary purpose of this line to help the new-born find their way to the mother's breast? She thought about the painting – the roots that turned out to be a tree, which Sammy had given her. Bright yellow in the earth that turned out to be the sky and blood-red in the beauty we produce that turned out to be blood that marks our beginning, and the tree itself painted in black against green, evergreen, and all around the dark.

Did she love that painting so much because she too had had a twin, and had lost him? But then she thought, no – she loved that painting because we all dream that we come from somewhere and that the place we come from will give us strength. And the painting had been just as good upside down because we all hope that we will rise – from our pain we will rise, and tower against the sky. The line dividing her stomach in two continued above her belly button, and then petered out. She remembered the name before 'Hebe' on the christening dress: 'Edward'. She thought of all the babies in danger who had visited her over the last nine months, the babies falling, the babies burning, the babies warning her, and she wondered if he had sent them.

And she saw the evergreen eyes of Neil, who had lain in this bed with her and who had said, 'You are no worse than anyone else.' He was right. And yet she had crawled here. She had erased herself to become what her mother wanted. She had let this madwoman tell her what her name was. She had let her insult her mum and slander her father with the foulest accusations. She had let her isolate her from everyone she loved and might love. She would, doubtless, be browbeaten into covering up the horrible end of this poor dead fool. She had allowed this woman to steal her hair and she could not see how she could stop her from stealing her baby. The baby, as if hearing the thought, stretched straight out across her womb, feet pushing one way and head pushing the other, ripping open the crusted-over wound. Anna thought that the wallpaper might peel off the walls and envelop her.

She did not know how to honour Tristan, who had lost his life at twenty-seven, so she sang softly, the only song she knew to say goodbye to someone taken too young, and as she sang it she also sang to the brother she had never known, 'Fly High, little darling. Fly High, my kindest friend, Fly High, pretty starling, your soul's taking flight and you're free in the end.'

A shaft of light from the window fell upon the repeated pattern of the paper. The woodland creatures gambolling and cavorting, apparently living in harmony, each one, presumably, a vegetarian – the deer, the badger, the owl, the squirrel, the wild boar.

Her mother came in at ten.

'What's the plan with the body?'

15

BIRTH

'There are several signs that labour might be starting. These may be different for different women – find out what signs to look out for and when to call your midwife.'

Anna had no idea how long Marlene would be gone, feeding the pigs. It was morning now. Her ankle was gently throbbing. Her throat was so sore. She opened her mouth to yell again. 'That's what she wants,' she thought. 'That's exactly what she wants.' Anna snapped her mouth shut. She would not shout any more. No one was coming. And that's the way it should be. All this time she had thought she needed her mother there to have a baby. But that was the opposite of the truth.

On the chest of drawers was the Moses basket Marlene had left for the baby: a Moses basket. A basket for Moses, who had been set adrift: for Moses, who had been found in the bulrushes, instead of a traffic island. Anna instantly could see her mum, her real mum, sitting on her bed next to her. The bed was not this bed, but the tiny single bed she had slept in as a child. And her mum was saying, 'Because his mother made the basket so carefully, that's why.' *I will lift up mine eyes unto the hills. I will lift up mine eyes unto the hills, from whence cometh my help*. Anna squinted into the light from the window. A Moses basket. The woods were still there. The world was still there. It was only her who was in this tower: her and the baby. She had to hide the baby. Maybe she could loop something through the handles of the basket and lower it out of the window? She'd got the window open before. She needed to find something which she could turn into a rope. And the word appeared in her brain: sheets.

There was a wardrobe in the corner which she had pushed over when Tristan had chained her. Anna thought she had seen sheets in the top of it. But she couldn't reach the top cupboard doors with the chain around her wrist. The chain went as far as the toilet one way and the wall the other, but the corner cupboard was just out of reach. It was just a bit further. Anna pulled at the chain, sunk into the ring in the fireplace, in a desperate attempt to stretch across and reach the handle to the cupboard. As she did, with the sound of centuries shifting, something in the hearth slid open. Anna turned. There was something behind the hearth, some emptiness, some horrible void, and Anna was going to go inside it.

'I'm a friend of your sister's,' the beautiful man said.

Hebe wondered if he was talking to her. Could he see her? Whenever she spoke to people now, they looked so concerned. Most people couldn't even see her, of course, but the ones who did were upset. Maybe it was because she was already dead.

'You have to get out! Go! Go!' The barista had waved

his arms at her and shooed her like he was wafting a ghost. But this man in front of her had locked his green eyes on her. There was nobody standing behind her, she checked, so he must see her. Maybe she wasn't dead yet. She was in the in-between place. She could see the world, but she could also see a veil across the world, where other things were happening, like a projection from somewhere out of sight. But sometimes the veil became the background, and the background was the veil. Sometimes, in the veil, she could see people reaching out to her to save them, setting off in dinghies from the tops of buildings, where the sea now reached, rowing through the air to the next bit of the skyline. Sometimes they fell.

'Hebe?' the beautiful man said.

Sometimes, when the people called out to her they were using the wrong name. Over the last – was it days or was it weeks? – since she'd followed Ziggy out into the dark, she had started to think that she shouldn't tell people her name. If she was meant to talk to these people, they would know her name already. It was a test. The baby psychiatrist hadn't known her name. But this beautiful man had said Hebe. That was the right name.

'I'm a friend of Anna's,' he said. So he knew Anna's name too.

Hebe's voice hurt when she spoke, because she hadn't used it for so long.

'Tell Anna I've cleaned my kidneys for the baby. The baby can have mine. Even if I'm dead.'

'What?'

'I stopped my pills. The baby can have my kidney. If the baby wants it. Tell Anna.'

The old woman with the grey hair started to join in. 'You heard her!' she yelled. 'Tell Anna! Tell Anna!'

The beautiful green-eyed man started to cry. 'I don't know where Anna is! Why do you have her phone?'

Perhaps he was an angel. He looked like an angel. Perhaps he was here to let her out of the in-between place and help her go to death, if she knew the answers.

'I took it. I was squatting at her flat. I didn't think she'd mind,' Hebe explained. But if she went with this angel who would look after Ziggy? 'Did she mind?'

'Anna's gone missing!' said the man, and his voice got louder. He held her arm. 'I can't find her!' The maybe-angel was looking at her through the tears hanging on his lower eyelashes, which curled all the way over. He was too beautiful to be real. 'I lost her.' He sobbed. 'I lost her.'

'I understand,' said Hebe, patting him kindly on the arm. 'I lost my cat.'

'It's OK,' said the man in a soft voice. 'I know where your cat is.'

As her eyes fixed on the cat scratches on the beautiful man's arm, the veil lifted and she knew with an absolute certainty that the man was real. His tears were real. The scratches were real. The arm was real. And if he was real, she wasn't dead, or in-between. She was alive and she needed to stay that way.

Anna examined herself. Her wrist was wounded where it had rubbed against the cuffs. Her right ankle was about twice as big as the left. Her finger was still stiff and strange. The baby kicked Anna hard. She looked at the wound on her belly. It was a big lump of dried blood. She was sure that when labour came, it would open again.

She knew that she had to sew it up. She had a needle; the strange curved upholstery needle, which Tristan had sterilised, was still sitting on the beach towel. But there was nothing to stitch with. Was there? Anna remembered, in the files, a client sewing himself up with dental floss. Who was that? She had a dim memory it was the twin, the mugger's brother. She had dental floss. She even had the whisky Tristan had been drinking to calm his nerves. She could drink that. What harm would it do now?

It was only eleven stitches. She was worried about bacteria from her hands getting on the needle and being driven into her flesh, but there was no choice. She ran the water in the bathroom sink as hot as it would go. She could just reach the tap. She rinsed the needle in the hot water between every stitch and washed her hands again with soap.

It was amazing how, once you'd decided to stick the needle through your flesh, it was bearable. It was the making the decision to stop avoiding pain that hurt so much. Once the pain was happening it was just pain. The needle through her flesh was so intense she hardly noticed the backache.

Layla went into the art room to get some paper. The art therapist was always swiping it from the stationery cupboard, and she needed to provide a hard copy for her letter to the hospital. Since Neil had called, her front brain had been chewing on how to spring Hebe without triggering an enforced section, and Anna's disappearance had been reduced to a throbbing worry at the back of her mind. She was not expecting to see Anna's flower necklace – a bellflower, and at its centre a tiny pearl. It was around the neck of that kid, the one who'd had such a magical family reunion. The girl saw her looking at her neck.

'What are you looking at?' She was all bravura.

Layla looked her straight in the eye. 'I'm looking at my friend's necklace.'

'That's mine,' said Sammy, 'my brother gave it to me!'

'No, he didn't,' Layla said.

The art therapist, Jane, came over, a twitchy white woman with terrible acne scars. She had a joke 'therapy' voice, irritatingly cooing. 'Can I help you, Layla?' Layla shot her a look. 'Sorry, Dr Pasdar?'

'No, but this young woman can.' Layla's voice was steely.

'We're in the middle of an art session,' the therapist objected.

'She's not,' said Layla, looking straight at Sammy.

'I'm doing my art!' Sammy was all fury.

'You can do your art again,' said Layla, 'when you tell me where you got my friend's necklace from.'

'I do hope you aren't accusing my client of anything,' said the art therapist in cooing tones.

Around the art room people were looking up with worried faces, their spider senses, finely honed over years of violence, alert to a fight.

'I'm not accusing her of anything,' Layla reassured them. 'I'm asking her . . .'

'For Christ's sake!' The art therapist's deliberately measured tones broke. 'Could we take this outside?'

Outside the room Sammy twisted towards Jane and whined, 'She's saying I nicked this!'

'Did you nick it?' Jane asked directly.

'No!' Sammy was a terrible liar.

'It's just,' said Jane in her super-gentle voice, 'you do nick a lot of stuff, don't you?'

'Fuck off!' Sammy turned back to re-join the session, but Layla stopped her.

'You know whose that is, don't you? It belongs to the one who found your brother.'

'What?' Sammy said.

'The person who found your brother is the person that necklace belongs to.' Layla added, 'You gave her your painting.'

This information drifted down and landed on Sammy like a ten-ton snowflake. She paused a second then started scrabbling at the clasp. 'Take it! Give it back to her! That's fine!'

'I can't!' Layla started to lose control of the volume of her voice. 'I can't give it back to her! She's missing!'

'What?' Sammy's tiny film star face twisted into a question mark.

'She's gone missing! For fuck's sake!' Layla swore. She looked at the little flower with a tiny pearl swinging from her hand. Suddenly, she felt exhausted. She sat down on the floor of the corridor and pulled off her black jacket.

'I'm sorry. It's just, I can't find her. She won't reply. She's disappeared.'

Sammy was squatting next to her, suddenly a little detective. 'What about her mum?'

'What?' Layla turned to look directly at Sammy's intelligent eyes.

'Well, if she's gone missing, I'd have a look for her mum because, as God is my witness, that mum is one hundred percent psycho.'

'Why would you say that?' Jane chimed in.

'How have you met Anna's mum?' Layla asked Sammy.

Sammy eyeballed the two of them. 'The mum came to find me. I didn't realise the lady who found my brother was the same one I . . . the lady whose necklace this is,' Sammy said. 'The mum – she wanted to buy all my paintings. She bought like four.'

The therapist, Jane, was absolutely winded by this. 'You sold your art?'

'Of course I sold my art!' said Sammy. 'I'm an artist!'

'It's meant to be therapeutic!' said Jane.

'Two hundred and fifty quid is quite therapeutic too,' said Sammy. 'But I asked for more. She was keen, so I was, like, I'm probably underselling myself, or maybe she's selling them on or whatever, and she went full psycho. She called me a bunch of sexist shit, then I came in here one day and she'd cut up my painting.'

'She what?' Layla needed her to repeat it.

'Yeah, babe! She cut the shit out of it. With serrated scissors!' Sammy nodded at the faces surrounding her. 'I mean,' said Sammy, 'what kind of a psycho destroys art?!'

It was clear now to Anna that she was having the baby. 'Labour was now established.' That was the phrase they used, wasn't it?

The sensation was as if the earth were cracking in two and each of her hips was a different side of the schism. Now a river ran through her and she knew with complete certainty that she would be borne along it all the way to the sea. The convulsion graunched through her back and she felt sweat roll down behind her ears. She would not bellow. She would not scream. She would only sweat. A river ran through her. Marlene would be back soon.

Marlene had been having a nice long soak. Feeding the pigs was a dirty job at the best of times and this was hardly that. In a way, it was serendipitous she'd been so busy with the baby, and they'd had less attention than usual. They were that much hungrier. But now her feet were in a terrible mess and doing a pedicure on oneself was so irritating. She'd miss Tristan for that. Perhaps Beth would help.

Marlene gathered her nail polish, toenail cutters and emery boards together before abandoning the nail scissors in case Beth was still cross. But she seemed perfectly amenable to doing her feet, so Marlene hoped the unpleasantness had been put behind them. She was positively friendly. Perhaps it had been Tristan's presence that was driving a wedge between them, and with Tristan gone there would be more of these mother-daughter moments. It was almost like a spa. Beth was not awful at foot massage, though her hands were a little sweaty. But then she had jabbed her a little with the clippers, and Marlene couldn't help feeling she was more than ham-fisted. It seemed deliberate. At least Marlene had got a nice photo for her Instagram.

She allowed herself to picture life after the baby was born. She loved babies so much. She saw herself, aged about twenty, feeding the baby, dressed in a gorgeous embroidered shirt, but she couldn't remember if the child was Beth or the new baby. Maybe she could call her Beth too, that would be less confusing for everybody. She remembered a baby crying and saw herself shutting the oven door on her to try to keep her quiet. Was that a fairytale or a daughter? She had a feeling it was Hebe, and she'd taken her out before it got too hot. Babies were lovely. Babies were perfect. She was going to have a baby.

The pains would be terrible now if she could feel them. Anna observed them from her perch all the way up in her brain, above the storm. Any minute now she'd be inside it again. She knew she had to dive, down, down into the tumult. Any minute now the waves would be buffeting her again, as the salt seared her bald spots. She wished she could stay here, above the pain, but she wasn't allowed. She'd forgotten why; oh yes, the baby. She had to fetch her baby. The stork was coming. The stork was coming. And she must be the stork.

There was a fancy European bidet next to the toilet. If the chain around her wrist could reach that far, perhaps she could have the baby over the bidet? Then she could wash it. It had to be clean, didn't it? Babies died from dirt. But she knew the chain reached only to the toilet. It was just long enough to allow her to pee at night. What about the water in the toilet, that was clean, wasn't it? If the toilet was clean enough, maybe the baby could be born into the toilet? No bleach, of course. She wasn't safe with bleach. But there was a cleaning spray. She had to clean the toilet. She began to crawl.

The next wave was rolling in, grey on the horizon, reaching the sky. She had to get there before the storm caught her again. Her feathers were wet. Her feathers? She didn't have feathers. She had hair but it was all gone now. She had to count it in, the wave, so she didn't make a sound when it arrived. She could count to fifteen before the pain reached its peak and she was drowning in it. She wouldn't drown. She was a sea bird. She could bear fifteen silently. She would ride it out. Don't fight. Don't fight it. She flew in the direction of the wind; let the wind take her, let the waves take her. She must not make a sound. Her beak was full. Full of fish for the baby.

Thirteen, fourteen, fifteen, sixteen – still coming – seventeen, eighteen. It wasn't fair; the pain was still coming, and she'd agreed fifteen with herself. Silence. Silence was necessary. It was naive, she thought, to expect fairness. There is no such thing as fairness. Her beak was shut.

Nineteen and she was clear again, above the maelstrom, the pain receding. This was the way. Her whole life had been a practice for this moment: don't swim against the stream, go with it, go with the current. She tried to open the toilet lid silently, but her hand was shaking. It clacked a little against the cistern. The wallpaper was tiny blue flowers: bellflowers, like her name. What was her name? But before she could pick up the spray cleaner the waters came.

It was just the sea; the sea was coming out of her. It was exactly right. She got on the toilet to catch the sea.

It wouldn't be long now.

She watched as the sea left her body. But it wasn't stopping. It kept coming. How long had the storm been raging? She couldn't remember.

The cord had to be cut, didn't it? Didn't some people leave it attached? Didn't they just let it pump into the baby? No blades. No blades anywhere – no scissors, no knives. Not allowed. And it had to be clean, the cord cutter. What about her teeth? She could bite the cord, couldn't she? Do storks have teeth? She should clean hers. She reached for the plastic cup with the tiny child's toothbrush she had been given.

But the knife wound at the bottom of her pregnant belly had sprung open a little and was bleeding. Perhaps she should sew it up again? With what? She fell on to her hands and knees. No time now. Another wave pulled her into the roiling water. It smelt familiar: salt and iron, and some terrible stink of an only recently disturbed pool. She opened her gullet. She was empty now. She swam into a long-buried shipwreck. Cannonballs lay in the green gloom and rust floated upwards. Where was the baby? Where was the baby? She knew, from the smell, that the baby needed to be found soon and brought to the surface, or it would be lost forever in the stinking water. And then she saw it: suddenly, the eddies threw her towards it, she almost smashed into her baby and then her baby was there, in front of her, upside down on the tile, covered in the contents of the standing pool. As it yawned and gawped, she crammed her breast into its tiny little mouth to keep it quiet.

Had she been quick enough? Were they safe?

There was blood on the tile, but Anna did not feel faint. She knelt on all fours with the baby under her. She did not know how long, just that she was in a state of suspension. Then the pains came again. The pains racked her but she stayed on the ground, with the pain and her new-born. What was happening? Was there another baby?

Something else was coming out of her. Anna had no idea it would be shaped like this, would look like this. Where had she seen that pattern before, the blood vessels branching across it? Everywhere – she had seen it everywhere – in the trees, in the rivers, in her own eyelids. It was life and she had joined it. So, someone else was born, that night, after the baby, but it wasn't another baby. It was a mother.

16

AFTER BIRTH

'Skin to skin contact really helps with bonding. Once the cord is clamped, you can continue to cuddle your baby.'

By the time the sun rose Anna was ready.

She then had an agonising wait. Marlene normally came between nine and ten. Why was she late? Anna counted her breaths, as she had all night. Her lower body felt strangely airy, open to the elements. The wind could blow through her.

At ten past ten Marlene knocked twice, gently, as if Anna could refuse her entry, and came in brandishing a breakfast tray.

'Wakey, wakey!'

She put the tray down on a spindly table next to the door. Anna was suddenly aware how hungry she was. Maybe she could eat something before Marlene found out.

'It's a gorgeous day!' Marlene was opening the curtains. She stood in front of the window, looking out on the woodland of the mansion house. For a moment, she caressed the wallpaper.

'Stay still,' thought Anna. 'Just stay still.'

'I've brought you some ointment for that wrist.' Marlene showed her a little green jar. 'I get the little man to make it up for me in the village. It draws out the badness.' Marlene opened the jar, and a foul stench came from it. 'Now, do you want some breakfast?'

'Yes, please,' said Anna.

Marlene brought over the tray. There was porridge with blueberries. It looked like Marlene was going to stay for a chat.

'Are you ready to apologise?' Marlene said. Anna searched in her brain for what Marlene could want her to apologise for.

'Yes, I'm sorry!' Anna said.

Marlene narrowed her eyes. 'What for?'

'For . . . being ungrateful!' Anna was confident and from nowhere, she meant it. 'For everything! For everything!'

Marlene's eyes swam with tears. 'Eat up!'

Anna ate. The porridge was the best thing she had ever tasted. 'Thank you!' she said.

'Do you know? That is the first time you have said sorry and I've believed it. Give me that wrist!' Marlene took Anna's wrist, which was fringed with pus. 'Here!' And for the first time in three weeks, Marlene unlocked the handcuffs tying Anna to the chain.

'There's something different about you this morning!' trilled Marlene. 'Perhaps I'm finally rubbing off on you!'

'Steady,' thought Anna. 'Hold on.'

Marlene began smearing the foul-smelling ointment on Anna's wound. Then she took a stretchy bandage from the pocket at the front of her dress and wrapped it around

Anna's wrist, securing it with one of the strange little metal clips, just the same as Charmaine had used when she was bandaging her hand. She was sitting on the bed, trapping Anna under the sheets. There was no way Anna could make a break for it.

'Cuddle?' she said. Anna smiled brightly and put her arms out to be hugged and Marlene leaned in to embrace her.

'She'll work it out.' Anna felt the realisation hurtling toward her: any minute now.

But it didn't come. Marlene was crying. 'I do love you, you know, even though you're a silly sausage!' She started tucking in the covers tightly around Anna, turning her into 'a little Swiss roll'. She stood back and surveyed her handiwork.

Marlene's eyebrows pulled towards each other and Anna thought, 'Here it is.' Marlene reached forward and yanked the covers off her, regarding the lake of blood and jelly underneath her.

Anna snuck her left hand under the pillow and her fist closed on what she had hidden there.

'Where . . .' Marlene was processing more slowly than Anna had expected '. . . is the baby?'

Anna rolled to her left, landing on her knees, and barrelled straight towards Marlene's legs and the open door. Marlene fell on and over her, cracking her knee on the bedframe, and as Anna pushed free and crawl-walked doorwards, she heard Marlene catch up with her and slam the door shut. Marlene stood over Anna for a second, then stamped on Anna's soft belly.

'Where's the baby?'

It was like the pain was happening to someone else. Anna looked up at her mother's bloodless skin. 'The baby's dead.'

Marlene's face crumpled.

'What?'

'She's dead.'

'No!' Marlene was crying now. 'She can't be! How can she be dead?'

'Some men came and took her.' Anna held eye contact with Marlene.

'What men?'

Anna was sure she was at least considering this. Think like Marlene. The world is full of threat – threat from outside yourself.

'I think they were foreign.'

Marlene was out the door and along the landing and already at the top of the 'main staircase'.

Anna pushed herself upright and followed her. She was through the bedroom door and past the first landing. Now she just had to get to the second one. That was all she had to do. Get to the second landing where Marlene's landline sat on a tall pedestal table made of mahogany next to her 'Lady'. But Marlene stopped a couple of steps down, her hands reaching out to the wall and the heavy banister, blocking Anna's exit. Marlene turned back.

'I bet you think you're clever!' Marlene said.

Anna stopped, breathing raggedly. Her womb hurt. It was still rhythmically compressing. She could still feel the echoes of her night on the rack. A few steps behind Marlene a short flight of three or four steps led to the second landing.

'You took it!' hooted Marlene. 'You took it somewhere! Where's the baby, Beth?'

'My name isn't Beth. I'm Anna.'

'You're a silly girl. You're a silly baby. You're a . . .'

But Anna ran forward and smashed her shoulder into her mother's hefty frame. Marlene was pushed back a few steps but fell heavily at the top of the stairs on to her knees with an audible crack, missed her footing and slipped on the stair carpet.

Anna ran forward and pushed Marlene down the short flight of stairs and turned to the pedestal to pick up the phone.

The phone wasn't there. There was just the nude statuette of Marlene in perfect white porcelain. The one cast by a lover of hers in her heyday.

Anna felt Marlene cuff the back of her head, hard.

As Anna turned around, Marlene pushed her backwards and dug her knee into Anna's bleeding abdomen. 'Silly, silly girl!' Marlene banged Anna's head against the floor.

It hurt. It all hurt so much. Anna returned to her body with a rush, so soon after the birth. Anna reached up to fend off her mother's blows with her left hand. With the other, she took what she was holding and wrapped it once around Marlene's neck.

Anna would never have believed it could be so strong. The cord. The baby's cord. She pulled, and the grip Marlene had on her ears loosened. She pulled again. And Marlene's mad eyes looked suddenly vacant. She just needed to keep pulling. The umbilical cord snapped. It sprayed bright blood-orange sap across Marlene's face and into her eyes. 'It's so bright,' thought Anna, 'it's too bright.'

'You little bastard,' Marlene said. And she and Anna rolled on the landing. Marlene heaved Anna off her and struggled on top of her, trying to blink the baby's blood out of her eyes. Drops of orange liquid hung on her eyelashes. She sat astride her daughter while Anna used the flailing end of the baby's cord to whip at her mother's face. With each whip gobs of straggly bright blood flew across the perfect decor and Marlene's expensive silk quilted robe. But Marlene flat-handed Anna across the face. Anna grabbed at her mother's hair, but it came away in her hand. What seemed to be her whole scalp came off, exposing a second scalp below, covered with nicks from a fresh shave. Marlene gathered some of the ample material of her huge bat-wing sleeve and stuffed it into Anna's mouth, smothering her.

Anna could see behind her and to the right, the top of the tall one-legged table. Anna grabbed the tripod base and pulled. The table fell towards Marlene, and, as Anna had hoped, she shifted her weight to rescue the statuette from shattering.

'No,' she said, 'not my Lady!' Marlene caught it with both hands and pushed the table upright. Anna was able to get her own arms free and, putting her hands over her mother's, pushed the statuette sideways hard into the wall. There was a splintering sound.

'You vindictive little girl!' Marlene screamed. 'You've broken her!' The statuette was in three distinct pieces. The woman's torso and head, her pelvis and legs, and the two children that had previously been attached to her. Marlene was desperately trying to rescue the pieces of her. She struggled up to put the sections of the broken mother into place on the table, steadying her hands against Anna's body.

Anna held on to one fragment of the dismembered lady, the legs and pelvis, and drove it forcefully into Marlene's stomach. Marlene screeched. The skin was broken, Anna was sure of it, though it was hard to tell with all the baby blood everywhere. She pushed Marlene backwards and shuffled up against the wall, so they both sat, at either end of the landing. There was a leg sticking out of Marlene's belly, as if she too had been pregnant, and the child had attempted to kick her way out.

They looked at each other, panting and in pain. And in the silence of the moment came the unmistakable mewling sound of a new-born's reedy cry.

'She's alive!' Marlene grabbed the frozen baby leg out of her belly and threw it on the rug as they both staggered to their feet. The sound was coming from Anna's bedroom or the bedroom which had served as Anna's prison for the last three weeks.

Anna was three steps behind Marlene. She stopped in the doorway as Marlene began to tear the room apart.

'Where is she?' Marlene flipped the cover over in the bed and knocked over the side tables. She opened all the drawers in the chest of drawers and ran to the wardrobe, dripping blood from her stomach on to the polished floorboards. As she opened the wardrobe, she pulled out the blankets on the shelves and the beautiful expensive little children's dresses which hung on the rail: nothing. The mewling stopped.

Marlene ran through into the bathroom, gripping her belly wound.

'Where is she?' she said.

Where had Beth hidden her? She needed to be held. She needed to be loved. She needed her mummy.

Marlene flipped the lid off the laundry basket, throwing the laundry out on the floor. She wasn't there. Where was she? Marlene felt something hot running down her leg. It was too much blood. It wasn't right. Was she miscarrying again? No, she'd heard the baby. The baby must have been born. Beth had had the baby.

Looking up, she saw the bath. The shower curtain was pulled half across, and poking out behind it was something bloody, something unspeakable.

One foot in front of the other. With each step more fell out of her, slowing her down. But she could not have stopped going to the bath now, not if armies had stood in her way. She ripped back the curtain.

There, in the white, was a mess of veined flesh. Was it throbbing? She bent over and scooped up the poor creature with both hands. It was still warm. It was still warm. She staggered to the doorway.

'What have you done to her?' she asked.

The crying started again. Marlene looked at what was in her hand, then at Anna, stupidly, like a character in a Sunday night drama being given a plot point. The noise was pulling at Anna's womb, making it contract. She felt it ripple.

'That's the placenta,' said Anna gently.

Marlene dropped it on the floor with a squashy thump. She looked around wildly.

'You won't find her,' Anna said.

Suddenly Marlene pouted like a little girl. 'Why are you being so mean?' she whined to Anna. 'Why won't you let me see her?'

Anna stayed rooted in the door frame, her eyes following Marlene's every move. Marlene sat heavily down on the bed. 'Are you OK?' Anna asked.

Marlene's face was ashen.

'Where's your mobile? I'll call an ambulance,' Anna said.

'Oh! You'd like that, wouldn't you?' Marlene spat. 'I'm going to die here, and you'll just have to tell them you killed me. See what a wonderful mother you make in prison, Miss Holier than Thou!'

'You need a doctor.'

'Oh yes! Call a doctor. Show them those wrists. And make me look like a bad mother!'

'You are a bad mother,' Anna said.

'What?' Marlene's face, which was now a pale grey, was genuinely startled. 'I'm a *what*?'

'You drugged me. And tried to have me raped. You stole my *hair*. And then you tried to steal my baby.'

Marlene scrabbled at the vast pocket in front of her robe and took out her phone. She stabbed at the screen with what Anna noticed for the first time was an arthritic thumb. 'Look! Look at this!' Marlene had opened Instagram and was pushing the phone towards Anna.

'Is this a bad mother?' Marlene said. 'Look at it!'

Anna took the phone and glanced at the carefully curated pictures. The post in front of her eyes showed her own pregnant belly and her mother's cheek leaning against it, taken when Anna had been in labour and she'd cleaned her mother's feet. Anna dropped the phone on the ground.

'This isn't real,' she said.

'The sacrifices I made for you!' Marlene said.

'What did you sacrifice? Goats? Other people's children? I'd believe anything of you,' Anna said.

'I gave you my love, my time, my home! And this is how you repay me?'

'I tried to be what you wanted,' said Anna, 'but nobody could. Nobody!'

'Well, forgive me for having standards!' Marlene exclaimed. 'You think motherhood is easy? I had to make you ready.' She shifted and an astonishing amount of blood spilled out of the hole in her belly. 'So ungrateful!'

'Yes,' said Anna, 'I was ungrateful.' She looked at her mother's face. It was a good face, despite everything. 'I'm not ungrateful any more.'

'I've taught you that at least.' Marlene plucked at the bedcover.

Anna was propelled forward. She picked up a pillow and stuffed it into her mother's belly to stem the bleeding. That wouldn't work. 'We have to get you to hospital,' Anna said.

'Silly girl!' said Marlene. 'I'm dying!'

She laughed and laughed and carried on laughing.

'You always thought you'd killed your mother,' said Marlene, 'and now you have!' She lay back on the bed, her skin almost translucent, the wound in her belly spilling all over the mattress. She grasped Anna's hand with her bloodless, bony hand, fringed in silver. 'Please! Please! Let me see the baby.'

Anna started to edge around the room, her back to the wall, her eyes on Marlene, until she reached the fireplace.

She backed into it and pushed the grate forward with her feet. She pulled hard on the ring and released the ancient door, disguised as the side of the hearth, she had discovered just twenty-four hours earlier. With her left hand she pulled her baby in her basket out into the fireplace. 'Don't look at her,' she thought. 'Don't look away from Marlene.'

'You found the priest's hole!' said Marlene.

'Yes,' said Anna, 'you can look at her.' Marlene sat up higher.

'Bring her closer. Bring her closer so I can see her properly.' Again, with her left hand, Anna pulled the basket a couple of feet to the right, to bring the baby into view. 'Closer . . .' Anna pulled the baby basket slightly closer to her mother. 'Thank you,' said Marlene. 'She is just beautiful.' And she closed her eyes.

Anna waited. Her mother's chest was heaving. As she breathed it made a strange creaking sound, like fingers on a nearly dry plate. The baby was still crying, and Anna had never wanted anything so much as to hold her baby and comfort her. Anna had a strange sensation in her breasts, as if they were being scratched at by invisible tiny hands. She felt suspended between the two sounds: the creak, creak, creak of her mother inhaling and the please, please, please exhalation of her child, crying to be held. They synchronised, so, for a moment, it sounded like one person: breathing in, breathing out, breathing in, breathing out. And then her mother's rasp began to slow down and uncoupled from the baby's cries, which became more frantic. Anna's nipples prickled. Not yet, not yet . . . Marlene's breath was still creaking out . . . still creaking . . . It stopped.

And Anna, released, squatted down and reached out her left hand to cup the baby's precious soft head.

Marlene flew off the bed towards the baby. Anna's right hand came up – and with it the shard of The Lady – and stabbed her mother's neck, just above her collarbone. She pushed Marlene back on to the floor and looked into her eyes. They were a wonderful rich brown, flecked with yellow. Blood was oozing out of the neck wound, although not much. She must have already lost all the blood she had to spare. Marlene gestured for Anna to come close to her puckered mouth.

'Good girl,' she whispered. 'Good girl.' And then, 'I'm flying!'

17

NEW-BORN

'You'll probably spend a large part of the first few days after birth looking at your baby.'

The cries were still clawing at her. Anna stooped to pick up the Moses basket the baby was lying in and the handle snapped off. Her tiny baby rolled straight out, over and over and on to the hearthrug. Anna's heart dropped. She squawked in horror. But the child just lay there, wrapped in the towel Anna had bundled her in, blinking, and shocked into silence. Anna threw down the basket and scooped her up, holding her against her neck.

She was still covered in waxy white stuff from the birth, and the little whorls of her hair were crusted with blood. Anna stood up, jiggling rhythmically, and the baby casually head-butted her, as if Anna knew what to do next. Anna was suddenly bone-tired. She lay down on the opposite side of the bloody bed from where Marlene had lain, with the baby cuddled up to her. The baby yawned and gnawed at her and found the nipple easily. Anna let her suck at her for as long as she wanted. The sensation was both totally new and completely familiar. After a few moments there was a strange electrical prickling in her nipple, as if she had been lightly dusted with a cattle prod, and her right areola, the one which was not in the baby's mouth, misted with yellow droplets. And before long, the baby, too, was asleep. Anna looked at the sleeping body of her baby and, beyond it, the dead body of her mother. It was perhaps two days since she had slept herself. And she fell into a deep, deep dream of spoons and optician's spectacles and vibrators and pencil sharpeners and curved needles, all riding to the saltwater of the sea.

Anna woke to the smell of blood. She got up carefully to open the window, the same window she had attempted to escape out of a lifetime ago, with its window lock three inches above the sash frame, allowing it to be opened only a little. Anna turned round to pick up the sleeping baby, put her close to her and she let out a noisy burp. At just that moment Anna heard a feathery rustling and when she turned back, perched on Marlene's corpse was a huge brown and white screech owl.

For a moment Anna thought she might still be dreaming, but the entrails hanging from the owl's beak were indisputably real.

'No!' said Anna. 'Get out!' she screamed. The owl blinked at her. And flew back directly out of the too-small crack in the window.

She needed to clean up. Anna touched her mother's corpse, on her shoulder. She was already stiffening. How long had she been dead now? Three hours? Four? Marlene's marvellous eyes were open and clouding over. It was no good. Anna sat down on the bed, looking at the body, fighting rising panic. Could she go to the police? After all, she still had the cut on her belly where Marlene had attempted to cut the baby out. Maybe they would believe that she had acted in self-defence? Had she acted in self-defence? But she looked at Marlene's body, with the bruise around her neck and the puncture wounds and knew there was no calling the police. She got up and pulled on the broken foot of the statue which was sticking out of Marlene's neck. A strange farmyard smell from the hole in her mother's abdominal cavity made her gag and for a moment she thought she might vomit, so she went into the bathroom to rinse her own face, taking the broken foot with her, and chucking it into the sink. She noticed her hands were covered in blood. Of course they were.

In the shower, the water created dimples in her too-big skin, and rinsed the flesh wound on her stomach. She uncoupled the shower from its holder and held it over the plughole to break up the clumps of black jelly that had escaped her. When she came back in the bedroom Anna looked at her mother's body. She was still propped up – her head resting on the end of the bedstead. She pulled at Marlene to lie her flat. As Anna straightened out her mother's torso, very clearly, Marlene hissed, 'Beth!'

She was alive.

No, no, it was just some trick of death, as the last breath was expelled from her lungs, pushing her lips apart for one final time. Anna touched her mother's face, meaning to close her eyes, which were fixed open. But she couldn't bring herself to touch the eyelids. The skin was too delicate there. Instead, she carefully removed Marlene's jewellery: the strange, curved rings, like talons.

The baby woke up with a hiccough, startled herself, and started bawling. To Anna the sound seemed to cut through everything, but if the neighbours had not heard her, they would not hear the baby. The baby smelt strange, like the hole in Marlene's abdomen, and Anna realised she needed a nappy. She went under the bed to where Marlene had stashed the disposable nappies she'd bought: a single packet of ten. How long would that last? And they were way too big. Scanning the room for something else she could use, it occurred to Anna for the first time how utterly unfit the room was for a baby. It was all fussy edges, iron curlicues at the edges of the hearth, dainty trays on pedestal legs, collections of fragile ornaments. There was literally a pile of painted eggshells. The basket Marlene had brought had already broken. Preparations had been made for a baby, certainly, but for a baby that was entirely imaginary, that didn't cry or shit, that had no needs. If Marlene had been looking after the baby it would be only days before she was overwhelmed – or gave it away. Anna was suddenly flooded with pity for Marlene: poor, poor Marlene, so disappointed by reality she simply denied its existence.

Anna laid the baby on the tiled floor in the bathroom and took off the soiled towel she was wrapped in. The poo was almost green. That was a surprise. The first one, on the bathroom floor, had been black. She hand-washed the towel. The bathroom was already beginning to look like somewhere else, somewhere normal. She looked through the bathroom door at her mother's corpse, lying in her weird pocketed mumu. She looked like she'd come dressed for her own funeral. But all the parts of her which identified her as

Marlene were already gone or going: the bright blonde hair, the huge jewellery, the amazing, starry eyes.

Anna felt the need to put Marlene's rings somewhere safe.

When she went into Marlene's room, the first thing she saw was herself. Her head was sitting on Marlene's dressing table. But as she neared it the vision resolved into her own hair, sitting on a long-necked wig stand. She might need that. The quilt she had made which said 'Mother' lay across an antique chair. The sketch she had drawn of Marlene was hung next to the mirror. On top of her jewellery box were the lace fingerless gloves.

Anna put the wig on. It was bizarre how like her old self she looked, when really she was quite new. She took the BMW keys from the hook by the porch. As she crunched across the gravel there was no movement from next door. These last weeks, she'd have done anything to see either of them, but now she was deeply grateful to be alone. Anna beeped the keys to Marlene's BMW and opened the boot, where the tyre lay in its little recess. Was this big enough to carry a corpse? As she lifted her eyes, though, she saw the neighbour, Sophie, sitting silently in the driver's seat of her SUV. Anna raised her right hand in a flat-palmed greeting, but Sophie stayed stock-still. Did she know? Was she watching Anna? Anna slammed the boot shut and walked over to her, pulling her dressing gown over her still large belly.

As Anna knocked on the driver's window Sophie visibly started. She wiped her cheeks and buzzed down the window, and as she did the song, 'Somewhere Only We Know' blasted out on to the drive.

'Are you all right?' Anna asked.

'Yes, I'm fine! I'm just listening to Keane.'

'OK,' said Anna.

Sophie clearly felt compelled to offer an explanation. 'There's nowhere to go . . . where I don't have to look after someone. Do you know what I mean?' Anna must have looked like she didn't know because Sophie added, 'You'll get it, when this one arrives! I mean, they are wonderful, but they do change you. Sometimes I just want to remember a time when I wasn't responsible for keeping them alive!'

Anna reached in and held Sophie's teary, skinny hand.

'I totally understand!'

Sophie looked at Anna's belly, which was still swollen. 'You must be due soon!'

'A couple of weeks,' said Anna.

'Well, if you need anything . . .' Sophie added, 'just yell!'

'Actually, I'm going home for the birth,' Anna explained.

'Oh?' said Sophie. 'Where's home?'

Anna looked her right in the eye.

'London,' she said, 'home is London.'

Anna was turning away when Sophie said, 'Oh! I've got that baby seat for you! You should take it now!' She registered Anna's confusion. 'Your mum asked me for it.'

'Great,' said Anna. 'Thanks.'

'No problem,' Sophie said. 'Be glad to get rid of it!' She looked at Anna for a moment.

'You look different,' she said. 'Have you done something to your hair?'

Of course, the solution presented itself the moment she returned to the tower room and the baby. There was no need to take the corpse anywhere at all.

She went to pick up Marlene's mobile. No! First, she had to find gloves. Anna knew there were none under the kitchen sink; no Marigolds, too common for Marlene. On the bottom shelf of Marlene's bathroom cabinet was a purple rinse for her hair. The prosaic secret to that beautiful pale blonde. Anna took the gloves out of the packet. Then picked up the phone from where it had fallen on the bedroom floor. The screen was smashed up. Anna had a dim memory of a lecture from her father about touchscreens working by the electricity in your hand. But the old ones worked by some other method. Would a dead thumb work? Anna tried to squat down next to Marlene but a searing pain in her womb forced her to half-sit, half-fall in the pool that surrounded her. She grasped Marlene's dead hand and held the thumb on the button. The mobile immediately blinked into life, and, sitting beside her, in her blood, the deadness of Marlene filtered into her for the first time. The phone was more alive than her mother. Anna scanned Marlene's messages. She'd been thorough, telling everyone she was going away, although entirely inconsistent in telling them where she was going. She must have been planning to stay here with the baby. Anna had no idea if she'd intended to keep Anna herself alive. How could she have?

Could she remove the thumb? Would the mobile unlock if the thumb was removed from the rest of the body? And wouldn't that be a sign, if they did find the body, evidence that something violent had happened? Anna shook herself. There was already plenty of evidence of violence. She was covered in evidence. She had to make sure the body wasn't found. She couldn't cut her mother's thumb off. She just needed no one to come here for at least a year. Her mother had already done most of the work.

Anna sent an email from her mother's account. The email was to her, Anna, and it said, *Bye Pickle! Please check on the house if you have time! Key's in the pot!* Then she pulled away the stone covering the priest's hole. She dragged her mother's body the four or five feet to the fireplace and propped her up. Struck suddenly by a thought, she checked the pocket at the front of her mother's dress. The keys to the handcuffs were there. Anna tried them and they worked.

She just needed to get the body inside the hole in the wall.

She allowed herself to look at her baby. The day was ending, and the baby was now lying in the shadows. Yet Anna herself was flooded with sunlight. And she knew without searching for the word what she felt. The word rose unbidden, unconjured, exploding from the depths of her like the little bubbles in her baby's belly: happy. She was fantastically happy.

Suddenly Marlene was weightless. Light as a feather. Slipping her away in her hidey-hole was the easiest thing in the world. Anna went into the bathroom to wash her hands.

'Hello!' Anna realised she hadn't spoken to the baby yet. 'Hello, little baby! Have you had a busy day? Have you? Yes, you have! Shall we go downstairs? Away from the lady?' Anna picked her up, holding her to her body, and went downstairs to put the kettle on. She laid the little baby down on a towel on the floor to change her. 'I think this calls for some hot chocolate.'

The baby fell straight to sleep. Anna left her propped between two rolled up towels and went back upstairs to review the hell-scape. Blood was spattered over much of the tower room. The placenta sat, like roadkill, on the wooden floor where Marlene had dropped it. Blood had pooled on the rubber sheet where Marlene had lain wounded, blood marked where she had died and traced her journey to the inglenook. Anna headed back downstairs and paused on the landing, at a loss. Great globs of blood marked where they had fought. Placental gore tracked in whip marks over the panelling which lined the staircase. She stared at the mess. How would she clean this up?

The doorbell rang under her feet. Anna gasped. It rang again. She drew the velvet curtains of the window which looked on to the front of the house and peered out into the half-light. She could see nothing but the porch roof, but beyond it she made out the dark shape of a car. She watched for a minute. Whoever was there wasn't going away. Anna crept down to the front door and peered out of the spy hole – a rare example of a convex lens: the image it produces is virtual, not real. Anna unlocked the door with her bloody gloves. It was only as she was seen that it occurred to her what she looked like, bloodied, ripped, bald, her belly still huge.

And the person on the doorstep said, 'Anna!'

Layla looked at the blood on the stairs, the blood on the landing, the blood on the bed.

'You sit down,' she said. 'I'll do it.'

'Put these gloves on,' said Anna.

'Not those,' said Layla. 'I've got some in my car.'

Anna fell asleep again on the sofa by the fire, waking briefly to find Layla holding the baby to feed from her breast. Anna slept-fed her. When Anna woke properly four hours later the baby no longer had waxy stuff and dried blood on her head. She looked more like babies do in adverts and less like a terrified frog dressed in a babygro that was much too big for her. She started making the strange reaching movements with her neck and head, which Anna was beginning to recognise as signs of hunger. 'Ten times a day,' she thought.

Layla nodded at Anna's lower abdomen, where the onesie Marlene had given her had popped open, to reveal the leaking knife wound she'd sewed up just a day, or a day and a night and day, earlier. Anna had lost all sense of time.

'I'm going to need to stick that together,' Layla said. 'I've found some stitches.'

'I already sewed it,' said Anna, 'with dental floss. I don't think I can bear the pain now.'

'Very clever,' said Layla. 'I just mean Steri-strips. They're stickers basically. It won't hurt much. How about your vagina? Does that need stitching?'

'I don't know,' said Anna.

Layla ran Anna a bath, which smarted horribly, and Layla inspected her. 'You've ripped but it's already healing,' said Layla. 'I'm more worried about the belly wound.'

So Layla cleaned the cut and backed up Anna's handicraft with the stuff she'd found in the medicine cabinet. Anna looked out across the garden, through the French windows, the same French windows she had fallen in front of just a month ago.

'We should get you to a hospital,' Layla said, glancing up and trying to meet Anna's eyes.

'I'm OK,' slurred Anna.

'I'm leaving the floss in for now,' Layla smiled at her. 'You did a good job.'

'I'm sorry about the tumour,' said Anna. 'In your desk. I think she put it there to punish you for not wanting me around.'

'Don't worry about it now,' said Layla. 'Don't worry about anything.'

The evening was fantastically, unthinkably beautiful. The last of the sun fell on the red bricks of the walkway, and the irises really were out. On the mantelpiece was the framed music Anna had given her mother for Christmas. The page of the music showed only a fraction of the lyrics: 'gold, seven for a secret never to be . . .'

Layla took the baby off her when she'd had another feed.

'I want to show you something,' said Layla. She led Anna along the landing, now clean, to the tower room, where everything was perfectly tidy, and the smell of iron had been replaced by the smell of bleach.

'Thank you,' said Anna.

'Looked like one hell of a birth,' said Layla. 'I've packed up the baby things.'

'Good,' said Anna, 'let's have tea and then we'll go.'

'Where to?' said Layla.

'The coast,' said Anna, 'I think I saw a map book. We can't use the Satnav.'

She handed Layla the lovely squirming body of her little baby. As she did so she felt a pulling at her chest, as if she and the baby were still part of one body, and she were handing over a vital organ: a lung, or a heart. The baby began to whine, a thin, high cry which meant she felt it too, this terrible parting.

'She'd better go with you,' Anna said.

'Anna!' said Layla.

'Don't!' Anna sobbed. 'Don't say anything. Please! Or I'll lose it. She'll be safer with you.'

They drove in convoy out on the A25 towards Whitstable, where Anna planned to say goodbye. Layla drove Marlene's car with the baby in Sophie's car seat. Anna drove Layla's, trying desperately to keep the BMW, with the baby, in view ahead of her. All through the journey tears poured down her cheeks. Maybe this was what being a mother was, to cry and not stop crying.

They pulled off Marine Parade, close to JoJo's café. She parked on the road, a little way away from Layla. She could see Layla's shape in the front seat, not moving. Anna couldn't see any CCTV cameras but there were bound to be some somewhere. She put on the crop wig that Marlene had worn during their last fight and pulled Marlene's coat around her before stepping out of the little car.

She turned away from Layla and the baby without saying a word. She walked fast along the Marine Parade – past the bowling alley and right towards the Harbour, opposite the car park. A series of fancy pop-up shops had appeared since the last time she'd been here, and she was momentarily confused. But behind them you could still reach the sea. The boat needed to be big enough to get to France – the sort of boat that might hide a human but small enough not to be searched. But when she got to the railing there was only one boat near enough. Anna threw Marlene's mobile the ten feet down among the fishing nets.

'Goodbye Ma,' she said.

By the time Anna got back to Layla's MG, Layla had fixed the baby seat in the back, and was putting the overnight bag with Anna and the baby's things into the boot. The orange handbag was sitting on the passenger seat.

'Where to?' said Layla.

'Golder's Hill Synagogue,' said Anna.

18

ONE YEAR OLD

'At twelve months old, your little one may begin to use words or take a few steps. Your baby may also start to cry when you leave.'

The baby was asleep on top of her.

In Layla's garden the cherry tree was blooming, almost masking the bins and exhaust fumes smell of London in March. Rabbi Altman, who Anna had studied with nearly every week over the last year, had said, 'That's a social occasion, there's no need for me to be there,' when Anna had invited him, but now he was tucking into Layla's mother's delicious pastries and basking in the sunlight of her beautiful smile.

'Delicious,' he said, raising the home-made baklava and his eyebrows simultaneously.

'Those were made by Hebe.' Layla's mother was scrupulous about crediting a cook.

Hebe jerked her chin in acknowledgement. She was slipping coasters under everybody's glasses. She was fiercely flat-proud since being released into Layla's protection. She was even strict with Ziggy, who was now fully furred, ring-worm free, and living in a multi-storey cat palace almost as large as the sofa.

Anna's father, Nicholas, was rescuing the tin foil beneath the snacks and putting it in his pocket. Her father saved everything.

Dermot clutched an orange juice and shifted back and forth on his massive trainers. He was the wiry thin of a runner. Dermot now ran with almost the same dedication with which he used to drink alcohol. He was clean-shaven, though his lovely hair was still long. He looked, to Anna, about ten years younger than when she'd been with him a year ago.

Anna's own hair, still wet from the mikveh, was just three inches long all over, the same length as Hebe's. They looked like twins. She must cut it, she thought. All these years she'd had it long and there were now all the hairstyles to try, so many hairstyles. She'd just had so little time, with the baby.

The baby was getting uncomfortable. Her hot face was pressed against Anna's neck, and Anna knew that when she woke the imprint of Anna's flower necklace would be on her cheek, as if she were the smallest, fattest hippy at Woodstock. Anna patted her back and she stirred and woke as she always did, one moment asleep and the next completely awake and staring adoringly at Anna, then out and around at the world with infinite curiosity. Anna unpeeled her sweaty little legs and plopped her down on the flagstones that made up the tiny seating area.

Straight away, the baby was on her feet, grasping the curved wicker edge of Layla's garden chair, swinging from step to step like a very pretty gibbon, and taking two or three steps before she fell down on her bottom again.

'Oh my God!' Dermot was impressed. 'She's practically running! We'll have to get her some trainers. Do you want some little trainers like your daddy?' He squatted down to look in her lively little face. She had beautiful eyebrows which made her look curiously adult, like a little facsimile of a grown-up rather than a baby.

'She's just cruising,' Anna said.

'What?' Dermot's face creased up. 'What did you say?'

'It's called cruising, that walking around holding on to things.'

'You're messing with me!' Dermot was delighted. 'Are you learning to cruise? I've got an app for that! Can I fill your plate, Anna?'

Nicholas pulled an envelope out of the huge pocket he had stashed the tin foil in. He offered it to her diffidently.

'You've already given the baby her birthday present,' Anna said.

'This one's for you. This is also a sort of bat mitzvah, isn't it?'

'Well, technically it's a conversion,' said Anna. 'The Rabbi calls it an adoption.'

Out of the envelope Anna drew a Book of Psalms, with a ribbon bookmarker. It fell open at Psalm 121. 'It was your mum's,' said Nicholas. Anna turned to the front page, where a nameplate displayed her new name: '*Anat bat Sarah Imeinu*' – Anat, daughter of Sarah our mother.

'Thank you,' said Anna, and she put the book into the black fabric handbag she now carried.

Layla handed Ben a glass of wine. He was wearing flannels and a straw boater. Anna wondered how long it would be before she told Anna that she was banging him. Some time yet, Anna guessed. She did not begrudge Layla her privacy. After all, everyone's entitled to their secrets. Layla's nephews, yelling, came too close to the baby.

'No, you little shits!' Layla yelled at them. 'Mind the bloody baby!'

The baby had been startled, but before her mouth could fully form into the 'O' which meant she was going to cry, Anna had scooped her up and put her on her hip.

'You're OK, aren't you?' she cooed. 'Are you OK? Yes, you are!' Dermot came back with another full plate for himself.

'Everyone's here!' he said, gesturing round the garden.

'Yes,' said Anna, rubbing the baby's back.

'Apart from the obvious,' said Dermot. He looked at Anna with soft eyes. 'I miss my mam too,' he said, 'even though she was a right shite. At least we named this one for your mother.' Dermot gestured at their beautiful baby. 'I mean, your real mam.'

Neil brought over the car seat and started strapping Sarah into it, her own tiny pilot's seat.

'Would you look at that?' Dermot said, staring straight at Neil's new belly, which was, without doubt, significantly larger than it had been a year ago. 'She always liked them chunky!'

'Fuck you, man!' Neil replied good-naturedly.

Anna slipped her hand into Neil's. He did not hook his hand around her little finger. No one ever would again.

She was the mother now. Anna felt the terrible slowness of growth; she felt her feet root down into the soil and her extremities stretch upwards, knowing they would never touch the sky. Only the dead and the mad can fly.

Neil turned to Anna, 'Shall we get Sarah home?'

'Yes,' said Anna. 'Say bye bye, Sarah!'

Sarah looked around. 'Bye bye!' she said. 'Bye bye!'

From the cherry tree came the unmistakable sound of a screech owl, howling into the three o'clock sunshine.

Hebe darted, blinking, outside, 'Did you hear that?'

'Ignore her,' said Anna. 'She can't hurt you now.'

EPILOGUE

The morning after Marlene Mather's BMW drove to the coast, a jogger called Camilla Fellows crossed Dunstan Road in North London, on her way to Hampstead Heath. She was listening to a podcast about a double murder in a small town in Wyoming. She saw something orange on the traffic island. The woman jogged on down the road for a full four minutes before she doubled back.

It was a very large leather handbag, clearly valuable. She looked up and down the busy road, still jogging to keep her heart rate up, then swooped down and put the bag over her shoulder in one movement like it was, and always had been, hers, and finished her run.

At home, fifty-five minutes later, Camilla opened the stolen bag and found two hundred and seventy pounds and a short white-blonde wig. She sold the bag on Vinted for two thousand eight hundred and forty pounds. The wig she threw in the bin.

The bag's twin sat on the passenger seat of Marlene Mather's BMW on Whitstable seafront for eight hours, before it too was stolen by a nineteen-year-old heroin user. He didn't smash the car window. It had been left open.

A year after the orange bag was sold on Vinted, Hebe Williamson reported her mother, Lilith Marlene Mather, missing.

On examining Prescott House, the manor in Woldingham, the police discovered large amounts of the blood of Lilith Marlene Mather. In the attic, which had clearly not been disturbed in some years, they discovered a noose which had traces of Tristan Meunier's skin cells. They also discovered a large collection of art, including five paintings by emerging artist Samyra Nour. Police dogs were used, and this led to the discovery of Tristan Meunier's remains in the pig pen. These police dogs also discovered a 'priest's hole' within the house; it was empty, though there were traces of Marlene's blood inside it, as well as evidence of putrefaction.

Police traced the final movements of Marlene Mather's phone. They worked on the hypothesis that Lilith Marlene Mather had had a fight with her then boyfriend, Tristan Meunier, with whom she had had a tumultuous relationship; during this fight she had been badly injured, hiding from him in the priest's hole. He killed himself and she disposed of the body. Following this she attempted escape via the south coast, drowning in the Channel. The smell of death they attributed to the priest's hole having housed corpses over the last five hundred years.

Layla Pasdar adopted a two-year-old boy called Matthew. She continues to live in her two-bed flat in Willesden.

Hebe Williamson inherited six million pounds from her mother, Lilith Marlene Mather, and paid for a fast-track medical degree for Anna Rampion. Anna became Dr Anna Rampion at the age of forty-one. Hebe also gave Anna a painting from her mother's estate. It was a painting of a tree, called 'من الدم أصعد' which translates as, 'From Blood I Rise'.

Acknowledgements

Thank you first to my mother, who taught me to write, because otherwise I'll never hear the end of it.

Thank you Nicholas Dunham for your invaluable legal advice, Gillian Mackay for your medical expertise, Caroline Blake for telling me about traditional Irish music, Joel Morris, Steven Adams and Matthew Hawn for intelligence on the music business, Paddy Screech and Ellie Crawford for talking me through the Mental Health Act, and the many women who opened your hearts to me about your abortions, adoptions and Jewish upbringing.

Thanks to my first readers Annabel Friedlein, Jonathan Dryden-Taylor and Kate Russell-Smith. Thank you Molly Ker Hawn and Ivan Mulcahy for being so generous with your time and knowledge of publishing.

Thank you Millie Hoskins, my unflappable agent, and all at United Agents, for taking a chance on me. And likewise, thanks to the team at Wildfire, especially my very perceptive editor, Jack Butler.

Thank you Robert Webb for taking care of the kids and laundry while I wrote the book, for putting up with me wittering endlessly about plot points, and for reminding me regularly to 'make the words good'.